AFRICAN AMERICAN

CORNERED

CORNERED

BRANDON MASSEY

PINNACLE BOOKS
KENSINGTON PUBLISHING CORP.
www.kensingtonbooks.com

PINNACLE BOOKS are published by

Kensington Publishing Corp.
119 West 40th Street
New York, NY 10018

All Kensington titles, imprints, and distributed lines are available at special quantity discounts for bulk purchases for sales promotions, premiums, fund-raising, educational, or institutional use. Special book excerpts or customized printings can also be created to fit specific needs. For details, write or phone the office of the Kensington special sales manager: Kensington Publishing Corp., 119 West 40th Street, New York, NY 10018, attn: Special Sales Department; phone 1-800-221-2647.

ISBN-13: 978-0-7860-2085-0
ISBN-10: 0-7860-2085-7

First printing: August 2009

10 9 8 7 6 5 4 3 2 1

Printed in the United States of America

*The keenest sorrow is to recognize ourselves
as the sole cause of all our adversities.*
—Sophocles

Part One

1

The morning that Corey Webb's past finally caught up with him, he was taking his daughter to a doctor's appointment.

Tuesday, June 10, began hot, windless, and bright. The clear sky was cobalt blue, the blistering sun giving it the gloss of a glazed porcelain bowl. Although it was two weeks before the first day of summer, the temperature was forecast to peak in the mid-nineties, the heat worsened by a strength-sapping humidity that would guarantee thousands of air conditioners cranked to the max throughout metro Atlanta.

Cool air humming from the vents of his black BMW sedan, Corey navigated the crawling rush-hour traffic on Haynes Bridge Road in Alpharetta. His wife, Simone, and their nine-year-old daughter, Jada, were debating an R&B song that had been playing on the radio, a track apparently titled "Get Me Some." Corey had changed stations within five seconds of hearing the song's lewd hook—and had been treated to Jada singing the rest of it word for word in a pitch-perfect voice, drawing a gasp from Simone and a blush from Corey.

"I can't *believe* you knew the words to that awful song, Jada," Simone was saying. "And you tell me you can't recall where you've heard it, which I simply do not accept."

Corey had to admit that even after all these years, he got a kick out of watching Simone play mom. With her penny-brown eyes, jet-black hair styled in a cute bob, milk-chocolate complexion, and prominent dimples, she might have been a fresh-faced coed, not a thirty-four-year-old woman with a PhD in clinical psychology.

She was a great mother, though. He liked watching her at work.

Twisted around in the passenger seat, Simone subjected Jada to her penetrating gaze and awaited a satisfactory answer.

"Mom, I said somebody at school played it on their phone," Jada pleaded from the backseat.

Keeping quiet, letting Simone handle this her way, Corey glanced in the rearview mirror. Jada had pecan-brown skin, gray eyes, thick dark eyebrows, black hair woven into tight cornrows. He'd once worn his hair like that when he was a kid. It struck him that the Corey from back then and his daughter looked so much alike they could have been twins.

"Who's this somebody?" Simone asked. Her voice carried a gentle breeze of her Alabama accent. "Give me a name. I want to talk to their parents."

Last month, Jada had completed fourth grade at Alpharetta Elementary. She currently attended a three-week summer program in Roswell for gifted students. Nevertheless, high-performing youngsters, like all other kids, obviously found the time to enjoy lascivious songs that would have shamed their parents, and they did it on their cutting-edge cell phones that performed every conceivable task short of whisking you to the moon.

Sometimes, when listening to his daughter talk about

what she and her classmates did these days, Corey felt as if he had grown up in the Middle Ages.

"Somebody," Jada said. "I don't remember who it was. Everyone in class has a phone except me. When can I get a phone?"

Corey held back a smile. His girl was a clever one. When you couldn't win the debate, change the debate.

"Don't try to change the subject," Simone said.

Jada frowned, caught red-handed. A chuckle slipped out of Corey.

Simone turned to him. "Why are you laughing? This is serious. Your daughter was singing about having *sex*."

"No, I wasn't, Mom," Jada said. "I was singing about getting some till the morning comes."

It took every ounce of willpower in Corey to hold back a laugh. Simone flashed him a deadly, *don't-you-dare-laugh* glower.

Corey cleared his throat. "Umm, that's not the kind of song you should be singing, Pumpkin. Seriously."

"Why not?" Jada asked.

"It's a song for adults, that's why," Simone said. "It's not appropriate for you to sing. Understood?"

"Okay," Jada said with a sigh. "Then I won't sing it any more."

"Good," Simone said. "And if you hear one of your friends play it again on their phone or iPod or whatever else, you'll tell me who did it, because none of the children in your class should be listening to that song, either."

"Yes, Mom," Jada said in a defeated voice. Then she piped up, "But when can I get a phone? Daddy said I could have one."

Corey cut a glance in the rearview mirror again. Jada was grinning at him. Nine years old going on nineteen.

"You told her that?" Simone asked him. "I thought we

had an agreement. No cell phone, at least for a few more years."

Corey shrugged. "All of her classmates have them."

"Yeah, Mom, everybody does," Jada said. "Everybody except *me*."

Simone shot him a rebuking look. "Baby, you know I don't agree with keeping up with the Joneses."

"Who are the Joneses?" Jada asked. "Do they live near us?"

"It's just a form of expression, Pumpkin," Corey said.

"It means getting something you don't need, only because everyone around you has it," Simone said. "It's giving in to peer pressure, which we've discussed before."

"But what if I need a phone?" Jada asked.

"You don't *need* a phone, honey," Simone said. "You *want* a phone. There's a world of difference."

"It could be a good security measure," Corey said. "We could get one of those phones for kids that would call only the numbers we program into it—like ours and your mother's."

"But if we're doing our jobs as parents and keeping track of our child, she would never have a use for a cell phone."

"Things don't always go as planned," he said. "I like to take extra precautions. At the end of the day, better safe than sorry, don't you think?"

Simone got quiet. They both knew she could never beat him in a debate about security. He was co-owner of a firm that installed alarms and surveillance systems in residences and businesses throughout the region, and their own house was a marvel of high-tech surveillance and monitoring. Debating the merits of security with him was like debating criminal justice law with a judge.

"You still shouldn't have promised her a phone before discussing it with me," Simone said.

"I didn't exactly promise her a phone." He looked in the

mirror and caught Jada's eye. "Pumpkin, did I promise you a phone? Didn't I just say maybe?"

"Yes." Jada nodded vigorously. "Daddy said maybe, Mom."

"Didn't I say that I'd have to discuss it with your mother, first?" he said.

Another eager nod. "Daddy said he'd have to talk to you about it, Mom."

"See?" Corey grinned at Simone.

"You two co-conspirators are full of it," Simone said.

She shook her head in what was meant to be an aggravated expression, yet a smile broke through the mask, accentuating those killer dimples. The disciplinarian role she played so well was only an act, Corey knew; her heart was as sweet and soft as melted caramel.

"So can I get my phone?" Jada said.

"Your father and I will discuss the subject later," Simone said.

"Can you talk about it now?" Jada asked. "Please?"

"Later," Simone said firmly.

Jada made a whiny sound, but Simone gave her a warning glare, and she fell silent. Simone settled back into her seat, mothering duties concluded for the moment.

Corey took Simone's hand, squeezed. Glancing at him, she returned the squeeze, lips curved in a soft smile.

On mornings like that one, Corey felt like the luckiest man alive.

Growing up, he'd never imagined that he would one day have a life like this. A beautiful wife. An adorable daughter. A successful business. Most people thought they never got what life owed them, but he considered his own story as proof that sometimes you actually got more than you deserved, that God smiled on sinners and saints alike.

He'd been raised by his grandmother in one of Detroit's

toughest neighborhoods. He'd never met his father, didn't so much as know the man's name. As for his mother, she had abandoned him when he was three to follow some long-forgotten Motown crooner to California. She'd died twenty-five years ago with a needle in her arm in a seedy Los Angeles motel.

Grandma Louise, a big-hearted woman from Arkansas with a penchant for quoting Bible scriptures and packing snuff inside her cheek, had done her best to keep him on the straight and narrow, but her old-fashioned teachings couldn't compete with the siren song of the streets. Considering the things he'd gotten into and the dangerous crowd he'd run with, he should have wound up either in prison, or dead.

But he'd been spared, had escaped the chasm that claimed so many black men just like him. Rarely did a day pass when he did not count his blessings.

Idly scanning the dashboard, he noticed that he had only twenty miles' worth of gas left in the tank. A QuikTrip convenience store was coming up ahead, the fuel service islands busy as people gassed up on their way to work.

He turned off the road and parked beside the only available pump.

"That time again?" Simone checked the price of the gasoline, clucked her tongue. "My goodness, remember when it was less than a buck a gallon?"

"Those bygone days," he said.

"Can I help you put the gas in, Daddy?" Jada asked.

"Sure, Pumpkin."

"Don't be too long, guys," Simone said. "It's twenty to nine. We can't be late for our appointment."

Outside the car, Corey let Jada slide his debit card into the card reader slot, enter his PIN, and select the grade of gasoline. He inserted the spout into the tank, and told Jada the total price he wanted to pay. Her gaze riveted on the digits climbing on the price display, she ran her fingers through her cornrows, absently adjusting the tiny black speech processor hooked behind her left ear.

Jada had been born with profound hearing loss. When she was two years old, Corey and Simone had arranged a cochlear implant, a modern medical miracle that served as a prosthetic replacement for the inner ear, electronically stimulating auditory nerve fibers to produce a sense of hearing. Years of intensive speech therapy had enabled Jada to attend mainstream school from kindergarten onward, and she enjoyed as active a social life as any girl her age—Girl Scouts, ballet, play dates, the works.

In spite of her social and academic success, she enjoyed hearing in only one ear, a condition that posed unique challenges when she was in environments where sounds came at her from all directions. That morning, they were taking her to a specialist in Marietta who would evaluate whether she was a good candidate for a bilateral implant: a cochlear implant in her other ear.

"Almost there, Daddy," Jada said.

Corey squeezed in a few more cents and returned the nozzle to the pump. Jada handed the receipt to him.

"Can I go inside and get something to drink?" she asked.

"Actually, I could use some coffee myself." He tapped on Simone's window. "Want some coffee or juice, babe?"

Simone checked her watch; the doctor's appointment was at nine fifteen, and she was a stickler about being on time. "If you can be quick about it, sure, orange juice would be great."

"You heard your mother," Corey said to Jada. "Let's be quick about it."

"Yeah!" Jada performed a happy dance.

Together, they went inside the minimart, Jada skipping beside him, her hand in his, swinging his arm around between them as if he were a piece of playground equipment. He directed Jada to the glass-fronted coolers at the back of the store, while he went to the hot beverage station adjacent to the cash register.

He filled a large Styrofoam cup with coffee and flavored it with cream and sugar. Checking his watch, he went to collect Jada.

Hands on her hips, she was examining the brands of orange juice inside the refrigerated display case.

"We've gotta go, Pumpkin," he said.

"I don't know what kind of orange juice Mom likes," she said.

Corey started to reply that Simone liked Tropicana, when he noticed someone standing in an aisle a few feet away, observing them.

It was a colossus of a man. Corey stood about five-ten and weighed a hundred and seventy-five, and this guy had at least six or seven inches and a hundred pounds on him. Fairskinned—what Grandma Louise liked to call "high yella"— he wore faded denim overalls over a white T-shirt, muddy work boots, and a tattered Atlanta Braves cap cocked on an unkempt, bushy Afro. A stubbly beard made his pudgy face look soiled.

The guy's brown eyes were oddly flat, as if they were painted on his face. But Corey realized the guy wasn't looking at him at all.

He was looking at Jada. *Gawking* at her.

Jada was a beautiful child, but this man's intense attention was far from that of an innocently admiring adult. His was the naked leer of a pervert, a parent's ultimate nightmare.

Oblivious to Corey standing there, concentrating solely on Jada, the man licked his lips, his tongue leaving a glistening trail of saliva.

Disgust and anger wrenched Corey's gut. He sat his cup on a shelf, grabbed Jada's hand and pulled her to his side, shielding her from the giant stranger.

The pervert blinked as if awakening from a reverie, and only then did he look at Corey.

His stare was as empty as a scarecrow's. A chill trickled down Corey's spine.

Something's wrong with this guy, he thought. *Dude's elevator doesn't go all the way to the top.*

"Daddy, what is it?" Jada asked. She hadn't noticed the man.

"We need to go, sweetheart." He nudged his daughter along with a firm hand on her back.

"But I wanted apple juice." She looked over her shoulder.

"Don't look back there. We have to go. We'll get your apple juice later."

He ushered Jada outside. The hot air was thick as cotton, but refreshing compared to the bone-deep chill he'd felt inside the minimart.

A man called out: "Corey? Corey Webb? That you, man?"

In midstride, Corey stopped. He knew that voice, that piercing falsetto. He had not heard it in probably fifteen years or so, but he would never forget it.

Could that be who I think it is?

As other customers brushed past him, he stepped away from the entrance and turned. Sunlight lanced his eyes. He lifted his hand to his brow to block the glare.

When his vision adjusted, he saw a man leaning against a late-model, blue Ford F-150 parked in front of the store. Brown as a paper bag, he was about six feet tall, leanly muscular, with long arms webbed with tattoos. He had shoulder-length dreadlocks as thick as cables, a bushy salt-and-pepper beard, and deep-set, fiercely intelligent brown eyes. He wore paint-splattered denim overalls and faded leather work boots.

A cigarette dangled in his spindly fingers. He took a puff

and exhaled a halo of smoke, and just the acrid scent of the tobacco stirred long-buried memories in Corey's mind.

"Leon?" Corey asked. He was out of breath, as if he'd been slugged in the stomach.

The guy flashed a gap-toothed grin, an expression that made his elongated face appear wolflike.

"It's moi, the one and only, the great man himself, live and in the flesh."

Corey was speechless.

Leon Sharpe, his childhood friend from Detroit, was the last person he'd ever expected to see again.

And for so many reasons, the last person he'd ever wanted to see again, too.

2

"My homeboy, C-Note, well, I'll be damned." Grinning, Leon pushed off the side of the truck and spread his arms to their full tremendous wingspan. "Gimme some love, man."

Corey broke his paralysis and gave Leon an awkward brother man hug—one arm looped around the back, a solid pound on the shoulder blades with his fist. Leon smelled of nicotine, hair oil, and stale sweat.

I've gotta be dreaming, Corey thought. *If so, someone please wake me up right this minute.*

Stepping back, Leon looked down at Jada. She gazed up at him, squinting, partly from the sun's glare, but mostly, Corey figured, from confusion. None of Corey and Simone's friends looked or sounded remotely like Leon. He could only imagine the questions tumbling through her mind.

"Who's this little munchkin here?" Leon asked.

"She's my daughter," Corey said.

"Hey, cutie." Leon extended his hand toward Jada.

Jada regarded his large hand doubtfully, gaze traveling across his dirty fingernails and up the colorful tattoos that adorned his forearm.

Corey touched her shoulder. "Go wait in the car with your mother, Pumpkin. Tell her I'll be there in a minute."

Nodding, Jada ambled across the parking lot, repeatedly glancing over her shoulder at them with a puzzled frown.

"Good-looking kid you got there," Leon said.

"Thanks," Corey said numbly. He cleared his throat, fighting to overcome a fuzzy sense of unreality. The last time he'd felt this disoriented, it was when he'd learned Grandma Louise had died of a heart attack.

But running into Leon after fifteen years, several hundred miles away from their hometown, had to be the coincidence to end all coincidences.

Leon looked much different than what Corey remembered. When Corey had last seen him, his head had been as hairless as a basketball, and he'd worn a goatee so meticulously trimmed it might have been drawn with a mechanical pencil. His complexion had been smooth, his eyes had been bright with wild, youthful exuberance, and he'd been a sharp dresser, known for sporting the latest fly clothes, the hottest new sneakers.

The Leon in front of him looked, in a word, tougher. There were crow's-feet under his eyes, and a netting of heavy wrinkles across his forehead and cheeks gave his face the appearance of sun-weathered leather. Dark hollows ringed his sockets, as if he rarely slept. And those eyes of his, always fiercely intelligent, glinted with raw, kinetic energy, reflecting a personality far more dangerous than the young man Corey remembered—and that was saying a lot, because the Leon that Corey recalled was no one that you wanted to piss off.

Leon took a draw on his cigarette and appraised Corey from head to toe. "You're looking good, too. How the hell you been? It's been how long? Fifteen, sixteen years?"

"Something like that," Corey said. "I've been . . . I've been all right."

"All right?" Leon snickered. "You look like life's been treating you exceptionally well, I'd say. Pushing the new five series Beemer, got the cute kid, the no-doubt lovely wifey? Do you live in a white castle in the clouds, too? When did you strike the Faustian bargain?"

Leon let out a high-pitched giggle that sounded as if he'd inhaled a dose of helium. Same old Leon laugh—he sounded like an elf on crystal meth. For a long time, Corey had used to hear that grating laughter in his nightmares.

"A lot of things have changed since I left Detroit," Corey said. He looked at Leon's Ford truck, and wondered, automatically, where Leon had stolen it from. "How long have you been in town?"

"Not long at all, a few weeks, I've been living the knock-about life, you know, dashing from pillar to post, painting houses, doing odd handyman jobs here and there, trying to make a dollar out of fifteen cents." He dropped his cigarette on the ground and snuffed it out with his boot. "Need any painting done at your house, man? Seeing you here, all grown up and spit-shined and polished, I know you've gotta be living in a mansion somewhere, most definitely, a palace, dozens of rooms, and no doubt the old lady's been on your back about repainting some of those rooms, a woman is never satisfied, *ever*, and what better way to get it done than to hire your old, trusty running partner from Motown to do the work? What do you say?"

Listening to Leon's mercurial patter as sunshine burned into his skull, Corey began to feel a migraine headache coming on.

"Listen, ah, Leon, we don't exactly need any painting done . . . right now. . . ."

"I'm only shittin' you!" Laughing, Leon slapped his shoulder. "I don't know how much longer I'm gonna be in town, anyway, it's about time to blow this pop stand and hit the road like Willie Nelson, although, damn, I've gotta say, standing here enjoying a tête-à-tête with my homeboy from back in the day . . . I might have to change my modus operandi and settle in for a spell."

Heart knocking, Corey looked toward his car at the gas pump. He could see Simone and Jada watching them, curious about his prolonged interaction with a man they had never seen before.

He'd given them only sketchy details about the life he'd left behind in Detroit. They knew that he had no close family left there, that he'd moved to Atlanta sixteen years ago, shortly after Grandma Louise's death. They knew that he'd never gone back to visit, on the claim that there was nothing there for him any more.

But they knew nothing whatsoever of Leon. They knew nothing about the past he shared with this man.

And he'd always wanted to keep it that way. There were certain forbidden boxes of memories that, over time, he had closed watertight by sheer force of will, and he'd dared not open them, for his family's well-being—and his own.

But now Leon was here. Driving a new truck that had to be stolen. Probably in violation of parole for something or other. Maybe hiding a gun underneath his overalls.

Those hermetically sealed crates of memories were already starting to creak open.

Corey squinted, listening. He could barely understand what Leon was saying, and that brought back memories, too. Leon spoke in dizzying run-on sentences so generously peppered with idioms, foreign phrases, and archaic pop culture references that Corey had often found himself totally confused, and agreeing with whatever he said just to get him to shut up.

Leon said, "Have you been back to Motown, recently? I haven't, I severed my ties with the Motor City a few years ago, cruised into that wild blue yonder and haven't looked back, but the last time I was there the downtown scene was exploding with casinos, nouveau riche tourists crawling through like so many cockroaches through the projects, and I'm of half a mind to go back to get a piece of the action for myself, a fresh and lucrative new hustle of some kind, though at this point if I ventured back someone might declare me non compos mentis, I'll think better of it and keep drinking the wanderlust Kool-Aid and seeing what life brings to my doorstep, that's the way I live, you know, in the moment, right, remember, huh?"

"Yeah, sure," Corey said. He made a dramatic show of checking his watch. "Listen, Leon, I've got to get going. We have an appointment."

"All right, all right, all right." Leon bobbed his head, dreadlocks swinging. "You have a business card? We should get together sometime, grab a Heineken or two, reminisce about how we use to rock and roll back in the day when we were strapping young bucks, yeah, give me your card, all right, all right."

Without thinking, wanting only to get away, Corey pulled out his wallet and withdrew a card. Leon read it. His eyes got as big as billiard balls.

"Gates-Webb Security Services? You own a *security company?* You?" Leon laughed his frenetic giggle. "The irony, my man, the irony is too delicious, the irony is downright scrumptious."

Corey felt blood rising in his face. "Good seeing you again, Leon."

"Yeah, yeah." Leon tucked the card into his pocket. "Yeah, yeah, it's been real. We gotta get that beer sometime soon, don't forget. We ran in to each other for a reason, there's no such thing as coincidence, nope, fate's slammed us together again and we definitely need to reconnect, uh-huh, all right."

Mumbling in agreement, Corey was turning to go when someone exited the minimart. It was the dull-eyed giant who'd been ogling Jada. Corey's chest tightened.

The giant tossed Leon a box of Newports and climbed in on the passenger side of the pickup.

Jesus. They're partners?

Leon slid a cigarette out of the pack and fished a brushed-chrome Zippo lighter out of his pocket. It was a vintage model, and it was the same one Corey had last seen fifteen years ago. He would never forget it; the image was fire-branded in his brain.

That old box of memories opened wider.

Leon caught him looking at it, and winked. He struck a flame, lit his cigarette, and took a slow drag.

"Your lovelies are waiting on you," Leon said, lips curved in a smug smile. "Adieu."

3

Corey got behind the wheel and gunned the engine. Mashing the accelerator too aggressively for a parking lot, like a hot-rodding kid, he peeled away from the gas station.

In the rearview mirror, he spotted Leon waving at him. He exhaled through clenched teeth.

He still couldn't believe he had run into Leon, of all people.

He felt Simone and Jada watching him, felt their questions. He tried to will his racing pulse to slow, but it was tough.

"Who were you talking to back there?" Simone finally asked.

"Who was that man, Daddy?" Jada said.

Ignoring their questions, as if by doing so they would go away, he rejoined the sluggish flow of traffic on Haynes Bridge.

That damn cigarette lighter. He couldn't get it out of his head. What the hell kind of point had Leon been trying to make? Was he taunting him? Making a joke?

With that sick bastard, you never could tell.

He wished he hadn't given Leon his business card. What had he been thinking? He had reacted to Leon's request as automatically as he did when someone extended their hand to be shaken or asked how his day was going. Responding in kind was the ingrained, socially correct thing to do.

But he worried about it. If Leon decided to stop by his office . . .

No, he won't do that.

But it was an empty attempt at self-assurance. The truth was, he didn't know what Leon might do—hell, from one moment to the next, Leon didn't know what Leon might do. In the past, that was partly what had made being his friend so exhilarating. Leon might, literally, do anything.

He wished he had gone to a different gas station. Then none of this would have happened, and that Pandora's box of old memories would still be buried in the cellar of his mind.

He took a slurp of coffee, and immediately wished he hadn't. His stomach was cramped in such a tight bundle that the coffee was likely going to give him indigestion.

He felt both Simone and Jada observing him intently now, and he wished they hadn't been with him that morning; he wished that he'd run into Leon on his own and they had no clue about any of it.

He took another sip of coffee, and grimaced. It seemed he was wishing for a lot of different things right then.

"Baby?" Simone asked.

"Daddy?" Jada said.

He blinked. "What?"

"We asked you a question," Simone said.

"Oh, right," he said. "That guy back there? Just an old friend from back home."

"From Detroit?" Jada asked.

"Yes, from Detroit."

"What's his name?" Simone asked.

"Leon."

"Leon who?" Jada asked.

Corey glanced at Jada in the mirror. Her eyes sparkled with curiosity. She'd inherited her inquisitiveness from her mother, and for her to have seen a man from her father's fabled hometown was probably unbearably thrilling for her.

But he wished she would let it go.

"His name is Leon Sharpe," he said.

"You grew up with him?" Simone asked, eyes as intrigued as Jada's.

"He lived across the street from us, for a while anyway."

"What's a homeboy?" Jada asked.

"A homeboy is a good friend."

"Oooh, oooh. Really? Was Leon your *best* friend, Daddy?"

"*Mister* Leon," Simone said, gently correcting Jada. "We don't call adults by their first names, honey."

"Was Mr. Leon your best friend, Daddy?"

He shrugged. "I guess so."

"Wow, is that so?" Simone asked. "You've never mentioned him before."

"Well, I haven't thought about him in years."

"When was the last time you saw him?" Simone asked.

He looked at her. Simone's interest was innocent, not suspicious. If he'd seen her run in to a former, admitted best girlfriend who she hadn't seen in a long time, he might have been asking her similar questions, too.

"Fifteen years ago, I guess," he said.

Jada's face bunched into a frown. "You haven't talked to your best friend in fifteen years, Daddy?"

"He's not my best friend any more."

"Why not?" Jada asked.

"Because I moved away from Detroit and came here."

"But you could have kept talking to him," Jada said.

"I haven't."

"Why?"

Their turn was coming up. Corey took it too fast. Simone

knocked against him, and Jada slewed sideways in her seat as if riding a roller coaster.

Simone lightly tapped his thigh. "Take it easy, Mario Andretti. We want to get there in one piece."

He bit his lip. "Sorry."

"Daddy?" Jada said.

"Yes?"

"Why didn't you keep talking to Mr. Leon?"

"I told you, because I moved here."

"But you never called him?"

"No."

"Why not?"

"Jesus, Jada." He clenched the steering wheel. "Do you plan to be a prosecuting attorney when you grow up? Lay off with the questions, all right? I don't want to talk about it any more. Period."

Simone stared at him, lips parted in shock. In the mirror, Jada's face crumbled.

"Sorry, Daddy," she said softly. She wiped away tears.

Guilt punctured his heart. He rarely raised his voice with her, and she didn't deserve to be rebuked. She was only a kid with a natural interest in his past.

"It's okay, Pumpkin," he said in a soothing tone. "I didn't mean to snap at you."

But Jada wouldn't look at him. Simone looked away from him, too, jawline rigid.

They were quiet for the rest of the drive.

4

At the clinic in Marietta, after conducting a series of tests and speaking with them at length, the specialist, Dr. Kim, declared Jada a suitable candidate for a bilateral cochlear implant. They scheduled her surgery, an outpatient procedure, for the end of June, a week after Jada's summer school program would conclude and two weeks before their family vacation to Disney World.

Corey's attention had wandered continually during the appointment. Simone had picked up the slack, asking the important questions that were on both their minds, and Jada had come prepared with a handful of questions of her own, too, which the three of them had brainstormed ahead of time. Corey was left looking like the only unprepared member of the family, and he could sense the disdain in the physician's gaze and an edge of irritation in Simone's tone.

But he couldn't help it. He couldn't stop thinking about the possible ramifications of bumping into Leon. Not one of them was good. Not one.

Around eleven-thirty, he pulled into the driveway of their home in Alpharetta. Simone would drop off Jada with her mother in Roswell and then go on to her own job, a solo therapy practice she ran in nearby Sandy Springs. He was heading to his office a couple of miles away.

He kissed Jada on the cheek, and she bounded out of the car and raced across the walkway to the front door of their brick, two-story house. Simone started to get out, and then she paused, glanced at him.

"You've been in a mood since you ran in to your old friend at the gas station," she said. "Is something on your mind?"

"It's nothing to do with that," he lied. "I've only been thinking about all the work I've got to do today."

She studied his face. "That's it, huh? Thinking about work?"

"That's it. Work, work, work."

Her brow crinkled. She counseled people for a living, and was alert to the signs of deception. Besides that, she'd known him intimately for a decade, probably could read his body language and moods as easily as a roadside billboard.

But he wasn't prepared to talk with her about Leon any further. Not right then. Maybe not ever.

She combed her fingers through her hair, shrugged. "Fine, I'll see you later, then. Have a good day, honey."

"You, too."

He reversed out of the driveway and took the smoothly winding road out of the subdivision. The community, quiet at that time of day, was full of homes like theirs: contemporary two-story residences with three-car garages, fussily manicured lawns, and expensive landscaping. The residents were mostly well-scrubbed, corporate-ladder-climbing types with young children and hybrid vehicles; many of the wives were stay-at-home moms who could be found supervising their kids on the neighborhood playground or swimming in the clubhouse pool.

They had moved in to their home seven years ago, faithfully paid their association dues, counted many of their neighbors as genuine friends, and participated in block parties and other community activities—but he suddenly felt as if he didn't really belong there. As if he were a bad actor playing a role, and that if these people knew the truth about him, they would give him the boot.

A sour taste rising in his throat, he turned out of the subdivision.

Gates-Webb Security Services, LLC, was headquartered in an office building on a bustling length of road that featured dealerships for foreign luxury cars, strip malls, and fast-casual chain restaurants. Corey parked in the shade of a blooming dogwood, grabbed his briefcase off the backseat, and went inside, taking the lobby's elevator to their reception area on the third floor, where they leased an office suite.

"Morning, Corey," the receptionist said. A perpetually cheerful, silver-haired lady named Lynn, she sat at an oval mahogany desk, a telephone headset clipped to her ear. She handed him a sheaf of yellow note slips. "Lots of messages for you."

"Thanks, Lynn. Would you mind holding my calls for an hour or so? I'd like to get caught up on a few things."

"Sure thing, hon." She cocked her head. "How'd the appointment go?"

For a moment, he had no idea what the hell she was talking about. Then it hit him—he'd told her about the procedure they were considering for Jada.

"We got the green light," he said. "Surgery's scheduled for the end of the month."

"Good, good. Your little girl's one smart cookie, I tell ya. She's gonna zoom her way to some Ivy League school, you just wait and see."

He smiled. "Let's hope she does it on a full scholarship, or else we'll have to take out a second mortgage."

He strode down the carpeted corridor, past the clusters of cubicles. On an ordinary morning, he stopped and said hello to each of their twelve employees, but that morning he did not slow, though a couple of workers noticed him and waved. He returned the greetings, but kept moving.

Todd Gates, his partner, occupied the large corner office across the hall from Corey's. Todd's door was closed, and through the sidelight panel, Corey saw Todd speaking on the phone.

Corey went inside his office and shut the door. He tossed the messages onto his desk and dropped into the leather chair.

Normally, entering his workspace relaxed him. It was spacious and tastefully furnished. Cream carpeting, soft almond walls. Track lighting. Live potted plants Simone had picked out. His bachelor's and MBA degrees, both from Georgia State University, and both framed, hanging on the wall, next to a laminated feature about Gates-Webb Security that had recently appeared in *Entrepreneur* magazine. Photographs of Jada and Simone gathered on the edge of his mahogany desk. A crayon drawing Jada had created for him was in a frame on the opposite edge of the desk, the picture a stick-figure representation of Corey in a shirt and tie and a heading that read, "Daddy, CEO" in her careful penmanship.

But as he looked around, he felt out of place there, too, a poseur.

He reminded himself that he'd worked hard to get this far. At the invitation of a family friend, he'd taken a bus to Atlanta with only a hundred dollars in his pocket and a battered suitcase full of clothes. He'd landed an entry-level job as a burglar alarm service technician at a large security company and worked his way up the ranks while going to college at night, eventually earning his MBA and launching his own business with his partner. For over a decade, sixty- and seventy-hour weeks had been de rigueur; vacations infrequent and short. No family connections had opened doors; no trust fund had provided cushioning. He'd earned what he had by

he sweat of his brow and the occasional assistance of people
kind enough to lend a helping hand.

In spite of all those things, that nagging feeling of being
out of place lingered.

He booted up his notebook computer. The machine was
inked via a wireless connection to the company network. As
t proceeded through the start-up cycle, he methodically
cracked his knuckles one finger at a time, a nervous habit of
his that drove Simone nuts.

Although a full e-mail in-box surely awaited his attention,
he first thing he did was open a Web browser. By default,
he browser automatically accessed the Gates-Webb Secu-
ity home page. He pulled up Google instead.

In the search field, he typed: *Leon Sharpe.*

He was honest enough with himself to know why he was
feeling as if his life were out of joint. His encounter with
Leon had freed troubling memories, recollections that made
his current life seem like a farce, and he had to know what
Leon had been doing since he'd last seen him. He desperately hoped to find nothing at all, or if anything, then something good, such as Leon having done something heroic and
selfless like saving an infant from a burning apartment. He
knew it was unlikely that he would find such a thing—but
for some reason, it was important to him to look, to discover
something that might somehow validate the path of his own
life.

Google returned several dozen hits. He was expecting to
find news stories that would describe how Leon had been
convicted of numerous felonies over the years, how he had
perhaps served time in a penitentiary or two. That was the
Leon he knew. That was the Leon he expected to learn about.

He was not, however, expecting the top search result.

Heart thumping, he clicked on the link.

A page materialized.

"Oh, shit," he whispered.

FBI TEN MOST WANTED FUGITIVE

UNLAWFUL FLIGHT TO AVOID PROSECUTION—
FIRST DEGREE MURDER, ARMED ROBBERY

LEON SHARPE

Aliases: Leo Smith, Leonard Sharpe, Len Starks

DESCRIPTION

D.O.B.s Used:	July 23, 1971; January 23, 1971
Place of Birth:	Michigan
Height:	6'0"
Weight:	160 to 170 pounds
Build:	Slender
Occupation:	Housepainter
Hair:	Black
Eyes:	Brown
Complexion:	Dark
Sex:	Male
Race:	Black
Nationality:	American

Scars and Marks: Prominent gap between front teeth. Several tattoos on forearms.

Remarks: Sharpe is an avid professional sports fan, and enjoys playground basketball. He has been known to frequent sports bars and is a heavy smoker. He has been known to alter his appearance through the use of disguises and has demonstrated a facility for faking a Jamaican accent.

Sharpe has ties to Michigan, Illinois, Ohio, Missouri, Wisconsin, and Indiana. In the past, he has traveled to California and Georgia. Additionally, he may be in the possession of a Glock 9 mm handgun.

CAUTION

LEON SHARPE IS WANTED FOR MURDER AND ARMED ROBBERY IN DETROIT, MICHIGAN. DURING MAY OF 2005, SHARPE ALLEGEDLY SHOT AND KILLED TWO ARMORED TRUCK GUARDS OUTSIDE A MOVIE THEATER AND THEN FLED WITH THE MONEY.

CONSIDERED ARMED AND EXTREMELY DANGEROUS

IF YOU HAVE ANY INFORMATION CONCERNING THIS PERSON, PLEASE CONTACT YOUR LOCAL FBI OFFICE OR THE NEAREST U.S. EMBASSY OR CONSULATE.

REWARD

The FBI is offering a reward of up to $100,000 for information leading directly to the arrest of Leon Sharpe.

5

Corey stared at the screen, cold sweat beading on his forehead.

There was no question that it was the Leon he knew. The profile included a black-and-white head shot that presumably had been taken a few years ago. In it, Leon was clean-shaven, with a short fade haircut. His features were pinched in a kiss-my-ass glower.

Allegedly shot and killed two armored truck guards . . .

Although shock had struck Corey like a hammer, he knew he shouldn't have been surprised to learn about this. He understood as well as anyone what Leon was capable of doing. Leon's elevation to the FBI's Ten Most Wanted status seemed, perversely, like the inevitable culmination of the path Leon had traveled since he was a kid: the crowning achievement of a life of crime.

And he'd managed to evade the cops for *three years*. Three whole years on the run. Wouldn't he have been featured on that show, too, *America's Most Wanted*? Face flashing on tubes all across the country? Flyers plastered in post offices nationwide?

To stay free for so long, Leon had to be either a genius, or incredibly lucky. Corey suspected a bit of both.

He cracked his knuckles. Think, damn it. He had to think.

At the bottom of the profile was a link to contact a local FBI field office. Corey clicked the link, entered his zip code, and received the address and phone number of the FBI's Atlanta branch.

He glanced at the telephone on his desk. Cracked his knuckles again.

Think.

He couldn't call the FBI. Not yet. He had to think about this further, mull over the consequences of getting involved. This wasn't as simple as making a phone call and reporting a sighting of a fugitive.

This could, for reasons he was loathe to admit, get complicated.

The memory of that cigarette lighter pulsed like a malignant tumor in his mind's eye. He was convinced that Leon had shown it to him that morning because he'd known what Corey would do later. He'd anticipated that Corey would go online to look him up.

And he'd delivered to Corey a clear warning. Keep your mouth shut. Or else.

A knock came at the door.

Corey bolted upright in his chair. But it was only Todd outside, waving at Corey through the glass sidelight.

I don't want to talk to him right now. I don't want to talk to anyone. I need time to think through this.

But he closed the Web browser and beckoned Todd inside.

"Morning, buddy," Todd said. "How're things going?"

He shrugged. "It's going. Just got in from Jada's appointment."

Todd slid into the wing chair in front of Corey's desk and crossed his long legs. He looked, as he normally did, as if he were en route to a photo shoot for a men's clothing catalog. In his late thirties, he was tall, fit, and tanned, with a finely chiseled, Greek god face and thick black hair that was never out of place. He wore a monogrammed white silk shirt, diamond-studded cufflinks, paisley tie, tailored charcoal slacks, and Italian loafers. A platinum Rolex glittered on his wrist; he wore a gold signet ring inscribed with his family crest on the little finger of his left hand that he claimed brought him good luck.

Todd was one of the first friends Corey had made when he'd moved to Atlanta. At Corey's job as a service technician, Todd had been his supervisor. He'd been less like a boss and more like a peer, and they became fast friends, grabbing beers after work, trading DVDs of their favorite action films, and competing in a weekly poker game with some of their other coworkers.

Ten years later—Todd had been promoted to vice president of sales by then, and Corey was regional director of operations—they decided to launch their own security services firm. Todd, who hailed from a wealthy family, had a trust fund that they used as collateral to swing a bank loan. Corey took out a second mortgage on his house to supply the rest of the start-up capital they required.

After five years in business, their little engine that could was operating totally in the black, with increasing revenues and recognition each year. Corey had a knack for the nuts-and-bolts of managing a business; Todd had a flair for sales. Working together as a team, they figured to retire wealthy in fifteen or twenty years, with a legacy to pass on to their heirs.

"The doctor give you the green light for Jada's ear implant thingy?" Todd asked.

"She's perfect."

"Cool." Todd fingered a nonexistent mustache on his

upper lip, and leaned forward. "Hey, I got off the phone with Douglas Homes a couple minutes ago. We've got a verbal commitment. Thirty-eight residential properties. Major coin. We took a gamble with our bid and it paid off, big time."

"Sounds good," Corey said, glancing at the computer screen. He wanted to pull up the profile again, wanted to have some time alone to think.

"Sounds good?" Todd reared back in the chair. "That's better than good—that's awesome! Douglas Homes is building in the Florida panhandle, remember? That's a whole new market for us, new territory to conquer. This'll lead to even bigger things, partner."

Todd's blue eyes danced. He lived for the major deal, the big gamble, the bold risk. More often than not, his maneuvers panned out in their favor, a significant reason why Gates-Webb was earning money hand over fist.

"You're right, it's awesome," Corey said, trying to put some enthusiasm in his voice. "We'll buy some champagne for the team when the contract comes in."

"You okay?" Todd frowned. "Seems like you're not here. Mentally, I mean."

"Can I pose a hypothetical question? Not work related?"

Todd shrugged. "Shoot."

"If you knew I had committed a crime and was wanted for it by the police, what would you do? Would you turn me in?"

"You mean would I snitch?"

"Yeah."

Todd shook his head. "Don't know. What kind of crime are we talking about?"

"Let's say I killed someone."

"Killed someone?" Todd's Adam's apple bobbed. "Killed them why? In self-defense? Because you were going through road rage? Because they did something to your family?"

"Let's say I was robbing this person, and then when I was making my getaway I killed him, because I had to in order to escape."

"Like a stickup?"

"Sort of like that," Corey said. He added: "Purely hypothetical situation."

"Purely hypothetical?" Todd grinned. "I don't think I'd snitch, but I'd probably try to talk you into turning yourself in peacefully."

Corey frowned. "Why would you do that? I mean, try to talk me into turning myself in, instead of snitching?"

"I couldn't snitch on a friend. I'm too loyal."

"You'd put loyalty over obeying the law?"

"Wouldn't you do the same thing for me?"

Corey bit his lip. "I don't know."

"Thanks a lot." Todd rolled his eyes. "Christ, I know who *not* to call if I commit a hit and run."

"Sorry, it's not personal. I just don't know."

"Okay, if you want to talk about an actual situation, we could've been busted for playing poker way back when. That's against the law in Georgia."

"True."

"You know I play in some pretty high stakes games these days, matter of fact." Todd tented his long, manicured fingers and gave Corey a measured look.

Corey was well aware of Todd's gambling habit. He hit Las Vegas or Atlantic City at least once a month, and he sure as hell didn't go to play the slots. Last summer, he had returned from a Nevada trip driving a spanking new Mercedes-Benz coupe, and had hinted that he'd won the pink slip for the car in an especially high-stakes, underground poker game.

Personally, Corey had little interest in gambling. Years ago, when he'd played poker with Todd and some of their friends from work, it had been a social thing, something to pass the time: drink beer with your buddies, munch on a few pizzas, and if you were lucky, you'd walk out the door with an extra twenty bucks, or at least break even.

But Todd had soon grown bored with their "pissant pots" as he'd called them, and ratcheted up to much bigger games, where someone had to vouch for you before you were allowed to buy in and the pots rose into a stratosphere far beyond the resources of the average gambler. He traveled to the country's gambling meccas for many of those games, but some of them took place right there in metro Atlanta, and there was rarely a weekend when Todd didn't play cards somewhere. The guy was probably long overdue for a twelve-step program at Gamblers Anonymous . . . but let he who is without sin cast the first stone.

"Listen, you're a grown man," Corey said. "At the end of the day, what you do with your money is your business."

"But you haven't snitched on me, even though you could."

"That's because I'm not a snitch."

"Exactly." Todd snapped his fingers and rose from the chair, but his eyes dwindled to fine points. "What's this all about anyway, Corey? Have you done something?"

"No, it was only a hypothetical question."

"Hypothetical, sure." Todd chuckled. "Seriously, if you need to talk, you can trust me. I ever tell you about my Uncle Jim?"

"I don't think you've ever mentioned him."

"No? Okay, so the story goes like this. About thirty-some odd years ago, my Uncle Jim got in a bar fight one night, back when he was a truck driver running routes through east Texas. He choked some guy to death in the parking lot, then got in his rig, and drove off. Just drove off. He never turned himself in, and the cops never came after him. Our family knows about it, but do you think we've ever reported anything to the cops?"

Todd winked, and then he left, closing the door behind him. Corey sat there, hands knotted in his lap, pondering his friend's words.

He pulled up Leon's FBI profile again.

But he didn't pick up the phone.

And loyalty had nothing to do with it.

6

Around one-thirty in the afternoon, Simone wrapped up an appointment and stepped out of the office for a quick lunch.

She ran her individual psychotherapy and relationship therapy practice out of one-half of a modest, one-story brick building on Roswell Road in Sandy Springs; a family physician leased the other half of the property. She'd opened her doors for business two years ago, and her calendar was consistently so booked that new clients had to wait three or four weeks for a session. If things continued along the present course, she'd soon have to look into bringing in another therapist to share the workload.

But she loved her job, and didn't mind occasionally working late or on weekends. Counseling individuals, couples, and families through life's crisis situations was not only a career to her—it was a calling. In addition to her office practice, one day a week she provided counseling at a community center in southwest Atlanta, working mostly with at-risk teenage girls and single mothers (they were often one and the same, unfortunately), and she offered her services to them gratis, happy merely to make a meaningful difference in someone's life—just as someone had once made a difference in hers.

When she was fourteen, her parents had divorced. Struggling to make ends meet on her own, her mom had uprooted her and her older brother, Eugene, from their home in Mobile, Alabama, and brought them to Atlanta, where her mother had a close girlfriend who hooked her up with a job. Although it had happened twenty years ago, it remained the most painful transition period of Simone's life. She'd vacillated between blaming her mother for the divorce, to blaming herself. She struggled to make friends in the new school; her class work suffered; she gained weight. And her mom had been too caught up in her own adjustment issues to deal with her.

A high school counselor, Mrs. Fletcher, had been the first one to listen to Simone with empathy, and without judgment. The genteel, soft-spoken woman had made such a profound impact on Simone that she'd decided by her senior year of high school that she wanted to become a psychologist herself. The day she graduated from Georgia State University with her PhD, with Mrs. Fletcher watching on in the commencement audience, was one of the shining moments of her life.

Waving good-bye to her office manager, Simone slid on her sunglasses and strolled to her silver BMW X5 parked in the corner of the small, elm-shaded parking lot. The hazy air was a stew, a smog alert in full effect. Although she was dressed for the weather in a white, single-breasted notch-collar pantsuit, a black cable-knit shirt, and black pumps, after only ten short strides she had a dew of perspiration on her brow.

As she opened the driver's door, she had the distinct sense that someone was watching her, a sensation like fingers pressing on the nape of her neck. She looked over her shoulder.

There was nothing but lunchtime traffic shuttling back and forth on busy Roswell Road. She was the only person standing in the parking lot; a blue Ford pickup, a Honda, and a compact Kia were the only other vehicles parked nearby.

Must've been her imagination. She climbed behind the wheel.

She drove to a Chipotle Mexican Grill down the street, a favorite lunchtime spot of hers. The chain restaurant specialized in gourmet burritos and tacos served in a fast-casual environment.

When the stocky Latino gentleman working behind the counter saw her in line, he started preparing a burrito bowl, her favorite. She gave him a thumbs-up and smiled.

He grinned and indicated his cheek. *"Muy hermosa, señorita."*

He was talking about her dimples, which men often complimented. Men with tact, anyway. Those lacking tact reserved their crude praise for other parts of her anatomy. Over the years, she'd grown so accustomed to hearing certain catcalls—"Can I get fries with that shake?" "Damn, your onion's got me wantin' to cry," "Shake that money-maker for a playa, mami"—that she'd learned to tune them out like so much white noise.

"Gracias," she said, and paid the cashier.

She carried her tray to a booth near the window and took off her sunglasses. She dug a recent issue of *Psychology Today* out of her purse and placed it on the table beside her tray, intending to skim it while she lunched. Although the magazine contained mostly pop-psychology geared toward nonprofessionals, she liked to stay abreast of the articles because many of her clients read them, usually in an earnest but misguided attempt to diagnose themselves or others.

Suddenly, she had that sense of being watched again. She looked around.

The man watching her stood just inside the doorway, hands buried in his pockets. He wore wraparound mirror shades and paint-soiled denim overalls. He had a lion's mane of a black beard streaked with gray, and his hair was woven into dreadlocks that swept down to his shoulders.

Corey's friend, she thought with a spark of recognition. *The one from the gas station this morning. Leon.*

For some reason, Corey had been reluctant to talk about his friendship with this man, and had rebuked Jada for asking questions. Simone had found his reaction strange, but clearly Corey and this Leon had not left off their friendship on the best of terms. You didn't have to be a licensed psychologist to read Corey.

As if by psychic osmosis with her husband, Simone felt tension twisting like a corkscrew in her own stomach, too. What was this guy doing there?

Leon smiled at her, showing a wide gap in his front teeth. He sauntered to her table.

Without asking permission, he took the seat across from her.

"I'm Leon," he said in a surprisingly soft falsetto. He extended his hand across the table. "Your hubby C-Note and I were thick as thieves back in the day."

She didn't want to shake his hand—something about him looked dirty—but she didn't want to be rude, either. She briefly shook his hand. His touch was damp and hot, as if he were cooking inside his own flesh.

And what was that C-Note nickname all about?

She cleared her throat. "I saw you outside the gas station this morning. Corey told me he knew you back in Detroit."

"We go back like rockin' chairs," Leon said. He slid a salt shaker toward him and batted it like a hockey puck between his hands across the table. "It damn near blew my cerebellum to run into him this morning. Like, whoa, my main man! All grown up now with the wife and kid, a captain of his industry, I'm so proud of him, 'cause where we came from, no one expected us to amount to shit. We were given the old heave-ho into the streets like malnourished puppies from a mutt's litter, every man for himself, look out for number one and don't step in number two, and now Corey's living the life of Riley. It gives me hope, it does, it's marvelous, beautiful, a stupendously beautiful thing."

Snickering, he rocked back in the seat, juggling the salt shaker.

Simone stared at him. She had met some colorful characters in her day, but was this guy for real?

As a long-standing rule, she resisted putting on her therapist's hat outside of her counseling practice, but Leon was so unusual that she inadvertently found herself doing an assessment of him. He was definitely hyperactive. She noted the hands in ceaseless motion. The lightning-swift, jittery speech pattern. Did he display poor impulse control and dramatic mood swings, too?

She wished he would remove those sunglasses so she could get a good look at his eyes. They would help her formulate a clearer read on him.

Stop it, she cautioned herself.

But it startled her that Corey had been friends with this man. *Best friends*, he'd admitted. Corey was solid and stable as the proverbial rock. If Leon had always behaved like this, she couldn't imagine him and Corey as anything more than casual acquaintances.

Why hadn't Corey ever told her about this unusual guy? Why was he so reluctant to talk about him?

She was intrigued . . . but Leon showing up in this restaurant, at this time, troubled her above all else.

"Do you eat here often?" she asked.

He bobbed his head, dreadlocks swaying. "Oh, yeah,

yeah, uh-huh, I rip through this little restaurante all the time, daily. See Julio, the pint-sized wetback working the counter? Mi amigo hooks me up nice with the burritos."

She frowned. "Well, he's very friendly, but I don't think he'd appreciate being referred to by the word you used. It's not exactly a politically correct term."

He shrugged and scooped up the pepper shaker, too. Juggling them both, he said, "How do you make your pesos, baby girl? The way you're dressed, the snazzy pantsuit, the understated jewelry, the French manicure, the makeup tight and just right, I know you're not holding down a minimum wage gig greeting welfare moms and their broods of Bebe kids at Wal-Mart. You're involved in a high falutin' profession that requires a spiffy *edumucation*, what is it that you do, huh, do tell, darling."

"I'm a psychologist," she said. Out of habit, she braced for a shrink joke.

"A psychologist, no shit, uh-huh, that's cool. Can I have some Ritalin?" He giggled.

"A psychologist isn't licensed to prescribe medication. Psychiatrists do that. They have medical degrees. My background is clinical psychology."

"Do you deliver a diagnosis from your high and mighty shrink throne, append a certifiable label on a hapless patient, and summon the men in the white coats to haul him off to the funny farm to live the rest of his pathetic little Walter Mitty life in a rubber room strapped in a straitjacket and sucking applesauce through a straw?"

She blinked at his torrent of words. "No, no. I've never had to commit anyone, thank goodness."

He dropped the shakers onto the table and leaned forward, thick veins rising to the surface of his tattooed forearms.

"So you sit around on that lovely, bodacious ass of yours gabbing to half-wits all day, is that right? Listening and nodding uh-huh, uh-huh, asking asinine open-ended questions to fill the allotted time, nail the poor suckers between their dumb bovine eyes with an inflated bill when the buzzer goes off, usher them into the great outdoors with a Coke and a smile?"

Her jaw clenched. "Excuse me?"

"If you were my lady, I wouldn't let you leave *mi casa*. You're too traffic-stopping fine to lift a finger." He adjusted the sunglasses on his nose, then whistled and pantomimed a voluptuous shape with his hands. "Brick house all day and night, it's hard for me to peep the package in that high-priced chic suit you're wearing, but I'll hazard a guess, you've gotta be thirty-six C, twenty-four, thirty-six, perfect pole dancer coordinates, no doubt provoking wet dreams and blue balls and sweaty palms every time you strut your sexy chocolate ass into a room. Corey's a lucky, lucky dog, I tell you that, take that check to a bank and cash it 'cause it's good."

She blushed, speechless.

His wraparound mirror shades offered a distorted reflection of only her own bewildered face, but she could feel his lecherous gaze crawling all over her.

Hands clenched into fists, she crossed her arms over her chest, covering her cleavage.

"Quiet now, huh?" His voice had lowered several octaves, and a predatory smile danced across his lips. "Are you quiet like that in the sack, too, or are you a screamer, a lady in the streets but a freak in the sheets?"

Her face burned. Enough. She'd had enough of this nonsense.

Trembling, she gathered her things, grabbed the edges of the tray, and slid out of the booth.

"Excuse me," she said. "I have to get back to work. I'll . . . I'll tell Corey I ran into you."

"You do that, señorita bonita, yeah, you make sure you tell him. Shalom."

He blew a kiss at her, and laughed in his strange, giggly manner.

She hadn't touched her food, but she dumped the entire meal into the wastebasket near the exit. She no longer had an appetite.

Without looking back, she hurried across the parking lot and to her car, feeling watched all the way.

7

Corey spent the rest of the day at the office, determined to stay focused on business.

He returned all of the messages that he'd received earlier. Sat in on a conference call with a current customer, a local electronics store, about installing enhancements to their surveillance system. Interviewed a candidate for a new sales rep position. Had a meeting with a vendor who wanted Corey to upgrade to the latest and greatest customer relations management software.

It was, all in all, shaping up to be a busy weekday, for which he was grateful. It allowed him to delay making a decision about his Leon problem. He promised himself he would think about this issue later, when his mind was uncluttered.

He knew, of course, that procrastinating was only a dishonest tack to keep from confronting the dilemma head on . . . but he just couldn't let himself think about it too much.

Because frankly, it scared him.

Around three o'clock that afternoon, a long-time friend, Rev. Otis Trice, paid him a visit. Otis was a stout, dark-skinned man in his midsixties, with a round, bald head, wire-rim glasses, and a neatly trimmed snow-white beard. He entered the office looking as impeccably dressed as usual: polished black oxfords, gray wool slacks, white dress shirt, burgundy silk tie. Corey could not recall ever seeing him wear anything more casual than a pair of Dockers, and he doubted the man had anything denim in his entire wardrobe.

Corey shook his hand and invited him to have a seat.

"It is good seeing you, Brother Webb, indeed it is," Otis said, easing into the chair. He smiled, revealing a gold-capped front tooth, a relic from his youth in his native Detroit, and dabbed at his shiny pate with a handkerchief. "We are certainly experiencing a sultry day today, are we not?"

Otis spoke with crisp, elegant diction that had earned him the moniker "The Great Enunciator" among his friends and family. An admitted hell-raiser in his youth who'd gotten drafted for Vietnam, Otis confessed that he'd found God when he'd miraculously avoided detonating a land mine that claimed the lives of two members of his platoon not ten seconds after he'd passed over it. Upon his return to the States, he earned a doctorate in theology and founded a small, non-denominational church in East Point, using his ministry to stimulate positive change in the community.

"It's a hot one out there for sure," Corey said. "Can I get you some water?"

"That would be excellent, thank you."

Corey fetched him a bottle of water from the mini-refrigerator nestled underneath his desk. Otis accepted it gratefully.

Sixteen years ago, when Corey had found himself homeless after Grandma Louise had died, Otis, a family friend, had offered to bring Corey to Atlanta and let him live with him and his wife. The offer had changed the course of Corey's life—and, almost assuredly, had saved it.

Leon had gone to prison barely a month before Grandma Louise's death, and with his grandmother's passing, the two major figures of Corey's young life were gone. He had been in a fragile state, as liable to go down for a felony as he was to win gainful employment. Soon after bringing him to Atlanta, Otis had helped him land a job as an alarm installation technician.

The rest was history.

Otis crossed his legs. "How is the Webb family?"

"They're great," Corey said. He glanced at the photos on the edge of the desk, felt a familiar rush of pride and love. "You'll have to come over for dinner sometime soon. I know they'd love to see you."

"We must do that soon, yes," Otis said. He sipped water, his face growing troubled. "Unfortunately, I'm afraid that I'm not here to pay a social call, Brother Webb. It appears that I must enlist the services of your company for my church."

"Did something happen?" Corey asked.

"Someone broke in this past weekend," he said. "We believe it occurred late Saturday evening. These thieves helped themselves to our audiovisual system—it wasn't much, mind you, about five thousand dollars' worth of refurbished equipment, according to our insurance estimates. Certainly, a pale echo of the impressive systems that many churches lay claim to these days. But it was, alas, all that we had."

"I'm so sorry," Corey said. "The cops have any suspects?"

"We suspect neighborhood youth." Otis shook his head sadly. "The very children that we strive so hard to impact with our ministry. We completed a police report, but the officer himself admitted that there's only a slim chance that our equipment will be recovered."

Even as Corey commiserated with his friend, he was

thinking about those "neighborhood youth" who had almost definitely perpetrated the theft. Young Leon Sharpes—and young Corey Webbs, too.

It made him sick.

"Our insurance company has threatened to cancel our coverage unless we install a burglar alarm system," Otis said, "a measure that, as you are well aware, I've long resisted, perhaps out of a naïve belief that if you perform righteous works in your community and genuinely seek to serve those in need, you generate goodwill that others will respect and honor."

"I wish things worked like that," Corey said. "Unfortunately, your story is becoming all too common these days. If I had a dime for each call we get from nonprofits and small churches who've been burglarized, I could buy both of us a nice steak dinner."

Otis offered a broken smile. "Can you help me?"

"Of course I can." Corey slid open a desk drawer and retrieved a preformatted form that they used to create profiles of prospective customers. "And with this one, installation's on the house, and I'll see if I can cut you a nice discount on the monthly monitoring fee. That's the least I can do."

Otis shook his head. "No, I can't allow you to do that, Brother Webb. Absolutely not. You have a business to run, expenses of your own—"

"If it weren't for you, I wouldn't *have* a business." Corey smiled. "Don't argue with me. Isn't there something in the Bible about not blocking your blessings?"

"I believe you're referring to the idiom, 'don't look a gift horse in the mouth.'"

"Yeah, whatever, don't do that. Let me do this for you, Reverend, please. It's my honor."

"As you wish," Otis said. "God bless you, son. Your grandmother would be so proud of you."

Two hours later, he had scheduled Otis's church to receive an emergency installation of one of their deluxe alarm and monitoring packages. He was tidying up a few more loose ends before leaving for the day when he called home. Jada answered.

"This is the Webb residence," she said in a polite, careful tone. She pronounced "residence" as "res'dence."

"Hey, Pumpkin. How ya doing?"

"Daddy!" she cried with glee.

Corey grinned. He never tired of hearing the excitement in his daughter's voice when he talked to her. Once she reached her teen years, she would probably enter a sullen, rebellious phase and avoid speaking to him as much as possible. He wanted to bask in her adulation while it lasted.

"When are you coming home?" Jada asked.

"I'll be home soon, sweetie," he said. "Can I speak to your mother, please?"

"'Kay, Daddy," Jada said. "Here she is."

Simone came on the line. "Hey, baby. We're having beef stroganoff for dinner."

Corey laughed. "Okay, you beat me to the punch."

"After all this time, I think I've figured you out."

Leon's face surfaced in Corey's thoughts. *Actually, you haven't figured me out at all, babe. How I wish you had.*

"You need me to pick up anything on the way home?" he asked.

"We're good. I stopped by the store earlier."

"Then I'll be there soon."

"There was one thing I wanted to mention," she said. "I was going to wait until dinner, but . . ."

He tensed, in anticipation of more questions about Leon. Or—horrors—that Simone had actually taken it upon herself to look up Leon on Google.

He cracked a knuckle, phone wedged between his shoulder and ear. "Go ahead."

"I ran in to your friend Leon at lunch today."

He almost shot out of his chair. "What?"

"You know the Chipotle on Roswell Road, near my office?"

"He was there?"

"I went there around one-thirty, and there he was."

"Did he speak to you?"

"Did he speak to me?" She paused. "Umm, yeah, that would be a bit of an understatement. He sat at my table and started running off at the mouth like a carnival barker. You know I prefer not to do assessments outside of the office . . . but he seems rather hyperactive."

"Like an Energizer bunny on amphetamine."

"Exactly! Has he always behaved like that?"

"For as long as I've known him, yeah." Corey popped another knuckle. He was afraid to ask his next question. "So what did he say?"

"Nothing important," she said after a moment's hesitation. "I was surprised to see him there, but he said he frequents the place so, whatever. Coincidence, I guess."

Coincidence, my ass.

But Simone didn't sound suspicious. He saw no reason to worry her and no reason to delve into more info about Leon, either.

"Well, stranger things have happened," Corey said. "I'll be home in a bit, babe."

"C-Note?"

He stammered, convinced he had heard incorrectly. "Excuse me?"

"Leon used that nickname for you. C-Note. What's the story behind that?"

"It was only a stupid nickname he made up for me. As you saw for yourself, he says a lot of nonsense."

"Hmph. No disagreement there."

"I'll see you guys soon," he said.

It required all of his self-control to keep from slamming the phone onto the cradle.

What the hell was Leon up to?

8

As Corey was walking across the parking lot to his car, a blue Ford truck rolled up behind him and honked.

It was Leon, again. Shit. Corey got a quivery feeling in his knees.

"Corey!" Leon waved from the driver's side window. "Slow up, man!"

Corey looked around to see if anyone was watching them. They were alone in the parking lot. Evening rush-hour traffic traveled back and forth on the adjoining road, the bleat of horns and rumble of engines like discordant music.

He approached Leon's truck. Leon wore a pair of wrap-around mirror sunglasses. He was the only one inside the vehicle. The dull-eyed pervert was gone.

"What're you doing here?" Corey asked.

"I was in the area, my man, thought I'd drop by," Leon said. He took a draw on a cigarette. "I figured we could grab a cold one and chitchat a bit."

Corey glared at him. "My wife told me she ran in to you at lunch. Why the hell are you following us?"

"Following you?" Leon grinned. "Don't be a paranoid.

Come on, it was pure, unadulterated coincidence. I've been going to that Chipotle spot for weeks. I love Mexican cuisine, *amo el alimento mexicano*."

"Whatever. That's bullshit. I know you better than that. What kind of game are you trying to run on me?"

Smirking, Leon pointed ahead with his cigarette, reflections of passing traffic floating across the lenses of his sunglasses. "There's a sports bar down the road, you still guzzle Heineken by the keg, I know you haven't changed that much, let's roll, vamos, climb up in the saddle here and let's go get that brewski, it's so damn hot and smoggy in this bitch, nothing'll hit the sweet spot like an ice cold lager."

Sucking in a breath, Corey looked around again. All clear.

"I'll take my own car," Corey said. "Follow me."

As he drove, he tried to think of what he was going to say to Leon. His earlier conversation with Todd replayed through his thoughts. *I don't think I'd snitch, but I'd probably try to talk you into turning yourself in peacefully.*

He decided, finally, that that was what he would do: he would convince Leon to turn himself in to the FBI. Leon had been gifted with the kind of raw intelligence that defied standardized tests and regimented school curriculums, and he had the cold-blooded cunning of a rattlesnake, but no one, not even him, could elude the FBI forever. The Feds had mind-boggling resources, highly trained professionals, and access to a worldwide intelligence network. Sooner or later, they would catch him—and Corey did not intend to find himself and his family caught in the crossfire.

They went to a sports bar called Shooters. Corey had been there once with Todd and their staff. They had a wide selection of beers on draught, good burgers, buffalo wings at five different levels of spiciness, and an abundance of big TV screens positioned to give you a prize view of a sporting event no matter where you sat.

At Leon's request, they took one of the high-backed booths in the far corner of the dining room, in the smoking section, near the restrooms and a rear emergency exit. Leon settled onto the side that gave him a direct view of the entrance.

He's positioning himself to see everyone who comes inside, Corey thought. *And to make a quick getaway, if he needs to.*

It was early yet, the happy hour crowd just beginning to drift in. Corey noted, for his own benefit, that none of the patrons were uniformed police officers.

An energetic young brunette stopped by to take their orders. Leon asked for two Heinekens, on draft. When the waitress flitted away, he removed his sunglasses.

"My man, C-Note," Leon said. He twirled the shades in his fingers. "Another day, another dollar, nothing like hitting the bar after putting in a hard day of honest work."

"You know all about putting in that hard day of honest work, I take it."

"You know it, I've had my nose to the grindstone all day, painting houses in this damn near tropical jungle climate is enough to make a grown man cry uncle, but I doubt you know anything about that, sitting up there as you do in your plush, air-conditioned office, looking out the window at the hoi polloi while you sip on chilled Perrier and monitor your stock portfolio."

Corey let the veiled insult pass. "What's the address of the house you were painting today, Leon?"

"It's on Wainwright Way, a stone's throw from here, a mansion, actually, stucco, eight bedrooms, five bathrooms, Jacuzzi, wine cellar, swimming pool, the whole nine. They had some annoying little rat dog skittering around all over the place. I almost had to kick that sucker in the teeth to get him out of my way."

"A Chihuahua," Corey said.

"Yeah, that's what they call them, one of those Taco Bel mutts. The bastard pissed on my paint brushes and could've wrung his scrawny goddamn neck like a towel, bu the lady of the house was there, fine bitch, old as Methusela but fine. Most definitely she'd had about a million dollars o plastic surgery done, she had these crazy perfect D-cup knockers that made me want to nurse like a newborn, you know what I mean, huh, huh?"

Corey could only shake his head. It was impossible to know whether Leon was telling the truth. He lied with a glibness that Corey had never seen before in anyone else.

There was likely a road nearby called Wainwright Way and there might have been a home that fit Leon's thumbnai description. Leon might have even driven past and observe a crew of painters at work there, too. But who knew whethe he had worked there himself or not, unless you'd seen him with your own eyes? That was what made him such a good liar. He spun his fabrications from a loom of reality and wove the threads as he saw fit to suit his purposes.

The waitress delivered their beers. Leon raised his mug "To the good old days."

Leon took a long sip, belched with satisfaction.

Quiet, Corey left his beer untouched. He was struggling to find the words to express himself, and as far as he was concerned, this meeting of theirs was by no means a celebration of anything.

"Ah, that hits the spot," Leon said. He grinned. "Remember how we used to do, how we'd kick back and lounge afte we put in *real* work?"

Corey slid his mug aside. "I don't think about those days any more, Leon. I'm a husband now, a father. I run a business, a *legit* business."

"All right, all right, yeah, yeah, I feel you. You're Mr. Home Security now." He giggled. "Ironic, still, you know, deliciously ironic."

"I'm an upstanding member of society. I have a reputation in the community. A good name."

Leon drank more beer. "A man's only as good as his name, uh-huh, yeah, that's what I always say, right, right, right."

"These days, when I'm faced with a decision, I do the right thing," Corey said. "It's not all about me any more. At the end of the day, I have responsibilities to other people that I have to keep in mind."

"Of course you do, that's cool." Leon fidgeted with his sunglasses. "It's all good, I like to hear this from you, stepping up to the plate for the family and the business, comme il faut, my man, you make me proud."

Corey pushed out a breath from the bottom of his lungs. "Listen, I don't know why you've been following me and my wife, and I don't know how long you have, and to be frank, I don't care—because it all ends here. I looked you up online, Leon. I think you know damn well what I found."

"What's that?" Leon fished in his pocket and withdrew the cigarette lighter. He flicked the striker wheel and brought the flame to a fresh cigarette. Taking a slow drag, he left the lighter lying in plain sight on the table next to the beer mug. "Share the fruits of your research, good buddy."

Corey cracked a knuckle. Prying his gaze away from the lighter was like escaping the gravity pull of a black hole.

"Turn yourself in peacefully," Corey said softly. "Please."

"Why should I?" Leon tapped ashes into a tray. "Believe it or not, I like how I'm living. I'm here in the ATL maxing and relaxing with my best partner from back in the day, having a cold brew. My life's all biscuits and gravy."

"Be serious."

"I *am* serious. I'm a celebrity, don't you know, this pretty mug has been cycling all over the glass teat. Hey, want my John Hancock?"

Leon pulled a square beverage napkin toward him, removed an ink pen from his pocket, and did a loopy scrawl of his signature. He slid the napkin across the table to Corey.

"Give that to the wifey." Leon winked.

"Listen." Corey crumbled the napkin in his fist. "You're putting me and my family in a very dangerous situation. I'm trying to help you."

Leon sneered. "Wrong, wrong, wrong, you're trying to help yourself, and in my informed opinion, you don't need any more help, Mr. Husband–Father–Hot Shit Entrepreneur. Matter of fact, it looks as if you ought to be doing like Mother Teresa and lending a helping hand to the less fortunate who remember you from way back when, when your only ride was a rusty little Huffy dirt bike and your dear old grandma dribbled water in the milk so you could eat Frosted Flakes till the first of the month."

Leon picked up the lighter again and thumbed the wheel. He balanced the palm of his hand on the flame's edge, savage eyes lacerating Corey as the heat singed his flesh. It was a morbid game he and Corey had played as teenagers, and Leon had always outlasted him.

"You want money," Corey whispered.

"You owe me. Remember all those things I did for you, wingman?"

Corey didn't want to remember any of it. "We did those things together."

"I did time for you, too, do you remember that? A three-year bid, we didn't do that together."

"But that was for something you did on your own! That was your own solo job."

"I could've brought you down to the sewer with me, and you know it, I could've brought you down for a whole truck-load of dirt that I haven't told anyone about—yet."

Leon flicked the lid shut on the lighter and slammed it onto the table. Corey flinched in his seat.

"You've done well for yourself, and I'm proud of that," Leon said. He exhaled a ring of smoke toward Corey's face. "But you've forgotten your roots, kiddo, it's time to pay the devil his due."

Understanding washed over Corey like cold water. "That's why you followed my wife today, isn't it? You wanted to prove you could get to someone close to me if I don't agree to what you want."

Leon smirked. "Did I say that?"

"I know how you think," Corey said. "You know what? I bet me running in to you this morning wasn't coincidence, either, not by a long shot. You planned that somehow—something tipped you off about me and my business. What was it, huh? Did you plug my name into Google, too, learn all about my company, and figure you could run some half-assed extortion scheme on me?"

"If you say you know how I think, then you should know I don't plan anything. I live in the moment."

"Bullshit," Corey spat.

"Think so? Okay—want to know what I'm planning at this precise moment? Do you? How about this. I'm planning to drop an e-mail to the law in Detroit describing a cold case that involves this upstanding citizen who lives in Atlanta but who actually has a quite unsavory past, and this e-mail will rather strenuously suggest that they investigate this particular individual, uh-huh, perhaps request a DNA sample from said person, 'cause, golly, the crime scene techs must have collected forensic evidence for this lingering, perplexing case, and it would be a simple process for them to pop all of it under the ole microscope and see if there's a match—"

"That's enough," Corey said. "I get it."

Grinning, Leon took another pull on his cigarette and chased it with a gulp of beer.

Looking around, Corey blotted his damp palms on his

khakis. With Leon's refusal to turn himself in, he saw only one way out of this. He didn't like it, but it might be the only way to spare him and his family further involvement.

He dug his wallet out of his pocket.

"You have seen the light," Leon said. "I have trained you well, grasshopper."

Corey passed Leon all of the cash in his wallet: a hundred and twenty dollars.

"This is all I have on me," Corey said.

"A hundred and twenty dollars?" Leon riffled through the bills, folded them into his pocket. His eyes burned. "You actually think I'm going to saddle up and gallop into the sunset for a hundred and twenty fuckin' dollars?"

"Look, man." Corey opened his wallet, showed it to him. "I'm telling you, that's all I've got."

"You've got more in the bank, a whole lot more. You think I'm the village idiot?"

Corey wiped sweat from his forehead. "How much do you want?"

"How much is your freedom worth to you?"

Corey had handled the household finances ever since he'd married. He did a mental calculation on how much he could withdraw from their accounts without Simone immediately noticing.

"I could give you five thousand tomorrow," he said.

"That's all your nouveau riche life is worth? Five thousand lousy dollars? You spent that much on window treatments in your McMansion. Do you realize how absurd and insulting that sounds, do you have any fucking clue how ridiculous it is, do you, do you, huh?"

Corey stammered. "Maybe . . . maybe I could get you six thousand, or seven—"

"Fifty large."

Corey thought he had heard him wrong. "Fifty thousand dollars?"

"You know what? Make it a hundred."

"Leon, I . . . I can't."

"Two fifty."

"It's not possible."

"Three hundred."

Corey was shaking his head.

"You know you have it," Leon said.

"That's not the point. Listen, I'm not paying you fifty thousand, a hundred thousand, two hundred and fifty thousand dollars, or some other crazy amount. Hell, no. I'm not doing it, Leon. You can't bully me the way you used to, forget it, those days are over."

Leon glowered at him, eyebrow twitching.

"You'll take what I'm offering," Corey said. "That's five thousand dollars, cash. I get it to you tomorrow, you take it, and then you stay the hell away from me and my family and we forget we ever ran into each other again. Okay? That's the deal, take it or leave it."

Leon was silent for a breathless moment—and then he hurled his beer mug across the dining room. It exploded like a grenade against a far wall, bits of glass and foam spraying everywhere.

People spun around, gawking. A hush fell over the room.

Getting to his feet, Leon stuffed the cigarette lighter into his pocket and snapped on his sunglasses. He pointed at Corey, spittle spluttering from his lips.

"You're gonna give me everything you've got, one way or another. You owe me, motherfucker, you're gonna pay up, one way or another. *That's* the deal."

Leon stormed to the doors. One of the bartenders shouted at him, and Leon flipped the guy the finger and told him to kiss his ass. He shoved through the exit.

Corey's heart had crawled halfway up his throat. He swallowed.

The waitress appeared beside the table, cheeks flushed red. "Someone has to pay for that broken glass, sir."

"I'll take care of it," Corey said. "And the beers, too, I guess."

With a sigh of disgust, he slid out his credit card.

9

Driving home, Corey took a less direct route, repeatedly checking the rearview mirror to see whether he was being followed. He didn't appear to be, but that gave him little comfort.

He didn't know for sure how long Leon had been watching him, didn't know the depth of Leon's knowledge of him and his family. Leon had demonstrated that he knew where Simone worked. There was no telling what else he might know.

Home was a welcome sight, as always. Blood-orange evening sunshine shimmered on the gabled roof, and the newly planted hibiscus fronting the bay window was blooming, pink petals as bright as cotton candy. The Bermuda grass, tended by a landscaping service that visited weekly, was so lush, green, and finely edged that it might have been artificial turf.

He and Simone had worked hard, and sacrificed much, to achieve this house, their piece of the American Dream. He could not bear the thought of losing it all.

He parked in the garage next to Simone's SUV and cut off

the engine. He hit the remote control clipped to the sun visor, and the big sectional door rumbled shut.

One thing was certain: he couldn't tell Simone what was going on. If he told her what had happened at the bar, she would insist on contacting the police. It was the logical, good citizen thing to do. He would be unable to explain to her satisfaction why calling the cops was out of the question, not without delving into the truth.

Listen here, babe, we can't call the police and report that we saw Leon because Leon has some dirt on me. Yeah, some old, serious dirt—the kind of dirt that gets you sent to prison for a long time. . . .

She would pressure him for full disclosure. Once he shared those sordid details, everything for which he'd struggled so hard all these years would come crashing down: his marriage, his business, his reputation.

How had his life ever come to this? Hadn't he paid his dues? Hadn't he rendered his pound of flesh on the altar of the golden rule, hard work, service to others, and sacrifice?

But you've forgotten your roots, kiddo, it's time to pay the devil his due . . .

Hadn't he done everything he was supposed to do to make peace with his past?

It all seemed so unfair that he wanted to punch the crap out of something. Leon's smug face would have been a satisfying target.

He snatched the key out of the ignition and went inside.

"Daddy!" Jada cried when he entered the kitchen. She catapulted into his arms.

"Hi, Pumpkin." He bent and kissed her forehead.

The touch of his daughter, the sweet, innocent smell of her, made his throat tight. He could not lose her; he would not. She meant more to him than any house, any business, any amount of money.

"How was your day?" Jada asked, gray eyes ever curious.

He merely smiled and ran his hand across her cornrows. "Hmm, something sure smells good. What're you and Mom cooking?"

"Beef stronoff!" she said.

"Stroganoff," Simone corrected. Dressed in a yellow tank top and black terry cloth shorts, she leaned against the granite counter near the cook top, nursing a glass of red wine. Fragrant meat sauce and egg noodles simmered in a pan. "This is a good pinot, baby. Want to try it?"

"In a minute, sure. Be right back."

He went to the security system's touch-screen command center mounted on the wall next to the interior garage door. With the tap of an icon on the graphical interface, he activated the sensors installed on the house's ground-level perimeter; the system sounded a series of short beeps, indicating the newly armed status. If an intruder lifted a window or pried open a door, the alarm would sound, and the police would be notified within sixty seconds.

Feeling more at ease, he returned to the kitchen.

Simone gave him a puzzled look. "Why are you turning on the alarm? It's sort of early for that."

Typically, he waited until they were ready for bed to activate the system.

"I'm running some diagnostics," he lied.

Doubt touched her features, but she said nothing further about it. She handed him a goblet of pinot noir. He thanked her, set the glass on the counter, and leaned in to give her a moist kiss. Her lips tasted of black cherries.

"Hmm, it's a good wine," he said.

She smiled, cinnamon-brown eyes full of bottomless love. He had looked into those beloved eyes of hers every day for ten years, and they had not lost their ability to captivate him; in fact, time had given them greater character, power, depth. It was because of those eyes that he believed he could be a good husband; because of them he believed he could be a good father to a child when he had never known his own father; because of them he aspired to be a man who was in all ways worthy of her love.

He couldn't lose her. He wouldn't.

He kissed her again. Her mouth opened wider to accept him, and she hung her arms around his neck. He slid his hands to her small waist, and lower still, to the sensuous flare of her hips. She pressed her pelvis against him, and he suddenly wanted her so urgently it was like a gnawing hunger in the pit of his stomach.

"Okay, guys," Jada said, face red with embarrassment.

Corey stepped back. "Cut me some slack, Pumpkin, that was only a PG-rated kiss."

As Jada rolled her eyes, Simone comically fanned herself with an oven mitt.

"Whew, honey, where did that come from?" she said.

"Glad to see my wife, that's all." He smiled. "I'm going to change into something more comfortable."

"We'll be ready to eat in five, ten minutes at the most," she said.

Their master bedroom was on the first floor. In the large walk-in closet, he changed out of his work clothes and dressed in a T-shirt with a character from *The Boondocks* on the front, denim cargo shorts, and Nike slides.

At the back of the closet, hidden on a shelf behind a stack of shoeboxes, lay an aluminum case with a combination lock. He lifted it off the shelf and sat on a stool in the dressing area. Placing the case on his lap, he thumbed in the combination and raised the lid.

A Smith and Wesson .357 lay inside in thick, dimpled foam.

From a shoebox, he extracted a speed loader bristling with hollow-point ammunition, and a DeSantis in-the-waistband holster, for concealed carry.

Although he had installed a top-of-the-line security center in their home, electronic measures didn't cover every possibility. As far as he was concerned, complete peace of mind could be achieved only with a firearm.

Simone knew about the gun, and he'd trained her in its proper use, but she didn't like keeping it in the house because of Jada. As a compromise, he locked it away in a safe place.

He loaded the revolver, secured the holster snug against his waistband with a belt, and buried the gun inside. He pulled his T-shirt over his waist.

He checked his profile in the full-length mirror that hung inside the closet. Looked good. Felt even better.

He didn't know what Leon might try to pull next, but if it involved crashing into their home, he was going to be in for a surprise.

"Honey!" Simone called.

Armed, he went to have dinner with his family.

10

After dinner, Jada took a bath and dressed for bed, and then they all piled onto the sofa in the family room and watched *Shrek*, one of Jada's all-time favorite movies. Although many of the adult-oriented jokes were way over her head, she nevertheless found it hilarious and insisted on watching it at least once a week.

Corey normally laughed at the film, too, but that evening he couldn't manage more than a lukewarm chuckle at the funniest parts. Sitting beside him on the sofa, Simone seemed to take note of his low-key mood, but she made no comment. If he knew her, she was filing away every detail of his behavior in preparation for a future conversation.

Let her file away all she wanted. He wasn't talking. He would keep his own counsel and take the necessary measures to protect his family.

At nine-thirty, Simone announced that it was past Jada's bedtime. Jada protested, but a huge yawn betrayed her. Giving in with no further argument, she kissed both of them and shuffled toward the staircase. She'd recently declared her independence as a "big girl," as she put it, and at bedtimes would kiss them good night, go upstairs, and crawl under the covers without asking to be tucked in.

When Corey offered to give her a piggyback ride to her bedroom, however—something he hadn't done in at least a year—she happily accepted. He lugged her upstairs, hiking up her feet to his rib cage to keep her clear of the holstered gun.

"Whew, you're getting heavy, kid," he said. Winded, he set her down at the threshold of her room, straightened, and massaged his back. "That might be the last piggyback ride ever."

"Do you think I'm fat, Daddy?"

She gazed up at him, eager for approval. Sometimes, Jada would make observations or comments that made her sound mature beyond her years, an old wizened soul trapped in a little girl's body, such as the time a few months ago when she'd approached him in the study and asked him, point blank: "Daddy, do you ever wonder what you would be like now if you had known your mom and dad?" Stunned, Corey had stumbled through an inadequate response and afterward spiraled into an hour of agonizing self-reflection.

At other times, such as that one, she was only an insecure kid who craved validation.

"No, no, Pumpkin," he said. "I didn't mean you were fat. I meant you were getting older, that's all. You're far from fat."

Her face twisted into a scowl. "Logan said I was fat."

"Who the heck is Logan?"

"He's a boy in my class. He calls every girl fat. He said Melissa is fat, but I think she's skinny as a matchstick."

He chuckled. "Skinny as a matchstick, huh? Where'd you hear that?"

"I read it in a book."

Jada was only nine, but she had probably read more books than he had. He put his arm around her shoulders and ushered her into the bedroom.

"Sweetie, don't pay any attention to this Logan kid," he said. "You're a beautiful girl. Always remember, that, okay?"

She nodded.

"Have you brushed your teeth?"

"I did that after I took my bath," she said, with a tone that said he should give her more credit. "But I have to feed Mickey."

Mickey was her one-year-old pet budgie. Jada had originally wanted a puppy, but Corey and Simone didn't think she was quite ready to train and care for a dog. The parrot had filled in nicely.

The domed birdcage stood beside a window on the other side of the room. Jada approached the cage, the little green-feathered bird on his perch, watching her with dark, beady eyes. She shook a packet of seed near the metal bars. "Ready to eat?"

"Bring on the food, dude," Mickey said, one of the comical responses she had taught the parrot to give on cue.

Smiling absently, Corey went to the window, parted the curtains and Levolor blinds, and looked outside.

The road in front of the house was dark and quiet. By then, their neighbors would be shut away in their homes, dinners eaten, dishes cleaned, children tucked under covers, everyone settling in for the night in preparation to do it all over again tomorrow, the predictable and oddly comforting cycle of suburban life.

Most of the tension that had been collected in his muscles throughout the evening finally drained out of him. He wondered if maybe he'd been overreacting. Leon was bold and impulsive, but he would not be reckless enough to kick in the door knowing that Corey would be anticipating him.

Maybe he should just relax. A house was a man's castle, after all—and his was exceedingly well fortified.

Jada finished feeding the bird, drew the cage cover halfway across the dome, the way Mickey liked it, and burrowed underneath the covers.

"Good night, Pumpkin," Corey said. "I love you."

"Night, Daddy. Love you, too."

After he kissed her forehead, she removed the speech processor attached to her ear and placed it within arm's reach on the nightstand.

Without the device, Jada was essentially deaf. In the event of an emergency such as a fire, Corey had installed a flashing, vibrating red beacon on the wall beside her bed; the beacon was wired to the security system, and when triggered, caused enough of a ruckus to rouse Jada from all but the deepest REM slumbers.

He cut off the light and drew the door shut, satisfied that his little angel was safely tucked away. For his own peace of mind, he'd needed to see her to bed, as if the ritual somehow guaranteed her safety from all outside threats.

He returned downstairs. He heard Simone in the master bathroom, brushing her teeth.

He took the opportunity to remove the gun from inside his waistband, and placed both gun and holster in the nightstand drawer on his side of the bed. Leon might not attempt anything while he was home, but he would sleep better with the piece close at hand.

As he was closing the drawer, Simone sauntered out of the bathroom wearing a red lace-up chemise that exposed a tantalizing amount of skin. She walked to the bed with the easy grace of a feline, hips swaying.

He kicked off his slides so quickly he almost fell down.

She laughed. "Easy, tiger, I'm not going anywhere. I thought we could resume what we'd started before dinner."

She peeled back the duvet from the mattress and slid onto the sheets. "Did you tuck in Jada?"

"Tight as a bug in a rug." He pulled off his T-shirt, dropped it to the floor.

"You haven't done that in a while."

"Done what? Taken off my shirt in front of you?"

A small smile. "No, tuck in Jada."

"Just felt like it." He rolled down his cargo shorts.

She drew her legs underneath her Indian style and cocked her head, studying him. "If there's something on your mind, honey, you know you can talk to me. I'm here to lend a listening ear whenever you need it—free of charge."

"There's nothing like having a therapist in the house. But I'm fine, babe, really. Want some proof? Check this out."

He pulled down his boxers. She did a double take at his rigid length.

"Well, that's definitely proof of something good," she said.

He climbed onto the bed, and she came into his arms.

He was captive to a heavy, urgent lust, the likes of which he had not felt in ages, as if he were a horny teenager again. Simone was gorgeous, of course, and they had a healthy sex life, made love often and with great passion and tenderness, but the desire he felt then was something deeper—a primal drive to connect with her, to reaffirm the realness and strength of their union, as if to do so would magically ward off all hazards and evils, then and forever.

I'm not going to lose what we have, he thought, as he entered her and she gave a small gasp of pleasure. *No one's going to take this away from us. Ever.*

What would happen the next morning, unfortunately, would prove him completely wrong.

11

Late that night, Ed Denning circled the wooded banks of the lake near his home, flashlight in hand, searching for one of his dogs.

"Here, girlie!" he called out, his raspy voice echoing across the lake's still waters. He blew three bursts on a rusty whistle. "Come, girlie!"

The dog he sought was a young female black Labrador–Great Dane mix, a sweetheart of a hound that he had found rooting through trash one day on the side of the road, her body so emaciated that every one of her ribs was visible. He'd offered her a meaty treat, coaxed her into his old pickup, and brought her home.

To live with the fifty-seven other dogs he'd rescued.

"I know you're out here, girl," he muttered, picking his way through the weeds with a gnarled wooden cane he needed to support his bum right leg. "Come on home to Ed. Ed loves you. Ed needs you. Come on home, please."

Ed lived to rescue dogs. Although he had dim memories of doing other things in life—he vaguely remembered fighting a war in a foreign land of rice paddies and fearsome enemies who wore hats that looked like lamp shades—his life had not truly begun until he'd launched his rescue mission, until he'd begun to fill his home with wonderful canine lives that, if it had not been for his intervention, would have been snuffed out by soulless bastards who thought "putting down" an innocent animal was a humane thing to do.

They were murderers, in his opinion, no better than Nazis running gas chambers in concentration camps. Cold-hearted killers. They were the ones who really deserved to die.

He often saw cats that needed to be rescued, too, but felines did not seem to like him, and would scramble away when he tried to cajole them near with treats. But he had a natural affinity for dogs.

In fact, he much preferred dogs to the company of people. All a dog wanted was food, a belly rub, and a warm place to sleep. People . . . well, he'd never been much able to figure out what the hell they wanted, and had long ago washed his hands of them.

He'd once had a people family, though. A wife with jewel eyes and a little girl with a smile like July sunshine. They had left him one day, and in spite of his best efforts, he could not understand why.

But the dogs were his family now. Although one or two sometimes wandered away, tempted by alluring scents or noises, it was only because in their innocence they didn't understand the dangers lurking out there in the world. The fast cars that would crush them and keep on moving. The malicious teenagers who would torture them for laughs. The Nazi patrols who would capture them and sentence them to agonizing deaths in their gas chambers.

If he could, he would save every stray dog in the world, bring them into his home and let them live in comfort as a member of his family. The thought of so many sweet-hearted dogs roaming the night, scavenging for food and suffering at the hands of a cruel world, filled him with a nearly crippling sadness.

He had to find his dog. He *had* to.

The night was dark and quiet. Ahead, a forest bordered the lake, and beyond the woods, They had erected their atrocious homes.

"Hope you didn't wander over into Their territory." He squeezed the cane's handle more tightly. "That's not a safe place for you, girl."

They had erected their monstrous creations some time ago. He couldn't recall when exactly because he didn't have a calendar. They had come in, ripping apart the earth with their mighty machines, leveling trees, driving out deer, foxes, and other natural wildlife as they raped the land.

And then, They put up those abominations they dared to call homes.

A railroad ran along the southern perimeter of some of the so-called homes, carrying freight train traffic that occasionally woke him in the middle of the night. But some of the other houses were smack-dab on the other side of the woods, not far from the lake.

His lake. Dog Lake, he called it.

What troubled him about the homes They had built was that none of them were finished. Once, feeling brave after drinking several cans of beer, he had ventured into the territory. He'd discovered almost two dozen residential plots, some of them completely empty, the red clay bare, other parcels occupied by huge houses that were missing windows or doors, and others that had only the wooden framework of the home completed and stood like the preserved bones of some prehistoric creature in a dusty museum.

But there were no people, anywhere.

It was strange, and deeply disturbing.

Shivering, he entered the woods and sounded his whistle several times. "Here, girlie!"

He blamed himself for the dog escaping the house. It was hard to keep track of fifty-eight dogs, but he managed to do a good job, had never lost one. He'd opened the door earlier that evening to sit on the porch and drink a beer, and a few of the dogs sat out with him, the lost one included, and she must have slipped away from the pack and gone exploring.

"Here, girl! Look what Ed's brought for you."

He removed a hot dog from his shirt pocket and waved it, spreading the scent through the warm air.

"Ed's got a hot dog for you! Come get it, girl!"

He heard a rustling in the undergrowth, on his right. He shambled in that direction, parting the weeds with his cane, tattered shoulders of his fatigue jacket bending back tree branches, long mane of gray hair billowing behind him.

In a small clearing, he found the Lab and two unfamiliar dogs tearing into the bloody carcass of a raccoon. At his approach, his dog's tail wagged.

"There you are, girlie," Ed said. "Who are your two new friends here, huh?"

He panned the flashlight across them. The new dogs, both female, looked to be barely older than whelps. They were some sort of Lab mix, like many strays he encountered. Based on their age, black coats, and similar white markings on their chests, he guessed they were litter mates.

Their poor bodies were gaunt and trembling. He felt a pang of anguish.

Drawn by the scent of the hot dog, the three canines approached. He broke it into pieces and shared the treat amongst them. They devoured the meat, licking their chops, drooling.

"There you go, now, girlies, there you go."

Leaning on the cane, he knelt to the ground, and the dogs crowded him. They licked his fingers and his cheeks, poked their wet snouts into his grizzled beard as if searching for more food in its tangled knots. He stroked them behind the ears, his chest so full of joy he felt he might burst.

God Almighty, he *lived* for this.

"You two beauties are going to come live with Ed, too. Come now, girlies."

He slowly got to his feet. He noticed a flicker of yellow light beyond the trees. He squinted, looking.

It came from one of Their houses.

"Oh, no," he said.

He walked closer, to the edge of the woods, but he dared proceed no farther. The dogs followed, but remained behind him, as if sensing the danger.

A couple hundred yards ahead, a white van was parked at one of the residences. The light glimmered inside the garage. Two dark figures were lugging items out of the van's back doors and into the house.

Ed chewed a fingernail. He didn't like this, not at all.

Someone was finally moving in.

12

For Simone, Wednesday began like every other normal weekday morning. She awoke at seven to the buzzing of the bedside alarm clock, groaned in protest to no one in particular, and rolled over and fumbled it off.

"Morning, babe," Corey said.

Blinking against the gray morning light, she wiped her eyes with the back of her hand. Corey stood at the dresser mirror buttoning his shirt, nearly completely dressed. An early riser, he typically would be up and out the door while she was still dragging out of bed. She'd never been a morning person and would have slept in till ten o'clock every day if she could get away with it.

"Morning," she said, throat scratchy from sleep.

"Sleep well? I know I did. Like a baby." He winked.

The memory of last night brought a smile to her lips. They hadn't gone at it like that since they were newlyweds. Corey had been insatiable, and his desire had lifted her to a feverish height of passion that, afterward, had shuttled her into a deeper sleep than any sleeping pill known to man could have provided.

She'd been pleasantly startled by his ardor. Yesterday, after that sleazy old friend of his, Leon, had shown up at the gas station, Corey had gone in to a funk, and when she'd confided to him that Leon had run in to her at lunch, he had sounded furious—reinforcing her decision to refrain from mentioning Leon's offensive remarks to her and possibly send him over the moon in rage. She had expected Corey to be moody all evening, and though he had been quieter than usual, he had been especially attentive to her and Jada.

She wasn't certain how to interpret his mood swings, but the end result had been good. Memorably good.

He came to the bed and took one of her hands in his, kissed it. "All right, I'm off to make the donuts."

"Got any lunch plans?" she asked.

"I don't think so. Why?"

She took his hand and placed it on one of her breasts, molded his fingers to its fullness. "I think I want a lunch date."

"Oh? I think that can be arranged." He squeezed her.

In the early days of their marriage, they'd often enjoyed "lunch dates." She couldn't recall why or when they had stopped having them. Perhaps they had merely allowed life's tiresome demands to get in the way.

"How about noon?" he asked.

"Noon it is. Be there or be square."

"I'll be there—and I'll be straight." He smiled, bent to kiss her on the lips.

She put up her hand to block him. "Hey, I have morning breath."

He kissed her anyway. "Call me when you get to work."

She didn't normally call him when she arrived at her practice each morning. Although he'd tried to make his request sound casual, she thought she detected a trace of concern in his gaze.

Is he worried about that Leon guy? She suspected he

was, but she was reluctant to ask. She didn't want him to shut down on her or get angry, not when they were enjoying a playful resurgence of some of their old passion.

"I'll be sure to call you," she said. "Love you."

"Love you, too."

He left the bedroom. She heard him go upstairs, where he would kiss Jada good-bye as he always did each morning before he left for work. A few minutes later, she heard his car pull out of the garage.

But not before she'd heard the beep of the security system, indicating that he'd activated the perimeter alarm again. If she asked him about it, she could bet that he'd repeat that dubious comment from last night about running "diagnostics."

What was going on? His reticence, so unlike him, was unnerving.

Glancing at the clock, she calculated that she had about half an hour before she'd need to get Jada into gear for summer school. She climbed out of bed and padded to the shower enclosure in the master bath.

As she showered, she tried not to think about Corey, but of course, he remained at the top of her mind. In her opinion, they had built a genuinely strong marriage. While they'd experienced occasional arguments like any normal couple, they'd been able to successfully navigate the potholes in the road by virtue of their willingness to communicate respectfully, openly, and honestly with each other.

She didn't want to worry too much about how he'd been acting lately, but she had a gut feeling that his apparent bad blood with Leon was only the tip of the iceberg, and that a much more troubling problem lurked beneath the surface. She didn't know what it might be. She wasn't entirely sure she wanted to know.

But try as she might to ignore it, her uneasiness had a lot to do with the question of why Corey had ever been friends with a clearly shady individual like Leon in the first place. Not merely acquaintances. Best friends, as Corey had confessed.

Your hubby C-Note and I were thick as thieves back in the day.

She wasn't naïve. She knew Corey had grown up in a rough area of Detroit; she could understand if he'd skirted the law a bit in his youth. Hell, her big brother, college-degree mechanical engineer that he was now, had experienced a couple of brushes with trouble as a teenager.

What disturbed her was the possible severity of Corey's misadventures with this Leon character. Those were the thoughts she was most reluctant to entertain—and were why she hadn't pressed Corey for more details. She preferred the comfort of willful ignorance.

Counselor, counsel thyself, she thought ruefully.

After about fifteen minutes under the shower, she dried off with a bath towel and began to apply a generous lather of cream to her skin. Her complexion showed ash easily if she didn't use lotion every day, and growing up, the threat of ashy knees or elbows being pointed out derisively by her classmates had made her obsessive about moistening her flesh.

She was in the midst of rubbing down her legs when she thought she heard the security system beep. It was the quick, five-chirp signal the alarm emitted when it was deactivated.

Had Corey forgotten something and returned home? Or had Jada turned off the system for some reason—unlikely given that Jada, like Simone, loved to sleep in?

"Corey?" she called out. "That you, honey?"

No answer.

Her skin glistening, she went into the bedroom, pulled panties and a bra out of a drawer, and slid them on. As she dressed, she checked the security system control panel mounted beside the doorway. The green "Ready" light shone, which meant the alarm had been disengaged by someone entering the PIN.

She wrapped herself in a terry cloth bathrobe and opened the bedroom door, Corey's name on her lips.

On the threshold, she froze.

Leon was coming toward her down the hallway. Unlike yesterday at lunch, he wasn't wearing sunglasses. His deep-set eyes held the predatory intent of a wolf eyeing fresh prey.

"Good morning, good morning, Miss Thang. My goodness, ain't you lookin' scrumptious?"

Upstairs, Jada screamed.

13

When Jada awoke and discovered the giant sitting on her bed, she screamed.

She'd been having a fantastic dream about her all-time fa-vorite movie, *Shrek*. In it, she was best friends with Shrek and Donkey, and they were traveling all over Duloc together getting involved in thrilling adventures. When Daddy had come into her room to kiss her good-bye, she'd smiled at him sleepily, reluctant to let the dream fade, and sure enough, she sank back into the marvelous cartoon fantasyland as soon as he went away.

It was the smell that woke her up for real.

It was the unmistakable scent of chocolate. She loved chocolate, especially Snickers bars and her Grandma Rose's double-chocolate cake, would have eaten it for breakfast, lunch, dinner, and every snack in between if her parents had allowed her to, but they were strict about the foods she ate and let her have candy and desserts only every now and then, because they didn't want her to get cavities. She could never remember waking up to the odor of chocolate in her bedroom, not even on her birthday, which was in September, three months away yet.

The smell came from *right beside her*.

She opened her eyes and found a giant man sitting on her bed beside her. He had light brown skin, a humongous head with puffy hair, and the biggest hands she had ever seen in her life—hands as big as shovel blades resting on the legs of his jeans.

Unlike Shrek, who was a funny, nice, giant ogre, this giant man was scary.

It wasn't his smell that frightened her, though the smell, she realized upon waking, was not just chocolate. It was the aroma of chocolate mixed in with something foul, like the way the poor man who asked her and her friends for money during their third-grade school trip to the aquarium had smelled, as if he hadn't taken a bath or used deodorant in ages. Combined with the chocolate, it was a disgusting, sickly-sweet scent. A *putrid* smell.

It was the way the giant looked at her that frightened her.

It was a flat stare, like he was a stone statue in a park. He didn't blink. He didn't move from beside her.

He just stared at her, as if he were in a trance.

A chill flashed down her spine. She immediately sensed from his odd stare that something was wrong with him. Daddy would have said the man's elevator didn't go to the top floor, but Mom said it wasn't nice to use that expression. Mom would have said that the man was "disturbed."

His mouth and chin were covered in dark smudges, and when he stuck out his fat tongue and licked his lips, she knew he'd been eating chocolate candy.

But the strange look in his eyes made her fear that he wanted to eat *her*.

She realized that she had opened her mouth to scream, but she didn't hear herself screaming, because she wasn't wearing her speech processor and couldn't interpret sounds without it. But she felt her frantic heartbeat pounding in her head like a drum, and she thought she was screaming, because her tight throat vibrated with words exploding out of her.

Mom, Daddy, help me, please! Daddy! Mom!

Across the room, Mickey went wild in his cage, wings flapping, the cover sliding to the floor.

The giant bounced off the bed and clapped his hands to his ears. He shouted at her, ropes of saliva flying from his mouth, but she didn't know what he was saying. She couldn't read lips, had never had to learn.

Why was this man in her room? Where were her parents?

She sat up, to try to run away. The giant thrust out his huge hand and shoved her in the chest.

She slammed against the headboard, striking her temple, and literally saw stars spin in her eyes, like in some of the cartoons she liked to watch.

Dizzy, she slumped onto the bed.

She wanted to scream again, if she could get enough air in her lungs, but she was afraid. She imagined the giant might flatten her with one blow from his powerful hand.

Where were Mom and Daddy? Did they hear her scream? Where were they?

The giant turned away from her and lumbered like a robot to Mickey's cage. Mickey was frantic, darting back and forth.

The giant opened the cage and stuck his hand inside. Mickey tried to escape his thick fingers by fleeing to the far corner, but there was nowhere else for the bird to go.

No, she said. *Leave Mickey alone.*

The giant's hand swallowed Mickey whole.

He's only a bird, he won't hurt you, leave him alone, mister, please, she begged.

But the giant ignored her. She wasn't sure that she was speaking loud enough for him to hear her.

Or maybe he heard her fine, but didn't care. He'd almost knocked her out when he'd pushed her, and hadn't seemed concerned at all that he'd hurt her.

The giant brought his hand out of the cage. He squeezed it into a fist for a few seconds, and then opened his palm. Mickey dropped like a stone to the floor, loose feathers fluttering in the air.

Tears of anger flooded her eyes.

You didn't have to kill him! she shouted. She was suddenly so furious she wished she were bigger, so she could teach this terrible man a lesson.

The giant studied a few of the feathers remaining in his palm, as if surprised to find them there.

Taking advantage of his fascination with the feathers, she jumped off the bed. She felt sort of woozy, and her head throbbed, but she was okay.

She balled her hands into fists and raced to the door.

But the giant was fast—he reached out and caught the sleeve of her Goofy pajama top. She automatically started to scream again, but quickly bit her tongue so hard that blood flooded her mouth.

If she screamed, he would hurt her bad. Those enormous hands of his would crush her.

Please don't hurt me, she said in what she hoped was a soft, calm voice. *Please, please. I'm sorry I screamed, mister.*

He stared at her with his statue eyes. His lips moved.

She thought he said, *We have to go.* But she could have been wrong. She hoped so much that she was wrong.

She didn't want to go anywhere with him. She would rather stick her hand in a beehive than go anywhere with this awful man.

Then he plucked her off the floor and slung her over his shoulder as if she were a stuffed animal he had won at a carnival, and she realized, to her horror, that she had been right

14

As Jada screamed upstairs, Leon swaggered down the hallway toward Simone.

Poised on the threshold of the master bedroom, Simone would not have been more shocked to see this man suddenly in her house if he'd materialized in a cloud of mist from a genie's bottle. But Jada's terrified shrieks made the questions of why and how he'd invaded their home irrelevant.

She had to protect her daughter. At the moment, nothing else mattered.

As Leon strutted toward her, grinning that gap-toothed Cheshire cat grin, limbs loose and cocky, she hissed, bared her teeth like a feral animal, and charged him.

It didn't matter that he was a man, taller than her, stronger, or that he might also have a gun. Her need to protect Jada was as imperative as the need to breathe.

She went to kick him in the groin. When she was a kid, her big brother had taught her that if she ever found herself in a fight with a guy, to call him first—and if he wasn't around, to kick the guy in the nuts and run like hell. A blow to the family jewels tilted the scales in a woman's favor.

Leon saw the kick coming and began to turn, but she still landed a solid blow with the ball of her right foot, and the feel of her foot smashing into him was savagely satisfying.

He grunted and doubled over. "Fuckin' . . . bitch!"

She dashed past him, but he snagged the hem of her bathrobe and yanked it. The front of the robe flapped open and her legs got tangled in the folds of cloth. She lost her balance, windmilled her arms, and crashed against the hardwood floor on her shoulder, a cry of pain bursting out of her.

Upstairs, Jada was still screaming, and Simone immediately forgot her own agony.

Oh, God, what's happening up there? Please, God, help us.

Heart swollen in her throat, she rolled over onto her stomach. She crawled away, the robe coming free, dragging behind her like a tail.

"Back here . . . bitch."

He grabbed her calf. She jerked her leg upward, and his fingers slid off her lotion-slick skin.

She got to her feet again.

My baby, I've got to save my baby.

She started running. She got no more than three paces before Leon roared and tackled her.

Together, they slammed to the hardwood. The breath flew out of her lungs. She tasted blood, and vaguely realized that she'd bitten her bottom lip.

It meant nothing to her.

"Get off me!" she screamed hoarsely. She squirmed beneath him, his weight crushing her. "Jada . . . Jada!"

Snarling like a rabid wolf, Leon was trying to get his hands around her neck. His eyes burned with fury. He was panting and swearing.

"Bitch . . . fuckin' bitch. . . ."

She clawed at his face, went for his eyes.

He pulled his head back, dreadlocks swinging. Her nails

scraped down his cheeks, gouging red trails, and her fingers got lost in the coarse thicket of his beard.

"Bitch!"

He backhanded her across the face. Her head rocked sideways. Pain fanned across her jaw, and the world swayed and briefly went dark.

As if from a great distance, she heard Jada's anguished cries.

Jada . . . my baby . . . no . . .

Fear reined her away from the brink and brought her vision back into sharp focus.

Grunting, Leon was attempting to turn her over, but was having a hard time getting a firm hold on her oiled skin.

"Let me go!"

She snatched her arm free of him and mashed the heel of her hand into the base of his throat. His teeth clicked in the back of his mouth, and he emitted a strangled gasp.

As he choked and gagged, she scrambled from underneath him and got up again.

On her feet, reeling with pain, her vision slanted drunkenly. She braced her hands against the wall to keep her balance.

Gotta get to my baby . . .

Pulling in snatches of air, she ran down the hallway, bare feet slapping across the floor.

She rounded the corner. The staircase was ahead, near the end of the main hallway.

Jada was shouting at someone. Who else was in their home? In God's name, who?

Mama's coming, baby . . .

As she grabbed the handrail and mounted the steps, a large object crashed into the back of her head, and her eyes exploded with brightness.

She fell forward against the stairs, and whatever had

struck her shattered on the floor behind her. In her hazy peripheral vision, she glimpsed shards of a brightly colored item.

A vase. Leon had thrown a vase at her.

Her head burned as if molten lava had been poured atop her skull. Her jaw was swelling from when he had slapped her.

But she wasn't going to let anything stop her.

Groaning and weeping, she clutched a baluster, and started to hoist herself to her feet.

Leon came around the corner. This time, he had a handgun.

He aimed the muzzle at her head.

She froze, staring into the dark bore of the pistol. It looked huge enough to launch a rocket.

"I . . . I only want to . . . help my baby," she said in a raw voice.

Although his face was red with scars and he was out of breath, Leon had the audacity to smirk at her. With casual dexterity, he flipped the gun to his other hand, drawing her gaze along with it like a pin to a magnet—and suddenly hammered his free hand into her solar plexus, a punch that felt like a spear boring through her midsection.

She buckled over on the steps. Her mouth gaped open to scream, but only a dry rasp of pain came out.

"That's . . . for fighting back, bitch," he said, chest heaving. "I'm not wasting any more . . . time with you . . . get up and make yourself presentable . . . time to hit the trail."

15

At the office, Corey sat at his computer, sipping coffee and searching on Google for information about guns.

He had brought his revolver to work with him. The gun was tucked inside the waist holster, hidden by his button-down shirt. He had a concealed carry permit, but except for the occasional visit to a firing range, he'd never taken the weapon out of the house.

Driving to work that morning, he'd decided that he was going to purchase another firearm, too. Perhaps two or three more. One to keep at home. One to keep in his car. One to keep in his desk drawer at work. One to keep on his person at all times.

His family was too precious for him to do anything less. He needed to be prepared for anything, anywhere, at any-time.

If Leon dared to show up again, he'd have something for him.

His desktop phone jangled. Caller ID showed his home number.

For no reason at all, an iron clamp of anxiety snapped

across his chest. Somehow, he knew that something terrible had happened at home.

He hesitated for a beat, and picked up the phone.

"Hello?" he said.

"You're a pupil of Ben Franklin, huh, home boy? Early to bed and early to rise makes a man healthy, wealthy, and wise."

Leon's voice blew through Corey like an icy breeze. He squeezed the handset, knuckles popping.

"Leon? What the hell—"

"I think you better come to the domicile with the quickness," Leon said.

"—are you doing, you—"

"I think your beautiful wifey and your cute little munchkin need you."

"—bastard, I'll—"

"I think you better not make me wait too long. Au revoir."

The dial tone drilled into Corey's brain. Heart booming, he stared at the handset as if it were a viper.

Then he slammed it onto the cradle and ran like hell out of the office.

16

Speeding home, he used his BlackBerry to ring Simone's
cell, got no answer, dialed her office number, but got no answer there, either. He called home again, too, to no avail—
the line rang and rang until voice mail picked up.

He desperately wanted to believe that Leon was playing
a cruel joke on him, that he'd jerry-rigged their home landline somehow to make it only appear that he'd phoned him
from their house. But his failure to reach Simone proved
that this was really happening. Whatever *this* turned out
to be.

*God help me, if he hurts either Simone or Jada, I'll kill
him, I really will.*

A few minutes later, he veered into the driveway with a
squeal of tires.

There were no cars parked in the driveway or in front of
the house. The only vehicle within a block's radius was a
white Ford van with an HVAC company's name painted on
the side.

He didn't know what Leon was doing, but he thought it

important to pay attention to everything. Every detail might prove meaningful later.

He got out of the car. Yesterday's summer weather had abandoned them. The sky was the color of faded pewter, and there was an unseasonably raw bite in the air.

Drawing his gun from the holster, he approached the front door. There were no marks of forced entry on the door frame, and all of the windows were intact.

He twisted the knob. It was unlocked. Using his foot, he nudged the door open and crossed the threshold.

He didn't see anyone. He heard the whispery hum of the air conditioner. But he heard no voices.

The house felt empty, too.

"Is anyone here?" he called out.

No answer.

Gun pointed skyward, finger on the trigger guard, he moved down the hallway.

At the corner, at the foot of the staircase, a vase lay shattered in a dozen pieces, a wedding gift from Simone's aunt.

Fear squeezed his throat. What the hell had happened?

He ran to the interior garage door and flung it open. Simone's SUV was parked inside, in its usual spot.

No, he thought, as a terrifying possibility began to brew in his mind.

He dashed to the master bedroom. The bed was in disarray. A couple of dresser drawers had been pulled open, and random pieces of clothing dangled from their edges and lay on the floor. Simone's clothes. As if she had packed in a hurry.

Jesus, no. Nausea wormed through him.

He ran upstairs, taking the risers three at a time. He rushed headlong into Jada's room.

Empty. The sheets on her bed were in chaos, too.

Mickey the bird lay dead on the floor in a heap of feathers, beady eyes fixed on oblivion.

He shook his head. *No, no, no.*

Jada's speech processor lay on the nightstand.

No, God, not my little girl.

A scream boiled at the pit of his throat, and it was only through sheer willpower that he kept a lid on it. If he let the scream escape, he feared he would never stop, and he had to hold it together. He couldn't fold. Couldn't break.

The lives of his wife and daughter might depend on him.

Nearly tripping over his feet, he sprinted out of the room, into the hallway.

"Is anyone here?" he shouted hoarsely.

Hollow silence answered him.

On rubbery legs, he descended the staircase, clutching the hand rail in a tight grip to keep from falling.

He thought of calling someone. He didn't know whom. Maybe the police. Maybe a friend. He didn't know who could help him. Or if anyone could.

He staggered into the kitchen and dropped the gun onto the table.

That was when he saw the new cell phone standing near the napkin holder, nestled within the black coils of an AC adapter. A Post-it note was attached to it.

The handwritten text read simply: *"Keep me on."*

He peeled away the note and carefully picked up the phone, as if it might detonate in his hands.

It was one of those inexpensive prepaid cell phones that you could buy at almost any retail store, the kind of phone that made it virtually impossible for the police to trace it to anyone because the purchaser bought air-time in blocks via calling cards, and didn't need to supply a name or address to the wireless carrier.

The phone was already on.

Two or three breathless minutes later, it rang. The Caller ID display read Unknown Number, but Corey knew only one person could be calling.

"I've got your wifey and the munchkin," Leon said. "Whether you ever see them again alive, old sport, depends entirely on you."

17

Phone glued to his ear, Corey paced across the kitchen on legs so numb they felt disassociated from his body, as if they had been injected with a local anesthetic.

Whether you ever see them again alive, old sport, depends entirely on you.

A postcard photo of him and his family from last year's holiday season was pinned by a magnet to the stainless steel refrigerator. The three of them sat on a love seat in front of the stocking-fringed fireplace wearing floppy Santa caps and cheesy grins. Corey hadn't wanted to pose for the picture; he said they'd done it the year before and it was time for something new, but Simone and Jada had insisted, and as he often did when his ladies wanted something, he gave in—they both found the sight of him dressed up in anything absolutely hilarious.

A knot of anguish rose in his throat. He already missed the sound of their laughter.

"Why?" Corey asked thickly.

"Why?" Leon said, incredulous. "Why what? You sound woozy, kinda off-kilter, are you losing your grip already, have you flipped your lid? I always recalled you as having nerves of steel, the Iceman, taking care of business, standing and delivering, and I think you better dig deep down and rediscover those reserves of iron nerves again, keep it Ziploc-tight, 'cause things have only just begun, hear me?"

Corey stopped pacing and pressed his hand to his temple. His skin was greasy with cold sweat. His head pounded.

"I mean, why are you doing this? Kidnapping isn't your style. You're a thief."

Leon released a ripple of manic laughter. "I'm broadening my horizons, expanding my repertoire, desperate times call for desperate measures. I have expensive tastes. I can't realize Cristal dreams on a St. Ides income."

"But I told you yesterday that I'd give you money! You didn't have to do this!"

"You insulted moi yesterday with that insipid pin money offer, that was the coup de grâce, I gave you a chance to do the right thing and you blew it. Screwed it up. Flunked out. Now you've gotta pay the piper, you've gotta do things my way or hit the highway, you dig, are we clear, huh?"

In the background on Leon's line, Corey heard a rumbling engine. Leon was in a vehicle, he realized, presumably with Simone and Jada. Where was he taking them?

"Let me talk to my wife," Corey said.

"Say the magic word, amigo."

"*Please.*"

There was a lengthy silence filled with the sound of the grumbling vehicle and tires humming against pavement . . . and then Simone's thin voice crackled over the line.

"Honey . . . I'm so sorry . . . I tried to fight back . . ."

"No." Corey squeezed his eyes shut, struggling to hold back tears. "No, no, baby, I'm the one who needs to apologize. God, I should have known . . ." He tilted his head back and stared at the ceiling. What good were his flimsy excuses now? "How are you, sweetheart? How is Jada?"

"She's . . . okay . . . she's with me . . . but she doesn't have her speech processor . . . she can't hear anything."

"I know, I know. I found it in her room. I'm going to bring both of you home safely. I promise you. You've gotta believe me. Okay? Please believe me."

A ragged sob escaped her. It tore into his heart like a filet knife.

Only an hour ago, he had been touching her in their bed, gazing into her beloved eyes. How had their lives been up-ended so abruptly and tragically?

She sniffled. "I love you."

"I love you, too, baby, I love Jada with everything I've got. I . . . I'm just so goddamn sorry this happened." His knees folded, and he had to lean against the counter. "Can you tell me where you are?"

"No . . . blindfolded . . ."

"Okay, okay." He pulled in a shaky breath. "I'm going to bring you home. One way or another, I just need you to stay strong for me, okay? Please, just believe me and stay strong."

"She's plenty strong, all right," Leon said, on the phone once more. "She put up a fight that would've made Laila Ali proud, no lie." He whistled lowly. "Tough as nails and sexy to boot, you know when I got into the house, she was in her drawers? Damn near made me forget what I was there for. You're a lucky schmuck having a fine piece like her to come home to every night, slammin' bod' on her, and that sweet chocolate skin makes me want to take a bite out of her as if she were a Hershey's bar, matter of fact, before this is all over I might have me a nibble or two or three."

Corey pushed away from the counter, hand clenching into a fist. "Don't you dare touch her, asshole."

"And if you could only see how my partner's been ogling your little munchkin, whoa, that boy sure do love him some chil'ren." Leon cackled.

Corey remembered the leering giant from the gas station. The thought of that monster within five hundred feet of Jada made him ill.

"For God's sake, she's only nine, Leon," Corey said. "She's a *child*."

"You never told me she was deaf. How'd you wind up fathering a kid like that. You squirting jacked-up chromosomes down the chute. Is there a glitch in the man milk factory?"

Corey grabbed the gun off the table. "If you or your pervert partner hurt my little girl, I'm going to fucking kill both of you."

"You aren't going to do shit, *comprende?* You've met your Waterloo. Let's be clear. I'm the one running the show, I'm the chief, I'm the HNIC. If I wanted to shoot your lovely ladies in their pretty heads right now and dump their bodies in the Chattahoochee River, there's not a damn thing you could do about it but start planning a closed casket memorial."

Clutching the gun, Corey fell silent.

"That's what I thought," Leon said.

Corey had to force out his next words. "How much will it take to get them back?"

"Let's cover the ground rules of this engagement," Leon said. "*Numero uno*. No cops. If I see a cop on my tail, if I even *suspect* that you've involved them in this private business matter of ours, I'm going to kill your family, and I'm going to make it *exquisitely* painful, worse than anything you can imagine, I promise, I'll have my way with your cutie pie wifey, and I'll let my partner do whatever he likes to your little munchkin, whatever unspeakable acts he can devise in that mysterious big cerebellum of his, and then we'll waste them both and leave you widowed and psychologically half-Nelsoned for life. Are we clear?"

Corey lowered his head. His voice was soft and tight. "We're clear."

"We should be," Leon said. "Because we both know there's another major reason why you don't want to involve the police. If by some miracle they nab me over this, I'm going to have quite a story to tell them about how Mr. Corey Webb was intimately involved in a certain unsolved case that went down in Motown sixteen years ago, which begs the question, actually—have you told your wife what we did?"

Gnawing his lip, Corey didn't answer.

"Does she know anything at all about how we used to rock and roll back in the day?" Leon asked.

"Let's keep this between us," Corey said. "Leave my family out of it."

Leon laughed. "Wait, wait, wait! The Webb domicile is built on a faulty foundation? How could you ask a woman for her hand in matrimony, yet not tell her the truth about yourself? I mean, seriously, what kind of man does something like that, something so deceitful, what kind of low-down dirty dog are you that you would omit such an essential piece of vital information from the woman you claim is the love of your life?"

"Shut up!"

"Wow, you haven't changed at all," Leon said with what might have been a trace of surprise. "The only difference now is that you've bought yourself some better window dressing, that's all, sweeter butter cream icing, the big house, the luscious wife, the precocious kid, the lucrative white-collar business, all the cozy superficial trappings of the American dream, but I know the truth about you, even if *su familia* doesn't. Once a hood, always a hood."

"I'm not like you," Corey said firmly. "I never was."

"Repeat that to yourself enough times, maybe you'll start to believe it."

"What will it take to get them back?" Corey asked.

"Five hundred thousand dollars brings the clan home safe and sound."

Corey was speechless, convinced his ears had heard wrongly.

"Why do I suddenly hear crickets?" Leon said.

"How much?" Corey said.

"Did I stutter? *Five hundred thousand.*"

Breathing shallowly, Corey said, "I don't . . . I don't have that kind of money."

"It's Wednesday, around eight o'clock," Leon said. "The money's due by close of business on Friday. Five o'clock. We'll work out the particulars of the exchange later."

"You're not hearing me, Leon. I don't have five hundred grand!"

"You'll find a way to get it, by hook or by crook." Leon snickered. "Hey, maybe you can rob a bank. Get your face on all the Most Wanted posters, walk a few miles in my shoes, feel my pain, deal with my struggle."

"I can get you . . . I can get you fifty thousand," Corey said, pacing again, mind spinning. "I can get that to you by Friday, I know I can pull it together. Fifty thousand dollars. That's a lot of money, Leon. It'll go a long way for you."

"The price is fifty thousand times ten."

Corey's head felt as though it would explode. "Listen to me, okay? I don't have that much money. I don't know what you think you know about me, but I don't have half a million dollars!"

"You didn't have the flyest new clothes and Air Jordans back when we were growing up, but that never stopped you from doing whatever was necessary to get them, did it? You know how we are, we don't wait for a handout, we *take* what we want, that's our code, that's how it always was, and nothing's changed—you haven't changed—so you do what you've gotta go, you get me my five hundred g's and you get it by Friday at five, no excuses, no games, no cops, better not see any cops, I got you by the balls, I got you up and down all day, hear me? No bullshit. Fail to deliver and they'll be in the river. I mean it, you know it, and I've got the record to show it. *Just do it*—and keep this goddamn phone on at all times 'cause I'm going to be checking in with you, got it, are we clear? Are we golden?"

Numb, Corey couldn't make his lips work to form words.

"Do you understand me, motherfucker!" Leon shouted.

"Yes," Corey said quietly. "Loud and clear."

"Outstanding, wonderful, superb, that's what I wanted to hear. Now get to work."

Click.

A tremor rattling through him, Corey placed the phone on the counter, the plastic display smudged with sweat.

He read his watch: 8:07.

The deadline was fifty-six hours away, and the clock was ticking.

Part Two

18

Panic gripping him in a vise, Corey rushed into his home office.

Control, he thought. To get his family back safely, he had to exercise self-control.

He had to stop the cold sweat oozing from his pores. Had to still his trembling hands. Slow his galloping pulse.

Simone and Jada were depending on him. He was the only one who could bring them back alive and unharmed.

Dropping into the swivel-base chair, he powered on the desktop computer and accessed the software he used to administer their household finances. The software was linked via a DSL connection to their financial institutions and provided up-to-the-minute transaction and market data.

He discovered, as he'd expected, that the total sum of money he could get his hands on by the Friday deadline was far less than Leon's ransom demand. The money in their checking and savings accounts totaled $54,972.14.

It was a handsome sum by anyone's standards. But it left him short of the ransom by approximately four hundred and forty-five thousand dollars.

Drumming the edge of the keyboard, he stared at the screen, as if he could increase the digits exponentially through sheer force of will.

The fifty-five grand was not the extent of their holdings. They had more money invested in mutual funds, 401k's, CDs, and a college savings plan for Jada, which, when all were totaled and added to the fifty-five thousand, came to about two hundred and fifteen thousand dollars.

A helluva lot of money. For a couple not yet forty, who'd started their family and careers without a trust fund or inheritance, he and Simone had done well, the fruits of a decade of hard work, sacrifice, saving, and investing.

But he couldn't lay his hands on the funds by Friday afternoon, because of paperwork requirements and processing times. Glancing at the wall calendar above the computer, he estimated that the earliest he could get it all would be the middle of next week, if not later.

And it still would not be sufficient to ransom his family, not by half. As successful as they'd been, it wasn't enough to save them.

He pushed out of the chair, paced across the room. Had to think. Think.

Equity. They had equity in their home. Nearly a hundred thousand dollars' worth, according to an appraisal they'd had done last fall.

But a home equity transaction would take weeks to process, and since he jointly owned the house with Simone, he would need her signature on any loan paperwork.

And it still would fall far short of the mark.

He collapsed back into the chair and cradled his head in his hands.

What the hell was Leon thinking? Why was he so convinced that Corey could raise half a million dollars in two days?

Hey, maybe you can rob a bank . . . once a hood, always a hood.

God help him, Corey actually began to visualize how he might pull off such a crime. He had a gun. He had a car. There were an abundance of bank branches within a short distance of their home.

Write a note, walk into the lobby, pass the demand to the teller. Show the gun so they know you're serious. No one has to get hurt.

He shook his head. No. Besides the fact that bank tellers probably kept nowhere near the amount of money he needed in their drawers, he could never do something like that, simply on principle. He wasn't a criminal—he'd long since left behind that life.

Perhaps that was what Leon wanted, though. To reel him back into the chasm. The old crabs-in-a-barrel syndrome. Leon maybe was furious that Corey had chosen a different path and was determined to destroy everything he had earned.

But he wasn't a buck-wild, easily influenced teenager unable to see beyond the moment. He was a thirty-four-year-old man with a wife, a daughter, a business. Real responsibilities. A real life.

There had to be another way.

Cracking his knuckles, he left the office. He passed the control panel for the security system, stopped.

The command center's status light was green, for "Ready." But he recalled activating the perimeter sensors before he had left for work that morning.

If Leon had abducted his family while they were still in the house—hadn't Leon said Simone was "in her drawers" when he'd found her?—how had he gotten inside without setting off the alarm?

And no windows had been broken, either, no doors pried open.

Manually disabling the security system would have been far more complicated than simply snipping the wires at the phone box on the house's exterior wall, too. Corey had installed the package himself. It included cellular backup that would have automatically contacted the police if the landline connection were severed.

Perhaps Leon had become a well-equipped, high-tech thief over the years. Gotten past the front door's lock with a lock-release gun of some kind, used some sort of slick electronic gadget to scramble the control panel. No system or lock was foolproof, and Leon certainly possessed the intellect for such expertise, if not the discipline and patience Corey thought necessary to master those skills.

As he pondered the question, the doorbell chimed.

Frowning, he went to the window in the living room. The wooden Levolor blinds blocked the daylight. He lifted one of the slats and peered outside.

He'd been expecting a courier or a door-to-door solicitor, but a black Ford Crown Victoria with tinted glass was parked in the driveway next to his car. Everything about the vehicle declared *cop*.

"Shit," he whispered.

What could the police want? Had a neighbor witnessed something that morning and called it in?

The doorbell chimed again.

If I see a cop on my tail, if I even suspect that you've involved them in this private business matter of ours, I'm going to kill your family, and I'm going to make it exquisitely painful, worse than anything you can imagine. . . .

He had no plans to contact the police, but he couldn't avoid them if they were at his door. His car was in the driveway—they knew he was there. Avoiding them would invite suspicions, would raise dangerous questions.

He pushed out a deep breath, wiped sweat from his brow.

Clasping his clammy hands, he walked to the front door and opened it.

An attractive young woman in a black pantsuit stood outside, flanked by a man in a gray business suit who Corey took to be her partner. The woman was as petite as a ballerina, with an olive complexion, raven hair knotted into a long ponytail, and large onyx eyes that reflected a degree of perception and experience that contradicted her apparent youth. The guy, perhaps in his midtwenties, was tall and broad-shouldered, with blond hair trimmed in a buzz-cut and glacial blue eyes buried in a marble slab face.

"Mr. Corey Webb?" the woman asked. She had a New York accent and a husky voice that didn't fit her diminutive stature at all.

"I'm Corey Webb," he said, pleased that his voice was steady. "May I help you?"

She offered a professional smile and flashed a badge.

"I sure hope you can, sir," she said. "I'm Special Agent Gina Falco, and this is Special Agent Robert March. We're with the FBI."

19

A fresh layer of icy sweat moistened Corey's hairline. *FBI. What could they want?*

He had not invited the agents inside. Although he realized that he probably should have asked them in to put to rest any suspicions they might hold of him, a lifelong distrust of law enforcement kept him blocking the threshold.

He folded his arms across his chest. "What can I do for you?"

Falco put away her badge. Her perceptive eyes made him uneasy; they would detect a lie quicker and more effectively than a polygraph.

"May we come inside, please?" she asked.

"That depends on whether I'm in trouble or not." He offered a short chuckle.

She smiled disarmingly, and he realized why she was doing all the talking. With that smile, her good looks, and those penetrating eyes, she would be able to coax the truth out of virtually anyone.

"We have only a few routine questions to ask you, Mr. Webb," she said.

"About what?"

"This individual here."

Although Falco spoke, March offered Corey the photograph. Corey took it, already suspecting what he was going to see.

It was the mug shot of Leon that was posted on the FBI's Web site.

"His name's Leon Sharpe," Falco said.

She awaited his reaction. Agent March's cold blue eyes measured him, too.

Corey kept his face blank, but his mind spun.

"Come in, then," he said, and stepped aside.

The agents filed past him. Agent March had to turn sideways to get his shoulders through the doorway.

"You can have a seat in there." Corey indicated the formal living room on the left of the foyer.

"Thanks." Falco swept her probing gaze around. "You have a very nice home, sir."

"Thank you."

"You might want to talk to your housekeeper, however," she said.

"Excuse me?"

She settled onto the sofa. Her gaze didn't leave his face. "There's a broken vase on the floor at the end of the hallway, near the staircase."

Damn.

"Oh, that?" He shrugged. "My daughter knocked it over this morning, running through the house. I hadn't gotten a chance to sweep it up yet."

"Kids, eh?" Falco said, with a smile and shrug.

March sat beside Falco, moving with surprising grace for a man of his size. He scanned the house, too.

Corey hoped that nothing else was out of place. He was eager to get them out of there as quickly as possible. He could only imagine how nervous he looked, and he worried they would interpret his rattled nerves as guilty behavior.

Forcing himself to breathe slowly, he sat on an upholstered chair across from the agents, placing the profile photo on the coffee table between them. He nodded toward it. "I saw Leon yesterday. I ran into him at a gas station, totally by chance. I hadn't seen him in at least sixteen years."

"You and Mr. Sharpe used to be good friends?"

"We were friends back in Detroit. He lived across the street from us for a while."

"From 'us'?" She took out a pen and pad.

"Me and my late grandmother. She didn't like Leon at all. Said he was pure trouble."

"Was he pure trouble back then, Mr. Webb?"

"Of course he was—that's why I never hung around him too much. When I ran into him yesterday, I knew he'd probably been involved in a lot of mess over the years. A leopard can't change its spots, as Grandma Louise liked to say."

"So you spoke with Sharpe at a gas station . . ."

"The QuikTrip on Haynes Bridge Road, not far from here. Around eight-thirty yesterday morning, maybe eight forty-five."

She jotted quick notes, looked up and gave him the full power of those eyes. "Kinda funny, don't you think?"

He frowned. "What's funny?"

"You running into an old friend from the neighborhood, totally out of the blue. Some coincidence, huh?"

He felt color spread through his face. Was she implying that he had planned to meet Leon? As if he would ever want to see Leon again, in this life or the next.

"Well, that's what happened," he said with an edge in his voice.

"What'd he look like?"

"He didn't look like that picture you've got at all. He had dreadlocks down to his shoulders, and a thick beard, too."

"Disguise, no doubt." She made notes. "What was he wearing?"

"Denim overalls, old work boots. He was dressed like a house painter, which he claimed was the kind of work he was doing these days."

She nodded curtly. "Fits his profile. He say where he's been, where he's staying in town?"

"He said he's been bouncing around, following work, but didn't name anywhere specific that he's been, and he didn't mention where he's staying. I didn't ask."

She scowled as if she'd bitten something sour. "Anyone else with him?"

"There was some huge guy, maybe six foot five, weighed about two seventy-five, three hundred pounds. A light-skinned black man, tall Afro, probably in his late twenties. He seemed sort of off."

"Off?"

"You know, like his elevator didn't go all the way to the top floor. That was my initial impression of him, anyway. I didn't get the guy's name, but he bought Leon a pack of cigarettes. I don't think Leon ever went inside the store."

"Using Lurch as the front man." She scribbled notes. "You guys got any other old pals from the neighborhood living here?"

"I don't keep in touch with anyone from Detroit."

The answer came out more defensive than he'd intended. Falco frowned slightly.

"Is this coincidental meeting at the gas station the only time you spoke with Sharpe?" she asked.

He paused. "Unfortunately, no."

Her dark eyebrows arched. "No?"

"Without really thinking, I gave him my business card. I'm co-owner of Gates-Webb Security."

"Ah, I thought the little sign in your flower bed out front looked familiar. I've seen those signs in yards all over the city. Business must be going well."

"I can't complain. But Leon came by my office yesterday evening as I was leaving. He insisted on grabbing a beer."

"He a pushy guy?"

"He can be. We went to a bar called Shooters, about mile down the road from my office."

"What time?"

"I'd guess about five-thirtyish."

"What happened there?" she asked.

Her gaze challenged him to lie.

"He asked me for money," he said.

"He asked you for money?"

He licked his dry lips. "Yeah."

"Why did he ask you for money, Mr. Webb?"

"He said he'd fallen on rough times. He knew about m business, so I guess he figured I had cash to spare."

"Did you give him any?"

"I gave him the cash I had in my wallet."

"How much was that?"

He rubbed his mouth, strained to remember. So much ha happened since then it felt like two weeks ago. "About hundred and twenty dollars, I think."

"Was Sharpe grateful for your generosity?"

Lie to me, those dark eyes of hers said. *I dare you.*

"Actually, he got angry. He wanted more—for old time sake, he said. When I refused, he threw a beer mug agains the wall and stormed out."

She blinked. "You kidding me?"

"I wish I were."

"I mean, gosh, the nerve of him to react like that whe he's the one asking *you* for a handout. He's a piece of work.'

"Leon was never one for tact."

"How much more money did Sharpe want you to giv him?"

"A few thousand."

"He hasn't seen you in sixteen years, yet he expects yo to give him thousands of dollars?" She cast a sidelon glance at her partner. "I've been paired up with this guy her

or eighteen months, work with him daily, and he's never
bought me more than a hamburger."

Silent, Agent March shrugged.

"Well, that's Leon for you, expecting the world to do him
favors." Corey cracked his knuckles. "What's he done this
time? He must've done something, or else you wouldn't be
here asking me questions."

Falco crossed her legs, eyes sharp as nails. "You don't
know?"

"Knowing Leon, I'm sure it involves a robbery or something."

"You ever watched *America's Most Wanted*?"

"I'm familiar with the show, but I haven't seen it recently.
I don't watch much TV."

"Lucky for us one of the bartenders working at Shooters
last night is a big-time fan," she said. "He positively ID'd
Sharpe after Sharpe pitched a fit—pardon the pun." She
smiled.

"What? Leon was on *America's Most Wanted*? Are you
serious?"

He hoped that his manufactured shock appeared genuine.

"We put him on our Ten Most Wanted Fugitives List
about six months ago. Three years prior in Detroit, Sharpe
robbed an armored vehicle, gunned down the two couriers,
got away with about thirty-five thousand."

"That's terrible."

"Those two men he killed had wives, children. Hardworking, honest men like yourself."

"Tragic," he said, and meant it.

"The bar had your credit card receipt from last night on
file," she said. "That's what brought us to your door this
morning."

"Oh, I was wondering about that."

"There are records of everything these days, Mr. Webb,"
she said. "It's getting harder and harder for the bad guys to

slip the net. Sharpe's been ahead of us for a while, but eventually he'll make a mistake. Maybe he already has. Scumbags like him always do sooner or later."

"I hope you catch him. He shouldn't be on the streets."

"We would appreciate your cooperation in bringing him into custody."

Corey swallowed. That word, *cooperation*, stuck in his mind like a thumbtack. What else did they know? Or did they know anything?

If I see a cop on my tail, if I even suspect . . .

Suddenly, the phone rang: the house landline. Nevertheless, Corey jumped as if pinched.

Falco raised an eyebrow. "You going to answer that?"

"I'll be right back," he said.

The nearest phone was in the kitchen. Caller ID displayed his office number.

It was Todd. "Hey, partner. Are you coming in today? We've got a conference call in fifteen minutes, nine A.M. sharp."

"I'm in the middle of something, Todd. Can you handle it?"

"*No problemo.* Everything okay? You sound stressed."

Corey choked back a laugh, thinking *Stressed? You can even imagine.*

"It's cool. I'll be in shortly."

He hung up and returned to the living room. Falco had picked up one of the photographs of Simone and Jada that stood on an end table, and March was checking out another picture, one of Jada at a ballet recital.

Such a powerful bolt of anguish struck him that he almost broke down and told them everything. The old, terrible thing Leon was holding over his head, what Leon had done to his family. Corey almost spilled it all, almost gave in to the urge to let these people shoulder his burden and do the tough, dirty work of somehow bringing his family home safe.

But his knowledge of Leon's ways kept his lips sealed. If e confessed to the agents, he would, in effect, be signing his vife and daughter's death certificates.

The agents looked up at his return.

"That was someone from my office," he said, standing be- ind the chair. "I have a meeting I need to sit in on."

"Of course, you're a busy person, as we all are." Falco re- urned the photo to the table. "You have a beautiful family. our little girl looks a lot like you."

Corey pinched the bridge of his nose, hiding his pain. Thanks. But I really need to get to work."

"In a minute, sure. What does your wife do for a living?"

"She's a therapist."

"Is that so? Where?"

"She has a private practice on Roswell Road."

"I was a psych major at NYU. The education comes in andy out in the field."

"I would imagine it does," he said. "But listen, I haven't een or spoken to Leon since last night. If I knew where he vas, I'd tell you."

"Was he driving a vehicle?"

"A blue Ford pickup. Looks brand new. It's probably tolen."

"Stolen?" She cocked her head. "Why makes you say hat?"

"I . . . I just know how he is."

"You know a whole lot about your old friend." She smiled hinly.

"Apparently not enough, or else he'd be in your custody ight now, wouldn't he?"

Falco laughed sourly. "Anything else?"

He shook his head. "That's everything I can remember."

She rose. Her silent hulk partner stood, too.

She passed Corey a card. "If you have any more informa- ion that might help us, Mr. Webb, please give me a call."

"I'll be sure to do that."

"We can't do our jobs without the cooperation of honest law-abiding citizens like you," she said. "We're all on the same team."

"We sure are, at the end of the day," he said.

She glanced down the hallway. "Oh, remember to take care of that vase before the lady of the house arrives. Otherwise, she might pitch a fit—oh, pardon that little pun again. I can be repetitive sometimes." She smiled.

He smiled back, but inwardly, he felt sick. "I'm on it."

The agents left the house. He stood in the doorway and waited until their sedan had driven off before he closed the door.

He went to the shattered vase.

Oh, pardon that little pun again. I can be repetitive sometimes.

Damn. Falco's message was as clear as the pottery shards on the floor.

She knew he was lying.

20

I'm the man, Leon thought.

Puffing on a cigarette, wraparound sunglasses perched on his nose, he rode shotgun in the white Ford van while Billy drove and James Brown sang "The Big Payback" on the radio. All he could think about was how impressed he was with himself. He was frequently flattered by himself, of course, was dazzled daily by his own brash brilliance, but this fine morning of all fine mornings, referring to himself as the man wasn't mere braggadocio—he deserved all the lofty accolades that he was heaping upon his crown.

He had never attempted a kidnapping, but he had performed like a champ.

The wifey had fought him like a lioness, to be sure, almost cracked open a jumbo-size can of whip-ass on him in her mad motherly frenzy to save her little deaf girl, but a vase upside the cranium had slowed her roll, and a haymaker to that smooth tummy had cowed her, and while he hadn't wanted to hit her—she was so fine that he would have been happy simply basking in her luscious loveliness—she had forced him to do it to get things back on track.

His throat and nut sack still ached, though, and her nails had left a jagged trail of red scratches on his face that had swollen up like tribal scars and made him look like goddamn Shaka Zulu.

Fuckin' bitch, he thought.

He'd hit her again if she pushed him.

He'd do worse things than hit her if she tested him again.

It had been three weeks since he'd had sex, an *eternity,* and the prolonged period of celibacy made him jumpier than usual, reduced his tolerance for bullshit—one of the most difficult things about being on the lam, in addition to cash shortages, were pussy shortages.

A tumble in the hay with the foxy wifey might be just the thing he needed to unwind.

He twisted around. The wifey and the munchkin were snuggled together like war camp refugees on the shabby cloth bench seat, the wifey in a rumpled Minnie Mouse T-shirt, gray sweats, and Reebok sneakers, the cute little crumb snatcher in her pajamas and fluffy pink house slippers.

They were restrained at the wrists, the wifey with handcuffs, the munchkin with duct tape. Tape had been applied to their eyes, too. Do no evil, see no evil, and in the case of the deaf girl—hear no evil.

Earlier, the wifey had asked him where he was taking them. He had told her Shangri-la, and she had shut the fuck up ever since.

But as he looked at them, *damn,* his mind jumped back to how utterly amazing he was.

He'd stolen the van ad hoc and painted it to make it appear to be a service vehicle for a local HVAC company. Summoned home by Leon's call, Corey had swerved into his driveway and hadn't paid any attention to the van parked halfway down the block that happened to be holding his family. It had given Leon a good belly laugh.

Now, here they were, about to arrive at their safe abode,

ight on time, and he wasn't much of a guy for schedules,
plans, boring things of that nature—man proposes, God dis-
poses and all of that—and that was partly why he was so impressed with his performance, too.

"Damn, I'm good," he said to Billy. "I'm rapidly becoming the enfant terrible of the whole world, you dig?"

Beefy hands guiding the wheel, Billy took his gaze off
the rearview mirror—he glanced in the mirror every few
seconds to adore the munchkin—and gave Leon his dull-
eyed look.

"Yeah," he said in his rumbling voice, like a grizzly bear
that had laboriously learned to speak.

"This kind of stuff is outside my modus operandi, but I
think I'm good at it." Leon exhaled a ring of smoke. "We
might have another career opportunity opening up for us,
amigo."

"Sounds good," Billy said, his response to most of Leon's
suggestions. He slurped from the sweaty bottle of Nesquik
chocolate milk he kept braced in the juncture of his tree-
trunk legs, and checked out the munchkin again with a lick
of his lips.

Billy being Billy, he didn't care much about money or the
finer things in life. All he cared about was his chocolate milk
and candy bars and perv kiddie pictures. Hey, to each his
own.

Leon had met Billy a year ago on a house painting gig in
Memphis. He knew virtually nothing about the guy's background, but he suspected that Billy was a registered sex of-
fender and had been forced to leave behind his hometown,
wherever the hell that was, for a nomadic existence on the
highways and byways of America. In that sense, they were
like peas in a pod.

Billy had never asked why Leon was running, either, and
Leon hadn't told him. Their partnership was based on the
Don't Ask, Don't Tell policy. Leon would dispatch Billy into

convenience stores, where they usually had surveillance cameras tracking visitors, and whenever they had to go through highway toll plazas Billy would drive and Leon would duck in the backseat of whatever vehicle he had boosted. But Billy never complained, never posed a problem. He was easy to control, and that made him a perfect partner.

Billy turned off the tree-lined road and into a subdivision. The big stacked stone sign at the wide entrance announced ARCHER LAKE in gold calligraphic letters. A blue-and-white sign standing nearby in the grass proclaimed: FROM THE 300S. NEW HOME SITES AVAILABLE!

It was a community of twenty-one upscale properties, gigantic brick houses on rambling islands of land. Corey's Mc-Mansion would have fit right in there, and the irony of it made Leon grin.

Unlike Corey's neighborhood, however, every one of these homes stood empty. None of them had even been fully built. They missed windows, doors. Others plots had no houses at all standing on them, were nothing but parcels of red clay cordoned off by orange construction cones and black plastic silt fences.

Leon could surmise what had happened there because he was abreast of all the business news, skimmed *The Wall Street Journal* and various mags just about every day. When the real estate market had tanked a little while ago during the subprime mortgage catastrophe, communities across metro Atlanta had fallen apart. Record foreclosures. Spiraling property values. People kicked out on the street like stepchildren with their furniture dumped on the curb. Housing subdivisions like this one stood vacant and incomplete for want of qualified buyers.

Too bad, so sad.

Such calamitous economic events were a strong argument in favor of the lifestyle he enjoyed. He wasn't bound by

mortgage or a lease or a car note or furniture, not him. He
walked the Earth like Caine from *Kung Fu*, came and went
as he pleased, where he pleased, when he pleased. He didn't
owe anyone anything, not a damn thing; he was as free as a
falcon in the great blue sky.

After this job was over, after his home boy paid what he
owed him—and he was *going* to pay him, of that Leon had
no doubt—he would be set for a long time, living back in the
lush and putting on the Ritz, free to do whatever he wanted.

Billy backed the van into the driveway of a four-bedroom,
two-story home in a cul-de-sac. They'd visited late last night
to organize things there, another bit of planning that wasn't
in Leon's nature, but which was required this time around,
hey, sometimes you did what you had to do when the payoff
was worth it.

Inside, everything was in place.

All he had to do was take the Webb ladies in, hunker
down, and wait for his money. He had a stack of stolen li-
brary books he could skim to pass the time—he was especially looking forward to a new text of Latin phrases—plenty
to eat and drink and smoke, and his Glock nine. Everything
a growing boy needed.

I amaze myself, I really, really do.

"Open the garage door," he said to Billy. "Let's get ready
to herd 'em in."

Billy looked longingly in the rearview mirror once more,
and climbed out of the van.

Leon extinguished his cigarette. He pulled off his sunglasses and hooked a glance over his shoulder.

"We're here, ladies," he said. "Welcome to Casa de
Harpe."

21

Simone had earned a doctorate in clinical psychology,
had counseled hundreds of individuals, couples, and families over the years through crisis situations, but here, in her
hour of need, all of her training, education, and experience
deserted her.

She was more frightened than she'd ever been in her life.

The vehicle in which they were traveling had ground to a
stop, and Leon had announced that they were home. They
had been driving for fifty or sixty minutes, she estimated,
which meant they were somewhere in metro Atlanta.

Given her fearful state of mind, they might as well have
landed on a different planet.

She was not frightened for herself—she was hardly thinking about herself—she was frightened for Jada. She'd overheard Leon when he'd spoken to Corey on the telephone.
Leon had said a lot to her husband, had spewed hundreds of
words that had troubled her, but one remark above all the
others had sliced through her heart like a hot stiletto blade.

*I'll let my partner do whatever he likes to your little
munchkin. . . .*

At home, before they had taped her eyes shut, Simone had seen Leon's partner. He was a mammoth of a man, with a disconcerting gaze that betrayed a low IQ, and possibly mental illness. She'd seen how he'd looked at Jada.

Please, Lord, keep my baby safe, she prayed. *Let no harm come to her.*

Throughout this ordeal, she'd kept her attention and energies focused on Jada. She'd whispered words of reassurance in her ear, trusting that Jada would feel her love even if she couldn't hear what Simone said. She pressed her lips to Jada's warm cheek. Buried her nose in Jada's soft hair.

Cuddled as closely together as their restraints would allow, Jada had been crying when they'd first been placed in the vehicle, but she'd soon quieted, drawing in deep breaths, soothed, Simone hoped, by her presence.

If she could stay close to Jada, they could get through this together. Jada gave her the best reason in the world to stay strong.

Although she had no clue how Corey would raise the staggering amount of money Leon had demanded, she would not let herself think about it. It was out of her control, she and her daughter mere pawns in this deadly match between Corey and this mad man. She would concentrate everything she had on Jada, and pray that Corey would somehow come through for them as he'd promised he would.

The engine cut off. She heard doors clatter open.

Cool air swirled inside. The air carried woodsy scents and the songs of chirping birds, none of which told her anything definitive about where they had been taken.

A damp hand grabbed her forearm, fingers digging like hooks into her flesh. She hissed in pain.

"Let's go, *ma cherie*," Leon said.

He wrenched her off the seat, away from Jada. Jada let out a terrified squawk.

"It's okay, baby," Simone said. "Mom's not going anywhere. We're staying together, we're only going inside the house."

Jada's protests quieted to a whimper.

"I thought she was deaf?" Leon asked.

"You'd never understand," she said.

He grunted and jerked her outside the vehicle. She swayed on her feet, her abdomen tender from when he'd punched her, her head aching as if she'd suffered a mild concussion when the vase had struck her. She wriggled her fingers. Her hands, chained in front of her, were numb from restricted blood circulation.

Leon pinched her butt. She flinched away.

"Keep your damn hands off me," she spat.

"My, my, my, so much junk in the trunk." He snickered. "All right, all right, let's go in, yeah, let's go."

Grabbing her by the bicep, he ushered her across a dank echoing space that sounded like a garage, and through a doorway. The air was cool and stale. She smelled drywall dust, paint. Her sneakers tramped across what felt like a hardwood floor.

"Where are we?" she asked.

"The love shack," he said, and giggled in his weird way.

He shoved her through another doorway. She stumbled forward and tripped over something, losing her balance with a small shout, and landed atop a large, cushioned surface. A mattress?

A door slammed behind her. She heard plodding footsteps in another part of the house, wood creaking. It sounded like someone climbing a staircase.

At the realization, fear clenched her.

"Where's my daughter?" she said.

"Sit up," Leon said, "and hold still."

"Where the hell is that sick bastard taking my baby?"

"Do you want me to remove the tape from your eyes or not? I can leave it on. I've got no problem with that, and I'll

et you sit here blind as Stevie Wonder if that's your choice.
Perhaps that would be poetic justice, your daughter deaf, and
you blind, what do you think, huh?"

She was almost hyperventilating. She sucked in her bottom lip, tasted blood from when she'd bitten it earlier, and
willed her heart rate to slow.

"Okay . . . okay," she said. "Please . . . take off the blindfold. Please."

He ripped the tape from her eyes, tearing away a thin
layer of skin and hair in the process. ,

"You bastard!" she screamed, face burning.

"There we go now, there we go." He knelt in front of her.
"Now I can gaze into those big, pretty brown eyes."

Wincing, she blinked her sore eyelids, and looked around.

They were in a master bedroom. It had plain white walls,
crown molding, a dusty hardwood floor. A large fireplace
with a marble mantelpiece. Two long windows barred with
thick planks of plywood, bands of gray light filtering inside.
A tray ceiling. Overhead, where a fan would have been installed, a bundle of wires dangled like a severed umbilical
cord.

There was no furniture except for the full-size mattress
on which she sat, and a plastic folding chair a few feet away.
A door at the other end of the room led to a shadowed bathroom.

Leon followed her eyes with his feverish gaze. "You like?
I would have booked a penthouse at the Ritz, but I had certain rigid privacy requirements. This'll have to do."

She glared at him. "I want my daughter in here with me."

"Billy's keeping an eye on her."

"That monster?" She shook her head. "No, he'll . . . he'll
hurt her."

"Look, I told him to keep his hands off her, and he listens
to me, obeys my every word, I'm the Alpha dog of our dy-
namic duo, so your munchkin'll be fine—unless you make

me angry, do something to piss me off and get on my ba
side, in which case, I'll tell him he can do whatever he want
to her, and who knows what'll happen, God only knows th
incredible perversities Billy could commit while he's alon
with the little angel, ya dig?"

Nausea surged in her throat. Swallowing with a grimace
she bowed her head and focused on breathing, one slow
breath at a time.

Soon, the sickness passed. But the fear remained like
kernel in her gut.

Leon touched her shoulder. She pulled away from hi
hand.

"Don't be cruel, my sweet," he said. "You and I are goin
to get to know each other very well here. That's right, we'r
going to become the best of friends, you and I, and wh
knows, maybe something more, maybe a whole lot more
who knows what surprises the future has in store for us."

Looking into his manic eyes, knowing the power this ma
held over them, she couldn't take it any more.

She broke down, and cried.

22

After the agents left, Corey snapped into action. He swept up the broken vase; he gathered up the budgie's frail corpse, perhaps to bury later in the backyard; he forwarded the house landline to his BlackBerry, in case a call somehow came through from his family; and, not wanting to miss a call from Leon, either, he attached the prepaid cell to his belt in a spare phone holster.

Then, under an oppressive gray sky, he drove back to work.

The visit from the FBI made him want to get away from home. Agent Falco clearly suspected that he was hiding something, and they would be checking into his story and checking into him. Loitering in the house, pacing the empty rooms full of so many painful reminders of Simone and Jada, waiting for something to happen, filled him with a paralyzing sense of powerlessness.

He had to *do* something. Something proactive, not reactive. The clock was ticking.

First things first. He needed to talk to someone about what was going on, someone he could trust, someone who could help him formulate a strategy. He felt incapable of logically thinking through the situation on his own—he was navigating such an emotional high wire he feared he might do something stupid, and with the lives of his family hanging in the balance, he couldn't afford to make a mistake.

At work, he found Todd in his corner office, the door half open. Surrounded by posters of his favorite casinos, Todd was tapping away on the keyboard and bobbing his head to a Jimmy Buffet song playing on his iPod, the music blasting through a pair of external speakers.

Corey envied his friend's good cheer. It seemed so damn unfair that while Todd was bopping along happily, he was going through his life's worst nightmare.

Corey rapped on the door. Todd looked up.

"Hey, buddy," Todd said. He lowered the music's volume and spun away from his PC. "Sure could've used you on the conference call. You handle whatever you were doing?"

Corey closed the door, pulled a wing chair closer to Todd's desk, and sat.

"Listen, Todd, I need your help in a major way."

"Okay." Todd tilted backward in his seat and crossed his hands behind his head. "I'm all ears. What's up?"

"You remember our conversation from yesterday? About a certain hypothetical situation?"

Todd grinned, exposing capped teeth. "You're telling me you really did kill someone?"

"Listen, I need you to be serious."

"All right, I'm serious, sorry." He pinched his upper lip, face growing solemn. "What happened?"

"First of all, this stays strictly between you and me."

Todd raised his hand. "Scout's honor, Corey. I won't tell a soul."

Corey paused, deliberating over his words. Then, in a faltering voice, he told Todd almost everything. He told him about running into Leon yesterday. He told him Leon had abducted his family that morning for ransom. He told him about his visit from the FBI.

The only thing he didn't tell Todd was what he had never told anyone: the details of the act he and Leon had committed together, a memory that churned like a thundercloud in the depths of his soul. Instead, he painted the unsavory past he shared with Leon in general terms, admitted that they had done things together that could pose a grave problem if the facts were to become public, and that Leon was using their history as leverage to bend Corey to his will.

Throughout Corey's recounting of events, Todd listened intently, blue eyes alternating between shock and anxiety. But when Corey reached the part about his encounter with the FBI, redness bloomed in his cheeks.

"Never, ever trust the freakin' cops," Todd said with disgust. "It's like how it is on TV, you know? If you'd told this Agent Falco chick what was going on, they'd be manipulating you across their little chessboard."

"That's what I was afraid of," Corey said. Now that he had confided in someone, he already felt better. Sharper, more clear-headed. "Lying to them was its own risk, but their involvement is riskier."

"No shit, it's riskier. They wouldn't care about getting your family back safe, they'd care only about pinching this Leon guy—and if your family gets trapped in the crossfire, big deal. That's what they do."

"If there's one thing I can tell you about Leon, it's that he's not afraid of a fight," Corey said. "He used to tell me all the time when we were kids that the only way he'll ever go down is in a hail of bullets, and he'll take plenty of people with him."

"Don't screw around with him, then. Screw the Feds, though."

"I'm glad we're on the same page. I had to talk to someone or else I'd go crazy."

"No worries, I'm with you now." Todd gnawed on the eraser of his pencil, glanced at the computer. "So I can find this guy's photo and stuff online?"

"Type his name into Google and see for yourself."

Todd swiveled to the keyboard, typed. His eyes grew large as he stared at the screen. "Whoa. Christ, he looks like a badass."

Corey smiled grimly. "Leon's the real deal, Todd. A bona fide crazy motherfucker."

Todd was shaking his head. "It's hard for me to picture you being best buds with this guy. You're so . . . so straight-laced and normal. Like Mr. All-American Guy. How'd you ever hook up with someone like him?"

"He moved in to the house across the street from us when I was maybe sixteen, seventeen. He was a couple of years older than me, slick and sharp, talked beaucoup trash about a whole lot of things I'd never heard of, seemed so wise to the ways of the world, you know? I guess he just sort of blew me away."

"You looked up to him then, like a big brother?"

"I didn't have anyone else. I had a few friends my age, but none especially close. No close cousins. No siblings. It was only me and my grandma. So yeah, I think I saw him like a big brother type, for a while anyway. But that was a long time ago—now I see him as he really is."

"As a psycho," Todd said.

"He has no morals, no fear. No inhibitions whatsoever. If he wants something, he just takes it, and he doesn't care if he has to shoot someone to get it. That's the kind of guy we're dealing with here."

Nodding absently, Todd chewed the pencil eraser, gaze far away.

"What're you thinking?" Corey asked.

Todd's eyes focused. "I hate to say it, Corey, but I think we have to pay him."

"What?"

"We have to give him some money."

Corey bounded out of the chair and paced across the office. "Did you hear what I said, Todd? I told you, I don't have five hundred thousand dollars!"

"I know, I know." Todd raised his hands in a placating gesture. "Work with me a minute, all right? I'm the sales guy of our management team, you're the business know-how."

"What the hell does that have to do with anything?"

"Christ, will you let me finish, Corey? What I'm saying is that we've got to sell this guy a deal."

"Sell him a deal? How? He's got all the leverage—*he has my family*."

"I get that. But it's not in his best interests to hurt them. This guy is a killer, sure, but he's primarily a thief. He doesn't want bloodshed unless someone forces his hand. Am I reading him correctly?"

"If you push him too far, he can explode."

"Of course, sure." Todd rubbed his hands together, warming up to his proposal. "But with the way I want to do this, no one gets pushed, no one gets hurt. It'll be a win-win for everyone."

"A win-win? How?"

"I say we give him what we give some of the customers we really want to woo—an in-home, risk-free trial."

"I have no idea what you're talking about."

"Check this out. The next time he calls you, we tell him we've pulled together the ransom payment. We arrange for the drop-off of the cash and the release of your family. At the drop-off, we give him a briefcase full of money."

Corey stopped pacing. "How much money?"

"I think fifty thousand would do it."

"I tried to talk him into that earlier. He wants five hundred thousand, Todd. Period."

"And I want a Ferrari Spider, but if someone gives me the keys to a Corvette and says take it home, I'm not going to turn it down. Do you see what I'm saying here?"

Fists bunched on his waist, Corey said, "I think so."

"This guy is a freakin' FBI fugitive. He's desperate, strapped for cash. He needs to get moving before the heat builds. Once he sees fifty grand staring him in the face, we'll seal the deal—like our customers who fall in love with our system and go to contract after we give them a risk-free trial. With that much cash in hand, he'll be happy to turn over your family and hit the road."

"Then what?"

"What do you mean, then what? You'll have Simone and Jada back, this Leon guy goes back on the lam, and the Feds catch him later, maybe. But your headaches are over."

Corey sat down again. He cracked his knuckles, thinking.

Todd could be right. In spite of his bravado and fast talk, Leon was a relatively small-time hood, limited by his innate impulsiveness to minor burglaries of homes and armed robberies of convenience stores; even the crime that had landed him on the FBI's radar, as tragic as it had turned out, had netted him only thirty-five thousand dollars, and Corey was certain that was the most Leon had ever scored in one job. With fifty grand in his possession free and clear, he might turn over Simone and Jada, safe and unharmed.

But what if Leon wanted more money? What if, after they paid him, he didn't go away like they hoped he would?

"It might not work," Corey said. "Even if he releases my family after we pay him, he might come around again. That's what thieves do, they're greedy. They'll hit the same spot over and over until it's totally tapped out."

Todd's gaze was direct. "You have a gun, don't you?"

Corey understood what he was getting at. He touched his hip, where his shirt concealed his revolver's bulge.

"It's right here," he said.

"If he comes around again, I think you'll be ready to deal with him a bit more aggressively," Todd said softly. "An altercation between a violent fugitive and a devoted family man and entrepreneur, respected in his community, who kills the bad guy in self-defense? Write your own headline, Corey, but it's all good for you."

Corey knew he was right. If he was forced to gun down Leon in a fight, he would probably be hailed as a hero.

"It still seems like a big gamble," Corey said.

"Life's a gamble, man. One giant roulette wheel. One crazy hand of cards. One pull of the one-armed bandit. You've gotta roll the dice."

"We're taking about the lives of my wife and daughter, not a wild night in Vegas. I can't afford to be wrong on this."

"Most definitely, these are the highest stakes you could ever have." Todd tapped the pencil against his chin. "Take some time to think it over. You've got until when to pay him? Friday afternoon?"

"Friday at five."

"If I can help in any way at all, let me know. I'm here for you." Todd grimaced. "I'm so sorry this is happening. You guys don't deserve this shit. I don't . . . man, I don't even want to imagine what your family's going through right now with that psycho maniac holding them."

Corey thought he had been keeping himself under control, but Todd's words stirred up a deep, cold fear that compressed his heart like steel calipers. Muttering thanks, he hurried outside—he had to get outdoors into the fresh air or else he was going to explode.

23

Shedding tears, Simone knew from her professional experience, could often be cathartic, a means of expelling deep-seated emotional toxins and blockages. In her therapy practice, she aimed to create a warm, trusting environment in which her clients felt free to cry if they were so moved. In many cases, a healthy bout of purgative weeping led to greater self-awareness of one's troubles—and, eventually, enhanced self-awareness led to healing.

After she gave in to her own tears, she felt cleansed, too. Liberated from pointless denials of her situation. Profoundly and sharply aware of her plight.

Now she could heal—by taking specific measures to get out.

Maybe fifteen minutes ago, soon after she had begun crying, Leon had abandoned her on the mattress in the bedroom. He tucked the folding chair under his arm, locked the door behind him, and barricaded the doorway on the other side with what sounded like a heavy piece of wood. He'd left without a word, his gaze unreadable, as if annoyed by her tears or preoccupied with other matters that required his attention.

He was an enigma to her. Why on earth did he think Corey could raise five hundred thousand dollars in two days? What was the real nature of Corey's history with him? How long had he been planning to do this to them?

One thing of which she had no doubt whatsoever: he was dangerous. There was a hungry, reptilian gleam in his eyes when he looked at her that convinced her that he would not hesitate to hurt her. That he might even get a sick thrill out of it.

She would have to be careful with him.

As for the shady past he shared with Corey, why he had chosen them for this scheme, and why he believed Corey could pay the outrageous sum he was demanding—she had progressed no further in figuring out answers to those questions, and any answers she came up were likely to be wrong, so she avoided pondering them too much.

She would focus on what she could control. Her own thought processes. Her own actions. With the singular intention of merging thought and action to save Jada. Nothing else mattered.

Except for the occasional whisper of wind through eaves, the house was eerily quiet. She had not heard any noises from upstairs. She prayed her baby was fine and that Leon's partner indeed obeyed his command to leave Jada untouched.

The alternative was just too horrifying to contemplate.

Her cheeks sticky with drying tears, she examined the handcuffs in her lap. They certainly weren't the flimsy, bedroom-play variety: the heavy-duty silver chain was a couple of inches long, and the cuffs themselves were made of durable, nickel-plated steel. There was a keyhole in each restraint.

All she knew about escaping from handcuffs was what

she had seen in movies. Perhaps she could have used a hairpin to pick the locks if she had one, but she didn't. She had thin, delicate wrists, but when she tried to twist them through the cuffs, she succeeded only in sending hot rivets of agony down her forearms. The cuffs were cinched too tightly for her to maneuver free.

With effort, she got to her feet. Needles of pain threaded across her abdomen, the side of her face ached from when Leon had slapped her, and the knot on the back of her head felt as fat as a walnut. She inhaled several breaths, steadying herself.

The shift in position made her aware of her full bladder. On feet that felt like leaden blocks, she shuffled to the bathroom.

It was full of shadow, spacious, but unfinished. The large garden tub was missing the spout and faucets; the basin held a short stack of ceramic tiles that matched the floor, but nothing that could be used as a weapon or a lock pick. The door to the glass shower enclosure leaned against a wall. There was a door for the bathroom itself, but where a knob should have been, there was only an empty hole, preventing her from locking herself inside.

There were three windows, but each had been barred widthwise with planks of plywood, leaving only thin slits through which to view outside. She peered through the narrow opening of the window above the sink. A rolling forest of pines, elms, and maples receded from the house to an ashen horizon, but the landscape told her nothing about where they were being held. Metro Atlanta was full of wooded areas.

The door to the walk-in closet was at the other end of the bathroom; the knob was missing from that door, too. She pushed it open, and found a vacant, musty space crisscrossed with cobwebs.

A roll of cheap toilet paper stood atop the tank lid. She flipped up the cover. The bowl was dry, no running water, but she didn't care.

She nudged the door shut with her foot, yanked down her sweat suit bottoms and panties—it took a bit of shimmying to do it with her hands bound—and lowering herself onto the cold seat she emptied her bladder.

She thought of Jada having to urinate with that giant pervert looming nearby. An almost crippling wave of rage crashed through her.

Hold on to that emotion, she told herself. *Bottle it up. Save it for when the moment is right.*

After finishing on the toilet, she checked out the double sink vanity. A big mirror, shaped like half a moon, had been affixed to the wall. Her reflection in the glass was murky, as if she were as insubstantial as a ghost that might fade into the shadows at any moment.

Vaguely troubled by the sight, she looked away and got on her knees. She opened the cherry wood cabinet doors. In the dimness inside, she noticed a faint glimmer.

She squinted, leaned in closer.

It was a length of drainage pipe, curved at one end like a candy cane, about six inches long and an inch in diameter.

She carefully dug it out. She hefted it in her hands, pleased by its weight.

If she swung it at someone and connected, it could do serious damage.

Returning to the bedroom, she concealed the pipe underneath the mattress, near the baseboard.

Like her rage, she would save it for an opportune time.

Getting to her feet again, she crossed to the bedroom door. Someone had hung the door so that the hinges and the lock were on the outside of the room. She turned the brass knob. As she anticipated, it was locked.

Next, she went to the closest window. Two strips of thick wood covered it widthwise, fastened in place by nails driven into the surrounding wall.

She gripped the edges of the bottom slat, braced one foot against the wall, and tugged with all her might. Her arms trembled from the effort, but there was no give in the wood at all. She might as have been trying to pry loose an iron bar.

She gave up and looked between the boards.

A big backyard of smooth, reddish-brown dirt led to a perimeter marked by tall maples and pines. In the dense shadows among the trees, about twenty yards away from the property line, she glimpsed railroad tracks. They curved through the trees and wound out of sight.

Chewing her lip, she stared at those tracks.

She turned around and looked at the bedroom as if through a fresh pair of eyes. She noted the hardwood flooring. The crown molding. The marble gas-log fireplace. The tray ceiling.

Why did she have the feeling that she had been there before?

24

They were back.

That morning, in his single-wide trailer situated high on a tree-dotted shelf of land above the banks of Dog Lake, Ed stood at a bedroom window with a pair of binoculars and observed the white van returning to the same home it had visited last night. Those same two men had climbed out, but he hadn't been able to see what they were doing because they pulled the van into the garage, out of sight.

It troubled him.

He had wiped clean a spot on the grime-filmed glass to facilitate his surveillance. The window was cracked open—he'd never had air-conditioning—and the dingy curtains, stirred by a cool breeze, rippled around his hunched shoulders. At least a dozen members of his family crowded around his legs, licking, chuffing, sniffing, snorting, whining, and moaning, all in a bid for his attention.

Normally, he spent his days playing with the dogs, petting them, feeding them, talking to them. That morning, however, he was oblivious to his canine family, riveted by the mystery unfolding across the lake.

He had been keeping a close watch since last night, when he'd returned home after finding his black Lab and the two young strays. He'd dragged a kitchen chair with a wobbly leg to the window and had fallen asleep staring across the dark water, a puppy curled in his lap. He figured the van had departed sometime after he dozed off, because that morning, it had come back.

In the grayish light of dawn, he'd read the words painted in big blue letters on the side panel: LB'S HEATING & COOLING.

It was, he was sure, the same van from the night before. What kind of heating company visited a house in the middle of the night?

For many years, he had strictly limited his interactions with people. He had not held a job since returning from the war, and for his wounded leg, he received a disabled veteran's check each month that covered his modest expenses. He paid his few bills through the mail, visiting the local post office every few months to purchase a new supply of stamps, speaking as little as possible to the clerks. He consumed only canned goods and carbonated beverages that he purchased from the supermarket where he cashed his benefit check, stocking up on such a huge amount of items during his visits that he shopped only a few times a year; the dogs, full-fledged members of his family, ate the same foods as he did. He never entertained company, and warned away all visitors with a NO TRESPASSING sign posted at the end of the long dirt driveway. People would not appreciate his important rescue work, and might summon Them to take away his family and sentence the beloved souls to the gas chambers.

Likewise, he didn't own a television set, computer, telephone, microwave, or radio. He didn't have electricity. Electricity and electronic devices were vehicles by which They could invade your mind, jam your mental frequencies, and make you one of Them.

You had to be cautious. You never knew who might be one of Them. That was Their power; outwardly, They looked like everyone else. But of course They were not.

They were unquestionably vile creatures who appeared to be human, and They were intent on world domination. They were the ones who captured innocent animals and gassed them to death; They were the ones who raped the land to erect awful homes; They were the ones polluting the air and spreading litter. They were everywhere, and the only way to ensure that you did not become one of Them was to reduce your risk of exposure.

His only interest, other than his dogs and avoiding possible interaction with Them, was his collection of phone books. He usually found them lying atop someone's trash, or sitting forgotten in plastic bags in driveways. He had accumulated tall stacks of the guides dating back over twenty years. Since he lacked phone service, he had no pressing need to call anyone listed in the directories. He kept the books on hand just in case, in some dire, unimaginable emergency, he should ever need to locate a phone and place a call.

In spite of his isolation from society, Ed knew there was something unusual about a heating and cooling company visiting a house late at night. It made no sense to him.

But if the employees of the heating company were actually working for Them, he shouldn't expect to understand it, as the things They did in secret were as alien as the dark side of the moon.

Although he hadn't seen anything happen since the van had disappeared around the house, he kept watching. He didn't want to miss a thing.

But he wondered if he should get closer, to look inside. The idea terrified him, but it would not go away.

What if They were bringing dogs inside that terrible place? What if They were torturing the innocent creatures? Butchering them?

Eating them?

A hundred horrifying scenarios revolved around his mind like some morbid carousel, and he couldn't make them stop.

But there was one way to check it out.

Placing the binoculars on the window sill, he grabbed his cane from where it leaned against the wall and waded through the wriggling knot of dogs. He left the bedroom, the dogs flanking him, the warped floor creaking underneath his heavy footsteps and their clicking paws.

Outside in the shadowed hallway, more dogs of various breeds greeted him with barks, wagging tails, shining eyes, and damp noses. They pressed close to him, sniffing his fingers, and he gently nudged them away with his cane.

"Ed's busy this morning, guys," he said. "Let Ed work. Ed thinks this is important."

Phone books were piled head-high along one wood-paneled wall, from one end of the hall to another. He had a system for organizing them: he always placed the newest directories near the front room.

Repeatedly muttering "LB's Heating and Cooling," under his breath, he lumbered to the stack where he expected to find the most recent book. He blew off the dust, picked it up, and cracked it open. Squinting to read the tiny type in the dim light, he flipped through the crisp pages.

There was no listing for LB's Heating and Cooling in the Yellow Pages.

The white business pages, as well, turned up nothing.

Shaking his head, he moaned. "No, no."

What could this mean? How could the company not be listed anywhere in the phone book? Everything was supposed to be in the phone book.

He checked through other directories, for previous years, with the same troubling result.

He'd always believed that They masqueraded under the guise of ordinary people, ordinary companies. But perhaps this was proof that They had gotten bolder in their deceit and no longer felt the need to keep up appearances.

Cold bands of fear constricted his chest.

For the first time, he wished he had a telephone. He would call the police and report this.

But, he realized with dismay, They could have infiltrated the police department, too.

There was no one to whom he could turn, no one he could risk trusting with this vital information.

Around him, many of the dogs' ears had perked up, and their tails went pole-rigid. They sensed his anxiety.

Perhaps they sensed the danger, too.

He shuffled back to the bedroom window and looked at the house again through the binoculars.

What was going on in there? Were dogs being maimed? Killed?

He shuddered.

Or could it be something worse than he imagined?

Since no one else could be trusted, he would have to take a closer look himself.

25

Jada lay on a narrow mattress in a shadowed bedroom that had big boards on the window, a dusty floor, and a musty smell in the air. Curled up in a ball, she sucked her thumb. She had been sucking her thumb ever since Giant had cut away the tape around her wrists and taken off the blindfold.

She could not remember the last time she had sucked her thumb. Mom and Daddy hated for her to do it and chastised her that big girls didn't do such things, but right then, having her thumb in her mouth to suckle made her feel a little bit better.

Still, she could barely stop shaking. Where was this place? Where had Mom gone? Why hadn't Daddy come yet?

Why had Mr. Leon, who Daddy had said used to be his best friend back in Detroit—his *homeboy*—tied them up and taken them away from home? Was Mr. Leon mad at Daddy over something? Was that why he was doing this to them?

She wished Mom and Daddy would come and take her away from there.

Most of all, she wished they would take her away from

e big man. She didn't know the big man's name, so she had
ecided to call him Giant.

Silent as a rock, Giant sat in a chair on the other side of
e room, in front of the door. The chair looked too tiny to
pport him, and it reminded her of when Daddy had tried to
de her bicycle. His knees had bumped against his chest,
d she had laughed at him.

The memory made her want to smile, but she was afraid
smile, because Giant kept staring at her with those weird
at-coin eyes of his, and she didn't want him to think she
as smiling at *him*.

If he believed she was smiling at him, he might take that
an invitation to come close to her, and the thought of him
ear her frightened her to death. When he had taken the tape
ff her wrists and eyes, his fingers had softly brushed against
er skin, for only a second. His touch was damp and cold,
ke the scales of a dead fish, and he had an excited look in
is eyes, as if touching her was the most thrilling thing in the
orld to him.

It creeped her out so badly she'd thought she was going to
int.

She didn't want to look at him at all, but she was afraid to
rn her head completely away from him, too. Without her
eech processor, if he moved, she wouldn't *hear* him move,
d the idea of him sneaking up on her made her queasy.

So she remained curled in a ball, sucking her thumb and
atching him out of the corner of her eye.

To make things worse, she had to pee. On the other side
f the room, there was a bathroom, but she didn't want to go
there. There was a hole in the door where the knob was
pposed to be, and she could imagine Giant putting his flat
e to it and watching her as she sat on the toilet.

No way. She would have to hold it a little while longer
d hope that, soon, he left her in there alone. There was an-

other door near where she lay on the mattress, but she wa
pretty sure that it was just a closet, like in her own bedroom

To keep her mind off peeing and her fears of Giant, sh
thought about their upcoming family vacation to Disne
World. She couldn't wait. It would be their second tim
going, and while the last time she had been excited abou
seeing Cinderella Castle—she was seven then, still a dum
little kid—this time she was most looking forward to the Fu
ture World pavilions at Epcot. Science was her favorite sub
ject in school, and she was thinking that she might become
scientist or a doctor when she grew up, so of course, she ha
to check out all the technology stuff—

In the edge of her eye, she saw Giant get up and sta
shuffling toward her. His plodding footsteps made the floo
quake.

She snatched her thumb out of her mouth, bolted uprigh
and scooted against the wall, pulling in her legs close to he
body and wrapping her arms tightly around her knees.

Please, don't hurt me, mister, she said. Or, that was wha
she thought she said. Her throat was so tight she couldn't b
sure the words got out clearly.

He advanced toward her with slow, heavy steps, lips parte

Her back pressed against the wall, she shook so badly sh
felt as if she might crumble into a million pieces. There wa
an awful, gritty taste in her mouth that made her want to gag

Please don't hurt me, she said again. Her head still hu
from when Giant had pushed her in her bedroom at home
and she would never forget what he had done to Mickey.

Giant halted before he reached the mattress. He stoope
to the floor.

She squeezed her legs against her chest, her feet cold i
her furry slippers. What was Giant doing?

She wasn't sure, but this close, that chocolate-sour odc
of his made her want to retch.

As he stared at her, his lips moved slowly. He was speaking to her.

What was he saying? She tried to read his lips.

Want . . . a . . . Something. Try as she might, she couldn't
read lips.

I don't understand, she said. She pointed at her ears. *I
can't hear you. I'm deaf, mister.*

His shiny brow furrowed. She wasn't sure he understood
what she had told him.

His lips moved again. She thought he said, *You have it.*

Have what?

He dug inside the front chest pocket of his overalls. He
fished out a candy bar. A Snickers.

Giant had the biggest hands she'd ever seen in her life,
but she could tell that it was the king-size Snickers, too.

Her stomach churned. Snickers bars were one of her favorite sweet treats ever, right up there with Grandma Rose's
double-chocolate cake.

As delicately as if he were putting a candle on a birthday
cake, Giant placed the candy at the edge of the mattress.
Slowly, watching her all the while, he got up and backed
away to his chair.

He was giving the candy to her.

Her parents had taught her never to take candy from
strangers, but she suddenly became aware of how hungry
she was. She hadn't eaten her normal breakfast of cereal,
fruit, and milk. She hadn't eaten anything since dinner last
night. She was *famished.*

She stared at the candy bar. It hadn't been opened. It was
totally wrapped up, like when you bought it brand new at the
grocery store.

Mom's voice replayed in her mind: *Jada, baby, never,
ever take anything from a stranger, okay, honey? Never talk
to strangers, never take candy from strangers. It's not safe.*

She had never in her whole life disobeyed that rule. But her mouth was literally watering.

What if she was kept in this terrible room for a long time? What if this candy was the only food she ever got there? Would Mom and Daddy want her to starve to death instead of eating a piece of brand-new candy?

But what if it had been poisoned? Grandma Rose had once spoken about that when she and Mom had been talking about why kids shouldn't be allowed to go trick or treating on Halloween. *Uh-huh, folks these days are too crazy,* she had said, *they put poison in the candy, razor blades in the apples.*

As she was trying to make a decision, her raging hunger abruptly made the choice for her; she snatched the Snickers off the floor and tore open the package with her teeth. She bit off a big chunk, and though the chocolate was warm from being kept in Giant's pocket, it was sweet and delicious, the best thing she'd ever tasted in her life.

She ate the whole thing, and licked her fingers clean, too. When she had finally finished, she glanced across the room at Giant.

He was smiling at her.

26

Around a quarter past noon, Corey pulled into the parking lot of his bank.

After a long bout of deep, agonizing thought, he had resolved to move forward with Todd's idea of paying Leon a smaller ransom. It was the least repulsive choice from a menu of ugly options.

With going to the cops out of the question, and being unable to pay Leon the outrageous amount he demanded, Corey was willing to chance that giving him fifty thousand in cash, tempting him to take the money and get the hell out of Dodge, might just work. Besides the fact that Leon had never pulled off a big score and would consider fifty grand a major jackpot, Leon was the kind of guy who liked to get the maximum return on a minimum amount of effort, which was why he'd become a criminal in the first place, instead of a law-abiding citizen who worked legitimately for the things he wanted. A briefcase full of more money than Leon had ever seen in his life, for relatively little work on his part, might bring a swift end to this nightmare.

Stubborn logic, however, argued that he might be taking a

foolish risk that could place Simone and Jada in greater jeopardy than ever.

But he didn't know what else to do—and the worst choice was to do nothing at all.

The sun had recently broken through the clouds, and in his anxious state of mind, he interpreted the sun's emergence as a positive sign. God was smiling on him in approval of his plan of action—that was what he wanted to believe, anyway. Although he'd never been particularly religious, that day he was alert for signs of Providence and was frequently murmuring desperate prayers under his breath.

Perhaps he was a hypocrite for calling on God during his time of adversity, but so be it.

He uttered another short prayer and then went inside the bank, leaving his gun in the glove box. He felt naked without the revolver's comforting weight riding his hip, but he seriously doubted that his concealed carry permit allowed him to bring his firearm inside a financial institution. Although he'd been skirting the law on several counts that day, he didn't want to toss all caution to the wind, either.

It was the lunch hour, and the lobby was full. Ten minutes had passed by the time he reached a teller and told her that he wanted a cashier's check for fifty thousand dollars, to be withdrawn from his joint checking account; before leaving the office, he had visited the bank's Web site and transferred all of the monies from their savings into the joint checking.

The teller was a stout, brown-haired woman with enormous bifocals that magnified her eyes to an almost freakish degree, and upon hearing his request, those saucer-eyes of hers squinted in skepticism. Undaunted, he produced his driver's license and checkbook and asked her the processing fee that he should add to the withdrawal. When she told him, he filled in the full amount with a shaky hand.

He had never penned a check for anywhere near fifty

thousand, but if he had the funds and the lives of his family were at stake, he would have gladly paid fifty million for their safe return.

When the teller asked to whom the cashier's check should be payable, he said, "Todd Gates."

Earlier, Corey had called the bank and learned that the largest cash withdrawal he could receive on short notice from any given branch was two thousand dollars, far short of the fifty he needed. Todd had offered a solution: Corey could pay him, and in exchange, Todd would give him the money in hard currency.

You have fifty grand in cash available? Corey had asked, incredulous.

When you run with the big dogs, you need to have major funds on tap, Todd had admitted with a shrug. *The guys I play poker with don't accept checks or credit cards, if you know what I mean.*

Corey knew what he meant. Todd played with the kind of people who gambled for high stakes, and they weren't exactly reporting their winnings to the IRS. Corey had known for some time that Todd swam in those murky waters, but he had avoided making a big deal about it, deciding that as long as Todd was on point at work, the man's private life was none of his business.

But a check-for-cash exchange for fifty grand was going to make it his business, like it or not. He would have to accept that. All he wanted was Simone and Jada brought home safely—anything else, he could deal with afterward.

The teller printed the check and slid it across the counter for his approval. He nodded, head swimming as he saw all those zeros and remembered the hard work and sacrifice it had taken to build up their savings.

All gone soon, courtesy of Leon. Anger flashed through his chest.

The teller inserted the check in a business-size envelope and passed it to him, and Corey marched out of the building, arms swinging.

As he was getting behind the wheel, the cell phone Leon had given him chirped. Corey fumbled the phone out of the holster.

"Guess who?" Leon said.

27

"Listen, I've got your money," Corey said.

"Word?" Leon said. "Now that was fast, I mean, whoa, you moved like the wind pulling together such an *exorbitant* sum of capital, so much for your woe-is-me claim that you didn't have the funds, I knew you were lying through your bleached teeth."

I'm lying to you now, you bastard. The key to pulling off the scheme was to let Leon think he was getting the full ransom payment. They trusted that when he actually counted the money, his glee at having fifty large in his hands would outweigh his fury at being shortchanged.

Pressing the phone to his ear, Corey strained to hear any background noise on the line that might give him an idea of where Leon was calling from. But there was only hollow silence, as if Leon were at the bottom of a well.

"Let me talk to my wife," Corey said.

"I can't go for that, no can do, you got the currency, you'll welcome her into your open arms soon enough. Take my word, she's cool, your munchkin's cool, we're cool, everybody's cool as cucumbers. I'm ready to do this, I'm ready to get my money and cruise into the boogie nights."

"How do you want to do this, then? How about I come to you, give you the money, and you give me my family?"

"No, no, no, no, no. Do not pass go, mi amigo. That's not how this is going to go down, no. We'll rendezvous this afternoon, sixteen hundred hours sharp, Lenox Square Mall, east side."

Corey's mind raced. "Where on the east side? It's a big mall."

"Be there at sixteen hundred, go inside the general mall entrance, wait near the doors, and I'll buzz you and give you the precise drop-off point coordinates, you dig? I need to scope the scene and make sure you haven't gone five-o on me."

A car pulled into the space alongside Corey: a police cruiser. Corey held his breath as a muscle-bound cop wearing yellow-tinted aviator glasses climbed out.

He felt the officer's mirrored gaze casually rake over him, perform a quick assessment, and judge him harmless. The cop moved on toward the bank.

Corey exhaled. He was so worried about the FBI that every cop was a threat.

"You got verbal constipation?" Leon asked. "Did you hear what I said?"

"Leon, I haven't gone to the cops. Why the hell would I? You know me better than that."

"Never been a snitch bitch, I'll give you that." Leon giggled. "I've missed you, C-Note. Don't you miss how we used to rock 'n' roll? How could you ever give it up and go legit? That crazy adrenaline buzz, that quick, easy loot, you've gotta reminisce sometimes."

"I'll deliver the money to you at four," Corey said. "But when are you giving me my family?"

"You get the address when I get the funds."

"I want them to be there at the mall."

"This isn't Burger King—you can't have it your way. You've got no leverage. All out of chips. Pockets turned out. Do what I say, how I say, when I say, where I say, and you can resume your merry fuckin' Heathcliff Huxtable life, comprende, hombre?"

Click.

Corey stared at the phone, gnawing his bottom lip. He didn't like the plan, but Leon was right. He had no leverage whatsoever.

A blanket of shadow spread across the car. He looked up at the sky through the windshield. The sun had vanished again.

28

When Mr. Leon came into the bedroom, he made Giant leave. Jada breathed a sigh of gladness. She'd been trying to ignore Giant after she ate the Snickers, but he continued to stare at her and smile that creepy smile of his, as if he expected her to do something as payment for the candy bar, and she'd been terrified that he was going to get out of that chair, shuffle to her, and *make* her do whatever awful thing he was thinking about.

As Giant lumbered out of the room, he said something to Mr. Leon—Jada thought his lips spoke the word *candy*—and Mr. Leon shrugged, closed the door, and approached her. In one hand, he held a white plastic bag with a Subway logo on it.

She loved Subway, but she scooted against the wall and watched him cautiously as he came near. Daddy had said he and Mr. Leon had used to be best friends a long time ago, but in some way, Mr. Leon actually scared her more than Giant, though he wasn't nearly as big. Mr. Leon made her think about the last time Mom and Daddy had taken her to

Zoo Atlanta. There had been a spotted hyena there, and the animal, which she knew from class was a vicious predator, had been pacing restlessly across the dirt, hungrily watching the people beyond the fence, pacing and pacing and pacing, and she'd known that if it hadn't been for that fence, the hyena would have pounced on them and torn them to pieces.

Mr. Leon was like that restless hyena, but there was no fence to keep her safe from him if he suddenly attacked, so she thought it best to be quiet and careful around him.

He dropped the bag onto the mattress. He said something to her, but his lips moved too fast for her to figure out what he was saying. She glanced inside the bag and saw it was full of food.

Thank you, she said, but she didn't say anything else. He left the room, and she was alone in there for the first time ever. *Finally.*

The food he'd brought was even better than a candy bar: a big sub sandwich with turkey and cheese and mayo, a bag of Doritos, and a bottle of cold water. The Snickers, as delicious as it had been, had only stirred her appetite. She was so hungry that she barely thought about her parents' warnings against taking things from strangers.

She was starved enough to eat it all, but she saved some of it in case she got hungry later. She drank some of the water, too. Normally she hated to drink plain water because it tasted blah, but her mouth was so dry the water tasted wonderful.

With all of the eating and drinking came the pressing need to go to the bathroom. She couldn't hold it any longer, and since Giant had left, she felt safe going.

The bathroom was really weird—*peculiar* was a word she'd recently learned that came to mind—like the people building it had left before finishing. The knob was missing, and there was no water in the bowl, so she couldn't flush. A roll of toilet tissue stood on the sink, though.

When she was done, she turned the faucet handle to wash her hands, and nothing came out of the spout. She frowned, tore off a piece of tissue, and cleaned her hands as best she could.

She decided to do some exploring.

There was nothing to see in the bathroom. No windows at all. There was only the sink, toilet, and a bathtub full of junk and cobwebs. She went back into the bedroom.

There was a door near where the mattress lay, and like the bathroom door, the knob was missing. She pulled it open, expecting a closet, and that was what she found. It was a small space, with lots of dusty cobwebs and a few pieces of wood stacked on the floor and leaning against the wall, but it held nothing interesting.

Next, she went to the bedroom door. The plastic chair in which Giant had been sitting was nearby, and being careful not to touch it—the idea of touching a chair in which he had sat grossed her out—she turned the doorknob. It was locked.

She went to the window, which was blocked with big pieces of wood. She peered between the slats. The sky was cloudy and gray, and there was a forest out there that seemed to go on forever.

Where was she? Where were Mom and Daddy? Was she all alone?

Tears trickled out of her eyes. Sniffling, she shuffled to the mattress and curled up on it. She slipped her thumb into her mouth, feeling like a big baby as she did it, but comforted nonetheless.

As she lay there tucked in a ball, she squeezed her eyes shut and whispered a prayer. *Dear God, please don't let anything bad happen to me. Please send Mom and Daddy here to get me and take me home soon, please, please. I want to go home, God.*

She thought about Giant, remembered that smile that gave her goose bumps, and shuddered.

Please keep me safe, God. Amen.

She hoped God was listening.

29

We've been here before. I know it.

Pacing the bedroom floor, periodically flexing her fingers to keep them from growing numb, Simone ransacked her memory, struggling to recall when she had visited this place and exactly where it was located. The railroad tracks curving around the perimeter of the subdivision and the master bedroom suite appointments had triggered her sense of déjà vu. Hadn't her family come there several months ago to tour the model homes? Hadn't something awful happened to Jada while they were there?

Although ritzy new subdivisions sprang up every day in metro Atlanta, some of which had nearly identical floor plans and features, she doubted that many of them bumped up against a freight train network. She knew she was right on this; her intuition was buzzing.

Was it coincidence that Leon had brought them here? Or did it mean something? What could it mean?

She didn't know. But somehow, she needed to get a message to Corey.

Footsteps approached the doorway. She swung toward the door, fingers bunched into fists.

She heard the barricade removed, and then Leon entered. "Bonjour, señorita bonita."

He grinned mischievously, one hand hidden behind his back. Fear fluttered through her, and she thought about the concealed pipe.

Wait and see what he does. Wait for the right time.

He approached the mattress and showed his hand. He was carrying only a small plastic Subway bag. With a chuckle, as if he'd relished her fear, he tossed it onto the bed.

"Time to graze," he said.

A spasm wrenched her stomach. She had not realized how hungry she was.

But she shook her head. She didn't want to be in debt to this man. "I'm not hungry."

He smiled derisively. "Don't lie to me. I scooped you and the munchkin from the Webb McMansion before you had a chance to eat your Special K and sip your café au lait. It's past lunchtime now, and with those child-bearing hips you've got on you, I know you don't miss one too many meals. Stop trying to be au contraire and dig your pretty little manicured fingers into this grub, 'cause I sure as hell ain't feeding your ass again. This is it, now or never."

Her mouth had begun to water, and he had raised a good point. She didn't know how much longer she would be trapped there. It could be several days before this ended, and how could she have the strength to fight back or escape if she were weakened from starvation?

Kneeling onto the mattress, she pulled the bag open. It contained a foot-long sandwich, potato chips, and a cold bottle of water.

"Thanks," she said.

He lit a cigarette with a brushed chrome lighter and exhaled a wisp of smoke. "Guess what? Your hubby came through for you."

"What?" She stared at him. "Corey's going to pay you five hundred thousand dollars?"

He scowled. "Why do you sound surprised? Don't you think you and the little munchkin are worth that much and then some, a king's ransom? You've got pitifully low self-esteem, sounds like, yet you call yourself a therapist, huh? But then I've read that all shrinks are prime rubber-room candidates themselves, so I figure you fall into that category, too, fits you like a wet T-shirt."

She was shaking her head. "It's not that, it's just . . ." She let the sentence trail off. She couldn't believe it, but what did it matter how Corey had raised the money? All that mattered was that this nightmare would be ending soon.

"When?" she asked. "When can we go home?"

He glanced at his watch. "If all goes well, mademoiselle, by this evening. I'm meeting him at four to collect the currency."

Hope swelled in her breast. They could be home by that evening. This could all be over. Praise God.

"Where are you meeting him?" she asked.

"Lenox Square Mall, sure you know it well, that's where you no doubt use the gold card to purchase the haute couture I peeped in the closet at *su casa*. You aren't the only one who's got love for the plush, you know."

In actuality, she rarely shopped at Lenox and bought most of her clothes from outlet stores and mail catalogs that specialized in inexpensive but stylish and quality wear, but she saw no point in sharing that information with Leon. She was only relieved to know that Corey would be meeting him in a public place, where things would be less likely to go wrong.

She glanced at the food, hesitated. "Does my daughter have food and water, too?"

"'Course she does, I gave it to her myself a minute ago,

Billy Boy was eyeballing her too hard after she munched his candy bar." He snickered. "Whoa, talk about a double enten-dre, huh?"

"He gave my daughter candy?" She tried to keep her voice level, but she wanted to scream.

Leon puffed out smoke. "She ate that sucker up, too. Probably made Billy Boy want to cream his pants as he ogled her. Poor guy, he only wants to be loved like we all do, you dig, there isn't enough love in the world, and I guess if he thinks he can only get love from a sweet little munchkin, who am I to say that's wrong?"

Her hunger, so sharp a moment ago, faded. Hungry, scared, and alone, Jada had no idea of the mistake she had made by accepting the candy, could not fathom the signal that she had unknowingly sent that sick man. She was in greater danger than ever.

Somehow, she had to get Jada out of here.

Smirking, Leon bent to his knees. "Aw, shucks, don't be sad, little lady. I told Billy Boy to make like a tree and leave. The munchkin's alone now eating her chow."

"Can I see her? Please?"

"Nope."

She glared at him. "For God's sake, what harm is there in letting me see my daughter? Corey's giving you what you want, isn't he? Let me see her, damn it!"

"No can do, señorita bonita."

He flashed a shark's grin at her through the cloud of smoke. He was enjoying his power over her, taking pleasure from her anguished pleading.

She wanted to grab the pipe and smash his damned teeth out.

If you try that, you'll be doing exactly what he wants you to do. Don't play his game. You're the psychologist, girl. You make the rules.

Without uttering another word, she turned away from

him. She dug the water out of the bag, carefully unscrewed the cap, and sipped. It was cold and delicious. She tore open the potato chips and popped one into her mouth. Gourmet cuisine had never tasted better.

"That's all?" he said. "No more begging to see your crumb snatcher, no more pleading, no casting yourself at my feet and beseeching me for goodness and mercy?"

Shrugging, she peeled the paper away from the sandwich. "Turkey and pepperjack on wheat. Yummy. Good choice."

She took a sloppy bite and chewed with gusto. Hunched in front of her, Leon watched her eat, deep-set eyes smoking like stoked coals.

"My mama used to do that shit," he said softly.

"What's that?" She kept chewing.

"Ignore me, tune me out, change the subject, give me the cold shoulder, like you did. I don't like that shit, baby girl, not one iota. Don't fuckin' play with me, bitch."

Bracing herself for anything, she swallowed, and regarded him with a purposely bland expression.

He slapped her across the face, hand as quick and sharp as a bullwhip. Her head slewed sideways, and the sandwich dropped out of her fingers. Pain rose in her cheek like a heat blister.

She clenched her teeth against a cry, and though tears hung in her eyes, she blinked them back. No more weeping. She would not give him the satisfaction.

He got to his feet, blew out smoke. "You better hope that Corey comes through for you and the munchkin, you hear me, bitch, you better hope you don't ever see me again."

She looked up at him and gave him a kiss-my-ass smile.

He snarled and flicked his cigarette at her. She raised her arms to protect her face. The glowing butt stung her forearm, and she stifled a scream.

He stomped out of the room and slammed the door behind him, the sound echoing through the house.

As he left, she was still smiling, even though smiling worsened the ache in her face. She had finally discovered a chink in his armor, a weakness for potential exploitation, if it ever came to that.

But she hoped to God that it didn't, and that Corey came through for them.

30

Corey arrived at Lenox Square Mall a half hour early. This was one time when he couldn't let Atlanta's crazy traffic jam up his plans.

Lenox Square Mall was located in Buckhead, north of downtown, a district of upscale restaurants and trendy boutiques, posh condos and gleaming office towers, and picturesque homes tucked away in tree-shaded enclaves. The mall itself featured a wide range of high-end stores and even offered valet parking. Considering Leon's aspirations to the finer things, it made a twisted kind of sense to Corey that he would have picked this place for the drop-off. Lenox was usually busy, too, a popular shopping destination for tourists, and would make it easy for someone to disappear in the crowd.

He parked at the far edge of the parking lot on the eastern side. As he waited in the car, cracking his knuckles obsessively, he checked out the sky. The sun had not only vanished, but the clouds had thickened, too. They hung low and dark over the city, threatening a storm, and a breeze had picked up, tossing scraps of debris across the asphalt and teasing the skirts of the young women sauntering in and out of the doors.

The black leather Hermès briefcase that Todd had given him lay on the passenger seat. It contained fifty thousand dollars, in rubber-banded packets of fifties and hundreds. When Corey had met Todd at his Midtown condo after leaving the bank, Todd had invited him to count the money, but Corey had given the cash only a brief glance. Looking at it, counting it, would have only pissed him off, would have reminded him that Leon had won.

By ten minutes to four, he was too antsy to wait any longer. He grabbed the briefcase and got out of the car.

Although it was probably only in his imagination, the briefcase felt so heavy it could have contained a load of bricks. As he walked slowly across the parking lot, he had a nightmarish vision of dropping the case and seeing the money spill out and scatter across the pavement, drawing the attention of security and eventually the police, the cops searching him, finding the gun on his hip, adding up the money and the handgun and assuming he was there for a drug buy.

Relax, man, just relax.

God, he hoped this worked, he couldn't wait for this to be over, Simone and Jada in his arms again, safe.

He reached the revolving doors. He couldn't remember if Leon had told him to go inside and await his call or to hang around outside, but he felt vulnerable and exposed outdoors, so he headed in.

Indoors, the refrigerated air crystallized the sweat on his face. He read his watch. Seven minutes to four.

He looked around. No Leon.

He drifted toward an empty bench not far from the entrance. He considered sitting, but his knees felt so watery he worried he wouldn't be able to get up. Remaining on his feet, he unclipped the cell phone from the belt holster and clutched it in a clammy grip.

A security guard walked past, but ignored him. Shoppers of all ages and ethnicities streamed around him, laughing and talking, chatting on cell phones, making dinner plans and hook-up plans and plans for who knew what else, going about normal everyday business, and seeing the casual happiness on their faces intensified Corey's aching desire to bring this awful episode of his life to a close so he and his family could resume their ordinary lives.

After what felt like an eternity, his watch hit four o'clock.

The phone rang. Before the ring completed Corey had the cell against his ear.

"I'm here," Corey said.

"Right on time," Leon said. "That's why I liked having you as a wingman. You're dependable as the day is long, yep, yep."

Squinting against beads of sweat dripping into his eyes, Corey looked from the lower level where he stood to the upper floor. "Where are you?"

"I'm all around you, I'm like the Force, I'm everywhere like chi, permeating the ether and the ozone and the oxygen you breathe, can you feel me?"

"Listen, knock it off, will you?" Corey wiped his brow with the back of his hand. "I want to do this, okay? Where do you want me to go?"

"What's my most favoritest thing in the whole wide world?"

"I . . . Jesus, I don't know. Cigarettes?"

"Man, you disappoint me. What would I be carrying around with me all the time back when we used to rock and roll? Have you forgotten, has it slipped that sputtering hippocampus of yours in your middle age, you coming down with a hard case of Alzheimer's?"

"Why don't you cut to the chase and tell me, Einstein?"

"Books, my illiterate brother, *books*. Iceberg Slim, Don-

d Goines, Chester Himes—those were my heroes, gave me
y joie de vivre, my inspiration."

Corey did recall that Leon would carry books with him,
ut Leon would boast that he never read any of them cover to
over, that he would skim them to find the juicy parts and
en toss them aside to pick up another one; he claimed that
s mind was so quick and brilliant that no author could keep
p with him and therefore even the best books failed to hold
s attention for more than a few pages.

Corey tightened his grip on the briefcase. "Okay, books,
o what? You want me to go to a bookstore?"

"There's one on the second floor next to an antique furni-
re boutique. Take the escalator behind you. Keep the
hone to your ear. Move it, my man, time is money and time
a wasting."

Corey moved toward the escalator. He scanned for Leon
gain, but didn't see him. Where the hell was he hiding?

He mounted the rising steps. There was a gaggle of ado-
scent girls ahead of him, gabbing on their cell phones and
iggling amongst themselves, and they made him think
out his daughter.

"Is my family okay?" Corey asked.

"They're snug as pigs in a blanket. That wifey of yours
as a hellified mouth on her, though, good Lord, I think
ou've been sparing the rod and spoiling the bitch. If she
as mine I'd be going upside her head on the regular like
lister from *The Color Purple*. Did you skip the part during
e exchange of vows when she was supposed to agree to
iss your ass?"

Corey tuned out Leon's meaningless patter and stepped
ff the escalator. "I'm upstairs now."

"The bookstore is a hundred paces ahead, forward march,
ft, left, left, right, left."

Corey strode forward briskly. "I see it coming up. But I
on't see you."

"I told you, you're not supposed to see me. I'm like th Matrix. I'm all around us."

"I'm standing outside the bookstore now." His finge were curled so tightly around the briefcase they had begun ache.

"Go inside," Leon said.

Corey walked inside the store. A handful of custome browsed the magazine racks, oblivious to him. A strawberry haired female clerk behind the counter was on the telephon flipping through a catalog, and she didn't notice him, eithe

"Now what?" Corey asked in a low voice.

"Walk to the rear, on the left-hand side."

Corey marched down the center aisle. All of the cu tomers were apparently gathered at the front; the rear sec tions were deserted.

The back of the store was devoted to children's literatur Colorful unicorns and dragons and other fanciful creature cavorted on the walls, and splashy floor displays advertise Dr. Seuss books.

On the left side, the area was set up for story time: te miniature green plastic chairs were arranged in a semicirc around a normal-size folding chair. A small, low woode bench stood against the wall, bracketed by shelves on eithe side.

Corey blew out a breath. "I'm here."

"See the bench?"

"Yeah."

"Slide the briefcase underneath it."

Sweating so much in the cool air he felt feverish, Core knelt in front of the bench, knees popping, and pushed th briefcase beneath it. The case disappeared in the shadows.

Lord, please let this work out for us, he prayed as he re leased the handle. *Please.*

Rising on unsteady legs, he clenched and unclenched hi

ore fingers. "All right, it's done. Now where the hell is my amily?"

"Not so fast, home boy. I've got to collect the currency rst. I've got to see the loot with mine own eyes, and when I ave, when I'm satisfied that you've held up your end of the argain, then I'll give you the coordinates for the other nembers of the Webb pride."

"So come get it then."

"Leave the store, and make a right."

Corey hurried headlong down the center aisle. Again, no ne appeared to notice him. He had left behind fifty thou-and dollars in cash in a briefcase in a risky gamble to ran-om his family from a maniac, and no one had the slightest lue what was going on. He would have found the scenario npossible if he weren't living it.

Outside the store, he cut to the right. "I'm out. Now vhere?"

"Mr. Webb?" a husky female voice said.

Corey turned. Special Agent Falco strode toward him, hort arms swinging. Her wide-shouldered partner, Agent Aarch, was close on her heels.

The bottom fell out of Corey's stomach.

"Who the fuck are they?" Leon asked, voice crackling in Corey's ear.

"Can we speak to you, please, sir?" Falco asked.

Numb, out of breath, Corey backpedaled.

Agent March peeled away from Falco and strode into the ookstore.

They had seen him go inside with the briefcase, he real-zed. And walk out empty-handed.

Oh, shit.

"You went five-o on me?" Leon said. "You went to the eds after we made a deal?"

"No," Corey whispered. "No, no, I didn't—"

Cursing, Leon hung up. Corey backed away from Falco.

"Mr. Webb, listen to me," she said, dark eyes like darts. "If you know what's good for you, you'll come with me peacefully."

"Stay away from me," Corey said. "Please . . . just stay away."

And then he ran.

31

Peeping the merde going down near the bookstore from the cool safety of a men's clothing shop on the other side of the mall, Leon headed in the opposite direction.

Using his singular gift for blending in to the crowd, he'd kept watch on Corey ever since his home boy had come inside. Corey had been looking around for him, of course, but his eyes had swept blindly over Leon as if Leon were draped in an invisibility cloak like a kid in a *Harry Potter* flick.

It happened, simply, because Corey was expecting someone else.

After leaving the Webb flock at the house, Leon had shaved off his beard, a little sad at watching four months of growth tumble into the sink of a local Mickey Dee's restroom. A bit of concealer had hidden the red scratches on his face. And he'd removed the dreadlocks wig, too, exposing his bald head, smooth and round as a baby's backside.

No beard, no dreads, Rasta man no more, kiss good-bye to his wisdom-weed toking brothers in the West End.

He'd dressed in one of his disguises: a crisp, long-sleeve

blue work shirt with an official-looking but meaningless in signia on the breast, dark slacks, polished oxfords, fak walkie-talkie holstered on a chunky utility belt, blac serge hat with visor, aviator sunglasses. He wore a Blue tooth apparatus clipped to his ear, to speak hands-free o his cell.

Chin up, shoulders thrown back, head ratcheting bac and forth, walking with a slow, I'm-the-man gait, he passe so well for mall security that someone flagged him down an asked for directions to the can.

When he'd passed Corey, he'd been close enough to sl his throat. In retrospect, he wished he had. He should hav slit his throat and snatched the briefcase, because onc Corey came out of the bookstore and those two Feds rolle up on him—Leon tagged them as FBI from their blan suits—he knew he would never get his hands on that cur rency. His El Dorado was gone, game over, hit the restar button or quit the game altogether and play somethin else.

As Leon swaggered away, in the corner of his eye h watched the refrigerator-wide agent stride inside the store going to retrieve *his* goddamn money.

His hands twitched. He wanted to break something.

For some reason, though, Corey started running from th pretty, pint-sized female agent. It puzzled Leon. If Core was cooperating with them—or if they were only followin him because they suspected him of being linked to Leon— why the hell was he running?

Bad move, C-Note, now you've got the mark of the beas Welcome back to the dark side.

Leon descended a flight of stairs and sauntered to a corri dor that led to the parking garage, where he had parked th van and where Billy awaited his return. He had no idea wha he was going to do next, but what else was new. He was a impulsive guy and rolled with the punches, danced on the cutting edge of life, lived in the moment.

As soon as he got outside, he lit a cigarette, hands jittering, heart banging.

At the moment, he realized, he felt like venting his anger.

32

Corey raced pell-mell to the nearest escalator going down, yelling at people to get out of his way, using his elbows and shoulders to clear a path. In his frenzy, he caused one guy to drop his ice cream cone and another woman to fumble her shopping bags, spilling shoes. Both of them shouted at him angrily and Corey muttered apologies, while on the walkway above, a red-faced Falco ordered him to halt.

He couldn't believe what was happening, couldn't believe he was running from the FBI. Jesus, how had this gone so wrong?

Nearing the bottom platform, he jumped off the steps and sprinted to the exit doors, shoes clapping across tiles.

All around, people turned and looked, alarmed. A pimple-faced teenager had his cell phone out and tracked Corey running. Just in case it wound up being a sensational crime in progress, someone had to capture video footage to replay on YouTube and the local news.

Corey shouldered through the doors. The sky had finally split open. Cold rain hammered the afternoon.

He dashed across the street to the parking lot, splashing

through puddles, rushing heedlessly through traffic. Cars honked. An SUV screeched to a halt, bumper less than a foot from him, the driver shaking his fist.

Corey ignored them and looked over his shoulder. He didn't see Falco coming outside, but that didn't mean she wasn't on her way, and she might have a whole team of agents stationed in the area. If they caught him, his life might as well be over—Simone and Jada would be gone forever.

No, never.

He ran across the lot, rain pelting his face and soaking through his clothes. He couldn't remember where he had parked. *Shit.* He wiped water from his eyes and whirled around in a circle, searching.

Wait, there. Over there. There, in the corner.

He finally reached the BMW, dove inside, and stabbed the key in the ignition, fingers trembling so badly it took three tries to get it in.

Drive.

He roared out of the parking lot, tires seizing traction on the slick asphalt, the turbocharged six-cylinder engine responding magnificently to pressure, steering responsive and tight, the perfect getaway car if ever there was one.

But he was going to have to get rid of it, and very soon.

Because now he was wanted by the FBI.

Part Three

33

As storm clouds darkened the sky and spat cold rain, Ed left his trailer to check out Their home on the other side of the lake.

Sitting at his bedroom window eating green beans straight from the can, he had watched the white van depart the house and roll away down the street, soon traveling out of sight. He waited for a while before he made his move, to be sure the vehicle didn't come right back and he was forced to confront Them on Their turf.

Convinced the coast was clear, he brought four members of his family with him, big, strong hounds. All of the dogs wanted to tag along, and he had to shut the door in their faces to keep the entire family from getting out. Scratching at the door, they yelped, whined, and barked in protest.

"Ed will be back soon, okay?" he said. "Ed's going to check on something around the lake. Don't worry, Ed's coming back."

He had a flashlight, the binoculars, his cane, and his bowie knife from the war, too. He hoped he didn't need to use the knife.

But if it meant saving a dog from Them, he would.

It was raining hard. He zipped his fatigue jacket and flipped up the attached hood.

Moving slowly, he picked his way around the lake and into the forest, mud squelching under his boots. As if aware of the gravity of their mission, the canines kept pace with him, occasionally halting to shake the rainwater off their coats.

The woods were wet, dense with the mingled odors of pine sap, wild flowers, damp earth. He lifted the binoculars to his eyes. The lenses were specially coated to offer a clear field of view even in rainy conditions.

Through the trees, he observed that no lights were on in the home, and he didn't see anyone inside through the windows, either.

He grunted, lowered the binoculars. Maybe he'd been wrong about this. Maybe the men in the van really did work for a heating and cooling company, and maybe they had left for good, their work done.

Maybe there were no dogs inside that needed to be rescued. Maybe They had nothing to do with this house at all.

He didn't know. Sometimes—most times, it seemed—he found it hard to think through things clearly. A fog often lay across his mind, obscuring his ability to reason logically. In the past, he'd only get that way after knocking back one too many cans of Budweiser, but these days he seemed to be like that all the time—except for the temporary, brief periods of clarity, like he was probably experiencing right then.

You've lost your mind, Ed, a harsh voice said. *What the hell's the matter with you? It's only an empty house, and those guys in the van probably had every right to be there. There is no Them; there never was. There is only the world and the ordinary people in it, and you've lost touch with the whole damn thing, and that's why Maggie took your little girl and left.*

Fear rose in him. He could literally taste it at the back of his mouth—sour and acidic, like bile.

This was why clarity of thought didn't visit him often any more. It scared the shit out of him. It gave him a frightening glimpse of what he had become: a bedraggled recluse who lived in a cramped, filthy trailer full of more dogs than he could possibly manage, nursing absurd delusions and quietly rotting away.

He shook his head. *No, no, no!*

He swallowed thickly, and the bitter taste faded off his tongue. He spat into the weeds, dragged the back of his hand across his lips.

Then, he raised the binoculars again.

He had to find out what They had been doing in that house. They had been there all day, and it could be only for some nefarious purpose.

Redoubling his grip on the cane, he trudged forward.

34

When Jada awoke, it was so dark in the room that she temporarily forgot where she was. She jerked upright, trembling, her pajamas damp with perspiration.

Mom, Daddy, where are you? she screamed. *Mom, Daddy.*

Crying, she ran to the door. She beat her fists against it, hoping her parents would hear her, though she couldn't be sure of how much noise she was making.

It must not have been enough, because no one came to get her.

She'd been abandoned.

Her chest swelling painfully, cheeks wet with tears, she felt a huge sob building in her stomach, and she pulled in deep breaths and struggled to keep it down. Her parents would want her to stay strong. That was what Daddy would say. *Stay strong, Pumpkin. You can do it. You can do anything in the world.*

The only thing in the world she wanted to do was to get out of there and go home.

There was a light switch near the door. She flipped it up and down a few times, but nothing happened.

She wiped her eyes, sniffled. She would have to handle being alone in the dark. She was nine. She was old enough to deal with it.

She padded to the window. Through the gap, she saw rain falling from the dark sky. "God washing the world clean," as Grandma Rose liked to say.

She stuck her hand between the slats of wood and touched the glass. It was cool. She could feel the steady thump of the rain as it struck the window. She tapped the glass with her fingers and tried to imagine how the rain sounded.

As she peered through the planks into the murky world beyond the glass, her eyes widened.

Someone was outside.

35

Ed emerged from the woods and entered the yard, which
was all sucking red clay, no grass. The dogs trotted ahead,
paws leaving tracks in the thick mud.

On this side of the home, the driveway curved to the
garage. There were long, narrow windows set in the sectional doors. Steeling himself for a gruesome spectacle, Ed
approached the windows, wet boots squishing, and peered
inside.

It was too dark to see anything. He panned the flashlight
in there.

He found a bare cement floor, nothing on the walls. There
were no dogs, maimed, dead, or otherwise.

He sighed with disappointment. Where had They hidden
their evil handiwork?

One of his dogs, the same female black Lab/Great Dane
mix who'd wandered off yesterday, left his side and circled
to the back of the house, ears perked.

"What is it, girlie?" Ed asked in a whisper. "Smell something? Hear something?"

The dog disappeared around the corner. He followed her, the other three canines at his heels.

From his observation point at home, he hadn't been able to see the rear of the house. There was a long concrete slab that served as a patio, accessible through a set of glass doors, and several windows on the ground floor level.

But the black Lab was watching an upstairs window. She glanced at Ed, looked back up there, and whined, tail wagging nervously.

"What's wrong, girlie?" he asked. "What's up there?"

He raised the flashlight, and looked.

What appeared to be bars covered the window.

He frowned, certain that his eyes were fooling him. Squinting against the rain, he took a couple of steps closer to the house, keeping the flashlight aimed at the window.

Yes. They *were* bars of some kind. What in the hell—

Suddenly, a small hand materialized in the darkness.

He screamed.

Spinning around, slipping-sliding in the mud, a ragged cry roaring from his throat, he fled back into the woods as fast as his sixty-year-old legs would carry him.

36

The rain's persistent tapping and the lengthening shadows had lulled Simone to sleep, warm thoughts of going home floating through her mind. But Jada's sudden, muffled cries snatched her out of slumber and lifted her off the mattress.

"Mom! Daddy! Where are you?"

Simone felt as if her heart had been clawed out of her chest. Jada sounded so frightened, so alone. She had to do *something* to let her child know that she was near, that everything would soon be okay.

"I'm here, baby!" Simone shouted to the ceiling, hoping beyond reason that Jada would hear her. She screamed as loud as she could, throat raw: "Mommy's right here!"

"Mom! Daddy!"

"Right here!" Simone yelled. She spun blindly around the dark room, looking for some means to communicate with Jada.

She heard, faintly, a pounding noise, as if Jada were beating against a door.

Simone balled her cuffed hands into fists, raised them, and slammed them repeatedly against the wall as if striking a gong. She prayed Jada would feel the vibrations through the walls and floor, and would be comforted that she wasn't alone, that her mother was close by.

But Jada fell silent.

Simone pounded the wall a few more times, the percussion reverberating through the house, pain barking through her hands and arms with each strike. But she feared the clattering rain was deadening the vibrations.

"Baby?" She struck the wall. "Mommy's here!"

Silence.

"Honey!" She hit the wall again. "Mommy's down here!"

Only the pattering rain answered her.

Breathing hard, hands tingling, Simone turned away from the wall. She charged the door, and, shouting, kicked it with as much power as she could muster. The door twanged in the frame, but the impact threw her off balance. She slammed to the hardwood on her shoulder, fresh pain sizzling through her muscles.

Meanwhile, Jada hadn't called out again.

Simone pulled in a hitching breath. *I can't take this any more, damn it. I can't take it, I can't wait. I have to get out of here!*

She rose on limp legs. Lifting her sore arms, she wrapped the chain that linked the handcuffs around the doorknob. She jerked, once, and the knob rattled slightly.

Emboldened, she braced her left foot against the door and pulled so savagely it felt as if her arms would tear from their sockets.

Come on, come on, come on!

The chain slipped free of the knob, and she tumbled backward and fell hard on her tailbone, an accordion of pain spreading across her lower back.

The doorknob was still in place, as impregnable as ever.

She sniffled, wiped tears out of her eyes. All of the assorted wounds and aches she had suffered that day suddenly intensified, as if a button had been pushed in her brain: her jaw from the slaps to the face; her abdomen from the punch; the back of her head from the vase smashed against it; the spot on her forearm from the burning cigarette butt; her wrists from the tightly cinched cuffs; her fists from banging the wall; her shoulders and tailbone from falling. Every tender point of pain throbbed in agonizing sync with the others, and she decided to sit there for a while, immobile, for she worried that if she moved again, she would black out.

A strange, guttural scream came from outside, somewhere near the back of the house. It sounded like some sort of wild animal, perhaps a bear.

A chill dripped down her spine. *What the hell was that?*

She hesitated. Then she got up, the movement making her head spin.

Woozy, she lurched into the bathroom. She peered through the slats on the window near the vanity, but she did not see anything of interest, no animal or person. There was only the wall of forest, the trees quivering in the downpour.

But something—or someone—had been out there.

She cocked her head to the glass and listened, but heard only the rain.

She questioned whether she had heard anything at all. What if she was beginning to hallucinate? From her studies, she knew the effects that extreme stress and isolation could produce. Even the most tightly wrapped individual, when subjected to enough pressure, could crack like an egg.

No. She shook her head firmly. She had spent perhaps seven or eight hours in this room, and though they had been the most harrowing hours of her life, she had not reached her breaking point. Not yet. She could handle much worse than this.

Soon, she got an opportunity to test her resilience. Leon came back, and he looked mad enough to kill her.

37

Speeding away from the shopping mall on Buckhead's mazelike residential roads, straining to see through sheets of rain, Corey was vigilant for government-issue sedans and marked police cruisers. He'd seen none yet, but the possibility of one lurking just around the corner kept him on edge.

He was still stunned at how the drop-off had turned into a complete fiasco.

By then, the agents would've found the briefcase he had left in the bookstore. They would've counted the cash. They would be cooking up a compelling theory—in their minds—as to exactly why he had left fifty thousand dollars hidden in a public place, when as recently as yesterday he had been spotted having a beer with a fugitive who had asked him for money.

Thinking about it curdled his stomach.

He couldn't figure out what had prompted Falco and her partner to follow him. Had they been tailing him since that morning? Or had they flagged his bank accounts, been tipped off by the large withdrawal earlier that day, and then decided to track him?

It had to be one or the other.

He'd sensed after their conversation that Falco had found his story dubious. In her eyes, he had just confirmed her doubts in the worst way.

In her eyes, he was aiding and abetting a known felon.

Windshield wipers ticking, he braked at a STOP sign. He checked both ways for suspicious vehicles, found none, and arbitrarily made a right, which carried him deeper into a labyrinth of tree-lined streets, the oaks and pines as blurry as watercolor images in the storm.

Worse than his situation with the Feds was his predicament with Leon. Now Leon would think he had betrayed him. What would he do to Simone and Jada in retaliation?

If I see a cop on my tail, if I even suspect that you've involved them in this private business matter of ours, I'm going to kill your family, and I'm going to make it exquisitely painful, worse than anything you can imagine. . . .

Tension twitched like a live wire across his shoulder blades, down his arms, and into his hands. He wanted to scream.

Peering through the rain-smeared windshield, he recognized that he was in a familiar area: a neighborhood that featured some of Buckhead's swankiest residences, behemoth houses that stood on rambling parcels of land behind wrought-iron gates and tall fences. In the early days of their marriage, when they were living hand-to-mouth in a one-bedroom apartment in Marietta, he and Simone had used to cruise this neighborhood on sunny Sunday afternoons and imagine someday building a dream home of their own.

That day had since come for them. He wondered if, after what had happened in the past twenty-four hours, it had also passed.

It was only a quarter to five, but the purple-black storm clouds had awakened the street lamps. He pulled into a cul-

de-sac near the gated drive of French-château style estate
and parked at the edge of a pool of light.

He would have called Leon and pleaded his case, but
whenever Leon had called him on the prepaid cell, his number was blocked. He would have to sit tight and pray that
Leon didn't go nuts—always a strong possibility, since the
guy already teetered on the edge.

He cracked a knuckle. He just couldn't think about it.

In the meantime, he took out his BlackBerry and called
Todd's cell.

The phone rang three times before Todd picked up. "I'm
afraid this is a bad time, sir."

Todd's voice was stiff, tense. What was going on?

"Listen, man, we've gotta talk," Corey said. "The drop-
off was a disaster, the Feds tracked me there, and I ran away
from them before Leon got the money—"

"Yes, sir, I'll e-mail you later this evening with the revised terms of the agreement. I apologize for the inconvenience. We sure appreciate your business, sir. Bye now."

Todd hung up. Corey lowered the phone, bewildered.

The answer hit him: the FBI was checking out Todd, too.

And why wouldn't they have? They might have watched
Corey drive from the bank earlier that day to meet Todd at his
condo. Besides, as Corey's business partner and friend, Todd
would have been on their short list for questioning, anyway.

He hoped Todd didn't tell them what was really happening. Based on Todd's loathing of cops and his own shady activities, he'd assume that Todd would keep his mouth shut.

Later, perhaps when the heat cooled a bit, they could
touch base again.

As Corey deliberated his next step, yellow light strafed
over him. Pulse kicking up, he whipped around in his seat
and saw an unmarked white sedan cruising in his direction, a
beacon spinning on the roof.

Not a police officer—a rent-a-cop. Residents of a neighborhood as pricey as this one would have retained a private security force.

The sedan crawled past him and moved on down the block, but Corey interpreted the security vehicle's appearance as a forewarning. He shifted into Drive and peeled away from the curb.

The next step was obvious. He had to find new transportation.

38

A few minutes past six o'clock, Corey parked around the corner from Otis Trice's house, sliding the sedan under the dripping boughs of a hickory tree.

Otis lived in East Point, a southwest Atlanta suburb, in a quiet neighborhood of ranches and split-levels with large, well-tended lawns, huge leafy trees, and gentle hills. It had taken nearly an hour to drive there from Buckhead in the evening's rainy, rush-hour traffic, but he had been determined to endure the hellish trip.

The truth was, he had nowhere else to go.

He couldn't go home. The FBI might be watching his house. Likewise, Todd was out. Ditto his mother-in-law—he could not even *begin* to imagine telling her what was going on.

With the princely sum of twenty bucks in his wallet, a hotel of any kind was impossible, and with the FBI presumably monitoring his financial accounts, he couldn't use any of his debit or credit cards for risk of giving up his location.

How the hell had Leon managed to elude the Feds for three years? He had been on the run for less than three hours and felt his wires unraveling. The only thing keeping him glued was the hope of holding Simone and Jada in his arms again.

He checked the prepaid cell for at least the tenth time. It was still on, the battery at three-quarters strength. But Leon hadn't called, and the prolonged silence worried him.

Before getting out of the car, he scanned the rearview mirror and the street ahead. Although he hadn't noticed a tail during the drive, he didn't want to lead the cops straight to his friend's front door, either.

He got out and dashed around the corner, rain leaking under his collar, one hand pressed against the gun riding his hip.

Otis lived in an immaculately maintained brick ranch with an attached garage. The square lawn was as neatly trimmed as the greens on a golf course, bordered by a bed of white hydrangeas that bobbed in the rain. A silver Cadillac was parked in the driveway, and warm golden light glowed at the front windows.

Corey rang the doorbell. He hadn't called ahead, not trusting himself to explain his situation on the phone.

Otis answered the door. He wore pastoral clothing: a long-sleeve black shirt with a white clerical collar, black wool slacks, oxfords with a mirror-shine. A silver crucifix pendant hung from his necklace.

Corey remembered that it was Wednesday night. Otis would be preparing to lead Bible study at his church.

"Brother Webb," Otis said, as gracious as ever, as if he had been expecting Corey's visit. "Come inside, please. It's so good to see you this evening, indeed it is."

Corey tapped off his wet shoes on the doormat and shook Otis's hand. "I'm sorry for dropping in without calling ahead. If this is a bad time—"

"Nonsense," Otis said, ushering Corey inside. "My door

is always open to you, son. It always has been and always will be."

Corey followed Otis into the living room. As always, the interior of the house was as orderly as the outside, everything in its precise place, a habit held over from Otis's years in the army. The aromas of spaghetti sauce and garlic bread spiced the air. Corey hadn't eaten all day and felt a pang of hunger, but he was so keyed up he doubted he could keep anything in his stomach.

"Please have a seat," Otis said. "Would you like supper? I prepared my world-famous spaghetti and meatballs."

"No, thanks. Smells good, though."

Otis pushed up his wire-rim glasses on his nose and scrutinized him. "How about a drink then? You look as if you could use a strong one."

You don't know the half of it, man.

"A drink would be great." Corey moved to the sofa, looked around. "By the way, is Anita here?"

Otis paused at the kitchen doorway. "Mrs. Trice is at the church this evening, facilitating a women's auxiliary meeting."

Nodding, Corey sat on the couch. Otis's wife was a good woman, trustworthy to a fault, but Corey had been hoping to talk to Otis in private.

Otis returned from the kitchen and handed him a tumbler full of ice cubes and a quarter-inch of an amber beverage. Corey sniffed it; the strong odor opened his nostrils.

"Whiskey?" Corey asked.

"Crown Royal," Otis said with a sheepish smile. "I thought it might help you relax."

"Thanks." Corey took a small sip. The liquor slid down his throat like simmering lava, warmed his heart, and spread outward through his bloodstream, burning much of the tension out of his muscles.

Otis eased into a nearby armchair. His Buddha-calm gaze rested on Corey, brown eyes glimmering behind his lenses.

"So, Brother Webb, how may I be of service?"

"Don't you have to be at Bible study tonight?" Corey asked. "I'm not sure there's time for me to get into this with you."

"My assistant pastors are immensely capable of filling in for me." Otis smiled. "You and I can hold a church service of our own here in this living room, if need be."

Corey smiled sourly. "For certain legal reasons, I don't think it would be a good idea for me to go into details. I'm sorry, but the less you know, the better."

A frown creased Otis's features.

"But I haven't done anything wrong," Corey said quickly. "Well . . . put it this way, the questionable things I've done the past couple of days, I've had a good reason for them. It's complicated."

Otis stroked his beard. "What do you need, son?"

Corey placed the whiskey on a coaster on an end table and stared at the rug under his feet. His head felt as if a ten-pound stone lay across the back of his neck.

Finally, he looked up and met Otis's patient gaze.

"I really hate to ask you this, but I need to borrow your car," Corey said. "And money, too . . . whatever you can spare."

39

When Leon tore into the bedroom, Simone immediately knew she was in trouble.

As she pushed away from the wall, where she had been pulling vainly at the boards on the window, he came at her like a cyclone. Shadow swirled around him, but could not hide his drastically altered appearance. He was clean-shaven, the beard shorn away. Bald-headed, no more dread-locks. Instead of the tattered denim overalls and T-shirt, he wore what looked like a police officer or security guard's uniform, right down to the walkie-talkie and gun nested in a utility belt.

She had no idea why he was wearing this costume—but those predatory eyes of his were the same. They flashed with fury.

"Come here, fuckin' wifey bitch," he said in a jagged voice.

Terror spiking her heart, she lunged for the mattress to dig the pipe from underneath, but he moved spider-quick and seized her arm in an iron grip. He flung her across the room. She crashed against the wall, her sore shoulder absorbing the crushing impact, and the pain dropped her to her knees.

Dizziness and confusion spun through her. What had happened between him and Corey? Why weren't they being set free?

Leon charged her again. She tried to scramble away, but he grabbed her around the waist, smoky breath hot against her neck. He tugged at her sweatpants, and the realization of what he was going to do shot through her like a burst of chilled air.

Rape, oh, God, he's going to rape me.

As he snatched her pants down, the fabric got knotted around her thighs. She swung back and forth wildly, got free, and pitched forward, her hands driving into her belly as she slammed against the floor, plunging a sword of pain so deep into her tender abdomen that she couldn't get enough breath to scream.

Grunting, Leon climbed her body like a ladder. One of his hands grabbed a fistful of her hair and mashed her face against the floor. His other hand yanked down her underwear.

"Fuckin betray me, home boy, I'm gonna get me a piece of wifey, see how you like that."

She had no idea what he was talking about, couldn't process his furious ranting. She heard his zipper unfurling. His fingernails dug into her buttocks like meat hooks.

In a far off, detached segment of her mind, she saw how it would unfold. He would fuck here right there on the dirty floor of an empty house, slobbering and cursing, hammering into her with punishing force, and she would never be the same afterward. She had treated many, many rape victims, had seen them struggle to regain a sense of dignity and, most of all, battle to overcome the fear. Some of them healed, but some of them did not, were scarred forever, prisoners of their past, and she could not know into which group she would fall—no one could, until it happened to them. . . .

No.

Blood boiling in her head, she gritted her teeth and put everything she had into rolling over. He was so strong, with the strength of the possessed, that it was like getting from underneath a crushing weight.

She squirmed. Shrieked. Wriggled.

Leon grunted, hand palming her hip, his hardness pressing insistently against her thigh.

No!

Finally, she tore free. She jerked her knee upward and felt a satisfying impact with his testicles. He let out a bleat of pain.

She log-rolled away, winding up on her back. Dizziness swayed through her as she sat up. Her panties and sweatpants were tangled around her legs. Frantic, she tugged them up, shimmying her legs and hips, while beside her, Leon was bent over, wracked with dry heaves.

That's what you get, asshole, a savage voice whispered in her mind.

As she got her panties and pants around her again, he reached for her. She clenched her hands into fists and swung them in a wide arc.

He ducked, dodging the blow. Her hands whacked against the floor, the attempt leaving her upper body twisted, and he quickly took advantage and dragged her toward him by her foot.

As she tried to pull away, he clamped his teeth over her ankle and bit her.

She screamed. Out of reflex, she drew back her other leg and kicked at his head. Her heel smashed into his chin, his head snapping back as if by whiplash. He let her go.

Using her elbows and knees, she crawled toward the mattress. She heard a tortured sound, realized it came from her. She was screaming, cursing.

Behind her, Leon was babbling incoherently, too.

She dug under the mattress, and for a terrifying instant, couldn't find the pipe, became certain that Leon somehow had taken it away, but then her fingers closed around it, the metal cool and heavy.

She whirled around just as Leon was lunging at her. She swung the pipe at him like a baseball bat. It whacked against his temple with a hollow, ringing sound. He tumbled backward, an almost erotic sigh escaping his lips.

She gathered her legs under her and pushed to her feet, ignoring the pulsing agony in her ankle.

"I'll beat your ass like your mama used to beat you!" she screamed. "Get the fuck away from me!"

He lay sprawled on his back, chest rising and falling slowly. Was he unconscious? She looked to the door, remembering that it locked from the outside. If she could get to it . . .

But then Leon groaned, sat up. He gingerly touched his head.

Bosom heaving, she hefted the pipe over her shoulder, ready to swing again. Keeping his eyes averted from her, he unsnapped the pistol from the holster and withdrew it.

"You're not going anywhere," he said in a paper-thin voice, as if he'd read her mind.

Grinding her teeth, she stared at the gun, wishing she had something more substantial than a pipe with which to defend herself. Leon weighed the pistol in his hand as if considering what to do with it, and she had the crazy notion—maybe it was wishful thinking—that he was going to put the muzzle to his head and pull the trigger.

She licked her chapped lips. "I don't . . . I don't want to fight you, Leon. I just want my daughter back . . . I-I just want to go home."

He didn't look at her, but his finger crept toward the trigger.

"Drop it," he whispered.

She hesitated for a moment, and tossed the pipe onto the floor.

He picked it up and tucked away the pistol. Without another word, and without glancing at her, he got up and walked to the door. His shoulders were slumped, his normally quick gait a slow shuffle, and she had the sudden impression that if he somehow lived to be an old man, he would look just like that, defeated by a long life of crime.

He closed the door and locked her inside.

She turned away—and her stomach suddenly convulsed. She doubled over and threw up onto the floor.

When she was done, she wiped her lips with the edge of her T-shirt and pulled the mattress across the mess. She carefully stretched out on top of it, her body mapped with a hundred assorted aches and pains.

Staring at the shadowed ceiling, she knew she had won a small victory. But the war was far from over.

40

In the quiet living room, Otis held Corey in his bespectacled gaze.

"You request money, and the use of my vehicle," Otis said. It wasn't a question.

"I know how crazy it sounds," Corey said. "But you're the only one I can turn to."

"Is there anything else you require?" Otis asked, as if Corey had not already requested enough.

Corey shook his head.

Otis fingered his beard. "You undoubtedly realize, Brother Webb, that I have *considerable* concern regarding the, ah . . . circumstances surrounding this unusual visit."

"Of course, sure," Corey said. "And I promise I'll explain everything, after it's over. You have my word, Reverend."

With a thoughtful grunt, Otis got up from his armchair, went down the hallway to his bedroom, and came back and gave Corey two hundred dollars cash and the key to his Chevy Silverado.

"Thank you," Corey said. "Thank you so much."

"Where is your car?" Otis asked.

"It's parked around the corner."

"I suggest that you garage it here as well."

"I don't know if that's such a good idea," Corey said. "The cops'll be looking for it."

Sitting across from him again, Otis folded his hands across his stomach. "I don't know anything about that, sir. All I know is that Mr. Corey Webb, who is like a son to me, visited me this evening distraught about a predicament that he declined to describe in detail. I've known Mr. Webb for sixteen years and trust him to be an honorable man, therefore, as you would expect, when he requested a favor, I offered him a small amount of money and the use of my vehicle. I also asked him to garage his own vehicle on my property, as I had the space available. I do not know where Mr. Webb went after he departed my residence, and I did not inquire. But as I stated, Mr. Webb is a man of esteemed character who has earned a sterling reputation in his community, and I can therefore only assume that whatever the nature of his situation, he is assiduously engaged in activity that will lift the light of suspicion off his hard-earned good name."

Corey smiled. "Wow. I couldn't have made up anything better than that myself. That sounds perfect."

"The truth tends to have that quality," Otis said.

Corey left the house to return to his car. As he dashed through the rain, he heard a siren warbling in the distance, and a cold finger of fear slid down his spine. He reached the BMW and waited inside for a minute, foot poised on the gas pedal, ready to blast away from the curb if he saw flashing beacons.

The siren faded somewhere far away. He dragged his hand down his sweat-filmed face. If this continued much longer, he was going to wind up a basket case.

He veered around the corner as Otis was backing his

truck out of the garage and onto the street in front of his house. Corey nosed the sedan into the vacated parking spot.

They met at the garage door and shook hands.

"Thank you so much, for everything," Corey said. "You don't realize how much you've helped me. I promise to pay you back as soon as I can."

"Do not concern yourself about that, son," Otis said.

"To put your mind at ease, I'm innocent—for this thing anyway. You'll see."

Otis's eyes glinted. "None of us is innocent, Brother Webb. We've all of us sinned every day, every one of us. But do we seek forgiveness for our sins? That is the question I submit to you."

His incisive gaze cut to the depths of Corey's soul, and Corey had the unsettling feeling that Otis knew everything he had done—every terrible, secretive deed. Corey turned away and gazed into the rain-swept evening.

"Listen," Corey said, still not meeting his eyes, "when I first moved in with you, I never told you about what happened in Detroit. You knew I was in trouble, of course, but you didn't know how deep. I—"

"I simply offered you a fresh start," Otis interrupted. "The same as was once given to me when I encountered 'deep trouble' in the jungles of Cambodia. You don't owe me an accounting of your past misadventures."

Corey glanced at him. "But I have to tell this to someone. I've been carrying this around for years."

"Confess it after you've come to terms with my question. Do we seek forgiveness?"

"You know I've never been religious, Reverend."

"Forgiveness may not always begin with us petitioning God for His mercy. It may begin with us. Right here." He tapped his heart with a thick finger. "Sometimes, we must orgive ourselves for our sinful acts before we are capable of accepting absolution from others."

"I do believe church is now in session."

"You know I can never resist a little preaching." Otis clasped his hand again and gripped his shoulder. "Be blessed, Brother Webb. I'll be praying for you."

41

Sitting on the mattress with a wad of tissue she dampened with a dribble of the water from the bottle, Simone did her best to clean the bite wound on her ankle. Leon's teeth had punctured the skin and drawn blood. She could only hope that it didn't get infected.

What the hell had come over him? What did he mean about Corey betraying him? What had happened at the mall?

Most of all, she wanted to know when they would be released. Or would they now?

Ink-black shadows had pooled in the bedroom. It was still drizzling outside, the clouds dark and thick. She guessed that it was midevening by then.

Her need to see Jada had become an ache in her breast. If she had only knocked Leon out . . .

She flung the tissue aside. What good did it do to worry about it? She had surrendered the pipe, her weapon of last resort. Now, she had nothing.

Head bowed between her knees, she dug her fingers into her hair, as if she could massage her brain cells. She ran the

ituation through her mind over and over, but came up with
nothing, no way out. So long as she was handcuffed, and
Leon had a gun, and his partner guarded Jada, she was at his
mercy.

Her sense of powerlessness nearly surpassed her fear.
She'd been raised to be an independent woman, fully capable
of fending for herself in a hard world. Even though she'd been
married for a decade, she retained a degree of self-sufficiency,
and never let herself lean too heavily on Corey for things
that she could do on her own. At least, that was how she had
long viewed herself. But maybe she had come to rely on her
husband more than she had realized.

Maybe her mistake was that, deep down, she'd trusted
Corey to somehow pull them out of this, that she'd given up
her own power in hopes of a rescue.

She snapped up as footsteps neared the doorway. By the
time Leon came inside, she had gotten on her feet, jaws and
hands clenched.

"Stay away from me," she said.

Leon said nothing. He carried what appeared to be some
sort of small, camping lamp. Eyes downcast, avoiding her
glare, he placed the lamp near the mattress and sat on the
floor beside it.

He switched it on. Soft golden light filled the room, pushing back the shadows.

She studied him carefully. A nasty purple bruise marked
his temple; she could not resist feeling a spark of pride.
Silent, gazing blankly at the wall, legs drawn up to his chest,
shoulders rising and falling slowly, Leon appeared to be a
defeated man.

She'd recognized in him the classic signs of hyperactivity,
a symptom of bipolar disorder. He had been manic since
yesterday, at least. Perhaps he had plunged into a depressive
state.

But she was hesitant to draw that assessment. She'd also spotted in him the qualities of a psychopath, and psychopath were nothing if not skilled at manipulating perception.

She slowly sat on the mattress, keeping several feet between them. He was quiet, looking into the shadows beyond the lamplight. Then he finally spoke.

"My mama . . . she used to beat me," he said, in an uncharacteristically soft, measured tone. "She said I looked and acted just like my daddy, and she hated the ground that man walked on and the air he breathed."

Simone paused, mulling over her response. His subdued demeanor reminded her of clients who came in to her office seeking help, but she was reluctant to assume the role of therapist with a man who had kidnapped her and her daughter—and who had attempted to rape her barely a half hour ago. Psychotherapy worked by the therapist establishing a dialogue that helped the client develop expanded awareness of irrational and harmful patterns of feeling, perception, and behavior, and for that breakthrough to occur, the therapist herself needed to have an open mind and spirit, but she had no interest whatsoever in helping Leon become more aware of anything. If she had the weapon and opportunity, in fact, she very well might have killed him.

But this could be a chance to establish a rapport with him that she could turn to her advantage. His mother, she believed, was his Achilles' heel.

She said, "Your mother beat you because she said you were like your daddy? That doesn't sound fair at all to me."

Grunting, he twisted around and hiked up the back of his shirt, exposing his lean, muscled back. There were faint, dark dime-sized marks scattered across his flesh, from the small of his back all the way up to and across his shoulder blades.

He glanced at her over his shoulder. "She did these with her cigarettes when I was a too small to fight back. Pinned me to the bed and branded me with her Newports."

"That's terrible, Leon."

"Mean, crazy bitch." Sneering, he flipped his shirt down. Like it was my fault that I reminded her of my old man."

"What was your father like?"

He shifted to face her. He tapped a cigarette out of a pack, lit it. He offered one to her, and she declined.

He blew out a wisp of smoke, gazed at the ceiling. "Daddy was a small-time hustler, he sold whatever was hot—jewelry, TVs, phones, whatever—bounced around from the joint to our crib or some other woman's crib, whoever he was messing around on her with at the time. Didn't help her with me or my little sister. He was a real positive role model. You know I'm named after him?"

"Is that so? I didn't know that."

"Yeah, they left that out of my profile. Sort of pisses me off, but I don't know why it does, 'cause my old man's been dead for ten years, and when he was alive I hardly ever talked to him anyway."

"What profile are you referring to, Leon?"

"Damn, C-Note's really kept you in the woods, hasn't he?" He squinted at her through the haze of smoke. "I'm on the FBI's Ten Most Wanted Fugitives list. Got featured on the TV show, post offices, the whole nine. You're looking at a celebrity, baby girl."

Her heartbeat skipped. She wondered if he was lying, but the pride in his voice led her to believe that he was probably telling the truth.

Jesus. Had Corey known this earlier and not said anything to her? Why would he have kept it secret?

"You've overheard some of my chats with your hubby," Leon said. "You've gotta know by now that he's got some skeletons buried twenty thousand leagues deep. You aren't that stupid."

She had come to that conclusion, but she didn't see the point of discussing it with Leon. Later, when the time was right, she would have a very frank conversation with Corey about his past with this man.

"You said your father is deceased," she said. "How about your mother?"

"She's dead," he said flatly. "She OD'd twenty-some years ago, she was a heroin addict, used some bad shit that got her sent to Sheol for good. There won't be any kissing and making up in this lifetime."

"Growing up with an abusive parent can be difficult on a child," she said. "So often, the child questions what he did to deserve such treatment. He worries that it's his fault."

"What if it is?" He stared at her. "Maybe he isn't worth shit, like she told him every day. Maybe he was born bad."

"Children aren't born bad, Leon."

"No?" He smiled. "I was six when I stole something for the first time. There was this mom-and-pop store on the corner where my mama would always send me to get her smokes. This one day, I got it in my head that I was going to steal a pack of Twinkies. You remember Twinkies?"

"I remember them. I used to love them until I found out how quickly they can add on the pounds."

He gave her a small smile. "So I put like three packs of them under my shirt, right? I go up to the register to get my mama's cigarettes, and they fall out of my shirt, right in front of the Pakistani guy who owned the place. He tossed me out of there on my ear and told my old man what I did—this was one of those times when my dad was living with us."

"How did your dad respond?"

"Daddy wore my ass out with a clothes hanger. Told me 'The next time you try to steal something, Junior, your black ass better not get caught!'"

Leon laughed so hard that tears squirted from his eyes. Simone offered a thin smile.

"That's quite a story," she said.

"I've got a million of them." He took a scrap of paper out

his pocket, folded it into a tiny bowl, and tapped ashes
to it. "You're a good listener. I dig that."

"It's easy to listen to someone who has so many interest-
ng things to say."

The moment the words left her mouth, she feared might
ave gone over the line and come across as insincere, but he
inked at her.

"Flattery will get you everywhere with an important man
ke me. I've got a lot of charm, a ton of smarts, to have been
orn bad, don't you think?"

"For the record, I don't believe you were born bad," she
aid. "I believe your environment played a major factor in
e choices you've made. If a child is constantly told that
's a bad seed, and punished for it, it's often inevitable that
'll grow to make decisions that reflect those low expecta-
ons. Children are like blank tablets—we can write anything
n them that we wish."

Leon was nodding. "Like blank tablets, huh? So I had the
isfortune to have some fucked up shit written on me,
en?"

"But those words that were written so long ago can some-
mes be revised, if you will."

"Revised? We're sort of like works in progress, I take it.
ike the novel I've been working on for the past ten years."

"All of us are like that, yes," she said, convinced that she
ad actually gotten through to him on a meaningful level.
None of us are irredeemable, with the possible exception of
ose suffering from severe mental illness, and even they can
e assisted to some degree with proper therapy and perhaps
edication."

"Like my partner, Billy." He tapped ash into the paper
ay and snickered. "Let me tell you, that dude needs *serious*
erapy and meds."

At the thought of his pervert accomplice in the bedroom
ith Jada, Simone's jaw tightened.

Leon blinked at her distress. "Oh, hey, sorry about that. Your little munchkin's fine. I'm serious, Billy won't touch her, he won't dare cross me."

"I thought Corey was going to pay you the money and we'd go free. Why are we still here?"

Anger twitched across his face, and she regretted that she'd asked the question.

"Why don't we ask Corey?" Leon said. He checked his watch, and flipped out his cell phone. "It's about time I tell him the rules have changed."

42

With a new vehicle and a wallet of cash, Corey was back
on the road.

His first priority was to eat. He'd eaten nothing all day,
and though Otis had offered him dinner, he'd thought himself too nervous to hold anything down; besides, he didn't
want to loiter too long at Otis's place and risk bringing the
cops to his door.

But he had to eat something, unsettled stomach or not. If
he didn't get food in him soon, he was going to spin off the
wave of adrenaline that had been keeping him going since
that morning, and he'd be useless when the next develop-
ment—and something was going to happen soon, of that he
had no doubt—came down the pike.

He found a Chick-fil-A restaurant on Camp Creek Park-
way, not far from Otis's place. Staring at the drive-through
menu, he thought wistfully about what Simone and Jada had
liked to order on those rare occasions when they dined there.
Emotion clogged his throat.

It's not as if they're dead, he reminded himself.

He bought two chicken sandwiches, a large order of waf-

fle fries, and the biggest Coke they had. He didn't kno
when he might have the willingness or chance to eat again

He parked in the corner of the lot farthest from the buil
ing, front end angled toward the nearby exit, in case a co
got too curious and he had to peel out of there. Although th
FBI might not have forwarded his description to every p
lice department in metro Atlanta, he saw no reason to tal
risks. At a time like this, a healthy dose of paranoia was ne
essary.

The interior of Otis's truck was as scrupulously clean
his house. Corey opened the bag of food and began to ea
taking extra care not to spill anything on the seats or floor.

The cell phone rang, and at the almost same time, h
BlackBerry hummed. Startled, he dropped a handful of fri
onto the floor. He swore softly and went for the cell phone

"Yeah?" he said.

"You've got quite a lady here," Leon said. He spol
slower, softer, and Corey figured that he was in a tempora
down phase. Back when they would hang together, Leor
hyperactivity often would be followed by prolonged perio
·when he would do little more than sleep and lounge arou
aimlessly, as if he were a kid crashing from a sugar rus
"We've been having ourselves a nice little chitchat."

That meant Simone was safe. Thank God.

"How's my daughter?" Corey asked.

"The munchkin's all good. She's in dreamland."

Corey exhaled, dared to relax. "Listen, Leon about wh
happened at the mall—I had no idea the FBI would be the
I never called them."

"You never spoke to them?"

Corey spoke in a rush. "They came by my house th
morning. I had to talk to them—someone ID'd you at the b
last night, when you threw the beer against the wall. Th
had my name from the credit card receipt. But I promi

you, I didn't tell them that you had my family, and I didn't tell them about the drop-off. I lied and said I didn't know where you were, but I guess they didn't believe me, because obviously they tailed me to the mall."

"Well, that's neither here nor there, is it?" Leon's voice was hushed, almost a whisper. "Still can't believe you haven't told the wifey here anything about our illustrious history. Don't think she appreciates being kept in the dark."

Corey's grip on the phone tightened. "I had my reasons."

"Why don't you give her those reasons?"

Corey heard a fumbling of the phone, and then Simone came on the line.

"Hey, baby," she said wearily.

"God, it's so good to hear your voice," he said. "How're you doing?"

"Remember when Jada was stung by a bee?"

He frowned, wondering where this was going. "Yeah, I remember. That was last fall, wasn't it?"

"That's how I am right now. That's how Jada is, too."

There was something about Simone's voice . . . something artificial that made him suspect there was a different meaning she was hinting toward. He had spoken to Simone every day for over ten years, and whenever he asked her how she was doing, she answered directly, with *I'm great* or *I'm doing okay,* or *not so hot.*

Remember when Jada was stung by a bee? That's how I am right now. That's how Jada is, too.

What was she trying to say?

He wanted to ask her to clarify, but if she was being cryptic, it was because she was worried about tipping off Leon. He would have to puzzle over her words on his own.

"Got it," he said. "Have you seen Jada?"

"No," she said, with a disappointed sigh. "But he tells me she's okay."

"I'm going to bring you and Pumpkin home. I just need you to hang on a little longer. We're going to get through this."

"I'm trying, baby, I'm really trying."

He had never heard her so exhausted and discouraged. She was hanging on, but by the thinnest of threads.

"I can't begin to explain how sorry I am for not telling you everything," he said. "I . . . I . . ."

He couldn't go on. His tongue felt stuck to the roof of his mouth.

"Explain later," she said. "Just bring us home."

"I will. I mean it."

Leon came back on the line. "Which gives us a perfect segue to the main purpose of this conversation. The rules of the road have officially changed."

Corey tensed. "What're you talking about?"

"You screwed up big-time at the mall. For my inconvenience and emotional distress, I've decided that I want more money."

"W-what?"

"I want a million dollars."

"You want a million dollars," Corey said, numb.

"That's a one, followed by six zeroes."

Corey pressed his hand to his sweaty forehead and stared out the rain-streaked windshield. Cars crawled through the drive-through line, people grabbing a fast dinner on a weeknight, single people on cell phones, mothers with kids bopping in the seats, families in SUVs.

He had never felt more isolated from the flow of ordinary life—and had never wanted it back so badly, high-calorie fast food with his wife and daughter and driving home to watch TV and carouse on the sofa, the whole thing. He'd never craved such simple things so desperately.

"Hello?" Leon was saying. "Earth to C-Note?"

"Yeah?"

"A million dollars," Leon said. "You've got until this Friday morning at ten."

"You want more money than you demanded before, and you're giving me less time to get it."

"Those are the new rules, amigo."

"Listen, you're crazy. I can't do it."

"I'll pass that on to your little munchkin. I'll tell her that daddy gave up on her and mommy before I shoot her in the head."

"*No*," Corey said.

"Then find a way to make it happen."

"I can't withdraw ten measly dollars from my account without the FBI knowing about it, Leon. Even if I had a million bucks—and I don't—I couldn't get it to you. They're on to me now."

"You'll work it out," Leon said with maddening calmness. "You don't have a choice any more."

Leon hung up. Corey slammed the phone onto the passenger seat.

A million dollars by Friday morning. It was totally impossible. Was Leon lying around picking outrageous sums of money out of the air? Where the hell was he getting this stuff from?

Sitting there, sweating and fuming, he remembered that his BlackBerry had vibrated. He checked it.

Todd had sent him a text message.

Can meet at 9pm 2 chat. 8126 Industrial Blvd, Covington.
Park in back. Watch out for feds.
See U there.

"You can bet your ass I'll be there," Corey said, and hoped that he and Todd, together, could find a way out of these suddenly darker woods.

43

Back in his trailer, Ed popped the tab on his third can of lukewarm beer and chugged half of it in a couple of gulps. He let out a loud burp as he slumped on the tattered La-Z-Boy, a spot from which he hadn't budged in over an hour.

Three beers in, a warm haze had settled over him, dulling the edge of his fear. He could not remember the last time he'd been so frightened. Probably, it had been during the war, when he'd seen many terrifying things, most of which, gratefully, had faded into the mists of memory.

The small hand at the window had sent him scrambling through the woods, around the lake, and into the security of his trailer, the dogs on his heels, yapping.

Ghost, he kept thinking, pulse pounding. *I saw a ghost.*

Or was it really a ghost? What if it had been something else?

Like a child, kept prisoner in the room by Them?

He wasn't sure.

Over a dozen canines swarmed around his recliner, wriggled between and beneath his legs, crawled into his lap, licked at the can in his hand, poked his face with their cold snouts. As he had lately, he scarcely noticed them, which made them vie even more enthusiastically for his affection.

Staring ahead into nothing, he rolled the questions over and over in his mind.

The problem with the ghost theory was that he had never seen a ghost before. He was sixty years old. If ghosts existed, and maybe they did, he figured he would have seen one before this.

Anyway, how had the dog sensed it? The black Lab had known before he had that something was at the window. Could dogs see ghosts, too?

That was why thinking it was a ghost troubled him. It stirred up more questions than it answered.

But a child, imprisoned by Them? That was an idea he could sink his teeth into.

The mysterious figures in the van could have kidnapped the child. They could be keeping the kid in the room. Why else would bars have been on the window?

He had been certain before that They had abducted dogs and were doing terrible things to them in the house. Why not a child? They were monsters, an evil race, and preyed on the innocent and helpless, which included canines and children alike.

He thought about his little girl with her long, silken hair, her smile like the sun. He could visualize her face, but he could not recall her name. He took a sip of beer, as if to lubricate his thoughts, but her name skipped around the edges of his mind, teasingly out of reach.

He groaned in frustration and flung the beer across the room. It clattered against the oak-paneled wall, foam spraying, and landed on the threadbare carpet. Several of the dogs immediately battled for possession of the can, snarling and barking.

Blinking groggily, he struggled off the chair and shuffled into his bedroom, the beers he'd drunk making him amble slower and more carefully than usual. The binoculars still hung around his neck. He fumbled them to his eyes and peered out the window.

The rain had subsided to a steady drizzle, the lake and woods layered in blackness. He saw the home in the darkness, though tall trees veiled the upper room at the rear of the house.

As he remembered what he had seen in there, fear quivered through him.

But he would have to face his fear. He would have to go back.

Because he was thinking that maybe the child at the window was his daughter.

44

The Silverado was equipped with the OnStar package, which included a GPS navigation feature. Corey entered the address Todd gave him and received turn-by-turn directions to the meeting point in Covington.

Located on the other side of the metro area, nearly an hour's drive, Covington was a booming eastern suburb in Newton County, off I-20. As he drove on the interstate, Corey was watchful for anyone following him, though he figured that if the Feds had him on their radar, by this point they would have closed in, without preamble, and taken him into custody. But staying on the alert had become habit that day.

After hours of slow drizzling, a thunderstorm was brewing. Thunder clapped across the low sky. Violent gusts whipped the trees, and jagged blue lightning forked the horizon.

His state of mind was as chaotic as the weather. He'd been mulling, sporadically, over Simone's weird remark during the last call: *Remember when Jada was stung by a bee? That's how I am right now. That's how Jada is, too.* He was no closer to understanding what the hell she was talking about—but with Leon's crazy ransom demand, the tighter deadline, and the upcoming meeting with Todd spinning through his thoughts, there was so much weighing on him that he simply lacked the mental capacity to decode Simone's words. Perhaps he and Todd would come up with something that would render everything else moot.

The navigation system directed him off the interstate through the creature comforts of suburbia—chain restaurants, subdivisions, strip malls—and into a desolate, industrial area of warehouses and tall, barbed-wire fences. Loblolly pines flanked the road, the pavement pitted with the occasional jarring pothole gouged open by rigs hauling massive loads back and forth from the highway.

As his watch ticked toward nine, his destination came up on the right, a rectangular sign standing outside a wide entrance, the letters in reflective white paint: GATES FOOD-SERVICE, INC., SERVING SINCE 1969.

Todd's family owned numerous businesses, and Corey recalled that the food distribution company was one of them. Since Todd hadn't worked for his father in years, Corey doubted the Feds would think to look for them there.

A chain-link fence fringed with barbed wire enclosed a complex that covered perhaps twenty acres. Slowing, he swung through the open gate. Two wide asphalt lanes curved to a long brick building, the windows dark. A fleet of half a dozen rigs were parked in a fenced area, and a large parking lot abutted the warehouse, empty except for a rusty Honda sitting on a flat tire.

Todd's text message had instructed him to park in the back. Corey took an access road around the perimeter of the building. Twelve loading docks lined the rear of the structure. One of the bay doors hung open, weak light sifting from inside.

Todd's black Mercedes-Benz convertible coupe was parked

at the open dock, glimmering like a beetle's carapace in the rain.

As Cory drew near, Todd got out of the Mercedes and motioned for Corey to park beside his car. Todd wore a black leather jacket and carried a briefcase that resembled the one Corey had left behind at the bookstore, which the FBI agents would have confiscated.

Corey made a mental note to buy Todd a new briefcase when all of this was over.

Outside the car, Todd greeted him with an enthusiastic handshake. "Is this not like a movie, or what? Meeting out here in the middle of nowhere 'cause we're under suspicion by the freakin' Feds? You"—he tapped the hood of the Silverado—"driving somebody else's ride probably 'cause the law is looking for your wheels? Wild, huh?"

"I'm glad you find this entertaining," Corey said. "Meanwhile, that bastard still has my family."

"I know, I know, the cash drop didn't pan out, sorry." Todd's eyes dimmed. "Sure you weren't tailed?"

Corey looked behind them. There was only the black sky charged with lightning, and the lashing rain. "Positive."

"Cool." Todd squinted at the sky, rain beading on his lip. "Let's head in to the office, then. I don't know about you, but it looks to me like it's gonna storm like a mother out here."

Nodding grimly, Corey followed Todd inside.

45

The warehouse was enormous, the lightbulb above the bay door revealing tall aisles of metal storage racks loaded with boxes and pallets, the rows dwindling into the darkness beyond. A bank of walk-in freezers and coolers stood off to Corey's right, green status indicators glowing in the dimness. The cool air smelled of cardboard and lemon-scented disinfectant.

The only sounds were the humming of refrigerators and air conditioners, and the dull roar of the storm.

"Are we alone here?" Corey asked.

"Just you and me," Todd said with a conspiratorial wink. The raindrops gave his dark hair a slick luster, and his tanned skin looked oiled. "The last shift leaves at eight, same way it has since the beginning of time. I haven't worked here since my college days, but I still have keys. Convenient, huh? I ought to host a Hold 'Em tournament or something here."

Todd pressed a button beside the doorway. The sectional loading dock door clattered down from the ceiling and thumped against the floor.

"We'll chat in the office," Todd said. "Follow me."

Walking with long, swift strides, Todd led Corey around a gleaming array of forklifts, stacks of wooden pallets, and a small crane. Their footsteps echoed off the concrete floor and faded in the deep, cavernlike shadows.

"You could garage a few 747s in here," Corey said.

Todd grunted, swept one hand around without slowing his gait. "The old man's got a million cubic feet of dry storage, five hundred thou of perishable storage, another five hundred thou for frozen goods. He distributes across Georgia, Alabama, Florida, and the Carolinas. It's a hugely profitable business—I'd be working here myself if I could stand being in a room with him for five minutes."

Corey remembered that Todd and his father had suffered a major falling-out soon after Todd had graduated college. Todd had struck out to make it on his own steam, to prove to his dad that he could build his own business empire. Corey seemed to recall, in an ironic twist, that a Gates-Webb alarm system secured the warehouse premises, which probably explained why Todd, in addition to having an old key, was able to get them inside after hours.

Todd led them around a corner. Ahead, there was an enclosed office space with plate glass windows. Todd opened the door and flicked on the lights.

The spacious office was furnished with a large metal desk and matching credenza, executive chair, and two armchairs. Industry award plaques adorned the walls, and Corey saw framed photographs of Todd's family on the credenza.

Todd set his briefcase on the floor and dropped into the chair behind the desk, propping his loafers on the desktop as if he owned the place. Corey settled into an armchair.

The overhead florescents sputtered, casting them in brief darkness, and then blazed back into life.

"Damn storm," Todd muttered with a glance at the ceiling. He blinked, looked at Corey, drew in a breath. "Anyway, so you probably figured out that the Feds were talking to me when you called earlier. Ass wipes. I told them I didn't know anything."

"Thanks," Corey said. "I didn't think you would."

"I don't think they believed me, but, whatever." He shrugged. "Between what you said on the phone and what the FBI dickhead told me, I know some of what went down at Lenox. Can you fill me in?"

"Basically, they tailed me into the mall," Corey said. "On Leon's orders, I left the briefcase in a bookstore, and the agents popped up as I was walking away. I guess they thought they'd find him hiding in the store. Of course, he wasn't in there, but wherever he was, he saw everything."

Todd was tapping a pencil against the desk blotter. "Does he think you snitched?"

"He sure does, and he's pissed. He's upped the ransom."

"He has? To what?"

"One million."

"One million? Are you kidding me?"

"And he wants it by Friday morning."

"This is nuts." Todd pulled his feet off the desktop and snapped upright in the chair. "I never saw this coming. Christ, I'm so sorry."

"I take full responsibility," Corey said. He lowered his gaze to his lap, clasped his hands together. "I took a gamble, the best idea I had at the time, and it didn't pan out. Now I've lost fifty grand and I've got the FBI thinking that I'm helping Leon."

Todd hissed. "Fuck, this really sucks."

Corey looked up at him. "Listen, I don't care about losing the money. At the end of the day, all I care about is getting my wife and daughter home safely. I don't have a million dollars, period. Leon's living in a dream world if he thinks I've got that much to give him."

"How much can you draw down?" Todd asked. "If you had, let's say, a week?"

Corey shook his head, massaged the back of his neck. "Man, I don't know. Minus the fifty grand I lost today? I'd guess somewhere in the range of a hundred and sixty-five thousand, if I liquidate all of our investments."

"Not even in the ballpark." Todd drummed the pencil against his chin. "At this point, since he's big-time pissed and feels some heat from the law, he's not going to settle for less. He's willing to go for broke now. We've got to give him what he wants."

"Todd," Corey said in a low tone, steel in his voice, "I just told you I don't have a million dollars."

"You sure about that?"

Corey frowned. "What?"

"Remember Gates-Webb Security, LLC? Do you know what our company is worth? I'll tell you—*three point eight million dollars*. As of last month. You know I love keeping tabs on the financials." Todd twirled the pencil in his fingers, eyes bright, like a student who'd solved a perplexing algebra problem.

"So?" Corey shrugged. "I figured the value was in that range, but I don't see your point. I can't tap into company bank accounts for this. That's highly unethical and probably illegal."

Todd tilted forward in the chair, elbows on the desk. He jabbed the pencil at Corey. "*That* is true. But *selling* your interest in the business is perfectly legal. You could sell your fifty percent share to me, and the company could cut you a check. You'd walk away with one point nine million—that's almost two million dollars, Corey. That's more than enough to send this jerk-off packing and get your family back, and you'd have plenty left over, even after Uncle Sam takes his cut."

A thick vein throbbed in the center of Todd's shiny forehead. He was smiling broadly, capped teeth gleaming, an almost lunatic grin that made him look like a used car salesman desperate to close a deal.

Corey felt a greasy coiling in his stomach. He looked at the briefcase standing beside the desk. The briefcase that Todd had conveniently brought with him.

The briefcase that, undoubtedly, contained legal documents that would facilitate the sale of Corey's share of the company to Todd.

His realization of the betrayal was so painful that he didn't want it to be true . . . but in his heart, he knew that it was.

"What's in the briefcase, Todd?" Corey asked softly.

Todd winked. "After the FBI clown left, I started thinking through all of the options we might be facing. On the remote chance that you'd have to come up with some insane amount of money to get rid of this Leon thug once and for all, I took the initiative to pull together a few documents." Rising, he grabbed the case, placed it atop the desk, and opened it. He withdrew a sheaf of papers held together by a butterfly clip and handed them to Corey. "If—*big if*—selling your interest in GWS is something you want to do, all the paperwork you need to sign is right there."

"That was considerate of you, Todd, to bring all of this for me," Corey said. His breath rattling in his lungs, he flipped through the pages, scanned the legalese-dense text. "Wasn't it last summer that you'd first asked me about selling my share of the company? Hadn't you said that you'd found some interested party willing to give us a few million?"

"I totally understand why you turned it down back then," Todd said. "You wanted to build a legacy for your family, I get that. But this time . . . you could use the proceeds from selling your share to actually *save* your family. How ironic, right?"

Corey glanced at the documents in his hand. "I'll need to have my attorney review this, of course."

"Oh, there's no need for that." Todd sat on the corner of the desk, crossed his long arms over his chest. "I wouldn't try to screw you."

"But business is business, right? We've gotta cross all of our t's and dot our i's."

"But you need to move fast on this." Todd stroked his upper lip, laughed nervously. "This thug, Leon . . . he's got your family. Can't waste time while some overpaid attorney drags ass through the paperwork. If you sign these papers tonight, we could process a check tomorrow, Friday at the latest, and I'm sure Leon might be willing to give a little on the deadline, if he knows you've got the funds on the way." Todd's gaze was electric, his Adam's apple bobbing as he spoke. "Think about Simone and Jada, Corey. Think about how you can finally bring them home safe. Tell me what kind of guy gives a shit about some company when the lives of his family are at stake, huh? You're a loving husband, a great father. Do the right thing, for them."

Corey pushed to his feet. His hands trembled as he dropped the papers on the desk. He was so angry he could scream, but in the calmest voice he could muster, he said, "Sorry, Todd, I'm not interested in selling out. I wasn't interested when you brought it up before, and I'm not interested now. If this is your idea of a plan, we've got nothing left to talk about. I'll see you around."

Heart thundering, Corey turned on his heel and walked to the door. As he put his hand on the doorknob, Todd grunted and said, "Park it back in the chair, partner. We're not finished here, yet."

Todd had a gun, and he was aiming it at Corey.

46

Corey slowly raised his hands, gaze riveted on the gun.

"It's a Walther PPK," Todd said. Although he was holding Corey at gunpoint, pride flushed his face. "James Bond's semi-automatic pistol of choice, a classic. Won it in a card game in Miami."

Corey's throat felt stuffed with shards of broken glass. "Listen, Todd, don't do this. Please. Let me go."

Todd's sculpted face hardened. "Do you still have the piece you had with you earlier at the office? Put it on the floor, now. Move slowly."

"Okay, just calm down, man." Corey lifted his shirt and withdrew the .357 from his waistband holster. Kneeling, he placed it on the tile floor.

"Kick it over here," Todd said.

Corey booted the gun. It skated across the floor and clanged against the edge of the desk. Keeping his eyes on Corey, Todd picked up the revolver and shoved it in his jacket pocket.

Corey swallowed thickly. He should have been shocked by Todd's betrayal, and he supposed that on some level he was, but the past twenty-four hours had been so crazy that nothing seemed impossible anymore.

More than anything, he was angry. Angry at Todd for stringing him along. Angrier at himself for failing to scope out the signs sooner.

"So how long have you and Leon been working together?" Corey asked.

Todd pointed the muzzle at the chair. "Sit down. Keep your hands up where I can see them."

Corey edged into the seat and placed his hands on the armrests, his sweaty palms dampening the fabric. As nonchalantly as possible, he scanned the desk and walls for possible weapons, something he could use as a distraction, and found nothing. To get out of this, he was going to need a miracle.

Please, God, cut me a break, he prayed. *Please.*

"Christ, you're so stupid," Todd said. He plopped into the executive chair, still clasping the Walther, muzzle angled toward the wall. "I gave you a chance to sell out and bring your family home, and you snubbed me. I ought to waste you right now for all of the headaches you've caused me."

Corey struggled to pull his gaze away from the gun. "I can't see you and Leon as partners."

"Tell me about it! Jesus Christ!" Todd pinched the bridge of his nose. "What a lunatic. I thought we could work this out together, you know? When he showed up at the office and told me he was there to see you, I knew you'd done some heavy dirt in your time, if you'd used to be buds with a thug like him."

"Leon came by the office? When?"

"Three weeks ago. I bumped into him in the lobby while you were out to lunch. He'd seen us on the Hot 100 list in *Entrepreneur* magazine."

The dots finally connected in Corey's mind. Leon read about him in the mag, decided to come to Atlanta and use the threat of going to the police about their past to shake him down for money. But Leon happened upon Todd first, who saw Leon, smelled dirt, and hatched a scheme.

It explained how Leon had "run in to him" at the gas station yesterday; he had simply followed Corey from home. It explained how Leon had encountered Simone at lunch; he would have found out from Todd where she worked and tailed her to the restaurant.

It explained, too, how Leon had skirted their home alarm system and gotten inside to abduct Simone and Jada. As co-owner of Gates-Webb, Todd had the highest security clearance, and could have dipped into the company's customer database and supplied Corey's pass code to Leon. And since Corey kept a key to his house in a desk drawer at work, Todd could have merely made a copy of the key and given it to him. Leon wouldn't have needed any high-tech gadgets, no lock-release guns. Invading their home would have been as easy as unlocking the door and deactivating the alarm.

Coldness swept through Corey. They had been so vulnerable . . . he knew it wasn't really his fault, but he couldn't help blaming himself for not taking more precautions.

"For someone who's stayed two steps ahead of the FBI for three years, Leon's got no brains at all," Todd said. "He was supposed to run an extortion job on you and keep upping the ante, kidnapping your wife and kid was the last resort. But he moved way too fast—and that crap he pulled at that sports bar with you, throwing the beer mug and tipping off the Feds . . . I'd had it with him there. I tried to cut him loose."

"By paying him fifty thousand dollars," Corey said.

"He would have split town for fifty grand," Todd said. "That's what he said, anyway. But that didn't work out, either, thanks to the Feds, so here we are. When you want something done right, I guess you've gotta fuckin' do it yourself. "

"You're unbelievable." Corey shook his head. "You teamed up with a career criminal, and risked everything, all because you wanted me to sell my share of the company?"

Todd's lips tightened. "When I tried to talk you into selling out the first time, you were too goddamn stubborn. You brought this on yourself."

"But the risk you took—"

"I *breathe* risk, partner," Todd said, a savage glint in his eyes that reminded Corey, chillingly, of Leon. "Leon's nothing to me, a burn card. The risk of using him was worth it. With you out of the picture, I can get five million for selling off GWS."

Corey stared at him. "Five million?"

Todd grinned. "I've been in talks with interested parties. Do you know the games I can get into with five rocks backing me? Do you have any clue of the crowd I can play with, the pots I could buy in on? I'm talking major league, more money than you'll ever see in ten lifetimes sitting on the table, one glorious, mega-pot waiting to be won."

Corey blinked. "Wait a minute. You're talking about gambling with the money you'd get from selling the company? Playing cards?"

"Of course." Todd glowered at him. "What the hell else would I be talking about?"

Corey's shock took his breath away. His wife and daughter had been kidnapped, severely traumatized and possibly abused by that maniac Leon and his pedophile partner, all so Todd could force him out of the business, sell it, and blow the wad on card games? *Fucking card games?*

The florescents flickered again, the darkness lasting for a couple of heartbeats, and then brightness returned. Todd glanced worriedly from the lights, to Corey.

"You're sick," Corey said. "You're as nuts as Leon."

"Spare me the analysis. You're going to sign these papers." Todd shoved the documents across the desk. "You're going to sign them, the company will cut you a check tomorrow or Friday, and Leon will give your family back and go away, after you pay him a fair portion."

"A fair portion? Not a million?"

"I told him to say he wanted a million to force you to come up with this bright idea of selling out all on your own. I thought it would lead you down that road, but I guess don't know you as well as I thought I did."

Corey smiled sourly. "Ditto."

"Give Leon a hundred grand or so, and he'll hit the road and be out of your hair forever. He's itching to go 'cause the Feds know he's in town."

"They aren't going to leave me alone, either. They're suspicious."

"Hey, that's your problem. But if you're thinking of cooperating with them and turning me in, well, your old partner in crime told me all about a certain unsolved case that went down in Motown. All it would take is an anonymous tip, know what I mean?"

Corey bit his lip. Once again, he was hemmed in by his past.

"Sign them," Todd said. He slapped an ink pen onto the desk.

Corey stared at the pen. "Tell me where my family is being kept."

"Leon will cover all that with you after you settle up with him. They're fine, trust me."

"Trust you?"

"You don't have a choice." Todd fixed the Walther on him. "I'm holding the royal flush. Sign the docs."

"No." Corey locked gazes with him. "You tell me where they're being held, or I'm not signing anything."

"Oh, you think I'm bluffing?" Todd's eyes crinkled with amusement. "I think you're the one bluffing, Corey. You always sucked at poker, you know." Todd pointed the pistol at

orey's head. "Stop screwing around and sign the goddamn
apers so we can get out of here."

Corey glanced at the documents, mouth dry as sawdust.
odd had him, and they both knew it. It was as simple as
at. He had no choice any more.

But he couldn't make himself reach for the pen. It was as
his wrists were strapped to the armrests.

Can't do it, he thought. *I can't give in, can't let them
in . . .*

The lights sputtered off again—and remained off, black-
ess falling like a tarp over the room.

"Fuckin' storm," Todd cursed.

Not thinking, acting purely from instinct, Corey shot out
f the chair, grabbed it, and heaved it in the general direction
f the desk. Todd shouted. Gunfire rang out, the muzzle spit-
ng fire. Corey ducked. Glass shattered behind him and tin-
ed to the floor.

Ears ringing, Corey scrambled through the darkness to
here he remembered the door to be and stumbled out of the
fice, Todd grunting behind him, furniture banging to the
oor.

The warehouse was dark as a moon cavern, and Todd was
oming after him.

47

Running through the echoing darkness, bumping again[st] hard-edged objects, shoes clapping against concrete, Cor[e] struggled to remember the location of the loading do[or] doors. His memory was a blur, as if it had been wiped cle[an] by the shock of Todd's betrayal. He was thoroughly lost, [a] mouse in a giant labyrinth.

He heard Todd's rapid footsteps somewhere behind hi[m]. Todd had used to work there, knew the warehouse's flo[or] plan well. And he had two guns.

Shit. When the hell would the backup power generat[or] kick in?

Pressing forward, one hand extended straight ahead, Cor[e] dug his other hand into his pockets. He felt the Leatherma[n] in his front pocket, a tiny utility tool he carried on his k[ey] ring, but it didn't include a flashlight. His fingers slid acro[ss] the cell phones holstered on his hip. Maybe the BlackBer[ry] would be good for a little light—

His shoulder slammed hard against something. A met[al] shelf of some kind. The collision knocked the breath out [of] him, and he staggered.

Adrenaline kept him balanced on his feet. Sticking both
ᴀnds out in front of him, he felt the sharp edge of a corner.
ᴇ sidled around it.

He spotted a door ahead, a crimson EXIT sign glowing in
ᴇ darkness.

He paused, listened, but didn't hear Todd's footsteps any-
ᴏre. Maybe he had lost him.

He sprinted toward the door. When he was halfway there,
ɡhts suddenly flooded the area, disorienting in their bright-
ᴇss.

Like some macabre jack-in-the-box, Todd sprang from
ᴏund the corner on Corey's left, pistol in his hand and a
ᴄath's head grin on his face. Corey shouted in surprise, and
ᴀrted to spin away.

Todd clubbed him with the gun, and his world went dark
ɡain.

48

Cold water splashed over Corey.

He came awake with a rasped shout. He wiped water o[ut]
of his eyes, blinked. Blinking made him wince. His head f[elt]
as if it had been split open like a coconut, soaked in gas[o]-
line, and set on fire.

He lay on a smooth floor that felt like a sheet of pe[r]-
mafrost. Todd stood above him in a cone of light, a red pla[s]-
tic bucket dangling from his hand, the pistol jutting from h[is]
waistband in an inverted "L." Veils of mist swirled arou[nd]
them, and the entire room hummed and pulsed.

They were inside a freezer.

It was as large as a two-car garage. Tall metal racks lin[ed]
the stainless steel walls and stood in rows throughout t[he]
chamber, every inch of shelving packed with boxes of a[s]-
sorted sizes, many of them dusted with frost. A galvaniz[ed]
steel door that looked as impregnable as the entrance o[f a]
bank vault hung half-open behind Todd.

Head throbbing, Corey sat up. Bone-deep shivers cours[ed]
through him. He was completely soaked with water, and a[l]-
ready felt it hardening into a shell on his skin.

Todd wore a good-humored expression, strings of frosty breath curling from his nostrils.

"I thought I'd let you chill for a while." Todd chuckled at his joke and cast a look around. "This is actually one of the smaller cold storage areas. I got trapped in here once when I was a teenager. Twenty minutes of sheer hell. Wouldn't you know my cheap-ass old man still hasn't fixed the handle?"

"Todd . . . no . . ." Corey's throat burned; his voice came out cracked. He grabbed the support leg of a nearby rack. The freezing metal numbed his fingers. Groaning, he started to pull himself to his feet.

Bucket swinging from his hand, Todd backed toward the door. "Chill out in here and think about making the right decision for your family, Corey. It's about five below zero. Better keep moving to stay warm, or you might lose some fingers and toes."

Corey's knees quivered and popped as he rose. "Listen . . ."

Todd's smile was downright sunny. "I'll be back in a bit. Gonna grab me a burger. We'll see if you're ready to deal then."

Corey tried to move forward, but dizziness swept through him. He swayed against a shelf, jarring a box to the floor.

Todd slipped outside and slammed the door, foam sealing the portal shut with a soft sucking sound. Shouting, Corey ran-stumbled to the door and pushed it.

It did not budge.

"No!"

His voice bounced back to him, muffled and flat.

Wincing at the pounding in his head, he studied the handle mechanism. There was some sort of mushroom-shaped cap as big as his fist that should have sprung the lock, but it was coated in a thick jacket of ice. When he pushed it, it didn't give at all.

No, no, no.

He hammered his fists against the door. Ice slivers cascaded from the door and ceiling and rained over his head. But the door held firm.

Call someone.

Fogged breaths spewing from his lips, he searched his belt. His BlackBerry and the other cell phone were gone. When he was unconscious, Todd must have taken them.

"No!"

He was trapped.

49

He refused to believe that he was trapped.

But there was no emergency alarm on the wall, no phone box, no other exit. When he shouted for help, yelling until his voice broke, no one responded.

I'm not trapped.

He attacked the door, kicking the frozen mushroom cap repeatedly, as hard as he could, pain jolting through his shins and knees. Tiny chips of ice wafted to the floor. But the cap did not give.

He kicked it again. "Come on!"

Nothing.

One more time. "Damn it, open!"

No good.

Panting, he bent over. His legs burned, as if razor blades had been driven deep into his flesh. They ached so intensely it was difficult to stand, but he welcomed the pain. Throbbing pain meant blood was circulating.

It's about five below zero.

Goose pimples rashed his arms. His damp clothes were getting stiff, freezing, and crackled when he moved. He thought of stripping out of them, but couldn't imagine how that would help. His entire body felt as though it were under attack by a thousand knives.

How long would it take before frostbite set in? A half hour? Minutes? He wasn't the kind of guy who spent his time roughing it in the great outdoors, and the temp rarely dipped below freezing in Atlanta. He had only a general idea of the symptoms of frostbite. Like tingling. Numbness. Pain.

And he knew the potential risks. Like tissue damage. In the worst cases, amputation.

Hard shudders wracked him. His teeth chattered.

Move, keep moving, keep blood flowing.

He paced back and forth across the freezer, weaving between the aisles, from the door to the back wall. He clapped his hands, pinched his nose, rubbed his cheeks, clenched and unclenched his fingers and toes.

He checked his watch. Ice crusted the face. He scraped it clear with his thumbnail. It read 9:34.

How long can I last?

Vaporous ghosts swirled and hissed around him. The freezer compressor hummed, a rumbling vibration he felt echoing in the core of his heart, as if he were turning into ice from the inside out.

Keep moving, keep moving, keep moving.

He paced, paced, paced.

I'm not trapped.

He lunged wildly at the door again. He bounced off as if it were elastic, slipped, and fell down, slamming against the floor with a grunt.

Get up. Get up and keep moving.

He tried to push himself up. His arms trembled. A pins-
and-needles sensation attacked his fingers.

I'm . . . not trapped.

He squinted at his watch. 9:49.

Not . . . trapped.

He collapsed to the floor.

50

Sprawled on the cold floor, shrouded in mist, eyes glazed, Corey saw not the walls of the freezer and the frozen boxes on the racks, but an eighteen-year-old and his older friend. . . .

Leon picked the house on that sunny April day as he always did: on the spur of the moment. His impulsiveness thrilled Corey, and when he found himself having doubts about his friendship with Leon, when he asked himself when he was going to go straight and find a job somewhere, or go to college, like Grandma Louise was always telling him he should do, he remembered that rush, that charge of adrenaline that came only from Leon picking the house to hit and not wasting any time about it—doing it right then and there.

"I cruised past it last week, man," Leon said. They crawled past a neatly kept, brick bungalow in Leon's Cutlass Supreme, Corey riding shotgun. A Public Enemy track boomed on the Alpine stereo, "Rebel without a Pause," the ceaseless trumpet glissando piercing Corey's brain.

Leon sneered. "Guy who lives there, shiny-headed, Humpty Dumpty, fried-pork-skin-eating motherfucker, he had a white

Cadillac parked out front. He was waxing it like it was some bitch's luscious ass."

"Why didn't you hit it last week?" Corey asked. Leon sometimes pulled house jobs without Corey. The revelation that he'd gone solo always left Corey feeling a strange mixture of disappointment and relief.

Shrugging, Leon took a drag on his Newport and exhaled a thread of smoke, a gold watch glittering on his wrist that complemented the scalloped chains around his neck.

"I didn't feel it then, you know I have to be in the mood, the golden gut has to be talking to me, C-Note—but I feel like doing the old one-two punch on his crib right now."

For no reason at all, Corey's stomach clenched. He was always a little nervous before a break-in, but nothing that felt like this. He had big-time butterflies.

Corey cracked his knuckles. "Maybe we should come back later. Or go somewhere else."

"Fuck that." Leon glared at him. "It's one o'clock in the afternoon on a Tuesday, no one's gonna be in there, you've got to respect my instincts, if I worked on the New York Stock Exchange I'd be a motherfuckin' billionaire, Dow Jones Junior, respect the hustle, hombre, or drag your black ass back to church and holler hosannas with Nana and pass the collection plate, you dig?"

Corey recognized that feverish look in Leon's eyes that made it clear he would not be denied, that look that said he was going to go through with it whether Corey was down or not. But if he backed out, Leon would never let him hear the end of it. He would be branded a punk, he would lose respect, and Leon would spread the word that he'd let his boy down, and among their crowd, there was no worse label to wear. No one wanted to deal with a punk except other punks, and who cared what they thought?

"All right," Corey said.

Leon flashed his gap-toothed grin. "That's my homeboy."

Leon swung around the corner and parked in the shade of a sycamore, across from an elementary school. Children at recess pranced and skipped on the playground in the afternoon sunshine, looking as if they would be innocent, young and carefree forever.

Corey found himself wishing that he were one of them.

"Pass the piece, chief," Leon said.

Corey sighed, looked away from the school. Two rumpled nylon book packs lay on the floor beneath his feet, one red, one blue. Corey handed the red one to Leon.

It contained a Glock 9 mm with a scratched off serial number. The blue one, which Corey picked up, held a crow bar and other tools. Both knapsacks bore ID tags with someone else's names on them. It was Leon's idea. His theory was that if they ever had to cut loose from the scene, they could toss the bags in the bushes somewhere, and the items they contained would be linked to someone else.

"Let's act like we've got a purpose, my man," Leon said, stubbing out his cigarette in the ashtray. "Time to get money."

Bags strapped over their shoulders, they strolled back to the house, walking confidently, as if they were high school students who lived in the neighborhood. Leon always said that was the key to not getting caught: act like you have every right to be wherever you are, and no one notices you. It's the skittish ones that get nabbed.

They swaggered right up to the front door of the chosen home. While Leon did look-out duty at the end of the walkway, Corey rang the doorbell, and knocked three times.

No one answered. No dogs barked.

He levered the forked end of the crowbar into the door jamb. In half a minute, he had pried the door open.

"Let's do this," Leon said, coming up behind Corey and slapping his shoulder. He withdrew the Glock and went inside.

Corey hesitated on the threshold. He thought about those children in the school yard, playing in the sun. Suddenly, he felt on the brink of tears.

Moving deeper into the house, Leon glanced at him over his shoulder. "You see someone coming?"

Lips pressed together tightly, Corey shook his head.

"Then get in here. You know the drill, C-Note, seven minutes to win it."

Corey pushed back thoughts of the children. He dug the stopwatch out of his sack and pressed the button to start the timer.

Seven minutes inside. That was their rule. Leon had made it up. He said that seven was a lucky number, so if they measured all of their break-ins by the seven-minute-rule, they would never go down—universal law would be on their side or some other metaphysical weirdness that Leon always seemed to be talking about.

Corey crossed the threshold and shut the door behind him.

The shadowed house was cool and silent. The living room was modestly furnished, but clean and orderly, the residence of someone who'd worked to turn a house into a home.

Leon marched down the hallway, headed straight for the master bedroom, where the jewelry would likely be, and where cash could often be found, too, tucked between pages of a Bible, secreted underneath a mattress, hidden in a nightstand drawer, or concealed in a shoe box in the closet. Corey followed. His gaze scanned across the photographs clustered on the end tables and walls.

A man, woman, and little girl appeared in many of the pictures. They were smiling, happy. And the man looked very familiar . . .

No, Corey thought, cold perspiration beading his forehead. God, no.

"Come on!" Leon yelled from the bedroom.

Corey hustled into the room. Leon had found a jewelry box on the dresser and was dumping the glittering content into his bag.

"*Check the closet,*" *Leon said.* "*I've got a feeling about what might be in there.*"

"*Wait.*" *Corey wiped the sweat from his brow.* "*I know the guy who lives here. He was one of my high school teachers.*"

Leon cocked an eyebrow. "*So? You graduated from high school last year, you don't owe him anything.*"

"*But he's a good guy, man. We shouldn't do this here. We should go somewhere else.*"

"*Good people have fucked up shit happen to them every day,*" *Leon said.* "*What else is new? You're a good little boy but look what kind of life you've got—your moms died a druggie and you don't even know your daddy's name. Right? Cry me a river some other time. Toss the goddamn closet so we can clear out of here.*"

Face burning, Corey turned away and yanked open the closet doors. It was full of men's suits and shirts on the left side, and women's dresses and outfits on the right; the women's clothing took up far more space. A double-stacked row of shoeboxes filled a shelf above the hangers.

Corey swept the shoeboxes to the floor and tore off the lids. Shoes tumbled out, heels and sandals and flats, oxfords and loafers and sneakers. But at the bottom of the pile, a Nike Air Jordan shoebox held a rubber-banded knot of cash.

"*Bingo,*" *Leon said, peering over Corey's shoulder.*

Corey heard the door creak open at the front of the house. A man shouted in shock and rage.

Terror squeezed Corey's throat.

We're caught, he thought. It's over.

But after the flash of fear, he felt unexpected relief. If he didn't have the guts to stop doing this on his own, then someone else could make him stop.

But Leon's eyes had dwindled to hard slits. He pulled the Glock out of his waistband.

"What're you doing, man?" Corey whispered.

"I'm not going down for this. Neither are you."

Leon stalked out of the bedroom.

Heart hammering, Corey left the money in the box and hurried after him.

A man was at the end of the hall. Bald-headed, with glasses, a walrus mustache, and a prominent belly, it was the man from the pictures, Mr. Rowland, Corey's junior-year English teacher. Corey remembered him fondly. Mr. Rowland brought donuts for the class on exam days and let the students select the books they wanted to read for book reports—Corey had once picked an X-Men comic, expecting a rebuke, and Mr. Rowland had actually praised him for his choice.

As Leon approached, Mr. Rowland raised his hands in surrender.

"Look, kids . . . take whatever you want," he said in a tremulous voice. "I-I won't call the police. No one has to be hurt here."

Corey slid behind Leon and turned to hide his face, but Mr. Rowland's eyes brightened in recognition. "Corey? Is that you? My God, son—"

Leon shot Mr. Rowland in the chest, the gunfire deafening. Corey's mouth flew open to scream, but no sound came out, his throat feeling completely locked up.

Mr. Rowland gasped and dropped to his knees. A dark bloodstain spread across the breast of his white dress shirt. He clutched his chest, wedding band glinting.

"Please, God . . ." he whispered.

With the cold efficiency of an experienced mercenary, Leon stood over him and shot him again, in the head. Mr. Rowland fell backward to the floor.

Corey moaned. His knees folded, and he slumped to the carpet in the middle of the hallway. His stomach convulsed, vomit clawing at his throat, and some of it escaped his lips and dribbled down his chin.

"I had to do it," Leon said, with a backward glance at Corey. His eyes shone, face glistening with sweat, and it struck Corey that Leon was excited—he had that same frenetic appearance when he was in a shooter's zone on the basketball court. "This guy knew who you were. He would have gone to the cops anyway soon as we left, we had no choice."

Corey tried to speak, couldn't. His head felt as if it were being crushed in a vise.

Leon searched Mr. Rowland's pockets. He found a wallet, he opened it and took all of the cash. He fished a brushed chrome cigarette lighter out of his pocket, too.

"Looks like an antique, probably worth something, I'm keeping this, uh-huh," Leon said, and shoved it into his bag.

Corey wiped his lips and finally managed to speak. "I . . . I can't believe you . . . you killed him."

Leon stormed across the room to Corey and jabbed his long finger in Corey's face.

"We killed him, you and me, get it straight," Leon said. "You're the one who knew the guy, I had to kill him. Because of you, he would have gone to the law and identified you and that would've led to me, too. We're equally responsible for this, joined at the hip, suck it up and deal with it. We did it and that's the end of it."

Corey's gaze dropped away from Leon and fixed on Mr. Rowland's body, watched the blood leaking from his head and chest and trickling into the plush carpet. As he stared, eyes glazing over, he strongly wished this was only a dream, a nightmare, from which he would soon awaken. . . .

When Corey blinked, he felt ice crusting on his eyelids.

and forming a hard ring around his lips. He had zoned out. He wasn't sure for how long.

It had felt like a lifetime.

He hadn't let himself recall the vivid details of Mr. Rowland's murder in many years. He'd restricted himself from reliving that day, as if by refusing to think about it in concrete terms, it would somehow fade away and become something that had never happened.

He had witnessed a good man murdered and done nothing. He hadn't gone to the police. He hadn't pressed Leon to turn himself in. They had walked out of the house, returned to Leon's car, and driven off, and when Mr. Rowland's wife discovered his body that evening, the police launched an investigation that never circled within ten miles of him and Leon.

It was the last time they pulled a job together. Leon, emboldened by the killing, his first, quickly grew impatient with Corey's reluctance to hang with him any more. He struck out on his own exclusively, and three months later finally got arrested when robbing a liquor store. Soon after, Grandma Louise died, and Corey relocated to Atlanta and started a new life.

But the past still trapped him.

Tears spilled from his eyes and streamed down his face. Sobs shook him.

"I'm sorry, I'm so sorry," he said, tongue thick, throat aching. "Oh, God, I'm so sorry."

He had never cried for what he had done. He'd been too frightened of what he might feel compelled to do if he let himself break down. After so many years of being repressed, the guilt, pain, and tears were like a great dam pent up inside him. He let it all out, and his tears were so hot they burned furrows through the ice on his cheeks and steamed on the floor.

I'm so sorry, please, forgive me, I'm so sorry.

He cried for Rowland and his family. He cried for himself, for the shame he'd carried for so long.

He would finally confess, he decided. He would find Simone, and he would tell her what he had done, for as his wife and his sworn life partner, she deserved to know before everyone else.

Then he would tell the police, and let them handle him as they saw fit. He would not carry this burden anymore. He would see justice served, even if it meant giving up his freedom.

But first, he had to get out of there.

He blinked away his tears, shifted. His head was nestled against his outstretched arm. A mantle of ice was forming where his cheek touched his shirt sleeve.

From his position on the floor, he could see beneath the bottom of the wire rack that stood nearest the freezer door. In the dim cone of overhead light, he thought he made out a faint outline in the wall against which the rack stood. Like the seam of some kind of panel.

Slowly, he sat up, ice crackling across his clothes and falling from his hair. His hands and feet tingled, but he could move them.

He checked his watch. It read 9:51. Amazingly, he'd been adrift for only a couple of minutes.

With effort, he got up and approached the shelves. He peered between the rear of the rack, and the wall.

There it was—a rectangular panel perhaps three feet long and a foot wide. The crevice was too narrow for him to fit his arm back there. He retreated a few steps, to get a full view. The shelves were stuffed top to bottom with frost-wreathed cardboard boxes, frozen foods of all kinds.

He began to pull the boxes off the shelves and heave them onto the floor behind him. His breath plumed in front of him as he worked, and blood pumped hard through his veins warming his limbs again, alleviating the tingly sensation, warding off the numbness.

Once he had cleared away most of the boxes, he had a complete view of the wall panel. It had a small knob in the upper right corner, and a sign hung in the center, a white background with ice-crusted red letters:

IN CASE OF EMERGENCY USE FIRE AX

Hope rose in him. He grasped the knob of the panel, and pulled it. It was stuck.

"Don't play with me," he said.

Two more hard pulls, and it squeaked open. A gleaming ax with a red head, sharp steel blade, and shiny yellow shaft stood inside, held in place with a clip.

The ax was heavy, and felt good in his hands.

He turned to the door and started swinging.

51

At 10:16, Corey hacked his way out of the freezer and stumbled onto the warehouse floor, ice crumbling from his shoes.

He let the ax drop beside him. Hunched over, hands on his knees, he sucked in the blessedly warm air, and felt waves of heat spread through his lungs and muscles. Latent ice crystals fell off him and melted on the concrete, and behind him, the ruptured freezer door bellowed cold mist, like some mortally wounded beast.

He'd spent nearly an hour trapped inside, but because he'd kept in almost constant motion, he didn't think frostbite had affected him. Except for the bruise on his temple, he felt good—rejuvenated, even, though this had to be the longest, most grueling day of his life.

He found the cell phone and BlackBerry sitting on a small table against the wall. He holstered them both.

Todd was nowhere to be found. Maybe he would return soon, but Corey was not going to wait around.

He believed he knew where his family was being held, and no one was going to stop him.

Part Four

52

When Jada awoke, Giant was sniffing her.

She'd fallen asleep sometime after she had seen the shaggy-haired man and the big dogs outside the bedroom window. She'd tapped her fingers against the glass, and the man had looked directly at her and shone a flashlight in her face—but then he'd run away, as if frightened by the sight of her, leaving her puzzled and alone.

Then, more darkness had steadily seeped into the room. Hugging herself, she'd lain back on the mattress and slipped her thumb into her mouth. She hadn't intended to sleep, but she drifted off.

She'd dreamed of Mom. Her loving face, her gentle voice, her warm touch. Mom was whispering to her in the dream. *It's going to be okay, baby, everything's going to be fine, Mommy's going to come and take you away from this place.* . . . Jada had been comforted.

And then she came awake to find Giant bending over her, his huge round face floating above her like a moon as he sniffed the front of her pajama top. He was so close she could see the dirt-packed pores on his pudgy cheeks, so close the awful stench of him made her stomach buckle like she was going to puke.

She screamed.

Eyes widening with alarm, Giant jerked up and crawled away from her. While she was sleeping, a small lamp had been placed near the center of the room, and he clumsily knocked it over with his big foot.

She was so scared she couldn't move, and her throat had closed up with such terror she thought she had probably stopped screaming, too.

Giant plopped onto the floor near the mattress and put his finger to his lips. Smiling faintly, he lifted his T-shirt, exposing his hairy chest and bloated belly, his skin ghostly pale in the light.

Her mouth hung open in a frozen scream. She was breathing so hard her chest hurt.

Giant pointed at several crude-looking, heart-shaped tattoos spread across his stomach. There was a girl's name printed in the center of each heart: *LaTonya . . . Ariel . . Kisha . . . Ashley . . .*

As she stared, paralyzed with fright, he pointed at her and then tapped his stomach. She read his lips slowly form her name: *Jada.*

He licked his lips, and grinned.

She broke her paralysis, leaped off the mattress, and ran. She went through the door nearest to her: the closet. Scrambling inside, she backed against the wall, knees knocking, fingers clenched and digging into her palms.

She screamed. *Mom, Daddy, help me!*

She didn't know if they heard her, didn't know if anyone heard her. This was like the worst nightmare ever.

There was an empty hole where the doorknob should have been that let a thin cone of light inside. Through the hole, she saw Giant shuffle toward the door, and she felt the floor trembling under his heavy footsteps.

Mom, Daddy, please, help me!

She pressed against the wall. A board brushed across the back of her legs, fell to the floor.

Giant stooped and peered at her through the hole in the door, eye shining, bulk blotting out the light.

She crouched on the floor and pulled her knees against her hitching chest, curling into a ball.

Giant began to open the door. Light sifted inside.

She shrieked hopelessly for her parents.

Giant stuck his head inside. He looked down at her. He licked his lips, and one of his hands dropped down to his private parts and squeezed.

She covered her head with her arms, wishing desperately that she could simply fold into nothingness, vanish.

Dear God, help me, she prayed, *please, please, please* . . .

The closet suddenly darkened again. She looked up. The door had swung shut, and she felt Giant's footsteps thudding away.

A painful, pent-up breath came out of her.

Maybe Mr. Leon had called Giant out of the room. Mr. Leon scared her, too, but he seemed to want to keep Giant away from her.

She didn't dare get up to look and see. For the moment, she was safe where she was, and reluctant to move.

As she sat on the floor, trembling, she felt something rattle behind her. Turning slightly, she reached behind her and raced her fingers across it.

It felt like another door.

53

As Jada screamed upstairs, fear propelled Simone to th
bedroom door. She beat her fists against it, shouting at Leo
to get up there and do something.

Leon had left her alone in the room some time ago, to d
whatever it was he did when he wasn't in her presence. She'
thought she overheard him speaking to someone—his par
ner, presumably—and she thought she'd caught him sayin
Corey's name and something about a freezer, but she was s
weary, and his words so muffled by the rain, that she couldn
be sure.

A couple of minutes after Jada began screaming, she qui
eted. Simone waited in front of the door, hands sore an
throbbing, uncertain whether her daughter's sudden silenc
was a good thing or not. Then she heard Leon's quick foo
steps approach, and she backed away to the mattress.

He came inside the room carrying a folding chair. H
winked at her.

Simone glared at him. "What the hell is going on u
there? Why was my daughter screaming?"

Leon placed the chair on the floor near the battery-powere

amp, and eased into it. He fired up a cigarette, took a slow pull.

"Everything's cool with the munchkin," he said. "Billy gave her a little fright, but she's all right, ain't nothing but a thing in the spring."

"You promised me that sick bastard wouldn't touch her."

"He didn't touch her. He only sniffed her." Leon snickered. "Technically, he didn't disobey my orders, he knows I'm the Alpha dog, the Omega, there's none greater."

Her mind reeled. That pervert had sniffed her baby? He'd gotten close enough to Jada to do that?

She felt cold.

"Leon, I want my daughter in here with me," she said firmly. "You can't control your partner. Clearly, he's testing the boundaries. God only knows what he'll do next."

"No can do." Leon tapped ashes into a paper tray. "I want to spend quality time with you, just you and me, I love having your undivided attention, Clair Huxtable, wanna build an effigy to you when we're all through, yeah, uh-huh, all right."

Since Leon had called Corey and named his new, ludicrous ransom, the depressive phase of his possible bipolar disorder had proven short-lived. He'd cycled back to a manic state, talking rapidly again, using convoluted sentences, gesturing frantically and chain-smoking cigarettes. Whatever bond she had forged with him a few hours ago had crumbled.

She could only pray that Corey understood the clue she had given him about their location. She estimated that it had been a few hours since they had spoken—it was maybe ten o'clock by now, maybe a bit later—and she wanted to believe that Corey was busy plotting a rescue. Although she reminded herself that she could not place all her hopes in Corey coming through for them, that she had to stay alert for an opportunity to take advantage of Leon.

But when Leon was manic like this, he was thoroughly

unpredictable, as difficult to pin down as a greased snake. And about as dangerous.

She sat on the mattress. Leon abruptly rose off the chair and dropped beside her, smelling strongly of sour sweat and nicotine. He touched her leg.

"No," she said. She jerked away, and stood.

He scowled. "Aw, why you wanna treat a brother so bad? We've been in here conversating for hours, getting to know each other well, I'm feeling our connection clicking, our rapport rising, you're becoming the yin to my yang, the hot to my cold, the white to my black, the east to my west, and that means *everything* to me." He pounded his chest with his fist. "All the confused little boy in me needs is some genuine love, Clair Huxtable."

She stared at him, barely able to disguise her disgust. "What is love to you, Leon?"

"Love is patient and kind, it doesn't boast, it isn't proud, isn't easily pissed off, it always protects, always trusts, always hopes, always keeps on doing the damn thing, love never lets you down." He sucked on the cigarette, flashed a proud grin.

He had just paraphrased the famous passage from the Bible book of Corinthians. She didn't know why she had expected a more believable answer. In truth, like most psychopaths, he likely had no idea whatsoever of love. All he could do was recite phrases and platitudes he'd read somewhere and try to pass them off as his own original thoughts.

"You feel a love that deep for C-Note?" he asked.

"Corey and I share a special bond of love, yes," she said, eager to deflect the questioning from herself. "When you say love is patient and kind, does someone in your own life come to mind?"

He sneered. "All right, there you go now with your dime store psychobabble bullshit, trying to put me under an electric tron microscope." He blew smoke at her. "Fuck that. Fuck you. That's why your hubby's a stone-cold killer."

She leaned against the wall, sighed wearily. She knew she shouldn't let herself get drawn in to this, knew that every word that came out of this man's mouth was highly suspect, but the bait was too tempting.

"What're you talking about?" she asked. "He's no killer."

"No? I've been doing the electric slide around the issue and I'm not going to hold back any more, Corey and I used to rock 'n' roll like Jimmy Hendrix back in the day, breaking and entering into domiciles all over Motown. That's right, yeah, you heard me right, Mr. Security Company used to be a B&E man, deliciously ironic, huh?"

From the phone conversations she'd overheard between Corey and Leon, she had suspected as much. She didn't know what to think about it, mostly because she had more pressing issues to deal with, and partly because she would accept only Corey's own admission of his past acts, not Leon's spotty stories.

"But you said he was a killer," she said.

"Patience, mademoiselle, I was getting to that, I wanted to paint the tableau. Anyway, so this one break-in we did on the east side, Conant Gardens. Picture a sunny spring afternoon in April. We busted into a brick bungalow on a quiet street, we were loading up on jewelry and cash, and the homeowner interrupted us before we finished. Corey was carrying the gun. He told me he wasn't going to go down. He popped the man twice, one in the chest, one in the head."

Her stomach turned slow flips. "You're lying."

Leon stared at her, half his face blacked out with shadow. 'You want to know why he did it? The guy recognized Corey, he was one of his old high school English teachers. The dude said he'd let us walk if we didn't hurt him, but Corey was worried that the guy would call the cops and ID him, so—bang, Corey smoked him like the Terminator, no pause, no hesitation. I couldn't believe it, baby girl . . . shit, still can't, first time I'd ever seen anyone murdered . . . it's stayed with me." Eyes watery, he sniffed, looked away.

"You're lying," Simone said again. "Corey . . . couldn't . . *wouldn't* . . . do . . . that . . ."

"Wouldn't he?" Leon's gaze snapped back to her. "Why do you think he's never told you about me? Huh? I remind him of a chapter of his life that he'd rather forget, swept under the rug, but homicide doesn't ever go away, there's no statute of limitations on murder. Why do you think Corey hasn't called the cops and told them you and the munch kin are here? Huh? Because he knows *I can snitch on him*, he knows he'd lose it all if I talk, and that's my leverage, the only leverage I've got on him, 'cause if I tell the truth he lose everything, his business, you, the kid, all of it, flushed down the drain, and joins the sewage system and he's serving a life sentence in a Michigan state pen. Rome has fallen."

"No." She shook her head adamantly. "I don't believe you."

"Face it, you married an ice-cold killer, and he's been lying to you ever since you've known him."

"Stop talking to me."

"Corey gunned down his old teacher like a dog in the street—"

"Stop it."

"Made me swear I'd never snitch—"

"No—"

"His whole life ever since has been a lie, and yours, too—"

"Stop it, goddamnit! Stop it! Stop it!"

Silent, Leon watched her through a shifting screen of smoke.

"Just . . . just leave me alone," she said, breathing shakily. "Please. Go away."

Shrugging, he stubbed out his cigarette, grabbed the chair, and walked to the door. Before leaving, he turned.

"Ask yourself what kind of man would lie to you like he has?" He tapped his temple. "Counselor, counsel thyself."

He left her alone in the room, the *thunk* of the closing door echoing in her heart.

54

As rain poured from the night sky, Corey sped away from the warehouse in Otis's pickup, the heater blasting out hot air at the maximum setting, drying his clothes and cooking the last traces of coldness out of his body.

Simone's words revolved through his mind. *Remember when Jada was stung by a bee? That's how I am right now. That's how Jada is, too . . .*

Finally, he understood.

Jada had been stung only once in her life. Last September, the three of them had been touring model homes in an upscale subdivision somewhere south of the city, and as they'd entered one of the decorated bedrooms, a yellow jacket had buzzed across the room and landed on Jada's exposed shoulder, attracted, perhaps, by the fragrance of her lotion. Jada went nuts, slapping at the insect and screaming, and the damn thing stung her before Corey swatted it to the floor and smashed it under his heel. Jada got a red, dime-sized welt on her skin that didn't go away for several days.

The community also stuck out in his memory because

ilroad tracks curved along the border of the properties. He
emembered that he and Simone had wondered aloud who
ould want to buy in to a neighborhood where a freight train
ight jostle you out of sleep in the middle of the night.

But the clincher, the reason he was absolutely certain his
nterpretation was correct, was that Gates-Webb Security
ad been in contract negotiations with the developer to pro-
ide burglar alarm systems in all of the residences, and the
eal had fallen through because the builder's own financing
ollapsed amid the nationwide mortgage crisis. The devel-
pment was most likely unfinished, half-completed houses
anding empty, lots bare and deserted; Corey had seen it
appen numerous times in the past couple of years.

Since he'd learned Leon and Todd were working as a
eam, he figured Todd could have told Leon the perfect place
o keep Simone and Jada on lockdown, with no fear of
eighbors interfering or noticing. He doubted Simone knew
f Todd's involvement—but she had known exactly where
ey were being held.

God, I love you, babe, he thought, squeezing the steering
wheel and pressing the gas pedal a little harder. *Sorry it took
e so damned long to figure out your clue.*

Although he knew he was right, he could not remember
e subdivision's address or name. He would have to check
ompany records.

To do that, he had to go to the office. Going there was
out as risky as going home, but he saw no alternative.

He took the entrance ramp onto I-20, heading west. At
at late hour, and in the rainy weather, traffic on the inter-
ate was light. But many of the drivers who were out rocked past Corey at speeds in excess of ninety miles an hour,
eedless of the slick pavement, typical Atlanta drivers who
ft their common sense at home when they hit the roads.

His BlackBerry vibrated. It was a text message from Todd:

So U got out, Im impressed. But I still have U.
Selling GWS is the only option. Lets make a deal.
Call me.

"Kiss my ass," Corey muttered.
He deleted the message.

55

As the windshield wipers swept back and forth, Corey passed by the office, checking out the building, parking lot, and the adjacent roads for possible surveillance vehicles or anything out of the ordinary.

The office windows were dark, as they should have been at a quarter past eleven. He didn't notice any suspicious cars in the parking lot or in the surrounding area.

He made a U-turn at the next traffic light and returned to the office. He parked in the back, between the building and a thick row of hedges, concealing the truck from the road.

He found an umbrella stashed in a storage space underneath the seat. Hail the good Rev. Otis Trice, always prepared.

He doused the Chevy's lights, but left the engine running. Warding off rain with the umbrella, he dashed to the side entrance. For an alarming moment, he thought he'd lost his keys, but then he located them buried deep in his front pocket.

He took the staircase to the third floor. The GWS office suite was empty, air conditioner and computer servers hum-

ming softly. A faint glow filtered inside from the stree
lamps, but mostly, deep shadows lay everywhere.

Avoiding switching on lights, he hurried to his private of
fice, to fetch a flashlight that he kept in a drawer. As he rum
maged inside, he tried to ignore the photos of Simone and
Jada clustered on the desk. His nerves were already so
frayed he felt capable of snapping with little provocation.

Flashlight located, he lifted his hooded windbreaker off
the coat hanger beside the door. He shrugged it on and went
to the lounge.

In a cabinet above the sinks, he found a bottle of Advil.
He tossed four tablets into his mouth and chased them with a
cup of cold water. The knot on his head hurt like hell, and he
needed something to dull the pain for a while.

Although they aimed to run a paperless work environ
ment, as a backup they kept hard copies of all contracts,
signed or not, in an administrative area next to the lounge.
He approached the wide, three-drawer file cabinet that stood
next to a laser printer and high-speed copier, and pulled out
the bottom drawer.

He thumbed on the flashlight and scanned the beam
across the file labels.

"Ah, here we are," he said.

He found the manila folder he wanted in the "Cancele
Contracts" section. The file included the subdivision nam
and the sales office address.

Archer Lake Homes
478 Archer Way
Fairburn, GA 30213

The contract had been canceled four months ago, with
note in his own neat handwriting describing the reason
"builder financing problems."

He tore out the page that listed the address, folded it into is pocket, and rushed out of the room.

As he was striding down the corridor to the exit, lights treaked across the hallway wall. Vehicle head lamps?

He ran to the nearest window and looked out into the ain.

Three stories below, a silver Crown Victoria roared across he parking lot. His stomach plummeted.

The FBI had found him.

56

Corey had come too close to finding his family to be hauled into FBI custody, questioned, charged, or otherwise delayed. He had endured too much struggle and pain in the past twenty-four hours to have the patience to deal with any more pointless roadblocks.

He would speak to the Feds later, but on his terms. All that mattered right then was getting Simone and Jada back.

Footsteps ringing through the stairwell, he took the stairs to the ground floor and whammed the exit door open with his shoulder. Rain snapped against his face. He lifted the umbrella.

The government sedan had swung behind the Silverado. Copying the license tag. Running it through the state's motor vehicles database, pulling up Otis's name and address, now going to get him involved in this fiasco, too.

Anger rippled through Corey, but it was mostly anger at himself. His own flaws had created this situation, had brought about these circumstances that jeopardized his family and friends. He had to deal with it now, head on.

He sprinted to the truck.

One of the agents climbed out of the sedan: a slender, dark-haired Asian guy so fresh faced he might have graduated from the academy that afternoon.

Squinting against the rain, the agent held up a badge and shouted, "FBI! Halt, sir!"

Without slowing, Corey went to the driver's door. The agent ran toward him.

"Mr. Webb, halt! That's an order!"

Corey opened the door. The agent lunged at him.

Corey thrust the umbrella like a sword toward the man. The pointy tip stabbed into the agent's abdomen. He grunted in pain, staggered backward.

Corey scrambled behind the wheel as another agent got out of the sedan. He was grateful that he had left the engine running, because every second was precious.

Outside the truck, both agents barked orders at him, drawing pistols.

Corey slammed the gears into Reverse. The tires screeched against the wet pavement, found traction, and rocketed backward. The truck's tailgate crashed into the side of the sedan, knocked the vehicle back.

Corey winced, worried fleetingly about how he'd explain the damage to Otis.

The agents had their guns out. Corey spun the wheel and slammed the gears into Drive, and the pickup leaped forward like a kicked mule. The men fled out of the way.

Standing on the accelerator, he thundered across the parking lot. He clipped a small dogwood, a flurry of blossoms raking across the windshield. He flipped on the wipers.

Gunfire shattered the night.

He cursed and ducked low in the seat, trying to keep the truck on course. Rounds ricocheted off the bumper, and then a tire burst with a *boom*.

The truck slewed hard to the right. Popping up in the seat, Corey wrestled the wheel.

In the rearview mirror, he saw the agents getting in their car, red taillights flaring.

They wouldn't have been working alone. They had been dispatched by Falco to keep a stakeout on his office, and would be on the horn with her that second to report the incident. She would loop in local cops, and they would issue an all points bulletin, throw down a net, and reel him in like a hapless fish.

No. To hell with that.

Rubber flapping from the ruined tire, he careened out of the parking lot and onto the street. The truck fishtailed, and he narrowly avoided hitting a Mustang speeding past. The driver honked furiously.

He risked a look behind him, saw the sedan stalled in the parking lot. The collision with the truck might have disabled the vehicle.

But more would be coming soon, and to have any chance of getting away, he had to find a new car.

57

The door Jada discovered in the closet when the piece of wood fell to the floor behind her was a small door, not a big one, but tall enough for her to go through if she crouched or crawled. When she pulled it open, it led to a dark tunnel full of thick, warm, musty air. It was much too dark inside for her to see where it went.

But she guessed: *attic*.

They had an attic in their house, too. Daddy was the only one who ever went into it, though she had gone with him once. He would pull a ladder out of the ceiling in the hallway outside her bedroom and climb up there to change the whatever-you-called-it, something that he said kept the air in their house clean. The one time she had gone into the attic with him, a piece of the fluffy pink stuff that covered the wood beams up there got stuck under her collar, and it itched terribly.

But she had never seen an attic like this one. How big was it? How far did it go?

She only wanted to go home. If the attic tunnel could only

help her get out of this house, she would be happy with that. Then she could find her parents or get help, and go home.

But as she stared into the passage, she held back, brow furrowed in thought.

What if she got outside the house and didn't know where she was? What if she got lost in the woods? There was a forest around the house. She knew that for sure from what she'd seen outside the window.

To be prepared for anything that might happen, she needed a phone.

Although she didn't have her speech processor on, she could still talk and make someone understand her. She could call Daddy.

She remembered yesterday—was it yesterday?—when she and Mom and Daddy had talked about letting her get her own cell phone. She wished they had done that before this happened.

But Giant had a phone.

She had seen it clipped to his belt. She had never seen him talk on it, but he always had it with him, maybe so Mr. Leon could call him and tell him what to do.

She crept to the closet door. She peered out of the door knob hole.

Past the glowing lantern, she saw Giant's huge, dusky shape in the shadows on the other side of the room. He sat in the chair, blocking the door.

It had been a while since Mr. Leon had made Giant leave her alone. Giant didn't appear to be moving.

Was he asleep?

She realized that she was sucking her thumb again. Annoyed, she pulled it out of her mouth and wiped it on the front of her nightgown.

She decided to keep track of how long Giant went without moving. Watching him, she counted silently to herself.

one one hundred . . . two one hundred . . . three one hundred . . .
four one hundred . . . five one hundred . . .

By the time she reached fifty one hundred, Giant still hadn't moved. All she saw was the gentle, rhythmic rising and falling of his broad shoulders.

He had to be sleeping. This was her chance.

She started to open the closet door, but her knees were trembling so bad that she didn't trust herself to walk. She bowed her head, put her hands together in a steeple, and whispered a prayer.

Dear Lord, please keep me safe, please keep Mom and Daddy safe and help us get home so we can be together again. Okay, God, please? I promise to do anything you want me to do if you bring us home safe. Thank you, God. Amen.

She was never a hundred percent sure God was listening when she prayed, but her knees quit shaking.

She slowly pushed open the door, hoping it didn't make a squeaky noise. She couldn't have thought of a better time for her to be able to hear, but she had to do the best she could and try to *feel* what was going on.

Giant didn't stir, so perhaps the door was quiet.

She was glad she was wearing her house shoes. She remembered that they never made any noise at all. *You're like a ghost, Pumpkin,* Daddy had told her one day, when she came upon him in his office at home and he turned to see her, startled.

That was how she imagined herself. Like a ghost. Floating quietly across the room.

As she drifted closer, she confirmed that Giant was definitely asleep. His eyes were shut, his face slack. A strand of drool hung from his parted lips, and chocolate stains spattered his white T-shirt.

Her nose wrinkled. Jeez, he smelled so bad it gave her a headache.

Giant's tree-trunk legs were sprawled in front of him, thick arms crossed over his belly. She remembered how he had shown her the girl's names tattooed on his big stomach, and she felt such a chill that she had to stop thinking about it.

The cell phone was in a holster on the waist of his jeans, right beneath his elbow.

Holding her breath, she tiptoed closer. She reached for the phone. She closed her fingers around it.

Giant stirred.

Arm extended, she froze, breath trapped in her chest.

I'm a ghost, he can't see me, I'm a ghost, he can't see me, I'm a ghost . . .

Smacking his lips, as if in his dreams he were eating candy bars, he sleepily wiped his mouth with the back of his hand, drool coming away.

His hand dropped from his face and fell across her outstretched arm.

She choked down a scream.

Giant's fingers were cold and wet with saliva. But his eyes remained shut.

Slowly, she lifted the phone out of the holster, his hand resting against her arm. Very, very slowly, she backed away.

His hand slid away from her and hung loosely at his side. He didn't wake up.

She let out a slow breath, and retreated to the closet.

She knelt to the attic hatch, but before she crawled inside she thoroughly scrubbed her skin where Giant had touched her.

58

The blown tire grinding against asphalt, Corey swerved off the wide thoroughfare, with all of its strip malls, car dealerships, traffic lights, and street lamps, and turned onto a darker, quiet residential street. As he rattled down the road, the truck's back end shimmied, and the steering wheel shuddered in his grip.

He needed to put distance between himself and the agents, but before he could do that, he had to lose the Silverado. With the ruptured tire it was useless in a chase, and every cop in metro Atlanta soon would have the vehicle description and tag on their hit list.

He didn't know what he would drive after he ditched the truck. He was counting on an opportunity presenting itself, a gift from fate or God or something. He had to believe this somehow was going to work out for him and his family—if he didn't believe it, he would have surrendered peacefully back at the office.

Running through a Stop sign, he veered onto another road, squinting to read the street sign. Rain-drenched oaks overhung the roadway, and large homes stood proudly on big, manicured lawns, windows darkened.

He ground to a noisy stop between a Colonial house and a brick ranch and cut off the engine. He jotted down the approximate address on a slip of paper, to reference later when he needed to relocate the truck.

As he was tucking the note into his pocket, his BlackBerry chirped. A call this time, not a text message. He expected to see Todd's number, but Caller ID read: *FBI—Atlanta.*

To reach him, the Feds had called either his home landline, which he had forwarded to the BlackBerry, or the cell directly, which was a private number. Either way, it made him uneasy. Wireless calls could be tracked, locations pinpointed.

He paused for a moment, and then answered. "Yeah?"

"Agent Falco here," she said, her husky contralto so distinctive she needn't have given her name. "Mr. Webb, look—"

"Why're you calling me at this number?" he shouted. "Do you have a warrant to tap this line or something?"

"No, sir, we got the cell number from your mother-in-law."

They'd visited his mother-in-law. Great. Talk about *real* pressure.

"Look, you need to stop running from us," Falco said. "We're on your side."

"Then why the hell were your guys shooting at me?"

"They only wanted to detain you, they got a little overzealous when you resisted. I apologize."

"They should have stayed out of my way."

"I know what's going on," she said.

"You don't know jack shit. You think I'm helping Leon."

"That's not what we think."

"He's got my family—did you know that?"

"Yes, we know, Mr. Webb. The fifty thousand you left behind in the briefcase was a ransom payment."

He fell silent, his surprise overtaking his anger. He didn't know how the agents had figured it out. Regardless, it didn't matter. They couldn't help him.

"We've been trying to locate your wife and daughter all day," Falco said. "When we couldn't find them, and factored in the money and your behavior, it finally dawned on me what Sharpe was doing to you."

"It took you long enough."

"Let us help you, Mr. Webb. Kidnapping is a federal offense, we're experts at this."

He shook his head. "I've gotta do this myself."

"No offense, but you aren't trained to handle these situations. We've got a great hostage negotiator, a crack team. We'll get your wife and daughter home safely. I promise you."

Her voice was smooth and persuasive. He didn't doubt that they had a top-notch crew. But he had created this hell for his family with his own deceptions and poor decisions. It was up to him to get them out of it.

"Listen, stay out of my way, all right?" he said. "I'll handle this."

"I can't allow that, Mr. Webb."

"I'm not asking for your permission," he said, and ended the call.

A few seconds later, Falco's number popped up again.

He shut off the phone, and for good measure, removed the battery, too. Falco had admitted that they weren't tapping the cell phone, but that didn't mean they wouldn't soon get a warrant to do so—and from his security work, he knew that cops could trace a wireless phone's location even if the cell was powered off, so long as the battery was plugged in. He couldn't risk their involvement.

Climbing out of the pickup, he flipped up the hood of his windbreaker against the rain. A large aluminum tool box lay in the truck bed, lid pebbled with water. He opened it with a key attached to the ignition key ring, rummaged inside, and found a lug wrench. He stashed the wrench against his ribs, between the waistband of his pants and his jacket.

Hands in his pockets, he marched down the sidewalk. He scanned back and forth across the street, looking for a car to borrow—he couldn't think of it as stealing. His days of stealing were behind him.

Most people in the neighborhood, however, appeared to garage their cars. He scoped a handful of vehicles parked in driveways or curbside, but they were newer models, most likely equipped with alarms and electronically operated ignitions, and he didn't see any keys in plain view or unlocked doors.

Reaching the end of the block without finding any prospects, he was deliberating which way to go next when he happened to glance behind him.

Half a block away, a city police cruiser had pulled up to the Silverado, and the officer was shining a light inside. The light panned in Corey's direction.

59

Corey turned away before the cop's high-beam flashlight found his face. A wave of brightness washed over the sidewalk, and then receded.

Casually, as if he were a local resident headed home perhaps after pulling a double shift, Corey strode forward. His teeth were clenched, and in his pockets, his hands were balled into clammy fists. The lug wrench felt like ice against his ribs.

He heard the police cruiser crawling behind him. Corey quickened his pace.

Keep moving, man. I'm nobody. Ignore me.

The bright light found Corey again.

Shit.

A megaphone-enhanced stentorian voice boomed from the car: "Excuse me, sir."

Corey didn't pause, and didn't look.

"Sir! I'm talking to you! Halt and turn around!"

Corey ran.

He sprinted into the front yard on his right. He dashed

around the garage and plunged into the backyard, thick we
grass pulling at his shoes and legs.

Behind him, a car door opened, slammed. One door
opening and closing meant one cop giving chase, and if he
had any luck, it would be one cop who'd spent too many
hours hugging the counter at the local donut shop.

A gigantic wooden playset dominated the back lawn.
Corey remembered that he'd purchased and assembled a
similar one for Jada a few years ago, a project that had taken
two tedious weekends. In the rain-distorted darkness, it resembled the skeletal remains of some prehistoric creature.

He circled around it and ran beyond the edge of the property, into a damp cavern of trees and undergrowth.

The cop shouted at him to halt. He sounded out of breath
but he might have backup on the way.

The land ahead of Corey sloped into a narrow creek. The
ground was muddy and slick, festooned with vines that
tugged at his pumping arms and legs. He nearly slipped, but
caught hold of a branch and saved himself from tumbling
into the creek. He reached the lower bank, jumped over the
creek, landed on the other side, and scrabbled up the slope.

Lights shone ahead, filtering into the woods. He wasn'
exactly sure of his location. But he kept running.

Somewhere behind, the cop cried out in pain. Probably
had fallen in the mud.

Panting, Corey exploded out of the trees and into the
glare of a street lamp. He was on another residential street. A
row of duplexes ahead on the left. An apartment complex a
quarter block ahead on the right.

He ran to the apartments. The wrought-iron gates hung
open.

He looked over his shoulder, but didn't see the cop following. Maybe the poor sap had twisted his ankle when he'
fallen.

The apartment complex was a series of several four-story buildings, the units featuring patios and balconies, a network of paved lanes serving the buildings. The parking lot was empty of people, but full of cars, SUVs, and pickup trucks, myriad possibilities.

He trotted past the vehicles, searching, thinking. He rounded a corner.

Ahead, parked in front of an end unit and sitting in a pool of darkness, he finally found a good candidate: a white, 1981 Oldsmobile Cutlass Supreme.

It was, ironically, the same model Leon had used to drive when they were living in Detroit, except Leon's was black. The body was spotted with rust, but the tires looked good, and the Georgia tag was current.

Best of all, the door was unlocked. It opened with a squawk.

He slipped inside. Cigarette burns scored the cloth seats, and the air stank of smoke and stale beer.

A pack of Newport Lights was nestled in the ashtray.

He grimaced. Newports. Just like Leon. He felt as if he'd traveled in a time machine back to Detroit, into some twisted alternate universe.

There were no keys in the ignition. He flipped down the sun visors. No keys there, either.

Blue lights suddenly whirled across the apartments.

He ducked in the seat, his nose almost aligned with the bottom of the faded steering wheel.

Raindrops plinked on the windshield. There was a leak in the seams of the roof fabric; cold drops fell and spattered on his head.

His heavy breaths soon fogged the windows.

Through the misted glass, he saw a searchlight playing across the buildings, tracking through the parking lot, raking across the vehicles.

Then, quick footsteps approached, splashing through puddles.

Corey reached inside his jacket for the lug wrench.

If they found him in the car, he would not go with them willingly. He didn't want to hurt anyone. He only wanted to save his family—and God help anyone who tried to stop him.

The footsteps went to the back of the car.

"Who the hell are the pigs after now?" a man's raspy voice muttered.

The owner of the car. Damn.

A key jiggled into a lock. The trunk creaked open. The guy grabbed what sounded like a paper bag.

Now go away, Corey thought.

The trunk lid thunked shut. The guy cleared his throat, spat wetly.

Corey held his breath.

Don't open the door, go back inside.

The guy spat again, muttered something under his breath about allergies.

Please, go.

Slowly, the footsteps splashed away. The searchlight moved on, too.

Corey closed his eyes, sighed.

He waited a few more minutes, and then he risked sliding up in the seat. The parking lot was dark and empty again.

He pulled out the lug wrench. He smashed the flat tip against the steering column and cracked it open.

Leon had boosted his Oldsmobile from a salvage lot. Every day when he wanted to drive, he had to hotwire it, and he'd taught Corey how to do it, too. Corey was not proud of the knowledge he'd picked up, but at the moment, it sure came in handy.

In the dark, he had to fumble at the rotation switch, but after a few tries, he had it. The engine rumbled awake with a dull roar, the muffler coughing like an old man with a bad case of emphysema. But the gas tank was almost full.

The subdivision where his family was being held was in Fairburn, a southwestern suburb. If he drove fast, he could get there within an hour.

60

In the bedroom, surrounded by soft lantern light, sitting on the mattress with her back propped against the wall, Simone struggled to stay awake. She had never been so exhausted in her life. It was late, perhaps midnight by then, but she was a night owl, so the hour had little to do with her weariness. Her fatigue came from the fact that she felt as if she had been fed through a meat grinder, in every way—physically, mentally, emotionally, spiritually.

The only thing keeping her awake was her sixth sense that things were somehow building to a head, that a major breakthrough was looming on the horizon, and that if she fell asleep, she would miss it.

But she wasn't sure how much longer she could hold on. Leon's story about Corey had wounded her more severely than any of the physical abuse to which he had subjected her. She knew she shouldn't have believed Leon, knew that he was a pure psychopath and, as such, every word he'd spoken could have been a lie calculated to hurt her—but her gut told her that his story had an ugly seed of truth. Corey might not have murdered a man in cold blood, but he had done *some-*

thing terrible, something far worse than burglarizing a few houses, and it was that suspicion, that awful doubt she now held regarding the father of her child, the man who had long been the love of her life, that threatened to break her spirit.

Groaning, she cradled her head in her chained hands. She squeezed fistfuls of her hair, her scalp burning.

Hold on, girl, she told herself. *Hold on a just a little bit longer. A change is coming, a breakthrough is coming. You've got to stay hopeful.*

Across the room, Leon opened the door. He carried a bottle of white wine, and two red Dixie cups.

His return jolted her to alertness as effectively as an electrical shock, tension coiling in her muscles.

"What do you want now?" she asked.

"Look what I've got." He grinned, raising the bottle as if it were a magnum of the finest champagne. "A little vino to pass the time, some for you, some for me."

She studied him carefully. His eyes sparkled; his movements were quick and jittery; his overall demeanor was jubilant. In his distorted perceptions, they might have been lovebirds who had gotten snowed in together at some log cabin in the Rockies. He appeared to have no idea that only a short time ago he had told her a story about her husband that had rocked the very foundations of her world.

With her last reserves of strength, she decided to toss her playbook of psychology theories and strategies out the window and go for broke. It was now, or never.

With deliberate casualness, she noted the gun holstered on his hip as he approached her. Somehow, she had to get out of these cuffs and get her hands on that gun. One without the other would not do. To get to Jada, she needed to be free, and once free, she needed a real weapon.

He sat in front of her on the mattress and poured her a cupful of wine, and then poured a serving for himself. A sweet, fruity aroma filled the air. She glanced at the label on the bottle: Arbor Mist, Peach Chardonnay. It was the same brand and flavor of wine her mom enjoyed, on those rare occasions when she indulged in drink.

It also gave Simone an idea.

Leon passed her the cup. "Cheers, *ma cherie*."

She took a small sip; it was cold and delicious. "Wow that's so good. This is my mom's favorite wine, too. Hmph. Probably the only thing she and I can agree on."

Leon lowered his cup, eyebrows arched. "You and your moms don't get along? You mean to tell me that Clair Huxtable and mommie dearest aren't best of friends, don't go shopping together for Blahniks at Bloomie's and brunch with the Links sisters on Sundays?"

"No." Simone shrugged, dropped her gaze.

"Whoa, why not, I sense a burden on your heart, a stone, a monkey on your back, something heavy, ease it off, darling, talk to me, come on, all right, unload those weighty feelings on your boy."

"It's kind of complicated."

"All right, do tell, do tell, do tell." He snickered like a child playing with matches. "Confessions time, this is gonna be good, spill those guts, I can feel it, oh yeah, lay it on me, sister."

"I don't know." She sucked in her bottom lip. "I've never told any of this to Corey."

"Good, good, good." He poured her more wine, liquid close to running over the rim. "This can be between you and me, baby girl, that's right, yeah, our little secret."

"Okay." She fixed him with a firm stare. "But if I tell you, then you've got to tell me something that you've never told anyone else, either."

"You got a deal, sweetheart." He nodded eagerly. "Spit it out now, lay it on me, my curiosity's killed the cat and the dog."

She took another sip, wetting her tongue. "Okay . . . well, was born in Mobile, Alabama. My parents divorced when I as fourteen. My mom moved me and my big brother here Atlanta, where she had girlfriends."

Leon watched her, captivated.

"Anyway," she said, "my mom's a high school teacher, d she actually taught at the high school I was attending. hen I was in eleventh grade—I'd just turned seventeen en—we got a new principal, Mr. Blunt.

"Mr. Blunt was—hell, I'll be blunt, no pun intended. r. Blunt was *fine*. He had this smooth caramel complexion, is tall, lean physique, this cute little gap in his front teeth at some kind of way made him look smart and sexy at the me time. He was single, too. All my girlfriends and some the female teachers would swoon over him every time 'd walk in to a room.

"My mom was right up there with them, too, going ga-ga. e'd talk about him over the dinner table with me almost ery night. Mr. Blunt is so this, Mr. Blunt is so that, Mr. Blunt, r. Blunt, Mr. Blunt. She was completely lovesick.

"Next thing I know, Mom and Mr. Blunt are going steady."

"For real?" Leon cackled. "She didn't waste any time, did e, girlfriend moved quick to snap up old boy, huh, like zoom, om, zoom!"

"Mom was fast." Simone paused for effect, and winked. But . . . I was faster."

Leon threw his head back and erupted into a body-shaking ugh. "Hold on, hold on, hold on. Hold the phone! What? d I hear you correctly? You were faster? What, what, what?"

"You heard me right." She grinned. "Mr. Blunt had his e on me from the first day he showed up at the school. ould you blame him? I don't want to brag, but umm . . . u've seen the curvaceous assets yourself, hmm?" She gave m a brief, flirtatious smile. Leon's mouth hung open; he

was literally drooling. "Now, Leon, imagine how luscious
was looking at seventeen, before these juicy hips and thigh
had ever carried a child."

"Wow." Leon chugged his wine in one gulp, burpe
shook his head. "The pictures I've got in my mind, the viv
skin flicks you've produced in my cerebellum with tho
words, have damn near rendered moi speechless, sugar pi
honey pie, goddamn, wow."

"Uh-huh." She took another sip. "But here's the best pa
My mom was clueless about me and Mr. Blunt, she thoug
he was her man and hers alone—until she walked in on us
his office after school. She found me riding that tasty tha
of his like a cowboy right there in his desk chair, Mr. Blu
moaning and groaning like he was having a stroke."

"Damn!" Leon shot to his feet, knocking over his cu
"That's the craziest shit I've ever heard! Damn! What d
Moms do then?"

Simone smirked. "What do you think? She kicked my a
out of the house. I had to go live with her girlfriend until
graduated. To this day, she's never forgiven me. Women ca
hold a grudge like you'd never believe, honey."

"Good God." He sat down again, laughing, tears runni
from his eyes. "My dear, you're something else, you're a ra
one indeed, a red diamond. I never would have imagine
Clair Huxtable as a bona fide high school freak of the wee
That is classic, in vino veritas, baby girl, straight up ar
down, no joke."

Simone merely smiled. The story she had told him,
course, was a total fabrication. She and her mother were th
best of friends, her mom wasn't a teacher, and she had nev
slept with her high school principal. But Leon seemed to be
lieve her; she had specifically concocted her tale to fit h
overall worldview of women as dirty, scheming whores.

Now came the difficult part.

Sipping more of her drink, she nudged his thigh with th

of her sneaker. "Now it's your turn to confess, Leon. Tell
e about something that happened to you when you were
owing up, something you've kept secret."

He rubbed his hands together. "I don't have any stories
at can measure up to that. I didn't even graduate from high
hool, mademoiselle. I dropped out at sweet sixteen. I didn't
ve patience for homework and schedules and sitting at a
sk all day. I was too hot for my teachers to handle, too cold
hold."

"Any stories about your family?" she asked gently. "Re-
ember, it has to be something you've never told anyone. A
cret."

Lips pursed thoughtfully, he poured more wine for both
them, emptying the bottle. He took his cup, swirled it
ound, inhaled deeply of the aroma.

She kept her foot levered against his leg and stroked back
d forth slowly. He glanced at her foot, his eyebrows
itching quizzically.

"Ready?" she asked, voice lowered to a pillow-talk hush.

"I need a cigarette, need that nicotine hit, got to get the
napses sizzling." Hands jittering like excited birds, he
ook a Newport out of the pack in his pocket. He took a
ep, luxurious drag.

Simone braced for anything. But she was not prepared for
hat he said.

"I killed my mother," Leon said.

61

On her hands and knees, Jada inched through the att[e] crawl space.

At first, she had tried to stand up and walk, but she ha[d] bumped her head against something hard, and the pain mad[e] her eyes water. Crawling was safer.

It sort of reminded her of the plastic tunnels you cou[ld] crawl through at Chuck E. Cheese, or on the playground [at] McDonald's. Except neither of those places had tunnels [as] dark and musty as this one.

A cobweb brushed across her lips. Her stomach churne[d] with nausea, and she wiped the back of her hand over h[er] mouth.

Chuck E. Cheese and McDonald's didn't have cobwebs [in] their play tunnels, either.

The walls and floor of the passage were wooden an[d] smooth, though, and except for the occasional gross spide[r] web, and the dust in the air that made her nose itch, it w[as] okay.

She only wished she could hear if she was making a lot

noise. She was trying to move slowly, trying to be careful not to bump against anything, but there was no way to know for sure how quietly she was going.

But Giant had not come after her yet, and that was good. The tunnel was probably too small for him to squeeze into.

The cell phone bulged in the pocket of her pajama bottoms. She wanted to use it to call Daddy, but she worried that if she turned it on, it would make too much noise, telling Giant or Mr. Leon where she had gone. She had to wait until she was somewhere safe before she turned it on.

But where was she? It was so dark in there she couldn't see anything. The tunnel sometimes slanted upward a little bit, and sometimes sloped downward some, sometimes curved around corners, and sometimes was straight, and occasionally, a thin trickle of light leaked inside through a small crack in the walls, but it was never bright enough for her to figure out her location in the house.

She hoped she wasn't going around and around in circles. That would be very bad.

Her heart was beating hard, so hard she imagined it was booming in the space like a drum, letting Giant and Mr. Leon know exactly where she was. She imagined Giant punching his big fist through the wall and grabbing her ankle, and snatching her into the room with him, licking his lips . . .

To calm herself down, she imagined, instead, that the tunnel walls were insulated with rubber, soundproofed, and that the passage actually led to her own bedroom closet at home. She would reach the end of it, find a door, push it open, and discover herself in the middle of her closet full of familiar clothes and shoes, and she wander out of it and into her room, and Mickey would greet her with a flutter of wings and a funny comment, and Mom and Daddy would be sitting on her bed, and Daddy would say, *Hey Pumpkin, where did you go? We've been waiting for you . . .*

She came around another bend, and found that the passage ended there. The tunnel was closed up with a sheet of wood.

So she hadn't been going in circles after all.

She traced her fingers across the surrounding walls. She felt what seemed to be a small door, like the one she'd entered through from the bedroom closet in the other room.

Where did it lead?

Sitting on her knees, she grabbed the edges of the hatch and pulled it open. Cautiously, she looked outside.

She was in a closet that looked exactly like the one in the other bedroom. The door hung open, soft gray light coming inside.

She inched out of the tunnel, into the closet, and out of there, into the room beyond.

No one was out here waiting for her. They must not have heard her crawling around.

The room was empty, and had two windows—there were no boards on those windows, she noted—and there was another, normal-size door just ahead. That door was partway open, and appeared to lead to another room.

Before going any farther, she brushed dust out of her hair and off the front of her clothes, holding back a sneeze. She also made sure she had the cell phone in her pocket and hadn't dropped it during her journey.

Then, she tiptoed to the door. It led to another bedroom. That one had a window, with no wood on it. A bathroom stood off to her right.

Yet another door stood on the other side of the room, half open. Faint light came from outside.

She crept to the doorway, and found it opened into a long shadowed hall. Two closed doors stood in the middle of the hallway, one on the right, one on the left. Light came from behind the door on the left. A staircase was at the end of the hall.

She remembered Giant carrying her up some steps when
he'd first brought her into the house. That meant Giant was
in the room where the light was coming from.

She chewed her lip, thinking.

The tunnel had taken her all the way around to the other
side of the house. But to get out, she would have to go down
those stairs, and to get to them, she had to pass the room in
which Giant was sleeping.

Keeping her eyes on the door, she stepped lightly along
the carpet.

Like a ghost, she thought.

She passed by the room, and Giant didn't come out after
her.

Reaching the staircase, she peered over the railing. The
stairs ended near the front door. No one was down there
from what she could see, but a pale glow came from somewhere out of sight.

Mr. Leon might be down there. He moved so fast she
doubted she could outrun him.

She would have to take her chances.

She moved to the far edge of the steps. If they were like
the stairs at her house, the far edge was where the steps
would make the least amount of creaky noise. Whenever she
had to sneak around at home, usually coming down from her
room to go to the kitchen to get just a little extra taste of
whatever delicious dessert Mom had baked, she would stay
way to the far side of the stairs, and Mom never heard her.

Like a ghost, she thought again, and began to creep
downward, one hand trailing along the dusty railing. She
risked a look over her shoulder, and didn't see Giant coming.

As she neared the bottom, she peeked over the railing
again. All clear.

Finally, she reached the floor.

The light she'd seen came from the end of the hallway. It
looked like a kitchen back there. She saw a plastic chair that

matched the one Giant had been sitting on, and a big blu
cooler standing on the floor, like the one Daddy put in the
trunk when they went on family picnics in the park.

There was another short hallway not far from the stair
case. It ended at another closed door, and light shone under
neath. A big piece of wood lay on the floor in front of th
door.

Mom is in there. She could feel it.

Mom would want her to get out, and get help.

She went to the front door. It was locked. She slowl
turned the dead bolt, praying that it was quiet.

No one came running after her.

She twisted the knob, and pulled open the door. Col
wind and rain swept inside. She would probably get sic
going out there without a jacket, but she figured her mothe
wouldn't mind if she did, just this one time.

She carefully shut the door behind her.

Outdoors at last, raindrops on her face, breathing in th
cool fresh air, she thought about the shaggy-haired man sh
had seen from outside the bedroom window, the man wit
the dogs who had run into the forest as if afraid of her, an
she decided that anyone who loved dogs was someone wh
would help her.

62

I killed my mother.

As Leon's confession rebounded through Simone's thoughts, the sweet wine turned sour on her tongue, and her stomach clenched so tightly she feared she might vomit.

But somehow, she maintained a cool facade. She continued rubbing the tip of her shoe against his thigh, and she kept her facial expression interested, nonjudgmental.

"How did it happen?" she asked, pleased that her voice was steady, fascinated.

"I said earlier that she OD'd." He squinted, tapped ashes into the floor. "I was being disingenuous, my moms was an addict of various vices, she sucked the glass dick, smoked a joint, did some heroin, hit the bottle, whatever she could get her hands on, that was her thing, you dig, that was her life, her raison d'être. Your moms spent her days teaching class and fantasizing about white picket fences and two point five munchkins with the principal. My moms spent hers drunk off her ass or doped up, lying in bed like a beached whale, fantasizing about her next hit of whatever she could get off on.

"So one summer afternoon, when I was eighteen, we had

a brouhaha, a real battle royale, 'cause she wouldn't let m
use her car. Normally I had my own wheels, did my ow
thing, but my Cutlass was in the shop at the time, and all
wanted was a little fuckin' understanding, you know? B
Moms' Saturday-love boyfriend, some popcorn-eating pun
named Tyrone, was supposed to be coming to the casa late
and she wanted to have her car for him to drive if he wante
to. Talk about ridiculous, stupid, absurd, right? Tyrone ha
his own whip, but when he'd come see my mother and the
want to go somewhere else afterward on his own, he'd driv
her car. He was playing her, probably running the same lam
game on three or four different dumb bitches just like m
moms, but Moms couldn't see it. I had business to handle a
the time, big money moves to make, a major score on th
horizon, and she wouldn't let me use her car because of thi
trifling Negro.

"That did it for me. Eighteen years of dealing with her bul
shit boiled over, and I wasn't gonna deal with her anymor
Next day, when she was out with that punk-ass Tyrone, I du
into her heroin stash, and I laced that shit up with fentany
created a combustible mix we called magic, and I hooked
up so potent I knew it would blow up a mushroom cloud i
her fuckin' mind like Hiroshima.

"Later that night, Moms hit it. Within fifteen minutes, sh
went into seizure. I waited it out a bit and then called 91
for appearances' sake, but by the time the paramedics g
there, she was on a boat floating across the river Styx. The
declared her dead by OD."

Leon took a drag on his cigarette and expelled a colum
of smoke to the ceiling.

"There you go, darling, true confessions," he said.

Simone sat still and silent. Stunned. She had heard man
disturbing stories in her years of practicing therapy, b
never a confession of cold, premeditated murder. She couldn
come up with adequate words.

Leon glanced at his cup, discovered that it was empty. With a mumbled curse, he flung it across the room.

"Why so quiet?" He turned a hot glare on her. "You scared of me now?"

"How do you feel about what you did?" she asked, finally finding her voice.

"I don't miss the druggie slut bitch. She deserved what she got for how rotten she treated me all those years. She's in hell where she belongs. Punching her ticket was the best thing I've ever done, it gave me the confidence to go out into the world and become the man I had the potential to be, be all I can be, now that I'm free, I don't have her steel albatross ass hanging over my head any more, holding me back and cutting me down like Tom Thumb."

Coldness shuddered through her. *No remorse. He's got no remorse whatsoever. Jesus.*

He smiled at her. In the lantern light, he looked like a grinning wolf.

She had to snuff out her fear. She could not back out now. The door to hell had been opened, a finger beckoned, and she had to follow it all the way inside.

She slid her toe along his thigh. "I thank you for sharing that secret with me, Leon. There's nothing like a man who can be open and honest with a woman. I find it very . . . attractive."

He lowered his cigarette. "You do?"

"Very much so."

"It doesn't scramble your brain that I confessed to offing my moms?"

"Was it shocking? Yes. Do I feel as if you were justified in doing it, considering the abuse to which she subjected you for so many years?" She shrugged, though inwardly she wanted to scream. "That's not my judgment to make."

"You're a believer in moral relativism, huh?" he said. "Nothing is intrinsically good or evil, you have to judge a man's choices by his life's circumstances. Spinoza said that."

"You're so smart." She scooted closer to him, and crossed her legs Indian style. Her knees touched his ankles.

He looked down at the juncture of their bodies. Redness crept into his face.

"Here." She took a sip from her cup, and passed it to him.

Never letting his eyes leave hers, he drank, and handed the wine back to her. She drank some more. Her mind buzzed, and the alcohol had nothing to do with it.

"Corey was never as honest with me as you've been," she said. "He's not a real man, not like you are."

Leon sneered. "C-Note's scared of his past, terrified of the skeletons lurking in the closet, the insects beneath the rocks. But I'm not, I can go there, I'm not scared of anything."

"Not you, Leon. Never."

"I'm stronger than him, always have been."

"Yes, you are."

Silence hung between them, as tangible as the smoke in the air. She thought about the community shelter where she worked once a week. There she had counseled many women who walked the streets, performing oral sex or other acts on men for ten bucks—sometimes less, if they were desperate—and one common thread in their heartbreaking narratives was how they'd learned by necessity to separate sex from emotion, from caring, from love, how they considered it a mere business transaction, and would go about the process, no matter how repelled they were by the john, with the mechanical indifference you might have used for washing dishes or folding laundry.

That was what she had to do now. Disassociate.

She gazed deeply into his eyes. The soul of a murdering psychopath lurked within them, cold and calculating, but she could not let that stop her.

She batted her lashes, flirtatiously.

"You've got pretty eyes, like freshly minted pennies," he said. He touched her cheek with his index finger, and she resisted the natural impulse to pull away, and instead, smiled.

"Thank you," she said.

"And those dimples . . . so adorable."

She edged closer to him, knees pressing firmly against his legs. Bending forward, she placed her hands on his crotch.

A soft gasp of surprise escaped him. She felt the hardness in his slacks, and gently kneaded it.

He groaned, eyes boring into her. "Don't do this unless you mean it. I haven't been with a lady in a while."

"And as I sit here with you, I realize that I've never been with a real man." She squeezed him, and pleasure flared across his face. "Until today."

"Wait a second, wait a second, wait," he said with hushed awe. He looked at his cigarette as if finally remembering it was there, and stubbed it out on the floor. He snapped his fingers. "Wait, I *get* this. This is like, what they call the Stockholm syndrome. You've heard of that? Where the hostage-takers and the hostage start falling head over heels in love with each other. That's what we're doing here, I think, I'm really feeling you, like, whoa—"

She cut him short. "Honey, are you going to take off these damn handcuffs so I can get out of these clothes?"

"Yeah, yeah, yeah, yeah, yeah, I got you, I got you." He fished a tiny silver key out of his pocket. As he reached for her wrists, she held her breath.

Then, he stopped. His eyes narrowed to slits.

"Are you serious, Clair Huxtable?" he asked. "Or are you just fucking with me, playing some kind of sicko, shrink game?"

"You're looking at the same girl who once rode her high school principal like a pony, sweetheart. What the hell do

you think? Huh? I'll tell you what I think, Leon. I think you'r
scared I'm gonna lay it on you so hard you'll forget you
damn name."

His suspicion faded, and he broke into a grin. "We'll se
about that, uh-huh, we'll see about that, that's right."

Hands trembling with eagerness, he fumbled the key int
each cuff, and unlocked them. He tossed them aside, th
metal clattering somewhere behind them.

Thank you, God.

She examined her wrists. They had purple-black rings o
them, and throbbed painfully. She massaged them—an
tried to keep her gaze away from the gun on his hip.

"There you go." He made a wild twittering gesture. "Fre
as a bird."

"Thank you so much. Now, I can do what I do best."

"Lay it on me." He started to unbutton his shirt.

She swatted his hands away. "No, I'll do that. You relax."

"Okay, okay, okay, do your thing, yeah, do it, do it, do it.

She rose to her knees and crawled onto his lap, straddlin
him. He licked his lips. She took his hands and placed ther
across her rear end, inviting him to feel the round firmness.

"Think you can hold on to these reins, cowboy?" she said

He dug his fingers into her and squeezed, forehead glis
tening with sweat. He was as hard as cement. Ignoring he
stomach-wrenching aversion, she sinuously ground her pelvi
against him. He closed his eyes, moaned.

"Thank you for calling me to the principal's office
Mr. Sharpe," she whispered in his ear.

Eyes closed in rapture, he clutched her as if holding o
for dear life. Starting from the top and moving down, she un
fastened each button of his shirt.

"Going to turn you out," she said.

"I can't wait, can't wait, can't wait, uh-huh."

"Better not be a minute man, baby."

His head whipped back and forth. "Not me, no way, nope, nope, nope, I stay long till the break of dawn."

She reached the last button, right above his belt buckle. She traced her fingers up his arms and rolled the top of the shirt down, making it snug around his shoulders and biceps. Like putting him in a straitjacket.

"I can't wait to feel you inside me," she said.

She playfully pinched his nipple, making him flinch, while she stealthily slid her other hand around his waist.

"I can dish out pain, too, I like to bite." He bared his teeth comically and growled. "Grrrrrr."

She chuckled, flicked his nipple with her thumb. Her other hand closed around the butt of the gun, quietly unsnapped the strip of leather securing it in the holster.

"I like to do all kinds of freaky things, honey," she said. "It'll be so nice to be with a real man who can respect what I've got to offer."

"I am so respecting you right now, *ma cherie*, like you wouldn't believe."

She snatched the pistol out of the holster and jammed the muzzle underneath his chin.

"That's so good to hear," she said, "'cause if you don't respect that I've got the gun now, I'll blow your fucking head off."

63

Summoning all of his courage—easy to do after he'd guzzled six cans of beer—Ed had resolved to rescue his daughter from Their house.

He'd been given a second chance to do right by his little girl. He had probably deserved to lose her before, but after years of saving dogs from the cruel streets and giving them a safe haven, proving his worth as a man, he believed God had finally deemed him fit to have his child again.

He did not know how to raise a child, but he had plenty of food, a warm home, and a loving heart. Surely that had to be enough.

He took a handful of dogs with him as he went out again into the damp darkness. The canines pranced around him in the muddy front yard, tails wagging. They seemed more excited than usual, as if they were aware of the importance of the mission at hand.

"Ed's going to get his little girl," he said to them. "We're going to save her from Them."

He'd watched Their house for hours. The white van had returned. He hoped that he would not have to fight Them

oped that he could reason with Them somehow, but just in
ase They did not listen, he had his bowie knife.

Feeling light-headed from all the beers he'd drunk, he
lunged into the woods. A fat moon gave the forest a ghostly
low. The rain had subsided, but the undergrowth was
renched from the hours of continuous rainfall, mud slurp-
g at his boots and splattering his pants.

It made him wonder how he would clothe his little girl.
e would have to go to her old bedroom and see what pieces
f clothing she had left behind when her mother had taken
er away from him. He hoped everything still fit her. The
ossibility of having to purchase new dresses and blouses
nd shoes and whatever else little girls liked to wear fright-
ned him so much he had to stop thinking about it, because
f he did, he would go back inside his house and convince
imself that it really wasn't his little girl trapped in Their
ome. It was a ghost, as he'd first thought, and he was simply
osing his mind.

Suddenly, the dogs went rigid.

"What is it?" he asked. Peering into the undergrowth
head, he listened closely for sounds. He heard only the
link and *plop* of rainwater ticking onto leaves and bark.
Someone out there?"

One of the dogs with him, the perceptive black Lab that
ad a knack for tagging along, bolted ahead in a dark streak.
he other canines followed.

"Hey, wait for Ed," he said.

The dogs ignored him. They disappeared in the shadows.

He ran after them as fast as he could with the cane, breath
vheezing from his parched lips, legs aching dully from
vhen he'd run through the woods earlier.

He pushed through a thick wall of shrubs. Ahead, under
ie leafy boughs of a maple, the dogs had gathered around
omething. They chuffed in excitement, tails swishing through
ie grass.

He lumbered closer. And dropped his cane in shock.

It was the little girl from the window.

Somehow, she had escaped Them on her own.

The Lab pressed close to the child, licked her face. Petting the dog behind the ears, the girl looked up at Ed, her eyes bright as bells.

"My name is Jada Webb," she said slowly. She pointed behind her. "I ran away from that house back there. My Mom and I are in trouble. Can you help us, please, mister?"

Ed blinked slowly. Her words had whispered like a soft breeze around his thoughts, and failed to stir comprehension.

Instead, his gaze was fixed on her pajamas.

A colorful cartoon image of a dog was on the front of her shirt. Her fluffy pink shoes were fashioned to look like little dogs, too.

His breath caught in his throat. Her clothing was the truest sign imaginable of her identity.

"Laura," he said in a voice cracked with emotion, speaking the name he thought he had forgotten. "Oh, Laura, my sweet baby."

The girl frowned. "Mister, my name is—"

With a cry of joy, he hooked his hands underneath her arms and plucked her off the ground. He swept her to his chest and hugged her.

"You've come home to me at last," he said. "Oh, thank you, God, thank you."

His daughter squirmed and kicked in his embrace, sending one of her fuzzy slippers hurtling into the bushes. A thin whine escaped her. He muffled her mouth with his hand.

"There, there, hush now, Laura, hush," he said. He buried his nose in her hair, and the sweet smell of her made his heart kick. "Don't you remember Ed? Ed's your daddy, sweetheart. Let's go home with Ed now. You'll love Ed's house, he has lots and lots of nice, friendly dogs."

Laura cried, but that was okay. It had been so long since they had seen each other, so many long, lonely years, that he couldn't help but shed wonderful tears of joy.

Warm tears streamed down his cheeks, gathered in his beard.

He was crying, too.

64

Halfway through his drive, Corey had pulled off the highway and found a Wal-Mart that was open around the clock. They didn't sell guns, unfortunately. The only useful weapon he could buy was a Buck hunting knife.

He paid cash for the blade, a compact flashlight, batteries, and a metro area map, and hurried back to the car.

The map spread on the passenger seat, he plotted the rest of his route. His BlackBerry had a GPS mapping feature, but he was reluctant to turn on the phone for fear of inviting an FBI trace.

Near the end of his trip, the rainfall tapered off. As the storm clouds dispersed, the moon came through, casting a bone-pale sheen.

Driving through a wooded area sparsely populated with old, ramshackle homes nestled deep within trees, he spotted an ornate, stacked-stone sign coming up on the right side of the road: ARCHER LAKE. Another nearby sign tempted: FROM THE 300S. NEW HOME SITES AVAILABLE!

His pulse quickened. This was definitely the subdivision he remembered.

He hung a right. The community was steeped in darkness, the street lamps shut off. The three contemporary models they had toured last fall were on his immediate right. They were shuttered and dark, with no indications of recent activity.

He crawled down the asphalt road, tires grinding over rocks and splashing through pools of water. All of the houses he passed by were unfinished. Many of the lots were only mounds of red clay bordered by black silt fences. Through a line of pine trees on his left, he glimpsed a lake in the distance, surface streaked with moonlight.

He arrived at a three-way intersection. To his right, there were more half-finished properties. To his left, more houses, too, a couple of which appeared closer to completion than the others he had seen.

He also saw, in the moon glow, muddy tire tracks criss-crossing to the driveway of one of the homes on the left. It was a large, two-story house with a side-entry garage and an elegant brick facade. It stood in a cul-de-sac, backed by a wall of forest.

A shiver coursed down his spine. *That* was the safe house. Even without the evidence of the tire tracks, it just felt right to him.

Not wanting to risk driving closer, he cut off the engine.

65

Blood pounding in her ears, Simone pressed the muzzle underneath Leon's chin. Her finger tingled on the trigger, and from Corey's lessons on handgun security, she knew enough about guns to know that you should never point a loaded weapon at anyone unless you were willing to fire.

She was willing, God help her. Considering the sheer hell this man had put her and her family through, he *deserved* a bullet to the head.

But Leon was smirking. "You won't shoot me, Clair Huxtable. You don't have the chutzpah, you lack the *cojones*, you're only some talented-tenth princess bitch in way over her pretty little bourgeois head, skinny-dipping in the Pacific with the white sharks now. If you've got any functioning brain cells at all you'll put down the Glock and finish what we've started, I'm getting blue balls sitting here with your bubblicious ass riding my dick. Put the gun down, all right, put it down and let me give it to you raw, how about back door, you ever had that, huh, I bet not, how about I introduce you to some new experiences, how about I shove my dick in your mouth and cum in the back of your throat, let you swallow my tasty kids, how would you like that, yeah, all right, huh . . ."

"Shut up," she said, greasy revulsion slithering through her. Clutching the gun in both hands, she lowered the muzzle from his chin, to the bulge in his pants.

Almost immediately, he gulped, quieted. For the first time, genuine fear crept into his fevered eyes. He was crazy, a psycho, but above all, still a man, more concerned about the head between his legs than the one sitting atop his shoulders.

She shoved the muzzle against him harder, and he gasped.

"Wanna bet that I won't blow your balls off to get my daughter back?" she said. "Wanna try me? Do you?"

"You're a crazy bitch, stupid motherfuckin' slut—"

"Raise your hands!" she shouted.

Lips quivering, he obeyed.

She felt jittery, drunk on adrenaline. But she had never in her life been so determined.

She slid off his lap and got to her feet. She kept the gun aimed at his vital parts. Watching her, he licked his lips nervously.

"Now, you're taking me to my baby," she said. "Get up, and keep those hands up, too. Do it slowly."

"Be cool, baby girl, all right? Be cool." He stood. "No one has to get hurt."

"Go open the door." She pointed to the doorway with the gun.

"Okay, okay, be cool, all right, Clair Huxtable. Be cool."

"Stop calling me Clair Huxtable. This isn't a damn TV show. My name is Simone Webb. *Dr.* Simone Webb. Now get your ass to the door."

"All right, Dr. Simone Webb, all right, you're the boss lady."

As he walked to the door, hands raised, heavy, rapid foot-steps pounded in the hallway outside. Before Leon could reach the knob, the door flew open.

Simone drew back, finger on the trigger.

Billy staggered inside the room. His dull gaze raked over her, but didn't appear to register the gun. He turned to Leon, face downcast.

"The girl is gone," he said flatly.

"What?" Simone and Leon shouted in unison.

Billy's round face reddened; he looked like a child expecting punishment. "I went to sleep. She was hiding in the closet. When I woke up, I looked in there. She was gone."

Shock deadened Simone's knees. "We've got to find her."

"You aren't running the show," Leon said with a snarl. He glanced at Billy. "Billy, get the gun away from this bitch. She was going to kill me."

The huge man turned on Simone. His enormous chest swelled, making him appear even more gigantic, and his nostrils flared.

Simone backpedaled a few steps, hands trembling on the gun. "I only want my daughter. I'll go find her myself. Just let me leave."

"Get her, Billy!" Leon said, like a dog handler unleashing a killer canine on a trespasser.

Billy charged her. He spread his tremendous arms and roared, saliva spraying from his mouth.

Screaming, she pulled the trigger. The gun's booming report hurt her ears, the recoil snapping through her already sore wrists.

A bloody wound appeared in Billy's abdomen, and pain seared his face, but he kept coming, implacable. Backing up fast, she squeezed the trigger again, at point blank range, and a round punched into his chest.

But he kept coming, and before she could get off another shot, he crashed into her.

It was like being hit by a bus. She slammed against the wall, struck her head against the plaster. Bright stars wheeled in her vision.

In the back of her mind, she realized the collision had knocked the gun out of her hands.

Groaning, Billy collapsed to the floor. She crumpled on top of him. Dizzy with pain, out of breath, she rolled away from his body. The coppery taste of blood filled her mouth. She blinked, pushing the stars out of her eyes.

Baby, I've got to get my baby.

She crawled toward where she thought she had dropped the gun.

But Leon had already picked it up. He towered over her.

"Slut bitch," he said.

He kicked her in the ribs. The tip of his shoe felt like an ax blade. She screeched and curled into a ball, folding her body around the agony.

In her pain, she could only think that she'd had her opportunity to save her baby, and she had lost it. Tears flooded her eyes.

Leon strolled to where Billy lay sprawled on the floor. The big man's T-shirt was saturated with blood, slow, ragged breaths bellowing out of him.

"Gut shot," Leon said blandly. "Helluva way to go. Thanks for your loyal service, amigo."

He shot Billy in the head, and the giant's breathing ceased forever.

The bedroom door was open, but Simone was too afraid to move. She lay contorted in fetal position, pain swelling across her rib cage with each breath she took.

Leon knelt beside her. He grabbed a fistful of her hair and wrenched her tear-streaked face upward. His eyes smoked.

"If I killed my partner, you should know damn well that I'll kill you and your little munchkin." He roughly shook her head. "Don't ever test me again."

She wept. "We've gotta find . . . my baby . . ."

Leon suddenly looked away from her. With a grunt, he released her hair as if she were an afterthought.

"Sounds like we've got company," he said.

66

As Corey prepared in the car, a series of muffled blasts, like gunfire, issued from inside the home that he had figured for the safe house, removing any lingering doubt about where his family was being held. There were two shots in quick succession, followed shortly thereafter by a third.

Ice spun through his blood. What the hell was going on in there?

He dropped his BlackBerry and the other cell phone on the Oldsmobile's passenger seat. He had no use for either of them any more, and he wanted to be as light and flexible as possible. He peeled out of his jacket, too.

Then he hooked the sheathed knife to his belt loop, grabbed the flashlight, and opened the door, wincing when it squawked. It was so damned loud he prayed no one heard it. He carefully nudged the door half-shut.

He hurried along the side of the road. As he neared the house, the muddy tire tracks grew more distinct. They looked fresh, as they would have if a vehicle had been traveling in and out of the garage all day.

There was a Palladian window above the front doorway.

Although the moon glow could have been fooling him, he thought he saw faint light inside. No light escaped the front windows, however.

He switched on the flashlight. Hooding the beam with his hand, he played it across the bottom of the front windows.

A black bed sheet appeared to be hanging inside, covering the glass.

He cut off the flashlight, heart thudding hard and slow.

There was no easy way to do this. Simone had said Jada was being kept in a separate area. Both Leon and his huge partner would be armed.

But with the recent gunfire, it was anyone's guess what the situation might be in there. His only advantage was the advantage of surprise. Leon would not be expecting him. If he swept in fast and furious, cutting and slashing, maybe he could take control.

It was a half-baked plan, and made him realize, as Agent Falco had told him, how completely out of his depth he was. The FBI employed entire teams of trained specialists to handle these situations. Here he was, a man alone armed with a knife, and he was about to do something that a reasonable person would have considered suicidal.

But this was his responsibility, his family. He could no more have turned away from this than he could have refused to draw his next breath.

He clipped the flashlight to his belt, and withdrew the knife.

He approached the front door, turned the knob. Unlocked. He pushed the door open. Since the hinges were new, they didn't squeak.

He moved inside, gently closed the door behind him.

The house was as still as a mausoleum. The cool air smelled of drywall, sawdust, paint, and faintly, of acrid gun smoke.

Clasping the knife, he looked around. There was an un-furnished living room on his right. The entry hall led past an empty dining room on the left, and beyond that, into a great room, and kitchen.

A small lantern glowed in the kitchen. He saw a plastic folding chair and a big blue Igloo cooler on the floor. But no one was in there.

A carpeted staircase on his right ascended to a darkened second level. Past the staircase, on the right, light slanted from another hallway.

He edged forward, past the stairs. The hallway terminated at a partly open door. The light came from inside.

The stink of gun powder was stronger over here, too.

He noticed that a thick block of wood lay beside the door, and bent nails bristled from both sides of the door frame. The hinges were mounted on the outside of the frame, limit-ing the door to opening outward, not inward, as would have been normal for a bedroom. If the slab of wood were placed between the nails, it would have proven a crude but effec-tive barrier to contain someone attempting to break the door down from inside.

Simone or Jada would've been held in that room. But where was Leon? Where was his partner? Who had gotten shot?

He swallowed. *Please, God, let Simone and Jada be un-harmed and alive. Please don't let me too late to help them. Please.*

Gripping the knife in one hand, he pulled the door open with the other.

Head hanging low, hair disheveled, Simone slumped in a chair in the center of the room, hands bound behind her. He thought she was dead, thought he was too late, but he real-ized her shoulders were rising and falling. She was breath-ing. Alive.

He gasped. "Simone . . . sweet Jesus."

She looked up, saw him. Her face was puffy and bruised, and her eyes flew wide with alarm. "Baby, run!"

Before he could react, a gun materialized from the shadows beside the doorway and pressed against his skull, the muzzle warm and oily.

Welcome to the soiree, motherfucker," Leon said.

Part Five

67

Gun pressed against Corey's head, Leon ordered him to drop the knife. Corey reluctantly let the blade clatter to the hardwood floor. Leon kicked it away and moved in front of Corey. He grinned, twirling the pistol in his fingers like a Wild West gunslinger.

Corey stared at him. Leon had undergone a stunning makeover. He'd shaved off the mad prophet beard, and the long dreadlocks were gone. Gone, too, were the dingy denim overalls. He was dressed, of all things, like a security guard or cop.

No wonder he hadn't ID'd Leon at the botched ransom drop at the mall. He'd been looking for someone else entirely.

See? That's why you should've called in the FBI, a smart aleck voice in the back of his mind chastened. *You're nothing but an amateur. Leon's a pro at this.*

There was a hideous purple-black bruise on Leon's temple, and Corey wondered what had caused it. He suspected Simone. Good for her, if so.

"Put those hands up, kiddo," Leon said.

Corey complied. "Listen, Leon, you don't have to hur
anyone. I didn't call the cops."

"I know you didn't," Leon said, and before Corey coul
protect himself, he slammed a crushing fist into Corey'
stomach.

Corey doubled over, grunted. Agony boiled in his mid
section and spread like fire through his extremities. Huggin
himself, he sank to his knees.

Through teary eyes, he saw Simone. Anguish twisted he
face, as if the painful blow echoed through her own body.

"My main man, C-Note." The gun holstered on his hip
Leon circled Corey like a prizefighter scoping out his nex
punch. "Not calling Johnny Nabb I understand, but I simply
can't believe you would show up to go mano-a-mano wit
moi with anything less than a bazooka. I'm downright of
fended at your insouciance. Did you forget all the lessons
taught you, grasshopper?"

Corey wheezed. "Fuck you."

Leon slugged him in the kidney. Corey choked on a
scream and dropped to the hardwood. It felt as if a sharp, ho
knife had been plunged into his side.

Got to take control, he thought, but saw no way at all t
turn the tables. He was unarmed, Leon had a gun, and Si
mone was subdued, too.

Leon massaged his fist. "You probably should've calle
in the cavalry, homeboy. Corporate life's made you soft a
the Pillsbury Doughboy, street smarts all shot to hell."

Corey moaned, started to get up. Leon charged him
bringing back his leg for a kick. Corey spun away, an
Leon's foot caught him in the ribs like a steel spike, sendin
him collapsing back to the floor.

Corey writhed in pain. In his peripheral vision, he notice
a large figure sprawled on the other side of the room, con
cealed in darkness. The body was as motionless as a piece o
furniture—and it looked vaguely like Leon's pervert partne

Dimly, he wondered if that explained the three gunshots e'd heard. What had happened here?

"I don't know how you found us," Leon said, pacing round Corey. "But it doesn't matter, I'm going to ring my uddy, the Todder, let him know you're here, and we'll clean p this icky-sticky situation."

"The Todder?" Simone said, frowning. "You mean, Todd? odd Gates?"

With effort, Corey raised his head and caught Simone's aze. "Todd and Leon . . . they're working together . . . Todd lanned all this . . . to try to force me to sell my share of . . . ie business."

"Oh, come on now, he didn't plan *all* of it," Leon said. Give the wunderkind here some credit. I added a few bril-ant flourishes, and hell, I did all of the dirty work, all the et work. Kenny Rogers didn't want to risk ruining his rench manicure."

"Todd?" Simone was shaking her head in disbelief. "They ut us through all of this . . . to make us sell the business?"

"So Todd could have . . . gambling money," Corey said. Vincing, he got to his knees and glowered at Leon. "Where's ty daughter?"

Leon shrugged. "That, old chum, is the most urgent mat-r at hand. It appears that the little munchkin has vanished, nd it looks like I'm going to have to go find the little deaf itch. I should have put a cowbell around her neck or some-ing, I don't have time for this bullshit."

Corey looked from Leon to Simone, blinking stupidly. Iada's gone?"

"I'm sorry," Simone said, glassy-eyed. "I . . . I tried to get • her."

Leon read his watch. "Hasn't been too long since she ipped the scene, those Oompa-Loompa legs of hers can't ave carried her very far."

Corey thought about his little girl wandering at night in

an unfamiliar area, scared, alone, and unable to hear witho▮ her speech processor. Fear seized his heart.

"I'll go look for her with you," Corey said, and Simo▮ nodded at the suggestion. "She'll come to me. She'll on▮ run away from you."

"She runs from me, I'll shoot her," Leon said, matter ▮ factly.

"Damn it, listen to me," Corey said, "I have to go wi▮ you, man."

Leon drew the Glock and leveled it in Corey's fac▮ Corey felt his bowels turn to water.

"Get down on the floor," Leon said. "On your stomach.▮

"Leon, be reasonable—"

"On the floor!" Leon aimed the pistol dead-center ▮ Corey's head, and his finger twitched on the trigger. "Now▮

"All right, all right, calm down."

Corey lowered to the floor, face turned sideways. ▮ clenched his hands into fists. There had to be *something* ▮ could do . . . how could he have suffered through so muc▮ only to get here and allow Leon to push him around a▮ keep control of his family?

As he strained to think of a plan, Leon went behind S▮ mone's chair and unlocked her handcuffs.

"Now you, baby girl, you'll lie beside your hubby ov▮ here, put your feet near his head, don't make me tell y▮ twice, don't test me, you know by now I'm *not* to be trifl▮ with."

Grimacing in pain, moving slowly, Simone stretched o▮ beside Corey, her sneakers near his face. Leon swagger▮ over to them, swinging the cuffs.

"What the hell are you doing?" Corey asked.

"Being creative with limited resources." Snickering, Le▮ grabbed Corey's right arm and secured one steel ring arou▮ his wrist. He snapped the other cuff on Simone's right ank▮

Corey lifted his arm, but could raise it only a coupl▮

inches without disturbing Simone's leg. Likewise, if Simone attempted to get to her feet and walk, she would have to drag Corey along by his arm—and she seemed to be in such a bad way that merely walking on her own, unencumbered by any extra weight, would be a challenge.

Leon stood over them, arms crossed over his chest, admiring his handiwork. "If I'd known you'd be joining us, C-Note, I would have bought another pair of handcuffs, but this ought to keep the two of you in situ while I go collect the little one. If the Todder gets here before I return, I trust you'll keep him entertained. Au revoir."

"Hey, don't leave us in here!" Corey yelled.

Leon picked up the knife and started to the door.

"You bastard!" Simone screamed. "Come back!"

Corey shouted at him again, too, but the only answer they received was the heavy thud of the wood block sliding into place, trapping them inside.

68

Jada had never seen so many dogs in her life.

She sat at a rickety table in Shaggy Man's tiny kitchen. A lantern stood in the middle of the table, showering the room with light that showed tons of crusty cans, other pieces of trash, and wriggling bugs that made her skin crawl.

And so many dogs. The dogs were everywhere.

As she'd cried and struggled, Shaggy Man had carried her through the woods, around a lake, and into his trailer home near the water. She had told him that she and Mom were in big trouble. She had pointed at the house she had escaped from. She had asked him to help, please.

But he didn't seem to understand anything she said.

He would speak to her, too, even after she'd told him at least three times that she couldn't hear him because she was deaf. He would keep on talking as if he heard something different from what she'd said, or if he didn't really hear her at all.

It was almost as if he were deaf, too.

But something else was wrong with him, she realized.

His hair was long and tangled. His clothes were tattered, dirty. His bluish eyes were strange and unfocused, ringed with yellowish crud. He was missing several teeth, and those that he had left were brown and crooked.

And he smelled very bad. He smelled like his house.

She'd long wanted to get a dog of her own, but Mom said that she'd have to wait until she was old enough to care for, train, and clean up after her own dog. Mom talked about the "clean up after your own dog" part a lot. It was a lesson that Shaggy Man apparently hadn't learned from his mother.

There was gross dog poop everywhere in the house. *Everywhere.* And pee-pee stains. *Everywhere.*

It made her want to throw up.

Shaggy Man had brought her in to the kitchen and sat her in a wobbly chair at the messy table. A cute, furry little dog had hopped into her lap and started licking her face. Two others clambered into the other chairs and crawled onto the table. Another dog rolled beneath her feet and licked at her toes; she'd lost one of her slippers in the woods. The dog's tongue was cool and tickly.

She loved dogs, but *jeez*. She had counted twenty-four so far, and she was sure there were more of them. New ones kept coming in to the kitchen, pressing against her, jumping on her and sniffing her, as if curious about whom she was.

Where had all the dogs come from? There were dogs of every kind, some furry, some short-haired, some big, some small, some old that walked slowly and had clouded eyes, and others that were still bright-eyed puppies. It was as if Shaggy Man was running a dog shelter in his house.

The animals swarmed around Shaggy Man, too, but he seemed to be used to it. Leaning on a gnarled wooden cane, he shuffled to a cabinet. He took out a can of something. He opened the can and stuck a fork inside.

Shooing the dogs away, he put the can and fork on the table in front of her. She glanced inside. Green beans.

Why was he giving her food? She wasn't hungry, and even if she were, she could never eat in a filthy place like this.

Shaggy Man was saying something. She tried to read his lips, but it was really hard because he had a fuzzy beard that covered much of his mouth.

But she thought he said, *Eat.*

I'm not hungry, she said, tears filling her eyes. *I want to go home!*

He pointed at the can of beans. *Eat.*

The little dog on her lap thrust its snout into the can. Shaggy Man said something and bent to pick up the dog, but it scrambled away, knocking over the can and spilling beans across the table.

Jada had the cell phone in her pocket; she had not lost it. She slipped it out and showed it to him.

I need to call for help, she said. *I need to call my Daddy.*

Scratching his head, Shaggy Man stared at the phone, as if trying to figure out what it was. Then his eyes flashed with recognition, and his face turned red. His mouth widened into what looked to be a shout.

They . . . something, she thought he said. He was yelling, shaking his head wildly, eyes frantic.

Frightened, she shrank back in the chair. For some reason, the phone made him angry. She didn't understand. It was just a phone!

She put it back in her pocket.

The redness drained out of his face. He patted her on the head and smiled.

But her heart raced. If she wanted to call Daddy, she would have to get away from this disturbed man first. That was what he was—disturbed. Only a disturbed person would ignore her words, let himself get so dirty, live in a filthy

ouse like this with all of these dogs, and be afraid of
hones.

Shaggy Man left the table and lumbered back to the cabi-
et.

He took out a can of peas, opened it, and returned to her
with another fork.

69

Corey's cheek rested against the cold hardwood, Simone's shoes inches away from his head. His bound right hand tingled; the rest of his body was an orchestra of pain from the beating he had taken from Leon.

He was unable to see Simone's face from where he lay, but he heard her heavy, pained breathing. He wondered if she was mad at him. If he were her, he would have been. She had every right to be furious at him for how things had turned out.

Plain and simple, he had fucked up.

He twisted around and looked at her over his shoulder, the movement stirring a rash of pain along his abdomen and ribs. Simone lay flat on her back, gazing at the ceiling.

"Simone," he said.

She looked up and met his gaze. In the lamplight, he got a closer look at the purple bruises on her jaw. The weary eyes veined with red. The cracked lips.

She didn't look angry, just exhausted and battered, as she had been put, literally, through a wringer. Guilt pinched him. *He* had let this happen to her.

"I'm sorry," he said, painfully aware of the inadequacy of an apology. "I'm sorry . . . for everything."

Sighing, she rested her head on the floor again. "At least you figured out my clue about where you could find us."

"Too late to be of any use." He wriggled the fingers of his cuffed hand and studied the restraint, thinking. "I have my Leatherman in my pocket, on my keychain."

"The little thingy with all the attachments, like a Swiss Army knife?"

"You gave it to me for Christmas a few years back, remember? If we can get it out of my pocket, I can try to pick the locks."

"You know all about picking a lock, huh?"

She didn't look at him when she said it, and she didn't have to in order to make her point. He knew exactly what she was talking about.

"I went to a lock-picking seminar a couple of years ago—for our business," he said. "Can't build a better mousetrap unless you know how the mouse is scheming to get the cheese. I remember a few pointers. A handcuff isn't like a door lock, but the general idea is the same."

"Anything sounds better than lying here waiting for that bastard to find Jada." She sat up with a groan. "Let's do it."

"My keys are in my right front pocket," he said. "I think I can dig them out, but I'll need you to move your leg with my arm."

"On the count of three, then. But move slowly. I'm in a world of pain, and I'm pretty sure you are, too."

He counted: "One . . . two . . . three."

Slowly and carefully, he slid his hand down his side, Simone moving her right leg with him, bending it at the knee. He rolled over onto his left shoulder, hot agony marching along the length of his midsection, drawing sweat to his brow.

His squeezed his fingers into his pocket, snagged the key

ring, and dragged it out, keys clinking. He gasped. "Got it Now I'm going to turn over and sit up."

"Okay. I'm with you."

He rolled until he was on his back. Then he sat up, Simone's chained leg lying across his lap. She scooted closer to lessen the strain of the awkward angle on her joints.

Hunched over, Corey opened up all of the Leatherman's attached tools—scissors, clip-point knife, tweezers, nail file, bottle opener, ruler, three screwdrivers of various sizes. He examined the locking mechanism on the handcuffs, checked his available tools.

"In the movies, people pick cuffs with bobby pins," Simone said.

"No bobby pin here." He picked the smallest screwdriver. "But I think this might work."

The seminar he'd attended covered mostly how burglars bypassed pin tumbler locks, commonly used to secure doors. The handcuffs were totally different—there were no pin tumblers. But if you understood how to analyze a lock's design, he'd learned, you could figure out its weaknesses.

Rivulets of sweat streaming in to his eyes, Corey noticed that on each cuff, the locking arm moved back and forth slightly, from the locked position to an even tighter clasp. In Leon's haste to hunt for Jada, he hadn't engaged the double lock that would have prevented the locking arm from moving in each direction, and probably would have made the cuffs harder to pick.

He slid the screwdriver's tip into the ratchet around Simone's ankle and worked at lifting the teeth.

As he worked, he felt Simone's gaze on him, but she stared at his face, not his hands. He braced himself. He'd been married to her long enough to know that a storm was rolling in, and nothing was going to stop it. Nor should anything—he deserved whatever she could rain down on him and then some.

"You said you were sorry for everything," she said. "What do you mean by everything?"

"Some of this situation's my fault," he said.

"Some of it?"

"All of it. All of it's my fault. I did something, a long time ago, and I never made it right."

"Leon said you killed a man."

Chest tightening, he looked up at her. Her eyes were hard as stones.

"*Leon* killed a man," Corey said. "His name was Mr. Rowland. Phillip Rowland. He was my high school English teacher. But I was there. I saw him do it. I didn't stop him. When it was over, I didn't go to the police."

He suffered her silence and searing gaze.

Finally, she said, "I knew you didn't kill anyone. He told me that story, but I couldn't make myself believe it."

"I've never killed anyone, never physically attacked anyone. But Leon . . . he's a cold-blooded killer. It's . . . it's almost like a sick game to him."

"He's a violent psychopath," she said. "Textbook. First one I've ever run in to face-to-face."

"You've seen the chrome cigarette lighter he carries around?"

"Yeah."

"He took that from Rowland after he killed him. Carries it everywhere with him like a good luck charm. Takes it out to taunt me."

She looked pained. "For God's sake, why didn't you ever go to the police?"

"I was scared."

"Scared?"

"I was scared to go to prison for accessory to murder. I was eighteen, I thought my life would be over if I snitched. I've been scared of it for sixteen years."

She was quiet for a few heartbeats. "He said you two used to 'rock and roll' back in the day."

"Leon and I . . . we used to break in to houses."

"How many?"

"At least a dozen."

"A dozen break-ins."

"At least that many, yeah."

Her lips twisted in disgust. "Why?"

"I've asked myself that question a million times over the years. Peer pressure, maybe? I'd let Leon manipulate me, tell me what to do. He has a strong personality, and I had self-esteem issues, I guess, and looked up to him. I would just go along with whatever he said."

"Breaking into houses and stealing other people's stuff."

"Most of the guys I knew back then got into trouble. I didn't exactly grow up in Bel Air."

"So that's your excuse? Growing up in the hood, nothing better to do than rob honest, hardworking people? 'Cause everyone else did it? That's bullshit, Corey, and you know it."

"Listen, I'm not making excuses. It was wrong, and I admit it. But you asked me why, and I told you."

"Hmph. Wish you'd told me ten years ago."

"So do I," he said bitterly. "I should have told you everything."

She closed her eyes, tilted her face to the ceiling. He wiped sweat from his forehead with the back of his free hand and resumed working on the cuff.

But his fingers were oily, and the tension between him and Simone made it hard to focus.

Her eyes snapped open again. "You ever consider confessing your part in what happened?"

"Not until tonight."

"You have to. Or I will."

"I'll do it, Simone."

"Justice deferred is still justice. I know that dead man's family would say so."

"They deserve justice, and they'll get it. I promise you. I'm not running from it any more."

She hesitated. "Is there anything else I need to know about you?"

"Wasn't all of this enough?"

A sour laugh escaped her. "Yeah."

"That's everything."

"One more thing."

He paused, not knowing what to expect. "Okay."

"Did Leon kill his mother?"

He stared at her. "What?"

"He told me he killed his mother when he was eighteen, that he gave her bad heroin and she died of an overdose."

Corey could only shake his head. "Leon hardly knew his mother. He and I had basically the same family situation, which is probably part of why we bonded."

She looked shell-shocked. "You're kidding."

"When he lived across the street from us, he lived with one of his aunts. And trust me, he didn't call her mom. What did he tell you?"

"Nothing that was true, apparently. Only proves that you can't bullshit a bullshitter."

Corey smiled thinly.

"He killed his partner." She indicated the darkened area behind them. "That big man? Leon shot him in the head, after I'd wounded him."

"You wounded that huge guy? That giant?"

"A lot's happened here."

"No shit."

He concentrated on the restraint. After a couple of intense minutes, he felt an easing of pressure in the ratchet. He'd shimmed the ratchet teeth clear of the pawl. The cuff popped open with a soft snick.

"Free at last," Simone said, rubbing her chafed ankle. "Thank you."

"Now for mine," Corey said. "We can move around as is, but I'd feel better with it off."

"Hurry," she said.

He switched the screwdriver to his left hand, and went to work on the cuff binding his wrist.

70

After chaining together the star-crossed lovers, Leon had
one upstairs to the room where they'd been holding the lit-
le deaf munchkin, curious to know how she'd escaped. He'd
ound a hatch in the closet that opened into a crawl space so
eep it had to feed into other closets on the second floor, and
e instantly put two and two together.

Smart little bitch. He hadn't even known the crawl space
xisted.

He did a cursory check of the other upper level rooms,
nd then hurried outside to find her.

The Todder was on his way, too. Leon had called him, and
e gambler said he wasn't far, that he'd anticipated this
ight happen, and he'd be at the house lickety-split to help
eon take care of things and arrive at a win-win solution.

Leon scowled. A fucking win-win solution. As if that
ere possible. Their entire master plan had gone to shit. The
eds were lurking around. The fifty large was gone. His part-
er was dead. Corey knew the deal.

Leon was of half a mind to just say fuck it, and to bounce.
ut the Todder had promised him a handsome payoff, and he

needed to get something for all his troubles before he wen
back on the road, wasn't going to put in all this hard worl
and risk his cover only to leave with diddly-squat, fuck that

Meanwhile, he was left to track down the little deaf bitcl
on his own. Doing the dirty work yet again.

If Billy were alive, at least Leon could have sent him ou
into the great wet and muddy outdoors to find her. But Bill
had gone bye-bye forever, too bad, so sad.

With his flashlight, Leon checked the neighboring house
for signs of the little munchkin. He looked inside th
Oldsmobile his homeboy had arrived in and parked at th
corner.

A Cutlass Supreme. Like his old ride. Too funny.

But the munchkin wasn't in there, either.

She was only nine years old and deaf as Helen Kelle
How far away could she have run on those itty-bitty legs?

He circled back to the safe house.

There was enough forestland beyond the lot to serve a
the setting for a *National Geographic* program. Could th
little one have gone back there?

Why not take a look see?

He crashed into the forest, knocking aside twigs and bat
ting away shrubs, heedless of the commotion he was caus
ing. The bitch was deaf. What difference did it make ho\
much noise he made?

He swung the beam across the undergrowth.

In a fall of weeds, not far from the house, he found a tin
pink house slipper.

He rang up the Todder.

"What's up?" Todd asked. "I'm maybe five, ten minute
from there."

"If you wanna know where I am, I'll be doing my wilder
ness tracker act," Leon said, scanning the trees ahead. "Th
little bitch's out here in the woods."

71

Bent forward, Corey worked at picking the ratchet around his wrist. It was a bit more awkward since he had to use his left hand and he was right-handed, but with the experience he'd gained from opening the other cuff, it shouldn't take him long to get free.

Simone had gone to the bedroom door, tried the knob, found it locked. She pounded it with a muttered curse. "How're we going to get out of here?"

"One thing at a time. Give me a minute."

Sweat dripped into his eyes. She came to him and, using a napkin she dug out of a bag, blotted the perspiration from his brow, a tender gesture that surprised him considering the shameful stuff he'd told her.

"Thanks," he said. He added, "Thanks for being you, I know you're angry—"

"You have no idea how pissed off I am, Corey," she said, jaw rigid. "No damn clue. So don't go there, all right?"

He lowered his gaze to the cuff, and the screwdriver.

She touched his arm. In a softer voice, she said, "But . . . I'm not leaving you. I'm not going to throw away the best ten years of my life. You're my husband, the father of my child. I have to find it in myself to forgive you."

He looked up at her, emotion squeezing his throat "Thank you. That means everything to me. Somehow, I'l make it up to you."

Her eyes glistened. "I'll make peace with this, Corey. I'l do that. But you have to forgive yourself, too, if you really want to grow past this. I know how hard you can be on your self."

He thought about the advice Otis had given him. *Some times, we must forgive ourselves for our sinful acts before we are capable of accepting absolution from others.*

"That might be the toughest part," Corey said.

"We'll work through it all," she said. "We'll go to the po lice together. We'll tell them the truth, about everything."

"And if I have to serve time?"

"I don't want to think about it." She exhaled through clenched teeth. "But if it comes to that, I'll be there for you So will Jada. You know she'll love you no matter what. You'l always be Daddy."

Tears fluttered in his eyes. He had never in his life wished so strongly that he had made different decisions. He migh earn a twenty-year prison sentence, but how many more years would pass before he could truly forgive himself fo his errors? Before he could come to terms with the pain tha he had caused his family and so many others?

He didn't know, but he only hoped that he got the chance to do better, to make up for all his wrongs.

He took the napkin from Simone and used it to dry his eyes. Teeth gritted in concentration, he worked the screw driver against the ratchet. In a minute or so, he finally, go the teeth up. Felt that wonderful soaring release as the cuf fell open.

He tossed the handcuffs aside. Simone helped him to his feet.

"We've got more work cut out for us." He nodded toward the door. "There's a thick piece of wood braced across the other side."

Together, they approached the doorway. He hammered the door with his fist. It rattled slightly in the jamb.

"Think we can break it down?" Simone asked.

"Since the door's set up to open outward, I'm pretty sure Leon hung it himself. I don't think he knew what the hell he was doing. He's no contractor."

"I kicked at it earlier. See?" She pointed out the scuff marks near the center. "It didn't give, obviously."

"I wasn't here to help you then. I've kicked down a door before."

He saw a question in her eyes.

"I locked myself out of my apartment once," he said quickly. "Kicking down the door was the only way I could get in."

She blushed. "Sorry. Stupid assumption."

"The door is weakest around the lock," he said, indicating the spot. "I'll boost you up on my back. Then you can use both your feet to hammer away. A few times should break it, and then we can both ram against it to knock away that board on the other side. It's resting against just a few bent nails."

"Then let's hurry up and do this."

Somewhere outside the room, a door opened. Footsteps clicked across a hallway.

They tensed. Corey sidled away from the door, prepared to launch an ambush. Simone edged away, too.

The footsteps stopped outside the room. "Hey, you guys in there?"

It was Todd.

Glancing at Simone, Corey took a couple of steps away and lifted the handcuffs off the floor. He tinkled them loudly for effect. "Listen, we're cuffed, man. Why don't you come in here and join us?"

"No time for chitchat." Todd chuckled. "Got places to go and things to do, partner. I'm here to wrap things up and cash in my chips."

"Cash in your chips?" Corey said.

"Don't you remember our partnership agreement?" Todd said. "In the event of the death of one of the partners, full ownership of the company automatically goes to the surviving owner."

"What the hell are you talking about?" Corey shouted.

"Settling up, my man," Todd said. "With everybody, including our good buddy, Leon. I realized that he's the perfect fall guy. A fugitive on the run kidnaps an old friend's family for ransom—"

"Todd, please!" Simone shouted.

"—and the whole plan apparently goes terribly wrong," Todd continued. "The incinerated remains of Corey Webb, his loving wife, and Leon Sharpe are discovered in a housing subdivision burned to the ground in the south suburbs . . . poor Sharpe, must have tried to torch the evidence of what he'd done and got trapped himself in a fire that blazed out of control."

The mention of fire raised the hairs at the nape of Corey's neck. He pounded his fists on the door. "Let us out, damn it!"

Todd paused. "Hmm, now that's interesting. You're supposed to be cuffed. What're you, like, Houdini? You keep escaping from tight places."

"Damn you, Todd, open the door!" Simone screamed.

"Anyway," Todd said, "as for our deaf little Webb girl . . . who knows where she is . . . but if I find her around here, I know certain people who'll pay good coin for a pretty little orphaned girl."

Shouting, Corey kicked the door repeatedly. The wood shuddered, splintered.

"How much you wanna bet you'll roast long before you bust out of there?" Todd asked.

Todd's voice sounded distant; he was leaving.

A second later, Corey smelled, distinctly, the pungent odor of gasoline. His heart trip hammered.

"Todd!" he shouted.

"Personally, I think I've got the high hand on this one," Todd said, voice fainter. "Think I'm going all in . . ."

A door slammed.

And Corey heard the crackle of flames.

72

To make Shaggy Man happy, Jada ate the can of peas while he stood over her and watched.

The sweet, big black dog that had found her in the woods had worked its way through the knot of other dogs around her and come to her side, sticking its wet snout in her face, sniffing at the can and licking her chin. She fed the dog some of the peas, and it gulped them without chewing and begged for more.

I have to eat, too, doggy, she said, and swallowed a forkful of the peas. They were cold, and she actually didn't like peas as all—spinach was her favorite vegetable—but Shaggy Man grinned.

If it makes him happy to see me eat, then I'll eat, she thought.

She didn't want to see him angry again. He did not seem to be a scary, bad man like the Giant or Mr. Leon—a bad man wouldn't have so many nice dogs in his house—but the fact that he was so disturbed gave her the feeling that he might hurt her without really meaning to hurt her, and in a way, that was almost as frightening as everything Giant had done.

Between her and the dog at her side, they finished the entire can of peas. She put the fork on the table. A yawn escaped her.

She went to cover her mouth as she yawned, but Shaggy Man suddenly seemed upset again. He started speaking.

She thought he said, *Bedtime.*

She nodded eagerly, and said it, too: *Bedtime. Yes, bedtime. I want to go to bed.*

She really was tired, too, "absolutely exhausted" as Daddy would say sometimes when he came home from work, but what she was thinking was that if Shaggy Man took her to a bedroom, she would be alone, and alone, she could finally use the cell phone.

He picked her up from the chair, as if she were an infant. He carried her through the house, though the sniffing, licking, probing pack of dogs. As he walked down a hallway lined with stacks of phone books, he stepped through several piles of doggy doo-doo, like he didn't even see them.

Gross, she thought, holding her nose. Mom would have a conniption fit if she could ever see this man's house.

He pushed open a door and brought her into a dark, musty-smelling room. He switched on a lantern on the dresser.

It was a room for a baby. There was an old looking crib covered in dust and cobwebs, and the walls had faded pink wallpaper with leaping white unicorns. An old box of Huggies stood beside the dresser.

It didn't look as if any of the doggies had been in there, though. There was no poop on the carpet and no pee-pee stains.

He placed her inside the crib, cobwebs wrapping around her arms and neck.

I'm not a baby! she wanted to say to him, but she knew he

would not understand. So she kept quiet. She curled up her legs to try to fit inside on the dusty bedding, the phone pressing against her hip.

The dogs tried to come inside the room, but he shooed them away, waving his arms frantically. They waited outside in the hallway, dozens of sets of eyes gleaming curiously.

Shaggy Man dug a diaper out of the box of Huggies. He stared at it, and then looked at her. He was frowning, totally confused.

He thinks I wear diapers? Jeez, she wanted to scream.

But she took the diaper from him, anyway. He smiled and his lips moved.

Good night, he said.

Good night, she said, and waved.

He backed out of the room and fastened the door behind him.

Finally, she was alone.

She counted to fifty. When he did not come back, she felt safe digging out the cell phone.

Hands shaking, she pressed the power button. As the screen brightened, she hoped the phone didn't make any beeping noises that Shaggy Man might hear.

Her parents had taught her to call 911 in case of an emergency, but she wanted to call Daddy first. She had decided that he was probably at home, wondering what had happened to her and Mom.

She punched in the number for their house. Out of habit, she put the phone against her ear.

She would not be able to know if Daddy answered the phone, but they had voice mail, and that would pick up if he didn't. She counted off ten seconds, and then she started talking:

Daddy, it's me, Jada, Mom and I have been locked up all day with bad people, Mr. Leon and a giant, they're partners, Daddy, and we need help, Daddy, we need you, I got away and I'm at a house on a lake, and there are dogs everywhere in here, and I hope you can find me, I'm with a disturbed man in his house on the lake, and I need you. . . .

Jada looked up, her words wilting in her throat.

Shaggy Man was standing in the doorway, and he looked furious.

73

Soon after the crackle of flames came foul black smoke. Serpents of it slithered underneath the door and inside the bedroom, writhed around their legs.

Corey coughed. He knew they had only a few minutes before smoke inhalation would kill them.

He turned to Simone, saw the same grim knowledge reflected in her eyes. Without needing to exchange a word, he boosted her on his back, her arms hooked in his.

She weighed maybe a hundred and thirty pounds. Not heavy. But in his battered condition, it was like having a refrigerator strapped to his back.

He clenched his teeth, ignored the pain.

She slammed both feet against the door, the impact rocking him forward. He heard the door rattle—but it held.

She hit it again. *Wham.*

Wood cracked, the best sound he'd ever heard in his life. *Wham.*

More breaking.

On his back, Simone was panting, her frantic breaths roaring in his ears. Tendrils of smoke curled around them.

Corey held his breath, lungs feeling as if they would implode.

Wham!

He heard wood thud to the floor on the other side of the door. The barricade.

The wafting smoke was blacking out the room, making his eyes water.

"Come on, damn it!" Simone screamed. She attacked the door with a fusillade of savage blows: *Wham-wham-wham-wham-wham!*

Finally, the door fell away and banged against a wall. Simone shrieked in triumph.

They unlocked their arms, and staggered through the doorway into the hall.

Hungry flames crawled up the walls and across the floor, most of them ahead in the foyer, but they were quickly spreading throughout the house. Fresh paint sizzled, bubbled, popped. Clouds of black smoke billowed in the air. The tremendous heat cooked the sweat on Corey's face.

He put his shirt to his mouth and grabbed Simone's hand. They shambled down the hallway, keeping clear of the overlapping tongues of fire.

The front door was like a blazing hoop in a circus, impassable.

"Kitchen!" Simone shouted, and tugged him in the opposite direction.

Smoke polluted the kitchen, snuffing out the lantern light. In the shifting veils, Corey glimpsed the cooler, the chair, duct tape, a stack of books, but no usable weapon. Damn.

A sliding patio door led from the kitchen to the backyard. They flung it open, the door screeching on the tracks.

The cool, damp air outside ballooned Corey's aching lungs, tasted delicious.

They staggered across the muddy yard and into the cul-de-sac. Bent over, they pulled in deep, replenishing breaths.

In the house, fire lashed the sheets that covered the front windows. The acrid fumes had begun to taint the air outdoors.

"Gotta call 911," Simone said, raspy-voiced. "It's stopped raining . . . fire might spread."

"My phone's in the car."

He led the way. Todd's Mercedes coupe was parked at the edge of the cul-de-sac. The car was empty, but the doors were locked.

"He's gone to find Leon," Corey said, remembering Todd's taunts.

Simone shook her head. "I don't care about Leon—I only care about our baby."

The Oldsmobile was parked where he had left it at the corner. Simone didn't ask any questions about the vehicle when she saw him open the door. They were past the point of explanations.

His BlackBerry lay on the passenger seat underneath his jacket, the battery and handheld separated. He plugged in the battery.

The other cell phone lay inside, but he didn't want to so much as touch the damn thing.

Arms clasped over her chest, Simone turned around and around, calling for their daughter in a pain-wracked voice.

Corey called 911 to report the fire. He gave the approximate address, and ended the call without answering any more of the dispatcher's questions.

"Now let's go," Simone said. "We've gotta start looking."

"Hold on," he said.

The phone's voice mail indicator stated that he had messages. Could have just been Falco harassing him, but he had to be sure. He punched in the code to access the mail box.

One message was from Falco; he skipped over it.

In the next, he heard Jada's voice. She was shouting, voice raw with terror.

". . . *Daddy, and we need help, Daddy, we need you, I got away and I'm at a house on a lake, and there are dogs everywhere in here, and I hope you can find me, I'm with a disturbed man in his house on the lake, and I need you. . . .*"

"She's at the lake!" Corey said. "A house on the lake, there are dogs everywhere, a house on the lake, she said. There's a lake here, *here*, in this subdivision."

Simone's eyes were huge. "Where?"

The boom of a shotgun echoed from behind them. It came from the woods behind the safe house.

"There!" Corey said, and started running.

74

Leon heard the shotgun blast as he was picking his way through the woods with the flashlight, tracking the little dea bitch. Buckshot took a big bite out of an oak not ten fee away from him, wood splinters arcing through the air.

Automatically, he dipped to the ground. He doused hi flashlight and drew his Glock nine.

Who the fuck was shooting at him?

It couldn't be C-Note, even if he and Clair Huxtable somehow had broken free of the cuffs and gotten out of the bedroom, they didn't have a shotgun.

Couldn't be Johnny Nabb, either, the law didn't fire or you without first issuing a warning, and though some ran dom, Negro-hating redneck might live in these boonies, tha just didn't feel right, either.

What felt right was The Todder. Good ole Kenny Rogers.

Leon's lips curled. He had never really trusted that guy Anyone who would make a major muscle move to force ou his business partner couldn't be trusted. Probably he wa aiming to ex out Leon so he could keep all the currency fo himself.

"Greedy motherfucker," Leon spat. Of course, he might
ave done the same thing if he were in Todd's high-priced
noes, but still. It was the principle of the matter.

Keeping low, he raced through the wet undergrowth, cir-
ling around, doing a flank maneuver.

Hidden safely behind a tree, he rose and peeped the
cene.

There was The Todder all right. Revealed in a splash of
noonlight, he wore a dark hooded jacket and gripped a shot-
un, stalking through the forest like it was hunting season
nd Leon was the big game.

"Son of a bitch," Leon muttered. "Gonna take me out, do
ou know who I am, huh, do you know what I've done,
itch, think you can whack the artiste, ice me, huh?"

The Todder was maybe thirty yards away, but he was
ooking in the wrong direction, a rank amateur, that's what
e was, didn't he know Leon was the crème de la crème in
is biz? You didn't get to be a superstar on the FBI's Ten
Most Wanted Hoods List by being a schmuck.

So Leon burst from cover and ran up on him, firing one round
fter another, gunfire echoing through the woods, the Glock's
ecoil snapping through his wrist, and by the time The Todder
urned, he'd already been shot two or three times. He went
own like a boxer dropped with a right hook, wasn't getting
p for the count, call the fight, good night, folks.

Leon took his time covering the rest of the distance be-
ween them. Swaggering like the Duke after smoking the
ad guy at high noon.

He felt electrified. Killing always gave him that crazy
yped feeling, a delicious experience better than blowing a
ut deep inside a fine-ass woman with a Ziploc pussy.

Giggling to himself, he came up on the Todder and shone
e flashlight in his face. Blood pasted his black hair to his
nned forehead. But his eyes were open, and he was breath-
g in shallow, whistling breaths through a ruptured throat.

When he saw Leon, fear rose in his baby blues.

"You're busted, disgusted, and shown why you can't l trusted," Leon said.

Blood dribbled from the guy's lips. He said something a whispery gurgle. It sounded like *fuck you.*

Leon smirked and lit a cigarette.

"I think I'll stand here and watch you *expire*, pilgrim Leon said. He took a drag on his Newport. "I wanna see tl chi fade out of your eyes, and then I'll rifle through yo pockets, get your keys, and go to *su casa* and see how mu(dirty gambling loot you've got socked away in there, 'cau: you're gonna pay me, hombre, one way or another."

A roar from close behind made Leon drop his cigarette. sounded like a bear, a tiger, something wild and inhum; and enraged.

What the fuck . . .

Leon spun, groping for his gun.

Eyes blazing, Corey exploded out of the darkness ar pounced on him.

75

When Simone and Corey reached the forest, they agreed
to split up. Corey had gone after Leon, angling in the direction of the gunfire.

Simone went to find their daughter.

She came out of the trees, to a surprisingly large lake.
Ambient moonlight shimmered on the tranquil surface. A
chorus of bullfrogs croaked and bellowed.

On the other side of the banks, she saw the mobile home.
It stood upon a grassy, tree-studded knoll, reached by a
crumbling set of concrete steps. The trailer's white paint was
so faded, the tin roof so festooned with kudzu and overhanging
branches, walls so buried within tall, dense grass, that it looked
as if it might have sat there for decades and was slowly being
sucked into the earth.

A couple of the trailer's windows were broken. But soft
light glowed in one of the rooms.

Her baby was inside that room. She could feel her.

Hold on, baby, I'm coming.

She raced around the muddy banks, heedless of the aches

and pains that wracked her body. Loose stones tumbled aw
beneath her shoes as she pounded up the steps.

She caught the smell before she reached the top of th
staircase. The stink of garbage, feces, and urine. The mi
gled fumes hung heavy in the air.

When she arrived at the top, she saw why.

76

Springing out of hiding with a battle cry, Corey swung a thick tree branch at Leon. It smacked solidly against his chest, and he flew backward off his feet with a surprised *uu-hhhh,* his pistol spinning away into the weeds.

Lifting the wood to his shoulder, Corey bared his teeth in a savage grin. This man had jeopardized his family, his life, everything, and he wanted to kill him, wanted to split his skull open until his brains oozed out and the crazy light faded forever from his manic eyes.

Shouting, Corey raised the branch and brought it down.

Leon rolled out of the way.

The wood slammed against the earth, sent painful tremors through Corey's arms.

As agile as a jungle cat, Leon launched toward Corey, tackling him. Corey's teeth clicked together as they collided, and he whammed to the ground.

They wrestled across the forest floor. Leon was grunting, cursing.

"Can't take me out . . . homeboy . . . can't take me out . . ."

Corey grappled him into a headlock. Wheezing, Leon got

a hand free and pounded his fist against Corey's same kidney that he had slugged earlier, and a burning poker of pain speared Corey's side. He howled, loosened his hold.

Their bodies tangled like the weeds in which they fought. Leon frantically rammed his elbow against Corey's chin. Corey's head whipped sideways, and he tasted blood, warm and salty.

Leon got on top of him. He was trying to apply a choke hold. Corey threw a punch, and it snapped into Leon's jaw. Leon dropped away with a grunt.

Gun, Corey thought, desperately. *Todd had a shotgun.*

He staggered to his feet. Leon grabbed his foot. Corey spun and kicked him in the head.

Leon groaned, went down.

On weak knees, Corey stumbled to Todd. Todd's eyes were glazed, as if he were daydreaming, but blood soaked his face and throat.

Was he dead? Corey didn't know. Didn't care.

He snatched the shotgun out of Todd's slack fingers. Turned.

Leon crawled away from him, tunneling like a badger through the undergrowth. Going for the other gun.

Corey aimed in his direction and pulled the trigger.

But nothing happened.

Jammed, jammed, the damn thing's jammed.

He didn't know how to clear a shotgun jam, and didn't have time.

Leon retrieved the Glock and fired. A round whizzed past Corey's cheek, the heat trail kissing his ear.

Corey fled in the opposite direction. Stampeding through weeds. Bouncing drunkenly off trees.

Another gunshot shattered the night, and a round smashed into Corey's shoulder.

He cried out, swayed as fire bit into him, and collided against a tree.

No, you fall, you die.

Somehow, he kept his balance and kept running. There was a lake up ahead. He sprinted across the banks and jumped in at a full run

As he catapulted through the air, he prayed the water was deep enough to hide him.

He plunged into the lake. He sank below the surface, kicked, and didn't feel a bottom.

Paddling his one good arm and kicking, he dove deeper.

Driftwood and vines batted against him. Fish wriggled by. Water flooded his wounded shoulder, felt like ice leaking into his bloodstream.

His lungs ached. He needed to breathe. But he forced himself to swim farther away from shore, stroking like crazy. When he could hold out no longer, he risked rising to the surface.

Gasping, he looked around, expecting to see Leon on the banks, taking aim at him like a kid in a shooting gallery.

Leon was gone.

The echo of warbling sirens rolled across the water. Through the forest beyond the lake, he saw flashes of red and blue light, and only then did he remember that he had called 911 to report the fire.

77

Moving toward the trailer, Simone had to choke down her gorge. So many heaping piles of dog manure filled the overgrown yard that she didn't know where to step. A big blue trash bin near the front porch overflowed with garbage. Four mongrel dogs were camped out in front of the can, picking through the trash.

A rust-eaten pickup truck was parked in the driveway beside the house. A gravel road led out beyond the property.

Who lived here? How could they?

The dogs' ears lifted at her approach. They turned to regard her, tails wagging.

Relief passed through her as she saw the animals' friendly demeanor because she wasn't going to let any number of canines stop her from getting inside that house to her little girl.

Other dogs inside began to bark, and she saw furry faces appear at the broken front windows. There were so many yips and barks it sounded as if a dog kennel were based inside.

The door sagged on weak hinges. She didn't bother with knocking. She turned the knob, found it unlocked, and went in.

The front room was dimly lit with a kerosene lantern, but t was difficult to see the furniture because there were so nany dogs. Dogs were everywhere, puppies and adults and eriatric hounds, of every breed and size, some in poor ealth, others fine. They swarmed around her, licking, pok- ng, sniffing.

The stench of feces and urine was unbelievable. She cov- red her mouth with her T-shirt.

Hoarder, she thought, recalling case studies. *Whoever ves here is a hoarder, obsessive compulsive, and because ogs are being hoarded, the resident is almost certainly a an.*

She wished she had a weapon. It would have made her eel safer.

A thumping sound reached her. It sounded as if it were oming from a back room, as if someone were going nuts ith a hammer: *thump-thump-thump-thump.*

Her heart pounding in sync with the sound, she forced her ay through the crowd of canines. She passed by a kitchen at was unbelievably foul. Roaches skittering across the oor and walls and counters. Mounds of feces everywhere. rine-stained tile.

Sweet Jesus.

She gagged into her shirt, longing for a gas mask.

Thump-thump-thump-thump.

She moved into a narrow hallway. Head-high stacks of hone books lined one wall. Light came from behind a door ear the end, on the right, and that was where the thumping me from, too.

She pushed the door open.

Dogs were in here, too, but compared to the rest of the ouse, the room was pristine. It looked like a nursery. She w a dusty crib. A box of diapers, a changing table.

Thump-thump-thump-thump . . .

A bearish, long-haired man in a fatigue jacket knelt in the

corner, his wide back to her. He was ruthlessly beating
something with a hammer and muttering a stream of gibber
ish.

Her blood froze. *Not my baby, no.*

Mesmerized with his task, he didn't stir at her entrance
She sidled closer and peered over his shoulder, her shir
stuffed in her mouth, her gut tight.

He was pounding what looked like a cell phone. He ha
smashed it, literally, to smithereens.

"Mom!"

Simone whirled as a closet door behind her slid open
Jada and a large black Labrador bounded out, the dog'
tongue lolling happily.

Jada leapt into Simone's arms.

"Oh, God, oh, my baby," Simone cried. She clasped he
daughter to her and sank to her knees, tears weaving dow
her cheeks. She sobbed into Jada's hair, smelling her, feelin
her, making sure she was okay, and she was, she was alive
everything was fine, everything was going to be fine.

78

Later that night, Special Agent Falco and her partner, Agent March, visited Corey at Grady Memorial Hospital in downtown Atlanta.

Although the bed Corey had been assigned wasn't intended to accommodate three people, Simone and Jada had slipped under the sheets and snuggled close to him, and the nurses on duty granted them an exception to hospital rules.

Otis sat watch in the upholstered chair near the bed, reading his Bible by soft lamplight. He had brought Jada's speech processor, which she had gratefully slid on. Jada normally didn't wear it when she slept, but Corey suspected that she would insist on having it on at all times for a while.

Corey had allowed himself to finally drift off when Falco and her partner knocked on the door. He snapped awake, tense, and Simone and Jada awoke instantly, too, clinging to him.

"Excuse me." Otis rose from the chair and moved to intercept the agents. "I'm afraid this is not an appropriate time for questioning. Please give this family some peace."

"It's okay," Corey said wearily. He wiped his eyes, looked at the agents. "Don't you people ever sleep?"

"Once a week, on Sundays." Falco strolled to the foot of the bed; March remained near the door. "How you holding up? Heard you took a shot in the shoulder."

"It's not too bad." Corey raised his good arm and tapped the dressing that covered his gunshot wound. "Considering everything that happened, I figure I got off easy."

"Gates certainly didn't. But I think you know that."

"I don't take any pleasure from it. I used to think he was friend. But that wouldn't be the first time I've been fooled, guess."

Falco gripped the railing at the foot of the bed. Her eyes were red with fatigue, but glinted with steel resolve.

"Where is Sharpe?" she asked.

"I don't know. He got away."

She scowled. "He got away? Again? After all of that Don't bullshit me."

"It's the truth. I'm sorry."

"I'm going to need a full, *very detailed* statement from you," she said. She cut her gaze at Simone. "And you, too."

"Happy to," Simone said. "We only want to put this behind us."

"What about me?" Jada asked.

Falco frowned at Jada. "That's up to your parents, sweetie"

"I don't think so," Simone said, with a glance at Corey "Our daughter's dealt with enough."

Corey agreed. Although a physical exam had confirmed thank goodness, that Jada had not suffered any abuse at the hands of Leon's partner, he'd seen the inside of the trailer where the dog hoarder, Ed Denning, had taken her, and was nightmarish and pathetic. The county's animal control services had been notified, and Denning had been taken into custody for psychiatric counseling.

"We'll chat tomorrow, then," Falco said. She straightened

anced at her watch, sighed. "Actually, that would be today.
ney ought to be discharging you later in the morning. Do
e a favor and don't skip town."

Falco turned to leave. Simone gave Corey an expectant
ok.

Corey cleared his throat. "I'm not finished yet, Agent
lco."

"No?" Falco retreated from the doorway. "I'm listening."

"You've been wondering all along why Leon came to me
the first place." He paused. Every gaze in the room was
ated on him.

He went on. "To put everything in perspective, let me tell
u what happened sixteen years ago. . . ."

79

Ten days later, Corey rented a sedan and drove to Detroit.

Simone and Jada stayed behind in Atlanta, under the vigilant protection of a private security firm and a black Labrador retriever–Great Dane mix with which his daughter had fallen in love during her ordeal at Ed Denning's house. For reasons only she knew, she named the dog Ophelia.

It was a fine day for a road trip. Under a warm sun and cloudless skies, Corey traveled I-75 North from Georgia into Tennessee, from Tennessee into Kentucky, from Kentucky into Ohio, and from Ohio, finally, into Michigan.

When the hazy Detroit skyline appeared on the burnt orange horizon around seven o'clock that evening, Corey felt an iron vise tighten across his chest. He had never thought it would feel good to come back home, but it did. It felt damn good.

He exited the interstate at 7 Mile Road, which would take him to the East Side. To Conant Gardens.

As the last vestiges of daylight surrendered to night, Corey parked in front of the house.

A FOR SALE sign stood in the weed-infested front yard.

he windows were boarded with plywood. The garage door, which had once protected a man's prized Cadillac, hung skew on damaged tracks like a lopsided grin.

Corey slung the strap of his overnight bag over his good shoulder, and went inside.

In the front room, he clicked on a flashlight. The air was warm and musty. The dust-filmed floors were bare of furniture, stripped of carpet. Cobwebs draped the walls and doorways.

He knelt to where a good man had once bled to death on his own living room floor. The carpet that had been soaked in blood had been removed, but as he traced his fingers across the faded floorboards, his skin tingled at the point of contact.

He sat on that spot, propping his overnight bag beside him. He dug a small, battery-operated lamp out of his bag and set it up a couple of feet away. It gave off pale, ethereal light.

And then, he waited.

He was prepared to wait all night and through the next day, and longer, if need be, but after he had been sitting on the floor for about an hour and a half, the front door banged open.

Corey straightened as Leon came inside. He wore glasses with chunky black frames, an Afro, and a thick, woolen beard. He was dressed in a black business suit, starched white shirt, black tie, and oxfords.

Trying to pass himself off as a college professor, a Cornel West look-alike, maybe? The disguise worked, except for the gun he was pointing at Corey.

"I've been following you all damn day, ever since you left ATL this morning," Leon said. He panned a flashlight around the room. "What the fuck did you come back here for? Haven't you heard that you can never go home again?"

"I'm doing penance," Corey said.

"What?"

"You surely know what penance is, Leon, a smart gu[*]
like you. Self-punishment, reparation for acts I committed—
or in this case, was accessory to."

"You need to get over it already." Leaning against th[*]
wall, face half-concealed in shadow, Leon tapped out a ciga[*]
rette and lit it with Mr. Rowland's lighter. Taking a puff, h[*]
shook his head. "I've never met someone so unable to pu[*]
the past behind him, to move on. You didn't even kill the bas[*]
tard. You were going along with me like your weak-wille[*]
ass always did, yet here you sit indulging in this ridiculou[*]
and overblown act of self-flagellation. It's not going t[*]
change anything, deal with it, suck it up."

"See?" Corey said. "You once said we were just alike, bu[*]
that's the difference between you and me. You can gun dow[*]
someone and then go grab a beer somewhere. I see some[*]
thing like that, and it haunts me for the rest of my life."

"The world's composed of leaders and sycophants, home[*]
boy." Leon tossed the lighter up and down as he spoke[*]
"CEOs and yes-men, too, uh-huh, wolves and sheep, that[*]
the way of the world, always has been, I'm the leader, th[*]
CEO, the wolf, you're the sycophant, the yes-man, th[*]
sheep."

"Maybe you're right." Corey shrugged. "Can I see tha[*]
lighter? Over all these years, I've never touched it."

Leon tossed it to him. Corey snagged it out of the air. H[*]
turned it around in the lantern light, struck the wheel, ignit[*]
ing a flame.

"I think Mr. Rowland's widow would like to have this,[*]
Corey said.

"Think so?" Leon snickered. He raised the gun. "If yo[*]
can make it out of the door alive, you can personally delive[*]
it to her."

"That's quite an offer." Corey pulled his bag in front o[*]
him, unzipped a compartment, and dropped the lighter in[*]

ide. He kept the bag positioned in front of his chest. "Unfortunately for you, homeboy, the Detroit PD and the FBI gave me a better one."

As a puzzled frown twisted Leon's face, hallway doors exploded open. Heavily armed FBI agents in dark tactical gear rushed out with a thunderous clatter of boots and shouts of "FBI! Drop your weapon now!"

But Corey knew Leon, knew he would never go down without a fight, without taking someone with him. As agents converged on him, Leon aimed at Corey and squeezed the trigger.

Corey shielded himself with the overnight bag. It didn't contain any clothes—it held a bulging plate of Kevlar armor.

Rounds punctured the bag, the impact rocking him backward, and then a cacophony of gunfire erupted, muzzle flashes brightening the room, the bitter odor of cordite infiltrating the air.

When it was all over, Leon's bullet-riddled body lay on the floor, the wig askew on his head, fake beard soggy with blood. The crazy light in those eyes had finally been extinguished forever.

Looking at his one-time friend, Corey felt no sense of pleasure or vindication. A vague sadness weighed on his heart, and he thought of how his life and Leon's might have turned out if they'd chosen different paths.

Agent Falco approached Corey. She wore tactical gear like the other members of her team. A walkie-talkie crackled on her hip; the operations vehicles they'd been holding at bay would be descending on the house like bees to a hive.

She extended a gloved hand and helped Corey to his feet.

"You got your man," Corey said.

"Wish it had been alive." She shrugged. "But it happens this way sometimes."

In exchange for his cooperation in bringing Leon to justice for the murder of Rowland and his other crimes, the FBI and Detroit PD worked out a deal with Corey's attorney that allowed him to remain free on all charges. The life Corey had built in Atlanta, and the testimony of character witnesses such as Otis Trice, had played a key role in the leniency he received.

"Here's your wire, for what it's worth," Corey said. He stripped away the miniature microphone taped to the inside of his shirt and dropped it in her palm. They had recorded the entire conversation to capture Leon's confession of the murder on tape. ·

It would, at last, close the case.

Falco shook his hand. "Thanks for working with us, Webb. It took a lot of courage."

"I'm no hero. I only did what I had to do."

A smile crossed her face. "Where you going now?"

"I owe a visit to a lady who would appreciate having this." He unzipped the pocket of the overnight bag and fished out the lighter. "After that, I'm going back to Atlanta. I've got a wife and a little girl expecting me home soon, and I don't want to keep them waiting too long."

Enjoy the following excerpt from

DON'T EVER TELL

Available now wherever books are sold.

Prologue

On the morning of the day he would taste freedom again for the first time in four years, Dexter Bates lay on his bunk in the dimly lit cell, fingers interlaced behind his head, waiting for the arrival of the guards.

He did not tap his feet, hum a song, or count the cracks in the shadowed cement ceiling to pass the time. He was so still and silent that save for the rhythmic rising and falling of his chest, he might have been dead.

Incarceration taught a man many lessons, and chief among them was patience. You either learned how to befriend time, or the rambling passage of monotonous days eventually broke your spirit.

He had long ago vowed that he would not be broken. That he would use time to his advantage. The day ahead promised to reveal the value of his patient efforts.

Resting peacefully, he thought, as ever, about her. About her supple body, and how easily he bent it to his will. Her soft skin, and how it bruised beneath his fists. Her throaty voice, and how he urged it toward raw screams of terror. . . .

Pleasant thoughts to dribble away the last grains of time he had left in this hellhole.

Soon, the metal cell door clanged open. Two correctional officers as tall and wide as NFL linemen entered the cell.

"Let's go, Bates," Steele said, the lead guard. Sandy-haired, with a severe crew cut, he had a wide, boyish face that always appeared sunburned. He had a green parka with a fur-lined hood draped over his arm. "Hurry up or you'll miss your last ride outta here."

Dexter rose off the narrow cot. He was nude—he had stripped out of the prison jumpsuit before their arrival. He spread his long, muscular arms and legs.

"All right, open that big-assed cum-catcher of yours," Jackson said. He was a stern-faced black man with a jagged scar on his chin that he tried to hide with a goatee. He clicked on a pen-sized flashlight.

Dexter opened wide. Jackson panned the flashlight beam inside his mouth, and checked his nostrils and ears, too.

"Now bend over," Jackson said.

"But we hardly know each other," Dexter said.

"Don't test me this morning. I ain't in the mood for your bullshit."

Dexter turned around and bent over from the waist. Jackson shone the light up his rectum.

"He's clear," Jackson said.

"How about one last blow for the road, Jacky?" Dexter grabbed his length and swung it toward Jackson. "You know I'm gonna miss that sweet tongue action you got."

"Fuck you," Jackson said.

During Dexter's first month in the joint, Jackson had tried to bully him. Word of Dexter's background had spread quickly, and there were a number of guards and inmates who wanted a crack at him. A shot at glory.

Dexter had repeatedly slammed Jackson's face against a cinderblock wall, fracturing his jaw and scarring his chin.

Although assaulting a guard would normally have resulted in a stint in the hole and additional time tacked on to his ten-year sentence, Jackson had never reported the incident. He had his pride.

Jackson searched Dexter's jumpsuit and boots for weapons, found nothing, and then Dexter dressed, shrugging on the parka that Steele gave him. Jackson cuffed his hands in front of him and attached the ankle restraints.

The guards marched him down the cell block. None of the inmates taunted Dexter, as was typical when an inmate departed. There were a few softly uttered words of support— "Peace, brother," "Take care of yourself, man"—but mostly, a widespread silence that approached reverence.

"These guys are really gonna miss you, Bates," Steele said.

"They can always write me," Dexter said.

They took him to inmate processing, where the final transfer paperwork was completed. He was being sent to Centralia Correctional Center, another medium security prison, to serve out the balance of his sentence. He had put in for the transfer purportedly to take advantage of the inmate work programs offered at that facility, and it had taken almost two years for the approval to come through.

The administrator, a frizzy-haired lady with a wart on her nose, expressed surprise that Dexter was not taking any personal items with him. Most transferring inmates left with boxes of belongings in tow, as if they were kids going away to summer camp. Dexter assured Wart Nose that he would get everything he needed once he was settled in his new home.

Paperwork complete, they walked Dexter outside to the boarding area, where an idling white van was parked, exhaust fumes billowing from the pipe. "Illinois Department of Corrections" was painted on the side in large black letters. Steel bars protected the frosted windows.

It was a cold, overcast December morning, a fresh layer of snow covering the flat countryside. An icy gust shrieked across the parking lot and sliced at Dexter's face.

He wondered about the weather in Chicago, and felt a warm tingle in his chest.

Steele slid open the van's side door, and Dexter climbed in, air pluming from his lips. Two beefy correctional officers from Centralia waited inside, both sitting in the front seat. A wire mesh screen separated the front from the rear bench rows.

"Sit your ass down so we can get moving," the guard in the passenger seat said. "It's cold as fuck out here."

Steele lifted the heavy chain off the vehicle's floor and clamped it to Dexter's ankle restraints. He nodded at Dexter, his blue-eyed gaze communicating a subtle message, and then he slammed the door.

As in police vehicles, there were no interior door handles. Packed inside and bolted in place, a prisoner bound for another concrete home could only sit still and enjoy the ride.

"Headed to our home in Centralia, eh?" the driver asked. He glanced in the rearview mirror at Dexter. "Just so you know, brother man, whoever you were outside won't mean shit there, got it? You'll be everyone's bitch, especially ours."

"Spoken like a man who's always wanted to be a cop," Dexter said. "Did you fail the exam? Or wash out of the academy?"

"What a piece of work," the passenger guard said, shaking his head. "You must want deluxe 'commodations in the hole soon as you get there."

At the manned booth, a guard waved the van through the tall prison gates. Dexter looked out the window. The snowy plains surrounded them, so vast and featureless they nearly blended into the overcast horizon.

By design, many state correctional centers had been erected in barren wastelands, to make it almost impossible for an escaping inmate to progress far before recapture. Dexter had heard rumors of inmates who managed to get away being tracked down within three miles of the joint, upon which they were brought back, weeping like babies, to an increased sentence and a long stay in solitary.

The two-lane road was crusted with dirty slush and riddled with potholes. It wound through nothingness for close to five miles before it fed into a major artery, which eventually intersected the highway.

At that time of morning, there was no traffic, and there wouldn't be much at all, anyway. The road dead-ended at the prison, a place most normal people preferred to avoid.

The guards switched on the radio to a country-western station. The singer crooned about seeing his lady again after being away for so long.

Dexter wasn't a fan of country western, but he could dig the song's message.

"What time is it?" Dexter asked.

"You got somewhere to be, asshole?" the driver said.

"I want to make sure we're on time. I've got a hot date with my new warden."

"Whatever. It's a quarter after nine, numb nuts."

Nodding to the music, Dexter dug his bound hands into the right front pocket of the parka.

A key was secreted inside, courtesy of his good man Steele. Correctional officers were even more receptive to bribes than cops, and that was saying something.

"I'm really feeling this song," Dexter said. "Turn it up, will you, man?"

"That's the smartest thing you've said yet," the passenger guard said, and cranked up the volume.

Dexter used the key to disengage the handcuffs, the loud music drowning out the tinkle of the chains. Leaning forward slightly, he stretched his long arm downward and unlocked the ankle restraints, too.

Then he sat back in the seat, and waited. He crooned along with the song, his intentionally bad voice making the guards laugh.

"You sure ain't got no future in music," the driver said. "Jesus Christ, you're terrible." Dexter shrugged. "A man's got to know his limitations, I guess."

After they had driven for about three miles, they came around a bend. There was a gray Dodge Charger stalled on the shoulder of the road. A blond woman in a shearling coat and jeans was at the trunk, apparently trying to lift out a spare tire. Her long hair flowed from underneath a yellow cap, blowing like a siren's mane in the chill wind.

"Would ya lookit that?" The passenger guard leered at the woman. "Pull over, Max. Let's help her out."

A green Chevy Tahoe approached from the opposite direction.

"You know we're not supposed to stop, Cade," Max said.

"You better not stop," Dexter said. "You're going to screw up my schedule."

"Shut up," Cade said. He turned to Max. "Look, it'll take ten minutes. That young broad can't change the goddamn tire by herself."

"You just wanna get laid," Max said.

"Hey, I'm a Good Samaritan. I gotta do my charitable deed for the day."

"To get laid," Max said. But he slowed the van and nosed behind the Dodge. "You got ten minutes. No word of this to anyone."

"I'll snitch on you," Dexter said.

"The hell you will," Cade said. He licked his fingers, patted down his eyebrows, and then climbed out of the van. Strutting like a rooster, he approached the blonde.

The oncoming Tahoe suddenly slashed across the road, snow spraying from the tires, and blocked off the van. Tinted windows concealed the occupants.

"Holy shit," Max said. "What the hell's this?"

On the shoulder of the road, the other guard noticed the Tahoe, and froze.

Dexter dug his hand in the coat's left front pocket and clutched the grip of the loaded .38, also compliments of Steele.

A gunman wearing a ski mask and a black jacket sprang out of the Dodge's trunk. The masked man shot Cade twice in the head with a pistol, and the guard dropped to the pavement like a discarded puppet.

Cursing, Max fumbled for his radio.

"Hey, Max," Dexter said. "Look, buddy, no chains."

When Max spun around, Dexter had the gun pressed to the wire mesh screen. He shot the guard at the base of the throat, just below the collar.

The guard's eyes widened with surprise, and he slid against the seat, a bloody hole unfurling like a blooming flower in his windpipe.

The passenger side door of the Tahoe swung open. A refrigerator-wide black man attired like a correctional officer scrambled out and ran to the driver's side of the van.

The blonde took the ring of keys from Cade's belt, and unlocked the van's side door.

"Morning, Dex." She smiled brightly.

"Hey, Christy."

Moving fast, Dexter and the ski-masked man lifted the guard's corpse off the ground and laid it across the floor of the van. In front, the guy dressed like a guard had gotten behind the wheel and was propping up the wounded guard in the seat to look like a passenger if one gave him a casual glance.

The dying guard was moaning entreaties to God in a blood-choked gurgle.

"Someone shut him up." Dexter slammed the side panel door. "Fuck it, I'll do it myself."

Opening the passenger door, Dexter shot the guard twice

in the chest, permanently dousing the struggling light in the man's eyes. Except for the splash of blood on his coat, he appeared to be sleeping off a hangover.

"Good to see you, man," the new driver said.

"Same here." Dexter nodded, closed the door. "Let's roll out."

The ski-masked gunner scrambled behind the wheel of the Dodge, the blonde got in on the passenger side, and Dexter hustled in the back.

Beside them, the Tahoe backed up and executed a swift U-turn, maneuvering behind the prison van, which had begun to rumble forward.

Both the SUV and the van were driven by longtime colleagues, upstanding members of the Windy City's finest.

"How long?" Dexter asked.

"Two minutes and fourteen seconds," Javier, his former partner said. He had peeled away his ski mask. A native of the Dominican Republic who had moved to the States when he was five, Javier was a lean, bronze-skinned man with dark, wavy hair and a pencil-thin mustache.

Javier flashed a lopsided grin that reminded Dexter of their wild days working together.

"We kicked ass, Dex."

"Like old times," Dexter said.

"How's it feel to be out?" Christy asked. Unlike every other member of the operation, she wasn't a cop—she was Javier's wife, and as trustworthy as any brother of the badge.

"Like being born again," Dexter said. "Hallelujah."

Christy passed him a brown paper bag that contained a bottle of iced tea and two roast beef-and-cheddar sandwiches wrapped in plastic. Dexter ate greedily. After four years of bland prison food, the simple meal was like a spread at a four-star restaurant.

A bag from Target lay on the seat beside him. He opened it, found a pair of overalls and a plaid shirt.

"The rest of the stuff?" Dexter asked.

"The duffel with all your things is in the trunk," Javier said. "But you need to get out of that ape suit pronto, man. Who would I look like giving a prisoner a taxi ride?"

Dexter peeled out of the prison jumpsuit and dressed in the civilian clothes.

When they reached the main artery that ran through town, Javier made a turn that would take them to the highway. The prison van, followed by the Tahoe, went in the opposite direction.

They would drive the van over a hundred miles away and abandon it, and its cargo of dead guards, in a pond. With luck, it would be at least several days before the cops would discover it.

Dexter settled back in the seat and dozed. He dreamed, as usual, of her. She was weeping, screaming, and pleading for her life.

It was a good dream.

When he awoke over two hours later, they were bumping across a long, narrow lane, freshly plowed of snow. Tall pines and oaks lined the road, ice clinging to their boughs.

Javier turned into a long driveway that led to a small A-frame house surrounded by dense forest.

"My mother's crib," Javier said, and Christy laughed.

Dexter laughed, too. The house was no more inhabited by Javier's mother than it was by the Queen of England. Javier had bought it in his mother's name to conceal his ownership, a ploy that many of them had used at one time or another to hide their connection to various properties and valuables they purchased—things decidedly *not* paid for with their regular cop salaries.

A car, covered by a gray tarp, sat beside the house.

"What's that?" Dexter asked.

"Something special for you," Javier said.

They parked. Dexter got out of the car and walked to the

covered vehicle, snow and ice crunching under his shoes. He peeked under the tarp.

It was a ten-year-old black Chevy Caprice, a model that was once the ubiquitous police cruiser.

Dexter laughed. "You kill me."

"Glad the joint hasn't taken away your sense of humor," Javier said. He opened the Dodge's trunk and handed a big olive green duffel bag to Dexter. *"Feliz Navidad, amigo."*

Dexter placed the bag on the ground and unzipped it. It contained a Glock 9mm, five magazines of ammo, a switch blade, a concealable body armor vest, a prepaid cell phone, clothing, keys to the Chevy and the house, a manila envelope, and five thick, bundled packets of cash in denominations of twenties, fifties, and hundreds, totaling approximately ten thousand dollars.

It wasn't a lot of money, but more waited in Chicago. Substantially more.

"Santa brought you everything on your wish list," Javier said. "In spite of how naughty you've been."

Dexter grinned. In the manila envelope, he found an Illinois driver's license, U.S. passport, and a Social Security card, all listed under the alias of Alonzo Washington.

"Alonzo Washington?" Dexter asked.

Javier smiled. "Sound familiar?"

"The flick about the narc—*Training Day,* right? Denzel's character was named Alonzo something."

"I thought you'd appreciate it."

"You're a regular fucking comedian, aren't you?" Dexter tapped the IDs. "These solid?"

"As a rock," Javier said. "The finest money could buy."

In the ID snapshots, Dexter's face had been digitally altered to depict him as clean shaven. Dexter rubbed the thick woolen beard he had grown in prison.

"We threw some Magic Shave and a couple razors in the bag, too," Javier said.

"I've had hair on my chin since I was fifteen. I'll hardly recognize myself."

He turned to the house. Although it offered perhaps fifteen hundred square feet, a decent amount of space but nothing spectacular, to a man who had lived in a seven-by-twelve cell it would be like having the run of the Biltmore Estate all to himself.

"Utilities are on," Javier said. "Christy went grocery shopping this morning, packed the refrigerator with everything a growing boy needs."

"Your loyalty," Dexter said. "That means more to me than anything. Thanks."

"Speaking of loyalty, we tried to track down your ex-wife," Christy said.

"Wife," Dexter said.

"Right. Anyway, she's dropped off the grid, like you thought. We got nothing."

"That's good," Dexter said.

"How the hell is that good, after how she screwed you?" Javier asked.

"Because," Dexter said, a grin curving across his face. "I get to find her myself."

GREAT BOOKS, GREAT SAVINGS!

When You Visit Our Website:
www.kensingtonbooks.com
You Can Save Money Off The Retail Price
Of Any Book You Purchase!

- All Your Favorite Kensington Authors
- New Releases & Timeless Classics
- Overnight Shipping Available
- eBooks Available For Many Titles
- All Major Credit Cards Accepted

Visit Us Today To Start Saving!
www.kensingtonbooks.com

All Orders Are Subject To Availability.
Shipping and Handling Charges Apply.
Offers and Prices Subject To Change Without Notice.

More Books From Your Favorite Thriller Authors